MW01415388

ACCLAIM FOR NOCTURNE IN ASHES

WHAT READERS ARE SAYING...

"A fast-paced, action thriller with a ton of suspense, distinct and memorable characters, and a unique setting."

~ ReadnGrow

"There was a twist in the plotline that I didn't see coming. It blindsided me."

~ Read With Me

"Joslyn Chase skillfully connects subplots, then injects a few surprises, then connects things again in an interesting cycle; weave, disassemble, weave, repeat."

~ Ron Keeler, Read 4 Fun

"I couldn't put this book down, reading late into the night and every chance I could sneak away from other things that people call important."

~ Monica Dannenberger (reader, Amazon.com)

GET YOUR NEXT JOSLYN CHASE BOOK FREE!

But catch up on your sleep now.
Once you start reading,
it'll be *No Rest* for you!

Get the book free when you join
the growing group of readers who've discovered
the thrill of Chase!

Get started now at joslynchase.com
OR
simply scan the QR code

Get The Ebook

NOCTURNE IN ASHES

Also By Joslyn Chase

Staccato Passage

Steadman's Blind

The Tower

The Devil's Trumpet

Falling For The Lost Dutchman

No Rest

What Leads a Man to Murder

Death of a Muse

Duet for Piano & Chisel

NOCTURNE IN ASHES

A Riley Forte Suspense Thriller

JOSLYN CHASE

PARAQUEL PRESS

NOCTURNE IN ASHES: A RILEY FORTE SUSPENSE THRILLER

Paraquel Press paperback edition, published by Paraquel Press, 2024

https://paraquelpress.mailerpage.com/

Publisher's Cataloging-in-Publication Data
Names: Chase, Joslyn.
Title: Nocturne in ashes : a Riley Forte suspense thriller / Joslyn Chase.
Description: 2nd edition. | University Place, WA : Paraquel Press, 2024. | Series : Riley Forte suspense thrillers ; book 1.
Identifiers: LCCN 2024905474 | ISBN 9781952647307 (pbk.) | ISBN 9781952647291 (ebook)
Subjects: LCSH: Widows – Fiction. | Pianists – Fiction. | Grief – Fiction. | Serial murderers – Fiction. | Rainier, Mount (Wash.) – Eruptions – Fiction. | BISAC: FICTION / Thrillers / Suspense.| FICTION / Thrillers / Crime. | FICTION / Women.
Classification: LCC PS3603.H37 N63 2024 (print) | DDC 813 C--dc23
LC record available at https://lccn.loc.gov/2024905474

Contents

Prologue

The summer he turned thirteen, he took his first life.

His first human life.

He'd killed scores of animals. His mother had taught him that.

"We're living off the fat of the land and sometimes that calls for slaughter," she'd told him as he watched her work over their latest kill, her long hair tangled and dangling, her arms bloodied to the elbow in the belly of the deer.

He'd learned to heed that call.

He gathered what he needed, sharpened the blade, and laid everything ready to hand. The small pile of sticks and stones, the strip of cotton fabric, the flint and steel. Squinting into the night sky, he dipped his head to the three-quarter moon peering down through the trees, smoothing a layer of silver over the crisped and browning leaves and waving grasses, gilding the rippled lake.

The last of the summer warmth came now in brief snatches, like the kiss of a capricious child. Autumn approached and with it, the familiar melancholy, the stirring ache of loss.

Still sharp, after so many years.

The mantle felt heavy upon him, bowing him down as he mourned the lonely course he was compelled to follow. So few understood his work. No one alive could appreciate his sacrifice.

Was it necessary, what he did? Must he carry on?

He asked the questions, as he had that first time, in his thirteenth year.

He asked the questions as he had every time since.

So many times. And every time, her voice comes back to him in a whisper.

Yes.

And so he plods on. He has seen the fruit of his works, his gift to the world. And yet the hunger, the need grows stronger. Always, more is required.

The killer let his gaze and his thoughts wander to the clump of bushes to his right. No sound or movement drew his attention, but he strained his eyes through the blackness and wondered if the slight shape he discerned was real or a product of his restless imagination. He forced himself to remain still, regulating his breathing and the beat of his heart.

Long moments passed before the scrape of metal against metal reached his ears, raising him from his seat against the smooth bark of an aspen. He watched through the low branches, his eyes focusing across the small clearing with the acuity of a hunter.

The sound was repeated, made by the door of an RV scraping across the ill-fitting steps which extended from it. A figure emerged and lurched down the steps, weaving and muttering as he staggered between the tall birch and whispering pines.

Into the silence of the night came the splash of an over-burdened bladder finding release, and it was under cover of this noise that the killer moved.

The man in the trees zipped up and dug into the pocket of his grungy, low-slung jeans. He came up with a twist of paper and lit it, puffing while he gazed up at the distant moon. Spread over his bare chest and biceps, a parade of inked figures swayed slightly with the gentle movements of hand to mouth.

Cricket song resumed. The night's gentle pulse beat out. The smell of marijuana drifted on the air.

The killer waited, letting the man finish his smoke. He listened as the man sang and repeated an unfamiliar phrase. He sang, revised, and tried again, staring up at the stars as if for encouragement or inspiration.

The man was a songwriter. Also a guitarist and a talented musician. Two nights ago, the killer had relaxed in the twentieth row of a half-filled auditorium, enjoying the man and his band in concert.

Rolling Stone had featured an interview with the man in one of last year's issues, and the killer had read every word with interest. But the great band's comeback tour was falling short of expectation.

Pity.

The singer flicked the butt onto the urine-dampened earth and blew one last lungful into the velvet air. The killer nodded. Gripping the knife, he stepped forward, moving fast and quiet.

The man stopped singing.

1

Riley stood naked on the dressing room floor.

She fingered the smooth black silkiness of the gown she would wear to cover herself on stage, knowing the very essence of her soul would remain exposed, uncoverable by any length of silk. It was what she always felt before a performance, and the knowledge both exhilarated and terrified her.

She slipped a robe over lace-trimmed undergarments, knotting the cord at her waist, and walked to the battered upright piano shoved into a corner of the cluttered dressing room. Sitting down on the bench, she touched naked fingers to naked keys, and shivered.

In Beethoven, there was no place to hide.

With Rachmaninoff, Debussy, even Chopin, the possibility of covering up a brief falter, a tiny misstep, without heralding disastrous consequences, existed. But the spare lines and disciplined elegance adhered to by the masters of the Classical era demanded the utmost precision, and Riley had always been known for accuracy.

Execution, interpretation, emotion—all are exposed under the stage lights at the piano.

For twenty-three months she had immersed herself in the music, studying, rehearsing, pouring herself into the work and thinking of little else. She was ready.

Certainly, she was ready.

There was a knock at the door and Helen entered, a sheaf of printed programs in one hand and a spray of roses in the other.

"They're lovely, aren't they?" she said.

"Which? The flowers or the programs?" Riley asked, inspecting the thick, ivory-colored cards that spelled out the evening's fare.

This concrete evidence that she was about to go under the spotlight kicked off a rush of adrenaline, bringing the heady mixture of anticipation and dread. *Why do I put myself through this?*

That thought was instantly followed by another—*what else is there?* Her very soul was made of music. Sharing it was all she knew.

Helen placed the flowers on a scratched wooden coffee table, pushing and pulling at the blooms, arranging them to her satisfaction. She was a tiny woman, plump in a way that rounded her features and made her look like a wise, old child. She came to Riley at the piano, dropping beside her on the bench, and squeezed an arm around her.

"You're gonna do great, kid. Jim would be so proud."

Riley nodded. She had no doubts on that score.

Helen patted her leg and switched to business. "Miller Cantwell is in the crowd tonight and I think a rep from Universal. Also, Frank Coston and Gabrielle Wilson, so keep your smile pasted on whatever you do. Now get dressed and warm up your fingers. It's time to knock 'em dead."

She waved and left the room, and in that interval before the door shut behind her, Riley heard the bustle of backstage, the faint chatter of the concert hall filling with people. Her hands were like ice against her skin as she pulled the silk gown over her hips and drew up the zipper on the low-cut back.

Pulling the pins from her long, auburn hair, she let it fall loose, filling in the space left bare by the fabric. At the piano, she ran through a series of scales, numbing out, drifting mentally to another plain. With an effort, she shook herself and wrangled her mind back to the little dressing room and the audience filling the auditorium.

Biting her lip, she tried to remember the initial notes of Chopin's Fantasie Impromptu, which opened the program, but came up blank. A jolt of panic speared through her, and she felt the urge to pull out the sheet music, study, cram, but she knew from experience that the notations would only turn to blurred Chinese characters before her face.

Heaven help me, what do I think I'm doing here?

She closed her eyes, exhaling into her hands to warm them, and brought her breathing into a slow, steady rhythm. Her grandfather, Zach Riley, for whom she was named, had been a jazz pianist doing USO shows during WWII. He'd played through bombshells and cannon fire and been injured more than once.

She fastened her thoughts on him, picturing him playing doggedly through air raids and enemy attacks. She thought of the orchestra members on The Titanic who went down with the ship as they played through, lending courage to others.

This was the heritage she claimed. She could do this.

She had to do this.

Applause flooded over her as she stood center stage and bowed her acknowledgment to a houseful of half-seen faces. Turning toward the piano, she took the first steps on what was always the longest walk, the distance stretching out and holding all the possibilities between triumph and tragedy.

Back straight, chin lifted, she seated herself, arranged her skirts, flexed her fingers, and began.

Striking the first chord, she let it resonate, floating up, drawing the expectant audience, and then the Chopin flowed out, her hands agile and dancing on the keyboard. Her heart pounded, pumping out adrenaline, speeding the tempo, and she pulled back just slightly, a gentle tap on the brake as her fingers raced.

The music enveloped her like a flurry of golden butterflies, filling her with a rush of pure excitement. She executed a perfect, rippling chromatic scale, spanning the keyboard and building to a series of crashing chords.

And then, a slight stumble as she crescendoed down the piano, one finger sliding off the slick surface of a polished key. None but the most distinguishing of ears would catch it, but it threw her concentration and she struggled to maintain the rhythm and balance of the piece as she transitioned into the central melody.

Drawing strength from the gentle, lyrical notes, Riley regained her equilibrium, preparing to face the second round of chromatics and thundering chords. She felt a blip of panic as she approached the section and fought to control the impulse to flee that always hit her when she lost focus.

She clenched her jaw, then released it, zeroing her attention on the keyboard choreography.

Her hands flowed up the keys like a wave on the beach and moved back down again, hitting the chords with determination. She navigated the passage without mishap, returning to the tranquility of the melodic line. As the last gentle notes faded, applause surrounded her, and she felt her face grow pink with pleasure and relief.

A good opening.

She sat tall on the bench, breathing in, breathing out, nodding her thanks to the audience. Lifting her hands to the keyboard, ignoring their palsied tremble, she straightened her spine and began the Tchaikovsky Barcarolle.

She watched her fingers almost with wonder as they produced the tones of heart-rending sadness, feeling the music pulse within her, building through the impassioned midsection before coming back to the opening theme.

The gondola rocked, moonlight rippled, the midway storm raged, and she conquered it. Riley was inside the music, constructing the image, living it, swaying and bobbing on the Venetian waters of the picture she played.

As the last melancholy notes drifted and diminished, applause burst over Riley, and it felt like sunshine.

This was her first concert in over two years, and she had designed a short program, without intermission. She floated through the Bach Prelude and Fugue, the Haydn Sonata, and the Scarlatti. Only the Gershwin Preludes remained.

And the Beethoven.

She tried to push the thought from her mind. It was always at this point, when the finish was in sight without disaster breaking over her, that she tensed up and mistakes loomed like jagged cliffs on the shoreline.

She focused, instead, on Jim, as she always had. He was her fortress, her rock, her support. He was her family, the father of her child, her anchor.

He was gone.

Jim was dead and Tanner, their son, gone with him. But she had practiced through this, prepared for it, playing through the pieces while holding this thought, this harsh fact, in her head.

She'd learned to draw strength from it, to make her work a kind of tribute, allowing her to hold them with her in the music.

But tonight, it wasn't working.

The fall was coming.

She felt its approach as the tension in her neck and arms increased. Her mind fumbled, small tremors at first and then increasing in intensity like the buildup to an earthquake. The flight impulse threatened again and she wrestled it, fighting to keep herself at the piano even while her mind was already fleeing out the door, down the staircase, into the night.

She was furious with herself, felt hot tears on her face and ignored them. She skittered along to the end of the last Gershwin piece, hardly hearing or acknowledging the applause as it rose and petered out.

Time to finish the program.

She sat motionless on the bench, stomach roiling as the silence stretched and grew, broken only by short, polite coughs and the rustling of paper. Riley took a deep breath and positioned her shaking hands for the opening chords. They hung there, frozen above the keys for an agonizing eternity.

Blood roared in her eardrums and a moan tore from her throat as she jumped up, tipping the piano bench. The swirl of her skirt caught in the adjuster knob, and she heard it tear as she ripped free and fled the burning spotlight.

The bench fell with an echoing thud, punctuated by the staccato clattering of her heels as she ran from the stage, leaving the shreds of her comeback performance drifting like the tatters of her silk dress.

2

"I'M NOT A GROUPIE, I'm his wife."

Detective Nate Quentin eyed the woman who claimed she was married to Coby Waters, bygone rock star and notorious bachelor. He raised his palm, pressing it against the air as if activating a giant pause button.

"Phoebe?" He tossed his voice to the fingerprint tech, but his gaze never left the witness. "What do you think, Feebs?"

"Married, huh?" The small black woman looked up from where she crouched over a powdery surface, rolled her eyes, and considered. "No. I didn't hear anything about a wedding."

Nate folded his hands on the table in front of him, waiting for a response. The woman seated across the scarred board that doubled as eating surface and spare bed in the spacious RV sent a searing look in Phoebe's direction.

The bones in her shoulders rose like hackles under the spaghetti-string tank top and a flush spread from her breast up and over her cheekbones. She seemed to be gearing up for an explosion but then the huff went out of her. She shrugged.

"We got married three and a half weeks ago, in Vegas. We kept it quiet." She paused, her pink-tinted cheeks going pale. "We didn't even make it to one month."

Nate leaned back against the bench seat, glancing at his partner, Rick Jimenez, who hovered over the kitchen sink with a notepad, taking down the details.

"I'm sorry," Nate said, holding her gaze. "I am. Will you tell us what happened?"

"I already told. Twice. It's not a moment I want to live over again."

Nate leaned forward. "Mrs. Waters, those other times you told it, that's for the record, well and good. But we," he gestured at Rick and back to himself, "we are the ones who are going to find the guy who did this. You need to be real clear on that and tell us everything."

"Okay, yeah. I get it."

She fumbled through a shoulder-bag on the bench beside her, pulled out a pack of menthols and lit up. Nate watched her eyes turn inward as she accessed the part of her brain that housed the terrible memory. She took a long drag.

"We got drunk, you know. We were sleeping it off." Puff and pause. "I woke up feeling like crap."

She shuddered and blew out a cloud, waving it away. "I brushed my teeth, got in the shower. Pretty soon, Coby comes hammerin' on the door."

"What time was this?" Rick interrupted.

She stared at him. "How do I know? It was the middle of the night. I got no reason to look at a clock that time of day. I had the door locked, you know, so I tell Coby to find a bush."

She hugged herself, blowing out another mouthful of smoke. "I sent him to his death."

Nate shook his head. "Don't shoulder that weight, Mrs. Waters. It's not your fault."

She gave him a bleak look and crushed out the cigarette, wrapping her arms tighter. "I put my wet hair up in a towel and went back to bed. Never saw Coby again until—"

Her hands clenched down on her own flesh, talon-like. "I woke up in broad daylight and came out here to the kitchen to put on the coffee. I looked at the clock," she threw Rick a glare, "and it was eleven forty-seven a.m."

Rick's gaze was impassive. "When did you go looking for your husband?"

"After two cups of coffee and three slices of toast. With jam. Let's make it a quarter past noon. I began to wonder what he was up to, so I went looking. Started off in the wrong direction and ended up walking down caravan way."

She flung her arm eastward to indicate the sprawl of buses, trucks, and vans that hosted the remainder of the band's entourage.

"I asked around. No one'd seen Coby. I got to talking with some of the girls, never dreaming anything was wrong, and then that chihuahua started sounding off. We thought he might have got himself hurt. You know, stuck in a trap, sprayed by a raccoon, something like that. But he'd found Coby and raised the alarm."

She fell silent and Nate decided not to correct her over the raccoon. He watched her rake the tabletop with miserable eyes as if searching for something to cover the awful scene inside her mind.

"He was cut bad, right across the neck, and it seemed every last drop of blood in him must have found its way out. The ground was soaked with it. Damn dog was standing in it, yapping his head off. Danny led me away, then, and I didn't see no more."

Nate let a respectful silence pass and then asked, "Why is your trailer separated from the others?"

Her washed-out blue eyes met his with reproach. "It's not a trailer. It's a motorhome. Coby'd kick your butt for calling it that."

She caught her breath and swallowed hard. "He liked to be apart from the crowd. It's a status thing, right? Heaven knows he got precious little respect any more from the band, but he took what he could get."

"Downed Illusion used to be a pretty big deal and I understand this tour was meant as a comeback. Can you think of any reason someone might have for harming your husband? Were there any disputes among band members, for instance?"

She stared. "You think someone here could have done this?" Her mouth fell open a little as she considered, then snapped shut with her emphatic head shake. "No way. Their arguments were small-time stuff. A punch in the face, maybe. Never this."

Nate's cell phone buzzed with his ex-wife's ringtone. "Thank you, Mrs. Waters. That's all for now."

He walked down the rickety metal steps and pressed the TALK button.

"What's up, Marilyn? I'm at a crime scene so make it quick."

"Quick as I can, but it does involve our daughter's welfare. Forgive me if I take up too much of your time."

"Come on, that's not what I meant."

"Yeah, I know. Sorry. I've got a lot on my plate, too." She paused. "Can you take Sammi next weekend? I want to head out of town for a few days. I need a break."

"Oh? Who's going with you? You don't like traveling alone."

A moment passed. "Brad is taking me to Vancouver."

"Geez, Marilyn. That guy? He gives me a bad vibe and I don't want him around Sammi."

"Sammi will be with you, I'm hoping."

"For the weekend, sure, but what then?"

"You're being ridiculous. Brad is a nice guy. The first guy I've really liked since I really liked you. And does this mean you'll take Sammi?"

Nate sighed. "I would love to have Sammi spend next weekend with me."

"Wonderful! I'll let you go. Bye."

Rick joined him and they sat at a picnic table in the twilight. Lunch and dinner time had come and gone, hours ago and unheeded, and they fell like wolves upon the coffee and sandwiches being passed around.

"Are you thinking it's the same guy they're after in Seattle?" Rick asked. "We got a serial case?"

Nate chased down a bite with a swig of coffee, wiped his mouth with a paper napkin, and nodded. "That's what I'm thinking. We need to get up to speed on those case files. Looks like we'll be joining the team on this one. Congratulations, partner. Your first case out and you draw the short straw."

"Hey, I'm happy with it. Go big or go home, right?"

Nate laughed. "Sure, but if you foul this up, you'll never be able to wash the stink out of your career. It doesn't even have to be you that falls short. We don't put this guy down, and fast, we're all gonna catch hell, but that first case can make or break you."

"Okay, so the pressure's on. Let me tell you what I got from the Specials." Rick flipped to a page in his notepad. "Hansen found a place in the trees where the guy must have waited. Except, get this, there are two spots. So, did he switch from one to the other, or were there two guys? Hansen's still working it out."

"We'll check the other cases, but I don't remember hearing anything about a second suspect."

"Also, there was a scattering of sticks and stones which might have been arranged like the cairn-type structures found at the other sites. It may have been knocked apart in the struggle, disturbed by animals, who knows? The makings were there, but unorganized."

Nate drummed his fingers on the table to accompany his thought process. "Okay," he said. "Continue."

Rick checked his notes. "Stevens went into the lake, turned up a plastic raincoat weighted with rocks. Shows traces of blood, no fingerprints. Guy wore gloves and probably galoshes. Heck, he'd have to be completely encased to escape that bloodbath. If he likes the water, there's plenty of holes around here where he could've dumped the gear and weapon, but nothing else has turned up."

Nate watched a couple of grid-searchers sign their findings into the evidence log. Karen Boggs glanced up, caught his eye, and walked over. She carried something carefully in her gloved hands. Nate hoped it was something good.

"Hi, boss," she said. "This was outside the perimeter, about a mile from camp, but I snagged it anyway. Figured it wouldn't hurt. Wanna take a look?"

Nate cleared a spot on the table and she opened the large paper bag and used it like a tablecloth, placing the item in question gently on top. It was a dark blue zip-front jacket, sized for a man. One hundred percent polyester, with a tiny red figure playing polo stitched to the left breast. Nate lifted the cuff of the right sleeve, angled it so Rick could see the smears of blood. In the pocket, he found a wrinkled score card with *Mountain Vista Golf Course* printed at the top and an eighteen-hole score of 93 penciled in at the bottom.

"Not bad." Nate liked to golf but hadn't had time for a round in over three years.

"If you say so." Rick was not a golfer.

"Relevant to our crime?"

Rick considered, head tilted as he thought. "Hmm. Found a mile away, in a direction traveled only by foot. The blood on the sleeve seems too small an amount and in the wrong place if our guy was wearing gloves and a raincoat." Rick tilted his head back and forth. "Ehhh...I'm leaning toward no."

Nate ran a gloved finger down the length of the jacket. "On the other hand, it looks recently dumped and blood is blood. My experience, and my gut, tell me it's important."

"Yeah? Okay," Rick said doubtfully. "Where's Mountain Vista?"

"Hell if I know, but be ready to head out there tomorrow morning."

3

Topper worked in the dark.

Ordinarily, he wouldn't go near the crater of an active volcano at night. Such an expedition, even in full daylight with a helicopter waiting, is fraught with risk. But there was nothing ordinary about these unfolding events and Topper's amazement outweighed his fears. He was riding the edge of this thing.

Like David had.

Early in the summer, Mt. Rainier had woken like a fussy baby after a long nap, gassy and petulant. She'd spit up and burped, raged and bawled, and then fallen back into an uneasy sleep. For two months she'd snored away, uttering only an occasional harmless grumble, and Seattle let out its tense-held breath and went back to business.

Topper's business was volcanoes, and his harvest of data suggested that Seattle's nonchalance was unwarranted. Geoscientists primarily monitor three predictive factors for volcanic eruption—thrust faults, earthquakes, and tiltmeter readings. When the three factors register critical levels, a warning is issued to the public and safety measures activated.

Last February, Mount Mayon in the Philippines had drawn the gaze of the world. Her thrust fault measurements and tiltmeter readings took drastic turns, but seismic activity remained low and stable. Two out of three tipped the scales, officials issued alerts, and media hyped the story.

Cities and communities were evacuated. Citizens put their lives and livelihoods on hold, perched in temporary housing, and watched the mountain puff serene on the placid landscape. Ten days and millions of pesos later, they returned to their homes and commenced recovery efforts from the damage not caused by the volcano.

Such occurrences are the land mines of leadership, and the political and economic fallout is harsh. Scientists may be willing to lay it on the line, but the political figures who hold the reins are more skittish, put in a position where they must weigh the potential for lost lives against the potential for lost dollars.

And where the bottom line is lost votes.

At Rainier's first sign of unrest, scientists had deployed an army of "spiders" and other devices able to monitor the mountain's activities remotely and their readings were followed with great concern. But as the weeks passed, public interest waned and only the scientists remained keenly aware of the volcano's activity while Rainier wrapped herself in a blanket of cloud and went back to sleep.

Topper clambered nearer the crater, his snowshoes making a rhythmic shushing sound. The light from his headlamp opened a little vista in the dark, pushing back the shadows which pressed in from all directions. Mt. Rainier appeared to be pulling a Mayon move, but he believed the end of this story would be far more dramatic than the instance in the Philippines.

The western flank of Rainier was primed to blow. For centuries, sulphuric acid had been mixing with rain and snow, seeping through the rock, altering it into a clay-like substance, unstable and susceptible to landslides.

The Osceola mudslide, 5600 years ago, had blown away the east side of the mountain, displacing the altered rock and making the west side the weak spot in the next major eruption.

Topper bent to collect samples of ash and snow, pressing the tube from a solution-filled gas sampling bottle into the vent, taking care to avoid a steam burn. He should have waited until daylight, but he was determined to make his case. His gut told him that Mt. Rainier was poised to erupt, and time was short.

He imagined he felt the hair at the back of his neck singe and crackle. He started down the mountain, headed for the panel of tiltmeters and beyond that, the four-mile hike to the snowcat.

At the tiltmeters, he paused to log in the readings. The figures were astonishing, and he made a note to check the calibration. Stowing the samples and logbook in his backpack, he climbed into the tracked vehicle, maneuvering it forward over the rough terrain, navigable in the dark only because he knew these trails so well.

He worked his way down the mountain until he reached the ranger station, where he parked the snowcat and transferred himself and his collections to his Jeep Wrangler. Firing the engine, he started down the road into the lower span of the mountain.

As he came into range of the nearby cell phone towers, his mobile blipped. He pulled it out of his pocket and squinted one eye at the screen, keeping the other eye on the road which became smoother as he neared civilization.

Four text messages and three missed calls.

He stopped the Jeep and scrolled through the texts. All of them were from Candace.

Call me.

Call me, it's important.

Urgent you call now.

Call now or die.

His heartbeat surged as his phone blipped again. He read the message.

If you value your paycheck, pick up the damn phone.

Candace was his USGS supervisor at the Seismology lab at The University of Washington, Seattle campus. He knew she was calling from the lab, and with this degree of urgency, he bet they'd hit the Trifecta.

Thrust faults, check.

Tiltmeters, check.

If Rainier's seismic activity was on the rise, that could bring attention in all the right places.

Before he could punch the speed dial, Candace's jazzy ringtone blared in the Jeep's interior. He pressed answer and heard the excitement in her voice.

"Get down here now. You gotta see this."

4

THE RISE AND SWELL of voices in the corridor seemed to Riley like the hum of angry bees.

She'd fled to the dressing room, locked the door, and ignored the persistent demands for entry. Her stomach churned and rolled under an enveloping wave of buffeting, suffusing misery.

She dreaded looking into any human face and longed for the unreserved championing of a dog. In human eyes, she would encounter disdain, resignation, or worst of all, pity. And before she could face that, she needed to wrestle with her own feelings, try to understand the mechanism underlying her disaster.

The wraith of some destructive force teased at the edges of her mind, refusing to come into focus. She could only return to the conclusion which she, and the world at large, had accepted for the last two years. That Jim and Tanner—beloved husband, treasured son—had been taken from her and that the hole they left is a maw which continues to consume her.

The pain was like stepping on broken glass beneath a threadbare rug. Riley sensed something sly and furtive, unwilling to be seen and dealt with, an unknown monster crouching in the shadows of her mind.

A banging louder, over and above the other pounding, shook the door and the theater manager's voice rose above the ruckus in the hallway.

"Mrs. Forte. There's an urgent matter we need to discuss."

He began a persistent clatter on the flimsy wooden door and Riley's mind shut out the sound, scooping her away to her fourteenth summer when she was a pale, skinny girl in a green one-piece swimsuit. She'd begged her parents to let her go with friends on a rafting trip down the Snake River in Idaho. A very rare treat in her world.

The life of a budding concert pianist yields few such occasions, and she remembered how peculiar it felt for her to do things, and eat things, and say things that ordinary teenagers did and ate and said. It felt almost like dabbling with another species.

She'd started the four-day trip with a surge of homesickness, wishing she hadn't come, feeling amputated from her piano. A day and a half later she'd become entranced with these creatures and their strange ways, wishing she could always live among them, like Ariel wishing for legs.

Enveloped by a heady passion, she was on a bender, drinking in all they had to offer.

She was scorched bright red by then, her fair skin beginning to blister at the shoulders from sunburn, no matter how much sunblock she applied. Pulling a tee shirt over her bathing suit, she paddled with the rest of them, laughing and splashing as the group pulled their rafts onto a sandbank.

She climbed out and felt the cool sand squish between her toes. In the still water near the river's edge, water striders flitted over the surface like skaters on a pond, and Riley watched them in fascination until some of the boys began to scale the rocks, pulling themselves like monkeys up the steep face of a cliff.

A shiver of apprehension rippled over Riley as she viewed their climb. "What are they doing?" she asked her friends.

The enquiry was met with a sprinkling of casual assurances.

"We all do it."

"It's fun."

"You'll love it."

"Come on!"

There was an alternate way to the top, which most of the girls chose to take, though it was still a rigorous haul up the rock face. A creeping unease began to settle over Riley. She was vulnerable to injury here; her hands could be damaged. Any kind of an injury could throw her piano schedule off track.

She was literally pushed and pulled to the cliff top amid laughter and chatter which fell like an alien language on her anxious ears. When she reached the pinnacle of the rock face, she was horrified to see the boys jumping off into the river far below.

Her horror intensified as she realized she was expected to follow.

When her turn came, she stood at the edge of the cliff and stared down into a circle of deep water, ringed by the boys and girls who had jumped before her. Their thrashing arms and legs had stirred it into a murky pool, opaque and distant.

Unthinkably distant.

There was no going back. It would be more difficult and dangerous to try climbing down the steep rock than it would be to jump. Yet, jumping seemed an impossible option.

A boy and two girls pushed past her, throwing themselves over the edge, and then Riley was the last one on the clifftop and still she stood, frozen. The cries of encouragement from below took on a tinge of impatience and then, as the minutes ticked by, outright disgust.

They rose up to her like the clamorous pounding on a door, like a persistent knocking, battering her eardrums and her soul. Becoming, at last, unbearable.

She pushed away the fear and jumped.

With a gasp, Riley forced herself back to the present and threw open the dressing room door. A crowd of people flowed in like a surge of murky water, sucking her down so that she felt she couldn't breathe.

Like cold water billowing over her, she felt darkness closing in. With sinking desperation, she searched the bobbing heads before her, focusing in on one face as it moved through the murk until it reached her.

Teren grasped her by the arm and drew her back into the dressing room, closing the door with a decisive snap. The human wave lapped against it, but muted and murmuring now, and over the sound of it rose Helen's voice. Tiny Helen, turning back the tide. She would handle the press and the fans and deal with the manager.

"Thank heaven for good agents," Teren said, hugging her. "Sorry I'm late. I left my conference early so I could be here, but my flight was delayed. I rushed straight from the airport, but I came in just as you were...finishing up."

Riley dropped onto the sofa, too weary to answer. Teren sank down beside her and took her hand, squeezing it gently. The door opened and Miller Cantwell admitted himself. His recording company had sponsored this event and even Helen knew better than to bar him entrance.

"Riley." He blew out an exasperated breath. "What was that?"

Riley rubbed a hand over her face. "I apologize, Miller. I just blanked. I couldn't remember how the Beethoven begins. I just...couldn't do it."

Miller sighed, stuck his hands in his pockets. "I just got the word from Henry. We're pulling our support. I'm sorry, Riley. We really thought you were ready."

Helen entered the room, slamming the door behind her. "Don't be hasty, Miller. The situation is salvageable."

She sent him a look that crackled with challenge as she took up a position behind Riley, rubbing her shoulders, like a trainer on a prize fighter.

"Let's consider. A few of our guests wanted their money back. Four of them, to be exact. If that's a fair representation of audience satisfaction, it's hardly catastrophic."

Miller opened his mouth, but she gave him a fierce glare and pushed on with her defense. "As for the press, Frank Coston will write a sympathetic story and garner support, making Riley the underdog. Curious concertgoers will queue up for tickets, just to see what she'll do."

"Okay, but—"

"And that novelty," she insisted, "will carry us through this crisis and soon Riley will be in top form. You'll see."

She waved down Miller's sputtered protest. "Yes, I know. Gabrielle Wilson will shred her to pieces in that rag she writes for. So what?

I think the bump in publicity from this will come out in our favor. Riley's a champ." She gave Riley's shoulders a squeeze.

Miller walked to the door, placing a hand on the knob.

"For what it's worth, I agree. You're a jewel, Riley." He paused and Riley watched his shoulders slump under his expensive suit. "I'm sorry. We'll have to cancel the remaining performances."

He went out the door and Helen swept off after him, her voice raised and cajoling.

Riley sat hunched on the sofa, steeped in misery, wanting the comfort of her own bed and a cup of hot chamomile, unable to believe it had ended like this. Concert pianists do not flee the stage. They simply do not.

She cowered there, in the crook of Teren's arm, until the voices in the hallway diminished, leaving behind a pervading silence.

Teren patted her knee and stood up. "I took a shuttle to the airport, so I don't have a car. Can I hitch a ride home?"

The thought of enduring the long drive and the terrible traffic was almost more than she could bear, on top of the deep disappointment and anguish of the night. She watched Teren assess her tired droop and felt a rush of gratitude that he'd come for her. Stretching out a hand, he pulled her to her feet.

"Give me your keys," he said. "I'll drive."

5

THE KILLER STRIPPED OFF his clothes.

He folded each item into a neat square, stacking them like a tower, with his shoes forming the foundation as a barrier against the dew-dampened earth. The chill of the early morning gripped him, raising gooseflesh as the watery, lemon-yellow sunlight filtered down through the sparse leaves and pine needles, slowing the flow of his blood to a sluggish stream.

He raised the bloody strip, letting it flutter in the light breeze. This is the way she'd taught him.

By blood and by fire.

He bent to the pile of sticks and stones and began arranging them, layering each of the three different types of wood in a distinctive pattern, using the rocks as cornerstones with the kindling on top. A small burlap sack yielded a nest of oakum, which he placed close at hand, and from a tin box, he removed a cut of char cloth and folded it in half.

A gust of wind shimmered through the little clearing, making the leaves dance in a flurry of orange and gold, raising an eerie whistle in the thinning branches. The killer shivered and picked up the stone flint.

He'd found the stone in the run-off from the Nisqually River and imagined it had spewed from Rainier in some long-ago eruption. It was smooth as glass, except for the sharp edge where it had shattered from the heat or from tossing down the riverbed. It felt oily to his touch.

He placed the folded char cloth on top of the stone and took up a thin strip of steel, curling it around the knuckles of his right hand. He swung the steel down at a thirty-degree angle against the sharp edge of the stone.

Again and again, he struck steel against stone, working to peel away a tiny sliver, waiting for the spark to catch and ignite the char cloth.

The steel was unresponsive.

In the distance, a dog barked. The inhabitants of the earth were waking, moving, swelling every finger and every vein of her. The killer struck harder, working faster.

A cold sweat now coated his naked body, chilling him further, gathering in his creases like a distillation of fear. The dog barked again, nearer this time, and accompanied by the faint droning of human voices.

He threw himself face down on the leaf-strewn forest floor, digging his hands and toes into the soil, feeling for the pulse of the earth. Pressing his moistened nose into the dirt, he drew shallow breaths through his mouth, and prayed.

His mind went away, drawn down into the bowels, the warm, sheltering channels of the earth. His need, and the primitive instinct for deep cover, would envelop him in her protective womb.

Time passed.

When he returned to himself, the filtered sunlight fell with more heat on his bare skin and the woods were as silent as woods can ever be. He scrambled to his feet and took up the flint and steel. It sparked right away, as he knew it would.

Transferring the burning char cloth to the oakum, he blew gently as smoke curled up from the nest of delicate fibers, catching and growing. He watched the tongue of flame lick and devour, felt his own answering arousal, the echoing fervor within himself.

Soon the altar fire was burning in earnest, sending long tendrils of dancing vapor up into the welcoming branches of pine, maple, and birch. The dry wood hissed and crackled as it burned, adding its voice to the proceedings. All was in readiness.

The killer held up the banner of blood and began.

6

RICK ENTERED THE EMPTY squad room.

He stirred cream into his coffee and took a tentative sip as he surveyed the bulletin board littered with notices, flyers, and bits of random information. The bitter-hot liquid stung his lip, and he placed the cup on the table amid a smattering of sticky rings.

The first to arrive, he made use of the time before his fellow officers entered by reviewing the Seattle PD files on the first two murders seemingly linked to the Coby Waters killing. He marveled that fate had drawn him into the very case he'd hoped to investigate. He was as green as they come, having just earned the rank of Detective, but he'd worked hard preparing for this over the last four and a half years.

He thought about that long-ago rainy day in the dingy, run-down taco joint. He mused over the memory of that meeting with Cal and how it had changed the course of his life.

After that day, he'd finished his third tour with the Navy SEALs, squeezing every bit of knowledge, training, and experience he could out of those years. He took an honorable discharge and entered the Police Academy, studied and earned a degree in Criminal Justice, and struggled his way up the ranks.

He worked and waited for further instruction, pushing back at the wall of doubt, the whispering voice that said Cal and his people had forgotten all about him.

And then two weeks ago, after years of no contact, Cal had called.

"You in the mood for tacos?"

"Do bears take a dump in the woods?"

They'd met again at Chico's and Cal assured Rick he'd not been forgotten. On the contrary, from the details of their discussion, Rick understood he'd been under close observation for much of those last four years.

He felt vindicated. And a little creeped out.

They sat in a dimly lit booth, eating fish tacos, dripping sauce from their chins and mopping it up with waxy paper napkins while they talked about the future.

Now, in the squad room, Rick's coffee had cooled to the perfect temperature. He drank it down and pondered the possibility that it had not been fate, but something more deliberate, that had maneuvered him onto this case.

He didn't want to over analyze. When the brass ring presents, you grab it and go.

All other considerations aside, one thing was clear—this was a test he must not fail.

The other members of the squad trickled in, cradling their own coffee cups while Nate herded in the stragglers and closed the door. Nate was the acting homicide supervisor, while the detective who carried the official title was out on emergency medical leave, undergoing back surgery.

He began by asking for updates on current investigations, inquiring into plans and making assignments. Rick was half afraid Nate would change his mind about letting a rookie homicide detective partner with him on such a high-profile case, but he sent the members of the squad about their business until only the two of them were left.

Nate scratched a few notes into the case book and flipped it shut. "Did you get an address for Mountain Vista?"

"It's clear out in Mason County," Rick told him. "You could just about stand on the eighteenth hole and cast a line into the Hood Canal. It'll take all day just to follow up that one lead."

He hesitated, unsure if Nate would appreciate what he was about to propose. "Why don't we split up, cover more ground?"

"Makes sense," Nate said in a tone that suggested he was willing to be reasonable, even with a guy who had no track record. "You comfortable with that?"

"I am. I'd like to comb through these files, maybe follow up with some of the witnesses. I also want to check if the specialists turned up anything more with the trace evidence and be Johnny on the spot if any new information comes to light."

"In other words, you still think the blood-stained jacket's got no legs."

Rick grinned. "Jackets don't, as a rule."

"Got me there," Nate said. "One problem, though. It's a long drive to Mason County and my car's got a bum radiator. I should have replaced it months ago, just never have the time."

Rick was assigned one of the unmarked Ford Explorers used by the department detective squads, but Nate was accustomed to riding shotgun when he was on the clock, so he drove his own car to the station each day.

"Leave me your jalopy and take the Explorer. Gas card's in the glove compartment."

Nate shrugged. "You sure?"

Rick felt a surge of confidence. "Absolutely."

Nate dug in his pocket and tossed over his car keys, accepting Rick's in return.

"There's a jug of coolant in the trunk and four gallons of water. If you need to drive anywhere, just keep an eye on the temp gauge. You might have to stop to let her cool down and top it off."

"Sure. I got it covered."

Nate slapped him on the back and headed for the parking lot.

Once he was gone, Rick walked down two floors and entered the men's restroom. He made sure he was alone and let himself into a stall, taking a cheap cell phone from his pocket and punching in a number he'd memorized but never called.

Someone picked up and invited him to speak.

"I'm in," was all he said.

7

Rainier was awake and screaming.

Topper stared at the data showing that the earthquakes had resumed, increasing in both magnitude and frequency, accompanied by harmonic tremor for the first time in six weeks. He was galvanized, nearly dancing with frustration over the unresponsive attitude of so many authorities in the vicinity. Seattle and many surrounding communities slept within reach of the volcano, filled with populations lulled into complacency.

Someone had placed a copy of *The Seattle Times* on his desk, opened to an inner page, a short article circled in red pencil.

PARTY'S WINDING DOWN

Mt. Rainer has entertained Seattle in grand fashion since mid-July, but her game has grown old and now government officials are scratching their heads over how to pay for the road closures and lost revenue. Yes, Daddy has taken the T-bird away. We can no longer afford to pay attention to Rainier's theatrics. The show's over, Seattle. It's back to business as usual.

The press had moved on, the briefings ended, excitement over.

Topper squeezed his eyes shut and took a deep breath. He knew when Rainier blew, it would not be lava flow or ash which posed the greatest danger, although these would be devastating. It would be the lahars, the rivers of mud created by landslides of melting snow mixing with boulders and debris, growing and picking up speed as they surged down the mountain like wet cement at forty miles per hour, destroying everything in their path.

Acoustic Flow Monitors, AFMs, had been installed on the mountain at the heads of major river valleys. These had sensitive microphones that can detect the sound of lahars traveling over ground and send the alarm. Scientists, working with local emergency services, had developed evacuation plans for the communities at risk, but time would be perilously short and the paths to safety were remarkably limited.

Some towns, directly in the flow channel, were equipped with a hi-lo siren signal and even the school children were drilled in how to react to it—run to high ground. But outside of these communities, few were prepared for the catastrophic effects of a big eruption.

The natural disaster would be eclipsed by man-made pandemonium.

Candace gave the wall of his cubicle a quick double-knock. "They've shut the mountain," she told him. "Moved the roadblocks down, restricted the area. The ball is rolling."

Topper pulled at his hair. "That's spit in the wind. No one's taking it seriously."

"It's progress," Candace said. "The Forest Service can close federal lands, but anything beyond that requires the governor's approval and she's under a lot of pressure not to close."

"This is crazy." Topper blew out a long, frustrated breath. "Private citizens assert their property rights and ignore the roadblocks. Logging companies sign waivers and send their people in. Thrill-seekers get their kicks sneaking in as close to the monster as they can get."

He seized a tension ball from the desktop and squeezed it hard.

"Rainier is going to blow," he said. "She's gonna blow big and she's gonna blow soon. The governor needs to issue a state of emergency and evacuate."

Candace banged her head gently against his cubicle wall, echoing his vexation. "I agree, and we're working on it." She ran a tired hand through her long, dark hair. "But it's like building a boat while you're rowing it, and the funds for dealing with it have been drained over the last two months."

"Someone's got to front the cash. This has to be done."

"No argument here, but we're dealing with 'the boy who cried wolf' syndrome. The mountain has been threatening and then not following through for so long that no one listens anymore. The Game Commission lobbies to keep areas open for fishing and hunting, so they don't lose license revenue. Business owners cry foul when closures affect their bottom line."

Topper started to protest but she held up a hand, cutting him off.

"On top of that," she continued, "we're dealing with multiple jurisdictions. Who's responsible for setting the roadblocks? Who pays to maintain them? Who's in charge? There's a lot to consider—"

"Wrong," Topper broke in. "There's only one thing to consider. How to get people away from the mountain as quickly as possible."

"Yes, and that starts with an official action. Like I said, we're working on it."

Topper smacked his fist down, sending a tub of paperclips skittering across the desk. "Put me in a helo. Let me go up and get some more samples. I'll bet the SO2 levels have spiked since last night."

"And what if they have?"

Topper saw that her chest was heaving under the white lab coat she wore. Her cheeks were flushed, her brows drawn down in a shape like a winging bird. He felt a little sorry for her. She was getting pounded from both sides.

Reaching up, he traced his thumb along her full bottom lip, where the red tint she always wore had gone a little smudgy. "I'll take care of this," he said.

She slapped his hand away. "What are you going to do?"

He sketched a salute and backed toward the door.

"Topper, stand down. Leave it!"

He ignored the alarm in her voice as he shut the door behind him. At the other end of the hallway, he entered the lounge and saw Jack Ridley drowsing on a couch after a long night running samples.

"Hey, buddy," Topper said, "You up for a road trip?"

They headed south on I-5, threading through the early Saturday traffic. The morning was cool, the air clear, and Topper could see Rainier rising in the distance, the tallest mountain in the Cascade range, part of the fabled 'ring of fire.' He kept his foot pressed down on the accelerator and watched for cops.

He heard paper crinkling as Jack peeled the wrapper off another Egg McMuffin from the sack on the console between them. "So, you're convinced eruption is imminent," Jack said through a mouthful of sandwich. "And yet you're taking us to the mountain? If you've got a hot date with death, why'd you have to bring me along?"

Topper munched a hash brown patty. "I need someone to help me put the fear of God into these people. I aim to cheat death, not cozy up with it."

Jack swigged some orange juice. "You know the old Sufi story, right? The Appointment in Samarra?"

"Let's say I don't."

"It happens in Baghdad, where a certain servant goes to the market and sees this scary looking dude and realizes it's Death. With a capital D. So, Death reaches out to him with his bony arm, and it scares the guy out of his wits. He rushes back to his master and begs for a horse so he can ride to Samarra and escape the terrible fate waiting for him in Baghdad."

Jack paused for another bite of breakfast and Topper waited for the rest of the story, though he had a fair suspicion about how it would end.

"So, the master is a decent fellow and sends him away on his fastest horse. Then he goes out to investigate and see if he can figure out what so terrified his servant. The master finds Death in the marketplace, and asks him, 'Hey, what's the big idea? Why'd you have to scare away my servant?' And Death says, 'I didn't mean to frighten him. I was just so surprised to see him here because I have an appointment with him tonight in Samarra.'"

Topper swallowed potato and opened his juice. "The moral being that you can't cheat death. I get it, but don't you think part of the human contract is to try? People do. It's an accepted practice."

"Of course," Jack said. "But then there are those who accept their fate with grace. Remember what David always said?"

Topper nodded. "If I die young, I hope it's in an eruption."

"Too bad he got his wish."

Volcanologist David Johnston was probably the first casualty claimed by the 1980 eruption of Mount St. Helens, perched on his observation post six miles away. David believed that scientists had to do whatever necessary, even at the risk of their own lives, to help protect the public from natural disasters.

And he'd walked the walk.

Topper had been six years old when David died and had never met the USGS scientist, but he'd modeled his career after David's example. David and his fellow scientists had convinced authorities to close down Mount St. Helens prior to the big eruption and their efforts had spurred huge evacuations and saved thousands of lives.

Topper's parents had let him watch as much of the news coverage as he could absorb, and he'd spent hours in front of the TV, transfixed and amazed that one man could have so much impact. He'd formed his life's ambition from that day.

He glanced in the rear-view mirror as he turned off on the Puyallup exit. "I feel like David's with us on this, riding in the back seat."

Jack bobbed his head. "No doubt." He swallowed and crumpled the sandwich paper into a ball.

They drove for a while in silence, miles sliding under the tires at a steady pace. As they approached the roadblock area, the atmosphere changed.

Pickup trucks scattered the side of the road, parked at crazy angles, tailgates open, lawn chairs out. Portable barbecues smoked and sputtered, and hot sauce flowed as folks served up "lava burgers" and "fire dogs."

Music blared, metal competing against bluegrass and hip-hop for volume points. Topper saw card tables decked with stacks of ball caps and T-shirts printed with pithy, volcanic remarks like "Me and Joe vs. The Volcano," "I reigned on Rainier," and "Just when you thought it was safe to go hiking..."

"Nice to know the spirit of capitalism is alive and well," Jack said.

"Sure," Topper agreed. "But these enterprising citizens may not live to spend the profits."

Makeshift displays offered vials of ash, pumice stones, volcano-shaped ashtrays. Buy two, get one free.

Artists with easels sketched and painted the mighty mountain, working from photos because there's no vantage point when you're this close.

Crowds of people strolled and laughed. Money changed hands. The volcano puffed.

Jack stared, mouth hanging open under his crumb-strewn mustache. "I'll be damned."

Topper nodded. "Welcome to hell."

8

From the kitchen, Riley heard the growl of a motor crawl into her driveway and putter to a stop.

Her stomach gave a lurch. Last night's disaster was sure to bring some media attention her way, and she wasn't ready to face the probing questions, the same ones she'd been asking herself. Teren had arranged to pick her up early and get her out of the house before the vultures descended.

She passed her wet hands over a kitchen towel and stepped across the cool tiles and onto the hardwood floor of the living room, peering out at the boxy SUV. The scowl she wore dropped away and she laughed as Teren's legs emerged and he strode across the lawn to the front porch. She walked out to meet him.

"Good morning, Riley. Nice to see you laughing. Will you share the joke?"

"I expected you to pull into the driveway with a couple kayaks strapped to the top of your miniscule smart car. The mental image is amusing me."

He grimaced. "Your derision is what I had hoped to avoid. I drive my sweet little Smartie on most occasions, but sometimes only a utility vehicle will do."

He ran his gaze over her. "You ready?"

"After last night's fiasco, I am more than ready. You promised this would melt away my stress and I hope you can deliver."

They climbed into the SUV and Teren drove along the lakeside road to the small boatyard used by the residents. Riley helped load and secure two kayaks to the overhead rack.

"Why is one long and skinny and the other short and stout?" Riley asked. "They remind me of my grandparents."

Teren smiled. "The long one is a sea kayak. It's fast, but harder to handle and tips easily. The other one is a recreational kayak. It's more stable and easier to get in and out of. What's your preference, first-timer?"

"I think grandma will be more my speed."

Half a mile down a steep hill, they arrived at the Case Inlet, part of the Puget Sound. Teren pulled down the broader, blue kayak and fitted it with a back rest, sliding it near the water's edge. He helped Riley climb inside.

"You're sitting in the cockpit," he told her. "And this," he said, indicating the lip around the large hole of the cockpit, "is the rim. Why is that important? Because that's where you attach the spray skirt if you want to keep dry." He paused. "Well, relatively dry."

He placed a thick, rubbery, apron-like apparatus over Riley's shoulders and stretched it snug around the rim of the cockpit. Handing her a paddle, he shoved her boat into the water before pulling down the narrow red kayak and fitting himself through the much smaller cockpit opening.

Soon, they were paddling across the smooth surface of the water, and it was much easier than Riley had feared. Like gliding.

Teren shot ahead, his sleek kayak slicing the skin of the inlet like a razor on wrapping paper. He showed off some fancy maneuvers and bowed to Riley's applause, then waited for her to catch up.

As they paddled side by side, Teren pointed out some of the plants that grew along the edge of the water. He kept her entertained with tidbits about birds and animals, but she was most interested in his stories about human activities, past and present.

They paddled past a house with imposing walls closing it off from the land side, but it was open to the bay and Riley gaped over the extravagance on display. She'd attended parties and events hosted by the affluent residents in the area. Her status as a concert pianist married to a handsome firefighter had opened a lot of doors, but she was by no means inured to such a high level of gloss.

"Smuggling money, there," Teren said, waggling a paddle at the house. "From way back. There are a lot of caves near here, hideaways and trading posts for smugglers. I wouldn't be surprised if some were still in operation."

"What were they smuggling?"

"Everything from bootleg whiskey to opium. The U.S. imported a lot of Chinese labor back then, to build the railroads, work the mines, run the laundries. They liked their happy poppy juice."

Dipping his paddle, he worked it against the subtle current, slowing his kayak's passage. He turned to squint at Riley. "You ever tried geoduck ice cream?"

"Never heard of it. What's a gooey duck?"

Teren let out an amused bellow, then cut it off abruptly when he saw her puzzled look.

"Oh, you're serious," he said, with a touch of awe. "How is it possible that you've lived half a mile off the Puget Sound for six years and never met the favorite phallic symbol of the Pacific Northwest?"

"Now I'm intrigued. And they make it into ice cream? What does that tell you?"

He laughed again. "It's all the rage at the Geoduck Festival." He scrutinized her more closely. "Really, you've never been?"

"In my defense, I must point out that during much of that six-year period, I was on tour in far-off places and for the last two years my social calendar's been...less than festive."

Teren grunted. "Point taken."

After a moment of silence, Riley said, "So, what's a gooey duck?"

Teren started paddling again, speaking over his shoulder as she followed.

"I take your education in such matters very seriously, so I'm going to give you the long version. The geoduck is a sort of clam, native to this region and distinctively shaped, as I think I mentioned."

He turned and waggled his eyebrows at her. Riley felt the blush on her cheeks and smiled.

"It might surprise you to know that it was also a hot ticket on the smuggling catalog and was traded with gusto on the international black market. The name comes from the native Nisqually language and means dig deep. And they weren't kidding."

He described the method for digging the clam out from the mudbed, shucking rocks and snails the size of softballs, the mollusk doomed but still resisting.

"You have to work for your supper, but so worth it. Although my first encounter with a geoduck was supremely unappetizing.

He wiped a hand over his forehead as if shining the memory to life.

"Shortly after we moved here, a neighbor took my wife and daughter clamming. They brought home a geoduck and instructions for cooking it. Wanting to immerse themselves in the local culture, they heated up a pot of boiling water and went to work."

He threw his head back, laughing as he recalled the occasion.

"When I came home, I was met with the most hideous smell and Beth and Amy were both in tears. I couldn't imagine what had happened. When they told me how they'd botched up the cooking of the clam, I thought it was hilarious and they were both furious with me."

He slapped the water with his paddle and watched it spurt up before finishing his story.

"My wife maintained that it was one of the most horrendous episodes of her life. They went to bed hungry, leaving me to clean up the kitchen and sample the seafood."

Wrinkling his nose, he said, "I don't know what they did wrong, but it tasted like raw sewage and smelled worse than that."

Riley couldn't get past the thought. "And they make ice cream out of it?"

Teren chuckled. "Lemon geoduck ice cream is not half bad. Don't knock it till you've tried it."

They'd been paddling through an open area and now approached an island. Teren gestured to it.

"Let's pull up there."

After they'd beached their kayaks, Teren surprised Riley by opening a hatch in her wide-bodied blue boat and pulling out a blanket and a cloth bag packed with a picnic.

"Brunch," he told her.

They spread the blanket on the grassy bank and Teren passed her a croissant stuffed with ham and asparagus. The day was fine, laced with a cool, light breeze and the marshy smell of muddy earth.

They munched, content and quiet. After a while, Riley swallowed and said, "I'm ashamed of myself, Teren. I've been so caught up in my own misery and struggles that I forgot other people have theirs, too."

She paused. "You never told me what happened to your wife and child. You only said you were in a unique position to understand my pain. What does that mean?"

Teren tore out little handfuls of tufted grass and threw them toward the water. For a long moment, he said nothing and when he spoke his voice sounded rusty.

"They died in a fire. A forest fire. It hit quick and moved fast...and they were caught."

The sun seemed suddenly to dim by a few degrees. Riley managed to murmur, "I'm sorry," before her throat closed, and a fresh spear of pain stabbed her under the breastbone. Teren's hand covered hers. She felt its warmth and strength as they sat listening to the lapping waves.

Doubt sucked at her, like a sinkhole. How do we survive? How do people manage after soul-searing disaster strikes? It's been two years, and I don't feel any closer.

Does anyone ever truly regain their footing? Does anyone ever feel whole again?

A flock of birds flew overhead, stirring the air. It was time to go.

Back in the kayaks, they glided over the water and Teren pointed to a rising hump of land in the distance.

“Herron Island,” he said. “Privately owned. About a hundred and fifty people live there and if you’re not one of them, you have to show an invitation in order to board the ferry.”

He looked up into the sky, noting the position of the sun, trailing his paddle in the blue-green water. “It’s time we headed home.”

Turning his kayak, he struck off toward the east. “Let’s paddle back along the opposite shore,” he called. “There’s something I want to show you.”

He led her into a channel with tapering sides which narrowed until the bank was only a paddle’s length away on each side. Drooping trees, willows perhaps, dipped their pale green fronds in the water and formed a leafy tunnel through which the sunlight filtered. A wavering, liquid gold.

Teren turned his kayak sideways, blocking the channel and bringing her to a stop against him.

“Hear that?” he asked.

Riley listened to the gentle slap of water against their boats, the faint gurgle of tiny waterfalls formed by branching, wayward trickles. A bird called in the distance and here, under the canopy of leaves, crickets chirped.

“The crickets, you mean?”

“Yes, the crickets. Isn’t it odd?”

“What’s odd about it?”

“Think about it, Riley. When do crickets sing?”

This was a subject she’d never thought much about, but as she listened, she began to realize that there was something strange about the cricket song.

“They chirp at night,” she said.

"Yes. They chirp at night."

They sat, holding against the current, listening to the creaky music.

"Do you know why they chirp at night?" Teren asked.

"I suspect you're fixing to repair another gap in my education."

He didn't respond and Riley feared she'd offended him. After a moment, she said, "I really am interested to hear about it."

In the shadow of the channel, she couldn't see his face.

"Male crickets sing to attract a mate. They chirp at night because, well, nighttime is the right time. And they shut up during the day to escape the notice of predators."

"So, why are these crickets making such a racket now?"

"Because they have nothing to lose. We've come to the very end of summer. The cricket has only a few days left to live. If he gets taken out in June, he loses the chance to mate dozens of times throughout the summer and leave hundreds of offspring. But to hold back now, what would be the point?"

"Make hay while the sun shines?"

"Make hay or make whoopie." He paused. "You are listening to the final, desperate song of the male cricket looking for a mate."

Riley sensed an undercurrent in his words and felt her cheeks go warm. Teren had been so much to her in the two years since Jim died. Friend, sounding board, punching bag. But not this.

She hadn't considered that he might have feelings beyond friendship for her and a pang of regret swelled within her, tinged a little by selfish anger. Why would he jeopardize what they had, putting it on new and shaky ground, when she still needed him so much?

He'd left her the option of feigning oblivion, and she'd grab it. At least until she'd had time to examine her own feelings and decide how to handle this new dimension. She was aware, in that moment, of no waking passion, only an abiding affection.

Forcing a light note into her voice, she said, “To me they sound...cheerful. Not desperate, but hopeful.”

He cocked his head, evaluating. “Hopeful, it is then.”

Looking away, he cleared his throat. “In Eastern cultures, crickets are a symbol of protection. They alert households to threats.”

“They set up a clatter, like a watchdog?”

“Quite the opposite.”

He let out a sudden harsh cry and slapped the water with his paddle. The cricket song ceased.

“They go silent, a complete and sudden absence of noise. That’s a sign. They sense danger and they stop singing to protect themselves. There are several Chinese accounts in which crickets have saved lives by alerting the family to intruders.”

He shifted in his seat, setting the kayak gently rocking. “Sometimes when danger threatens, it’s best to be still. Like the crickets.”

They sat in silence for a moment, the air around them heavy with significance.

Riley stirred. “You make them sound quite useful. Do people keep them as pets?”

“Absolutely. They fashion cages from bamboo, ceramic, even gourds.”

He released the kayaks from their holding position, and they proceeded through the channel. “I’m surprised you haven’t seen this in your world travels.”

“I spend so much time rehearsing and sleeping, I miss a lot. I have seen some amazing things, but not crickets in cages.”

They paddled homeward while Teren delivered an entertaining stream of wildlife trivia. Riley tried to regain the lightheartedness she'd felt earlier in the day, but a layer of melancholy descended over her once again, refusing to be dispelled by the glorious sunlight breaking through the trees overhead.

9

THE KILLER TURNED HIS vehicle off the main road and pulled into the tiny parking lot at the deserted trailhead.

He parked in a spot half hidden by a drooping profusion of multi-colored leaves and listened to the motor ticking as it cooled. Turning up the radio, he scanned through the channels, listening to snippets of songs, a brief snatch of Mariachi, the ranting of a talk radio host.

He flipped over to FM and paused as the plaintive strains of guitar and violin reached him and he recognized the song by Kansas. *Dust in the Wind.*

It conjured a memory, shimmery at first, then solidifying until he smelled the hot french fry grease, felt the pinch of his too-small tennis shoes, and he was there again.

It was his birthday. He turned nine that day and he wanted a hamburger.

They'd left their place in the woods—he and his parents—and hiked to the highway to wave their thumbs at passing cars. Most sped by, drivers studiously ignoring them, curious passengers sometimes staring from the back seat.

When a car pulled over to collect them, his dad laughed and said his mother's long legs had done it. His nine-year-old mind had been confused because he thought you did it with your thumb.

They rode in a car with big yellow curves, singing *boom-di-ada, boom-di-ada, boom-di-ada, boom-di-ada, boom-di-ay* and trailing their fingers out the windows in the warm breeze.

They stopped at a road-side burger stand and his mother had smooched their driver on the cheek as he dropped them off. The man had turned red and tapped the horn in a merry toot as he'd motored away.

The burger joint rose up from the dust, a garish pink and white box with bright green trim. The lurid colors had dazzled him, nearly knocking him over after weeks of nothing but shady browns and grays in the forest.

He followed his parents as they joined the line of customers at the order window. Stumbling over a loose stone on the pavement, he reached out a hand to steady himself, laying it on the rear fender of a shiny, cherry-red convertible with its top down.

A foursome of teenagers filled the car, bubbling with talk and laughter, and music blasted from the car's speakers. He felt the beat of it through his fingers on the car's fender, absorbing the *ooh, ooh, ooh, ooh* that was the essence of *Stayin' Alive.*

He smiled. It felt like a gift. For his birthday. This sun, this music, these vibrations in his hands.

Standing there, grinning, he shuffled his feet in a private sort of dance. He looked at the backs of the teenagers' heads and saw sleeked hair, turned-up collars, a blue ribbon tied around a blonde ponytail.

And then the ponytail twitched, and the girl turned her head, saw him shambling side to side on the pavement behind the car, a silly grin on his face.

She froze, a french fry dipped in ketchup hovering an inch from her mouth.

"Alan," she said to the boy at the steering wheel and tilted her head toward the rear of the car. Her voice sounded like the bray of the donkey he like to pet in the paddock at the edge of the woods. The boy peered over the back of the seat.

"Watch it, kid. Get your hands off my car."

The couple in the rear seat turned around also.

"Oh, look," said the pretty dark-haired girl, laughing. "He's dancing. Can't you see he's dancing?"

The back-seat boy popped up on his knees for a better look and shouted, "Hey, queer, if you gotta pee, the john's around back."

They all broke into laughter, the donkey girl's brays floating up and up, like soap bubbles you made with a wand.

The music from the radio changed to melancholy strains, sounding unutterably sad. He stopped smiling and dropped his hands, stepping away from the car, looking around for his mom and dad. They were standing at the order window, nearly at the head of the line. The woman in front had her big, brown purse open, counting out change.

Guitar and violin sang together, and the mournful words of *Dust in the Wind* imprinted on his mind as he watched his dad step forward and push the woman with the big purse aside. He grabbed two filled bags off the counter and turned, sprinting away.

His mother, already running, reached him where he stood behind the shiny fender and grabbed him, pulling him along.

"Let's go, baby."

Holding hands, they ran.

"Hey!" the woman shouted after them, surprise and anger in her voice. "Those are my burgers. Come back!"

Deep into the trees they dashed, his parents whooping victory shouts. When it seemed safe, they sat on logs and his mother opened the grease-stained bags to see what they'd got.

"Here's your hamburger," she said, handing him a foil wrapped packet. "Happy Birthday, honey."

The burger tasted like sawdust on his tongue. He worked to swallow each bite, wanting to spit it from his mouth as he wanted to spit the ugly memory from his mind.

He'd forced down every morsel.

Now, he pushed the scanner button on the radio, scrubbing the images from his thoughts, and found a news station.

"*...since Mount St. Helens in May of 1980, though scientists predict a Rainier eruption could be far deadlier. The mountain continues to rumble, but no time frame has been specified and no official warnings have been issued. Also, no word yet from the Governor's office regarding what actions will be taken.*"

The announcer made a slight shift in tone as he turned his attention to a different news story.

"*Police continue their investigation into the brutal slaying of Coby Waters, the singer and songwriter who took Downed Illusion to the top of the charts in the late nineties. The killing occurred early Friday in a wooded area outside Bellevue. Investigators are following a number of leads and declined to comment whether this case is connected to two similar murders in the Seattle area in recent weeks. For breaking news and developments keep your dial tuned to...*"

He continued scanning through the stations, but it was all the same. One thing was clear.

His work was not finished.

Grabbing a duffle bag off the seat beside him, he opened the car door and set off along the path. A quarter mile down the trail, he veered off the marked route and searched for three kinds of wood, deadfalls that would be waiting for him.

They were always waiting for him, laid ready, he believed, by a benevolent hand.

He gathered the stones and the broken branches, using his knife to pare down where necessary, arranging them in the duffle, checking that all items were in place. A tuneless humming passed between his pressed lips, accompanying his movements, allowing him, in some way, to be both distracted and focused on his own actions, like a man whose left hand didn't know what his right hand was doing.

He knelt and zipped the bag. He was ready.

No footprints showed in the pine needles and springy undergrowth beneath his feet. They disappeared instantly behind him, erasing his presence as he headed back to the car. He saw no birds, no squirrels, nothing to witness his passing.

He was like dust in the wind.

10

Topper watched as an object hovered in the sky above his Jeep.

It cast a brief shadow over the hood and then swooped, hitting the windshield with a smack. A frisbee. The shirtless man who scooped it from the ground gave the hood of the car a double thump and a grin by way of apology.

Jack's hands were braced against the dashboard, and he stared out the window as if they'd just crash-landed on another planet.

"This reminds me of that scene from The Ten Commandments, when Moses brings down the word of God from the mountaintop and everyone's dancing around the golden calf."

"I'm no Moses," Topper replied, "but I guess I know what he felt like."

They left the car and waded into the festival atmosphere. Two young women, their long hair threaded with daisy chains, drifted by with dreamy expressions and the faint scent of cannabis. Another woman moved through the press of people, handing out free hacky sacks, and groups of teenagers stood in circles, kicking the tiny footbags back and forth.

Topper watched a grizzled-looking old guy in a pair of mud-spattered dungarees weave through the crowd, clearly under the influence.

The front of his T-shirt featured a picture of the mountain. It read, "This is Rainier," and as he passed, Topper turned to read the follow-up: "This is Rainier on crack." The letters were dripping with lava and fire shot out the top of the volcano.

Children raced each other up and down the road, gleeful and carefree, tagging the orange and white striped barrier as the finish line. The roadblock was unmanned. Whatever authority had placed it there had abandoned post, and the crowd surged freely on both sides of it.

Topper scanned the throng, pushing his way through, waiting for inspiration to guide his next move. A voice wavered above the general din, belting out an off-pitch rendition of *Bohemian Rhapsody*.

Someone was set up for karaoke.

Topper set his course in that direction and got in line behind a woman who looked like Susan Boyle. He hoped it wasn't, because that would be a hard act to follow, and he needed everyone's attention. When the woman's turn arrived and she dove into the first verse of *Livin' on a Prayer*, she set his mind at rest on the matter.

Belting out the final chorus, she finished to applause from what must have been her family, a thin, balding man surrounded by three plump ginger-headed children. Beaming, she handed the mic to Topper and left the stage.

"Whatcha singin' buddy?" asked the man at the control board.

Topper waved him off and held the microphone to his mouth. "Ladies and gentlemen, please listen to this important announcement. Mt. Rainier is about to erupt. I repeat, the mountain is going to blow any moment now."

Loud boos burst out from every corner of the crowd. Topper raised his voice and continued his appeal.

“Please pack your things and leave in an orderly fashion. You are in danger here and you n—”

Rough hands invaded his armpits as two men hefted him from behind and dragged him away amid the laughter and cheering of the throng. Another man stepped forward and snatched the microphone.

“Cue up some John Denver for me, Sid. You got Grandma’s Featherbed?”

His assailants dragged Topper outside the circle of revelers and tossed him down with more amusement than derision. Topper lay where they left him, squeezing his eyes shut against the noonday sun overhead. At length, he rolled over, and sat up. Jack joined him, trying to stifle a grin.

Topper scowled. “It’s not funny.”

Jack shrugged, still smiling. Raising up on an elbow, Topper watched the gaggle of men relegated to the outskirts of the reveling mob. One grungy guy was fitted out with a sandwich board printed in large, blood-red letters: DOOMSDAY IS HERE! THE END IS NEAR!

Another grim-faced man wore a flowing robe and long, white beard. He carried cardboard tablets—a replica of the Ten Commandments—and waved them around at intervals while uttering dire warnings.

“Moses showed up after all,” Topper said. “What do we do now?”

“I could go for a lava burger.”

Topper’s phone vibrated in his pants pocket. He pulled it out and read the text from Candace.

We got the green light. Come help me.

"Grab it to go," he told Jack. "It's time to make like the Red Sea and split."

11

NATE HATED TRAVELING AROUND the Point of Tacoma.

The flow of traffic, compressed between waterways onto the I-5, was difficult to navigate and passing the dull, ugly hump of the Tacoma Dome depressed him. He tried dialing Anita's number again, but when he heard the standard voicemail message, he disconnected.

Anita Graham had been a presenter at a conference he'd attended last year in Florida. A large woman with a vibrant personality, she'd impressed him with her confidence, knowledge, and expertise. Anita was a criminal profiler, and the seminar she'd conducted had been interesting and eminently convincing. Nate had cultivated her contact and consulted her three or four times in the months following their meeting, finding her guidance helpful and insightful.

Except for the last time he'd called, a month ago.

His phone buzzed and he picked up the call. Anita, with her usual efficiency, offered no preamble. "Nate, how can I help?"

"Hello, Anita. I'm on a case that's right up your alley. I'll send you the details, but I hoped you could give me a preliminary opinion on what I might be dealing with."

Nate outlined the salient points of the case and gave information for the two prior murders he believed were connected.

"What is it with Seattle?" she asked. "You guys seem to grow more than your fair share of cereal crops. Sorry," she added, "I couldn't resist the pun."

Nate understood the question was rhetorical and didn't bother formulating an answer. He knew her mind was busy processing information, and her astute conclusions would soon pour forth.

After a short pause, she said, "Okay, this is just my initial impression. I know you're looking for a starting point and I'll give you what I can."

"Anything, Anita. Thanks."

"You've got three victims. A corporate exec, a right-wing senator, and a rock star. Your victims are all male, no discernible sexual component. Disparate demographics and physical descriptions. Am I tracking so far?"

"Perfectly."

"All three had their throats cut with what appears to be a similar, sharp-bladed instrument. All three crime scenes were remarkably clean as to trace evidence. No fingerprints, only undefined footmarks. The first two scenes had an arrangement of sticks and stones that might have been an altar of sorts or might contain some kind of message."

"Correct."

"And the third scene had a scatter of similar sticks and stones that might have been in the same arrangement and subsequently disturbed. Did I get all that right?"

"You got it, Anita. Sharp as ever."

"Hmm. You're dealing with a very organized killer, Nate. I'd say you're looking for a white male, probably mid to late thirties, possibly a little older. A planner, and shrewd. He could have a prior record of arson, burglary, or assault, but my gut says no. He's probably committed any number of crimes over the years, but he's smart and methodical. Chances are, he never got caught."

"Any idea why he does it?"

"I see no suggestion of a sexual motive, no signs of torture or overkill like you find with someone who enjoys inflicting pain and taking life. I'd say you've got either a thrill-seeker or a mission-oriented killer. All the victims were high-profile, so that suggests your guy likes attention. It may be a game for him."

"Wonderful," Nate said, shifting down and trying to angle into the right lane for the turn-off toward Gig Harbor.

"Nate, last time we talked...is everything alright?"

He growled and goosed the accelerator, cutting in front of a pickup hauling a boat. "I've got to go, Anita. Traffic. Thanks for your help." He ended the call and signaled for the exit.

How much stock should he put in Anita's assessments? She'd hit it spot-on the first time he'd asked for her help and come darn close the second time.

The last time he'd consulted her, it had been about Brad, the man spending time with his ex-wife and daughter. Her evaluation had instilled in him the disturbing impression that his family was becoming wrapped up with a dangerous manipulator.

Marilyn dismissed this, furious that he'd insinuate such a thing. He was jealous, she said, making excuses for his own inadequacies. This was true, of course.

But it didn't mean he was wrong.

That Anita was wrong.

If he trusted her judgment on a serial killer, he'd have to also accept that her assessment of his ex-wife's new boyfriend was likely to be accurate as well. The thought left him feeling helpless and irritated.

Scowling down at the steering wheel, he pounded it with his fist. He'd successfully navigated the freeway exit, but now the road split and he was in the wrong lane. He watched in angry silence as his turn-off slid past in the rear-view mirror.

"Cripes."

Fuming, he downshifted and braked, pulled inexorably into the tangle of midday weekend traffic in the congested shopping district of Tacoma.

12

Shielding his finger with a handkerchief, the killer rang the doorbell and waited.

A seagull flew overhead, screaming into the sky, and he heard the muted response of its mates. The door opened and he was surprised to see that the big man himself had answered the summons.

"Oh, hello." The homeowner gave a sheepish shrug. "You caught me on butler duty. Dixon is out on errands and it's just me and the cook for now."

He smiled and gestured the killer into his house. "I'm just about to leave for a meeting so I'm a bit rushed, I'm afraid. Is there something I can do for you?"

"It sounds like this is a bad time. I hoped you might show me your atrium. We spoke about it at the library fund-raiser after Better Homes and Gardens featured that layout and you mentioned—"

"Oh, sure, sure. I can give you a quick look now and we can schedule a more in-depth tour for another time. Come on back."

The killer shouldered his duffle bag and followed. He noted, as they passed the security control panel, that the alarm system was deactivated. He lagged behind just long enough to use his handkerchief to press the button for video surveillance, turning that off, as well.

He knew how to watch for cameras and had used oblique angles to keep his face hidden as he'd walked on to the property from a neighbor's empty house. He'd bargained that the man wouldn't be able to resist showing off his new pet project, and he'd guessed right.

He followed his host to the core of the house, a large glass cube with a vaulted framework ceiling, left mostly open to the sky. Beautifully landscaped miniature lawns merged with beds of plants and seating areas on raised, hardwood decks. In the center, a marble-trimmed rectangular pond housed exotic koi and lily pads.

"This is spectacular. Did you have a hand in the design?"

A modest flap of the arm. "Conceptually, yes, and a few of the little touches are mine, as well. For instance..."

He turned and bent over an arrangement of pygmy palms, pointing out a network of bamboo boxes. The killer was curious about the boxes but resigned himself to never knowing their purpose. He deployed the taser into the broad back and watched the electrodes attach, one under each shoulder blade as the man went down.

He had to work quickly now. Pulling on thin latex gloves, he fastened waterproof booties over his shoes and donned a plastic raincoat, zipping it to the chin. He reached into the duffle bag for the knife and felt a feeble tug at his left shoe.

The homeowner had made a grab for him. An uncoordinated and doomed attempt, but the killer checked the elastic enclosure of his shoe cover to ensure it was intact. He rolled the man onto his back, tipped his head as if about to deliver CPR, and drew the blade across his throat in a quick, smooth motion.

A spurt of crimson jetted across the front of the plastic raincoat, but the fountain quickly waned and soon the man sprawled in ultimate relaxation on the soft grass of his prize-winning atrium, his blood watering the earth, eyes turned heavenward.

The killer brought forth the sticks and stones, arranging them as he'd been taught. He swiped the cotton blood banner through the river of red and returned it to the duffle.

Now for the cook.

He found her at the butcher block, slicing carrots. He watched for a moment as she added disks rendered from one carrot to the growing mound of vegetables and reached for another. Inhaling appreciatively, he enjoyed the combined aromas of crushed garlic and freshly grated ginger.

A mound of smooth, pink chicken breast rested on a cutting board and glass pinch bowls held spices, rich in color and fragrance. A small measuring cup held a dark liquid he guessed to be tamari and a bottle of wine stood beside it.

The cook was efficient and a joy to watch. Her knife produced a rhythmic chopping sound, half mesmerizing him, and might have saved her life if she hadn't suddenly turned and stared at him, as if sensing his presence.

He used his own knife, then, and she dropped to the clean-scrubbed floor, uttering a keening wail that hung in the air with the smell of garlic and ginger.

Kneeling over her to retrieve his blade, he caught a flash of movement from the tail of his eye. He ducked but took a blow to his left shoulder that sent him sprawling. Dropping beside the dead cook, he rolled away and came up into a crouch, clutching his knife.

The butler was back.

The manservant held a heavy saute pan in one hand and a cell phone in the other.

"You're done for," he croaked in a warbling voice, brandishing the fry pan. "I've called the police. They're on their way."

13

Riley watched her blood mix with water and swirl down the shower drain.

It ran down her leg from where she'd cut herself shaving and slipped away, into the void. The sight compelled her. She tore her gaze from the bloody mess, but the image remained, imprinted on the layers of her mind.

Down the drain, into the void.

Wrapping herself in a towel, she stepped from the shower. She avoided looking in the mirror while she ran a comb through her hair, staring instead at the specks of granite in the countertop, counting the shades of gray.

She pulled on jeans and a light sweater, fighting a heaviness that threatened to drag her to the floor.

In the kitchen, she put on the tea kettle and sat at the table, flipping through a stack of letters and bills, pushing them aside, unread. Silence stretched through the house, filling the cracks and spaces, pressing on her like a stone.

Jim used to fill these spaces, and Tanner. In place of silence, there was laughter and music. Riley tried to keep her mind from wandering to Anne Naysmith, but it refused to be reined in. It went, like a tongue wanders to a sore spot in the mouth, prodding, waking the pain.

A movie called *The Lady In The Van* had premiered in theaters shortly after her husband and son were killed. Riley had steered clear of the cinema and avoided any talk of the film, but she already knew more about it than she cared to. It came far too close to representing the disaster of her own life and she didn't want to end up going down the same road as the title character.

The movie's subject, Miss Mary Shepherd, had been a gifted pianist on her way to a successful concert career which was derailed by trauma and mental instability. She'd spent the rest of her life living in a van parked in the driveway of a man who'd befriended her.

As horrifying as this was for Riley to consider, it was really Anne Naysmith who haunted her.

In the 1960s, Anne had been a promising concert pianist, studying at the Royal Academy of Music with Harold Craxton and Liza Fuchsova. Something had gone wrong for her, like something had gone wrong for Riley, and she ended up a bag lady on the streets of London, where she wandered for decades until she was hit by a lorry in the Chiswick High Road and killed.

The development of Anne's career, her performance repertoire, the critic's assessments of her strengths and abilities, in many ways paralleled Riley's own. And her pianistic demise, like Riley's, involved the loss of the man in her life.

Riley thought about Anne a lot, though she tried not to, because this mental path always ended in melodrama. Perhaps she, Riley, should cut out the years of wandering and just get right to the truck.

Her chair squealed across the floor as she abruptly pushed back from the table and went to the stove, switching on the countertop television as she passed to stem the flow of silence. A news program came up on the screen, a special edition covering Seattle's hottest topics.

"...continue to draw connections?"

"Well, Lisa, at this point we can only speculate how the Puget Sound Slasher chooses his victims.

"True. Everyone in the region should be exercising an extra degree of caution. We have the Slasher on one hand and Mt. Rainier on the other. What's a citizen to do?"

"You make a good point. Volcanologists say that if Rainier erupts, it could be the biggest natural disaster ever to hit the U.S."

"Scary thought. I did a little research this morning—"

"No! You? Research?"

"Yes, I did, Lisa. I buckled down and discovered that the Indian name for Mt. Rainier is Tahoma. It means 'giant slumbering in a cave'. What does that suggest to you?"

"It suggests that with Rainier's cloud cover, the giant could wake up howling and we'd never see it happening. We might not know until—"

Riley hit the off button. The prattle was worse than the silence and she just couldn't stuff another worry into her head at this point. At least the volcano and the so-called Puget Sound Slasher pulled media attention away from her concert fiasco. Not that she rated high enough for a morning news show.

The tea was too hot, but she drank it down, burning her lips and tongue. Letting the cup and saucer clatter into the deep granite of the kitchen sink, she stared out across the yard in back of the house, eyes passing over the thinning branches of the cherry tree, the spindly shrubs and yellowing grass.

Part of her understood that beneath this maudlin sulking lay the bedrock of some deeper grief, something she just couldn't get over. The bones of it poked through her misery and she dug her fingernails into the tender flesh of her wrist until the pain focused there, shutting out the rest like a numbing blanket. Lethargy seeped through her, so heavy.

Like wet cement filling her skin and hardening, pressing down.

A loud *thunk* from the living room shattered the weight holding her, allowing her to move. With a shriek of rage, she turned and ran toward the front door as two more solid thuds echoed through the empty house.

14

"Go home, Topper."

His boss laid a gentle hand on Topper's shoulder, but he brushed it off, irritated.

"This is insane!"

Grabbing at his hair, he pulled it up by the handful, releasing it to stand at attention atop his head.

"This is ludicrous. Absurd. The mountain is set to blow. Today or tomorrow, or sometime very soon. It's not going to wait politely for the go-ahead from the red tape boys."

Candace dropped some coins into the hallway vending machine, considered her choices, and pressed a button. Lips pursed, she watched her selection wriggle off the hook and fall into the tray below.

"Thanks for helping me craft the press release, Topper. There's nothing more you can do right now, so go home. Or better yet, get out of town."

She pushed back the flap on the vending machine and fished out a Danish pastry. Turning away from Topper, she walked back to the lab, high heels clacking on the tiles like the jabs of an angry typist.

Topper slammed his fist against the machine, felt the vibrations through his forearm. He'd crafted the press release, but the USGS protocols took hours to implement, and the media was jaded on Rainier, using it for filler and joke material on late-night TV.

The breaking news was focused on the serial killer, milking the story for all its sensational details, stealing attention from lesser news items. Like the biggest natural disaster in U.S. history.

He returned to his cubicle and switched on the radio to hear the latest. He understood, with great clarity, that upstaging the bloody killing of a rock star would require a lot of drama.

He had a plan.

The office area was deserted. Anyone there on a Saturday afternoon was in the lab, where the action was. Candace's office door stood open, and Topper went to her desk and woke her computer. They were required to change their passwords monthly and he knew she wrote hers down on a sticky note under her pencil tray.

Entering her password, he pulled up her official email account and copied the press release he'd written into the body of an email, making a few alterations, giving it the juice it needed to top the breaking news. He addressed it to a guy he knew at the Associated Press and hit send.

He exited her email and willed her screen back to sleep. No one appeared as he left her office and returned to his cubicle. He picked up the phone and dialed his AP contact.

"Hey, the boss lady here just sent you an email. You should give it your immediate attention. It's a bigger story than your slasher murders. Much bigger."

This reporter, Topper knew, was a bit of a rash actor and his salivary response to the dangling T-bone was almost guaranteed.

He hung up the phone and grabbed his jacket off the back of his chair. Switching off his computer, he watched it shut down while he processed a few more thoughts. He walked down to the lab and poked his head in the door.

Avoiding Candace's notice, he caught Jack's eye and beckoned him to come out into the hall.

"I'm heading out," he told Jack. Shrugging into his jacket, he patted the pockets for his wallet. "A legendary crap wad is about to hit the fan and when it does, I just wanted you to know...I'm the one who laid it."

He grinned.

"Oh, man. What did you do?"

"Candace sent a press release to the AP and authorized its dispersal which will activate a number of emergency procedures."

"She did?"

"Sure. She just doesn't know it yet. When all is said and done, she'll either be the hero or in the hash."

"Either way, you're wise to hit the eject button. When Rainier erupts, you're going to want that rampaging flow path between you and her. It's the only thing that will save you."

"Amen."

15

THE KILLER WATCHED THE butler with interest.

The man's hands, both the one holding the fry pan and the one with the cell phone, shook with dramatic intensity, his eyes wide and darting like a cornered animal. The poor fellow could barely stand.

As if repetition could make it so, the butler stammered out his pronouncement again.

"I called the police. Any minute, they'll be here."

The killer came out of his stance and let his knife hand drop limply to his side.

"Well, that's a relief," he said, letting out a groaning sigh. "I'm so tired of doing this. It's too hard lying to my friends, trying to act like everyone else, hiding what I am. I just want it to be over."

The butler's head thrashed up and down in a frantic nod.

"Well, good. It's over." His head continued bobbing, as if he'd lost control over it.

Shaping his mouth into a frown of regret, the killer said, "I've cost you a job, haven't I? I'm sorry about that, but then, you called the police on me, so that makes us even."

The butler took a step back, his eyes shifting, looking for escape.

"Yes," he quavered. "We're even."

"You did call the police, right?"

More frenzied head bobbing.

The killer smiled.

Raising the knife, he charged the butler. The fry pan glanced off his shoulder and fell to the tiles with a ringing thud as he rammed the blade up into the man's rib cage. The butler let out a strangled gurgle as the killer pulled the knife free and plunged it in again until the man stopped moaning and lay still.

He hated doing it like this. It meant wasted effort and wasted life. But he always did what the situation called for. He could be counted on for that.

He pulled at his knife, but it was lodged in bone and when he tugged it free, the blade wobbled in the handle, the fastening broken. He'd have to find a new knife, but now was not the time to do it.

He needed to clear the scene.

Prying the dead man's fingers from the cell phone, he pushed the call button and watched the display.

No bars, no service. No police.

Still, it was time to go.

He left the house and walked into the wild greenbelt where he removed the bloody raincoat and shoe covers, stuffing them into a garbage bag along with the broken knife. He'd dispose of the bundle on his way home.

16

"Yo, Jimenez!"

A passing officer hailed Rick, jerking a thumb over his shoulder. "They got something for you in Evidence."

Rick snorted. This was like watching for a pot to boil.

He'd hovered in the crime lab most of the morning, driving everyone crazy, learning only that processing the minute pieces taken from the crime scene is a slow and exacting task. He retired to his desk where he'd spent the last two hours drawing parallels between the three crime scenes, trying to make connections, combing for anything they'd missed.

And now, it seemed, the pot was boiling.

Rick headed back to the lab, eager for a new lead to follow. As he entered, the fingerprint technician beckoned him over.

"I got a partial print off one of the stones collected at the scene."

"I thought you couldn't lift fingerprints off a rock."

"Normally, we wouldn't even try. But this is chert. It's nonpermeable, almost like glass, and sometimes you can raise a print off it. A little powder, a little superglue, and voila! By itself, it doesn't mean much, but it's a ninety percent match to another print submitted from the scene."

The man paused, flipping through the pages of a notebook, sniffing loudly at regular intervals. He closed the book, freed a tissue from an industrial-sized box, and blew his nose.

"Have mercy," Rick said. "Fill in the blank."

The technician gave him a bleak look. "I got a cold, alright?"

The man finished wiping his nose, aimed and tossed the sodden tissue at a nearby wastebasket, and missed the shot. Rick swallowed his irritation, recognizing that the technician was toying with the newbie. He watched the man unwrap a cough drop and pop it into his mouth.

Reopening the notebook, the guy found the page he wanted and pondered it while sucking the cough drop. "Okay, the matching print was pulled from a scorecard found in a jacket pocket."

"You're kidding me," Rick said.

"Would I yank your chain?"

I'm a foul-up. Nate is the one on track while I've been spinning my wheels all day.

Rick turned and hurried for the exit, cursing himself, thoughts tumbling inside his head. The technician's voice caught him as he pulled open the door.

"Hey, Jimenez, don't you want the name?"

Rick reined himself in, returning to the worktable, forcing himself to speak in even tones. "Of course, please give me the name."

The man regarded him with amusement, enjoying the tease. "I ran it through a couple of databases and the computer came up with this guy."

Rick reached for the printout, but the technician pulled it just out of range.

"What are we, in fifth grade?" said Rick.

The tech smirked, holding the paper high.

"Yeah, all right." Rick hooked an arm around the box of tissues and made for the exit.

"Okay, okay. Lighten up, man."

Rick traded tissues for the printed report and scanned the information, pieces of the puzzle starting to coalesce, forming the beginnings of a plausible picture in his brain. A rush of electric energy pulsed through him.

This was the break they needed. He felt it in his gut. Things were coming together and best of all—he had a name.

He punched Nate's number on his cell phone but lost the signal before he could connect. After three failed attempts, he pocketed the mobile and picked up a station land line. He dialed the number and listened to an expanse of mute stillness.

Growling with exasperation, he slammed down the receiver and ran for the police radio, pressing the transmit button with an impatient thumb. He tried for several minutes to reach Nate, fidgeting with frustration, praying Nate would pick up.

He heard the urgency in his own voice, the need to convey this critical information to his partner.

But all he got back was static and silence.

17

"People who live in glass houses shouldn't swing a club," said Nate, "but apparently, they do. How often do you have to call in the glazier?"

The pro shop manager smiled and gave three raps on the oak countertop.

"I've been here seven years, have a house in the neighborhood, and we've never had a golf ball go through a window in Mountain Vista."

Nate whistled. "Straight up?"

The manager shrugged. "The great advantage in telling the truth is that nobody ever believes it."

Nate's drive through the golf course neighborhood had revealed a mass of well-kept houses on tidy lawns, each composed largely of glass and offering a spectacular view. From both sides of the window.

Occupants could look their fill at a distant Rainier or the local lake, but outsiders could also stare into the fishbowl habitats.

Nate introduced himself and showed his badge. The manager's demeanor altered slightly, a little flag of caution waving behind his eyes, lips tightening, fingers flexing. The man was nervous, but anything from an unpaid parking ticket to a basement full of bodies can produce such a reaction in some people.

Nate peered at the name stitched into the man's polo-style shirt. "Mr. Johanson," he said, placing photos taken at the crime scene on the counter. "What can you tell me about this jacket?"

"Call me Cappy. Let's see what you got."

Cappy Johanson donned a pair of spectacles and fiddled with the pictures, pushing them around on the counter with a stubby finger, the flesh of his forehead creasing under the blond crew cut as he concentrated.

"It's hard to tell much from a photograph."

He rounded the counter and walked to a circular rack at the back of the shop. A slice of neon pink cardstock inserted at the top read: *25% off, discount taken at the register.* Cappy Johanson slid a few hangers back and forth, then selected a jacket and returned to the counter where he spread it out for Nate's inspection.

"This jacket's like the one in your picture. I think. Is that what you wanted to know?"

"So, the jacket could have come from this shop?"

"And about a thousand other places. There's nothing in particular to tie it to Mountain Vista."

"Except that this was found in the pocket." Nate produced photos of the scorecard.

The man scrutinized the images. "Oh, yes, that's one of ours. Ninety-three, decent score, no name. Could be anyone. Sorry I can't say fairer than that."

Nate didn't reply, letting the silence stretch out, letting the man's nerves jangle, waiting for him to dump something into the gap and hoping for something useful.

Cappy Johanson scratched his nose, blinked faded blue eyes, and looked out the window at the line of golf carts. After a moment, he pursed his lips and offered an idea.

"What about the pencil?" he asked. "Was there a little pencil with the card? Might have a fingerprint on it you could use."

Nate clamped down on the sarcastic reply that played behind his lips. He shook his head and gathered up the photographs.

"No pencil," he said, passing over one of his business cards. "If anything more comes to mind, please give me a call."

"Sure thing."

Nate left the pro shop. He walked down the cart path, pausing at the driving range to assess the swings and marvel once again over the yardage of intact glass. He veered off the pavement and onto a dirt path covered in springy wood chips. Strolling beside a narrow creek which trickled through moss-covered rocks and over a series of short waterfalls, he considered his next move.

Had he wasted a trip? Was there a connection between Mountain Vista and the death of Coby Waters? Or had the jacket been dumped by someone unrelated to the case, as Rick believed?

He returned to the Explorer, started the engine, and pointed her nose down the road he'd come in on. Crossing the bridge which spanned the channel between the lake and the trout pond, he passed the clubhouse and crested the hill before the long drop down to the inlet.

On the side of the road, he saw a plum tree gracing a front garden gone slightly wild and beneath it, a teenage boy stooping to retrieve a windfall plum, the tail of his shirt pulled out to form a makeshift basket full of the fruit.

The door of the house burst open, and an auburn-haired woman boiled down the front walk, waving her arms and shrieking at the boy, who dropped his load of plums and ran into the road.

Nate jammed on the brakes. The car skidded, stopping six inches from the youth who gave the hood a disdainful thump with his fist before disappearing into a stand of pines across the street.

The woman shouted after him, her chest heaving, a high blush on her cheeks. Nate pulled to the side of the road and got out, walking around the car to meet her.

"Take it easy, lady," he said. "They're just plums, going to waste on the ground."

Eyes like green fire fixed on him.

"Yes, and welcome, if he intended to eat them. It's *that* I object to," she said, pointing to the massive plate-glass windows high above the driveway.

Smashed plums adorned the glass like Rorschach prints, dripping juice down onto the cream-colored siding beneath.

Nate felt foolish. "I see your point," he said. "I should have nabbed the fellow and made him clean up this mess. Instead, I let him get away. I'm sorry."

The woman stood, arms folded across her chest, emerald eyes still narrowed in indignation. Despite her annoyed expression, Nate found her powerfully attractive.

He bowed his head. "I suppose I'll have to stand in for the boy, do penance by proxy."

The woman's eyes traveled up and down the length of him and she gave a curt nod to hide the tiny lifting of one corner of her mouth.

"Yes, you will."

Turning, she walked down the sharp-sloping driveway to the double garage. She punched in a code and one of the doors slid open with a grinding noise that spoke of something out of place in the works. Nate joined her and they assembled the equipment, filling a bucket with cleaning solution, placing a ladder on the slanting driveway.

"Now that I'm down here, I can see why this is a chore you'd want to avoid," Nate said.

The steep driveway offered no level surface and even with the ladder and the telescoping cleaning wand, it would be a stretch to reach the window, much less scrub it clean.

The woman gathered auburn curls and secured them with an elastic band she drew from her pocket. She held out her hand. "I'm Riley."

Nate shook her hand, taking in the tilt of her cheekbones, the ivory skin, the lovely curve of her brow. He thought he understood the boy with the plums.

"Call me Nate."

He surveyed the situation. "I'm not sure where I'll be the most use," he said, "at the bottom of the ladder or on top."

"Oh, you're going up. Your arms are longer than mine and we're going to need those extra inches."

She was right. He anchored himself atop the ladder and stretched to the utmost, taking care not to overbalance. From his perch, he could see the front room of the house, the mahogany grand piano centered between the two enormous windows, glinting red in the sunlight.

He reached and scrubbed, cleaning away the mess of plums. Looking down, he saw her at the base of the ladder, straining to hold it steady on the uneven surface.

"Are you about done?" she said, a flush staining her face, sliding down her neck.

"Yes Ma'am. Coming down now."

In the empty Explorer, still parked on the road, the two-way radio squawked, sending out static, demanding attention.

No one heard and no one answered.

18

THE KILLER PLACED THE blood-soaked strip of cotton on the burning altar.

He watched it singe and catch fire, black holes burning through the fabric, disintegrating the whole into shreds and, from there, into oblivion. He sank, naked, onto the earth, face down, burrowing into the carpet of soft-crinkled leaves, breathing in the scent of dirt and loss.

He lay, crumpled and inert, remembering.

The smell was the same. It sent him spiraling back to that October cold snap.

The day she died.

He'd been playing Dragon, stalking along the stream bed as it tumbled over speckled rocks, growing sluggish along the edges with lumps of forming ice. He bellowed smoke from his dragon mouth, watching it curl in the frosty air, imagining the fire in his belly that had formed it.

He roared to the sky and heard a returning echo. Only, it was his father's voice.

He turned, frost-stung eyes searching the woods, and saw the red bob of his father's cap approaching. With dawning dread, he watched his father's frantic beckoning as he broke through the line of trees.

Together they ran.

His father's horror lifted him like a wave, carried him along in its wake. As they reached the edge of the camp, his father stopped dead, as if hitting a barrier.

Side by side, they stood on the fringe of the future, staring at the spitting fire, guttering and nearly gone. At the gray tent, utterly still and silent in the clearing. At the frosted laundry, shirts and underwear spread on spindly branches to dry in the frigid air.

His father snatched the cap off his head, clutching it to his chest. He fell to his knees, sounds escaping his throat like those of a mournful coyote.

And he—no longer a dragon, but only a boy—had stood in the autumn stillness, listening, and understood that his mother was gone.

He'd been afraid to enter the tent, afraid to leave that fluttering edge of forest, wanting to cling to things as they were. But he'd done it, walking stiffly, lifting the flap, seeing the surprise and hurt frozen into her face, recognizing the betrayal she'd felt in those last moments.

October had always been her friend.

He'd tasted salt and knew that he was crying.

As he was crying now.

The tears dripped onto the leaves beneath him, and he brushed them off his face with an impatient swipe of his hand. Rising from the ground, he began to dress. There was more yet to do, many things that demanded his attention.

He needed to be ready.

19

The shoes puzzled her.

Riley watched Nate's feet as he descended the ladder's rungs and dumped the bucket of dirty water down the storm drain. He wore nice shoes—good quality leather, sturdy, black, and understated. Three or four notches above the serviceable suit he wore.

The shoes of a man who needed to be quick and sure on his feet.

A cop.

As he squatted to tap the last of the plum fragments from the bucket, she glimpsed a peek of shoulder holster, clinching it.

Riley dipped her head, gathering cleaning supplies as she surreptitiously inspected her assistant, taking in his long, lean build, dark hair and dimples. The dimples would do her in if she wasn't careful.

He handed her the bucket and gripped the ladder, manhandling it into the garage, returning it to its place in the corner.

"So," Riley said, keeping her tone casual, "what brings you to the neighborhood, officer?"

Nate turned, raising an eyebrow. "Aren't you the bright, observant one?" He ran his hands down his suit pants, brushing off the dust. "I'm just looking to protect and serve."

"A cop that does windows. My lucky day."

He shrugged and smiled, looking away, eyes scanning the road above the slope of the driveway.

"Could I trouble you for a glass of water? I've got a long drive ahead."

"Of course. Come on up to the patio."

They climbed the steps that led from the lower level of the driveway to the yard and a small hexagonal patio above. Riley invited Nate to sit and went into the kitchen for drinks, returning with a tray of bottled water, cans of soda, and a plate of Scottish shortbread.

Nate thanked her and screwed the top off a bottle of water, draining half of it in one long swallow.

"That hit the spot."

His eyes roved over the rhododendrons, past the plum tree, up and down the street, always moving. He turned them next on her, a quick survey which lingered for a moment on the gold wedding band.

"Anything else I can do for you before I go, Mrs...?"

"It's Riley, remember? Riley Forte."

"Well, Mrs. Forte, I couldn't help but notice your piano through the windows and with a name like Forte, you must be in music. Am I right?"

Riley laughed. "It's the first thing about my husband that I fell in love with. Although it's pronounced for-*te*, with the emphasis on the second syllable and the music term stresses the first, as in *for*-te."

"What do you do, then, Mrs. For-*te?*"

Riley felt the misery settling over her again. He asked a good question.

Was she now only a former concert pianist?

On hiatus, or finished for good? She didn't know how to answer.

"I'm a classical pianist. I rehearse mostly, do a little teaching."

She'd been unable to keep the tension out of her voice and he'd heard it. Her face grew hot as an awkward silence stretched between them.

Nate broke it. "And with a name like Forte, what does your husband do, Riley?"

She pulled her water bottle into her lap and sat twisting the cap. "He was a firefighter. He died...in a fire."

"I'm sorry. How long ago?"

"Just over two years now."

A pained look crossed his face as he ran a hand through his hair. "That must have been tough." He hesitated. "Is it any comfort to you that he died in the line of duty?"

"No, it isn't."

The two hot patches that always bloomed on her cheeks when she got upset burned bright and Riley pulled in a deep breath. She'd been through this moment so many times before.

People trying to be nice, fumbling for something consoling to say, often seized upon this question. She'd formed an armored shell, but this one still got through the chinks. She swallowed and straightened in the chair.

"He died while he slept," she said. "In a house fire. With our son."

Nate looked stricken. "Oh, Riley. I'm so sorry."

Before she could think how to respond, Mrs. Newcombe from next door ran across the lawn, dressed in tennis whites. She gripped Riley's hands, clearly distressed.

"Riley, dear, it's happened. Rainier is erupting. Please come over."

She pulled Riley from her chair and dragged her along, beckoning to Nate. As they approached the open front door, they were joined by a couple rushing over from across the street.

Mr. Newcombe waited for them inside a large glass-walled room designed for gatherings. Groupings of sofas and chairs were scattered throughout. A wet bar occupied one corner and a smallish screen above it held the image of Mt. Rainier, wreathed in smoke and cloud.

It was the other end of the room, with its massive flat screen TV, that dominated the space, overwhelming Riley with the spectacle. No one sat. They were all too dumbfounded at the footage passing over the screen.

Mt. Rainier wore a cap of vaporous clouds, masking its summit. Far above the cloud cover, a black plume rose in a dark and ominous column, and below the white clouds is where the real horror unfolded.

The mountain had exploded, its western flank bursting in a vast horizontal spurt, spewing gas, ash, and hot rock for miles, setting off forest fires and sending a wave of destruction into the valleys below.

The pyroclastic eruption produced temperatures more than a thousand degrees Fahrenheit and the many square miles of ice and snow resting atop Mt. Rainier began to melt, mixing with dirt, rock, and all manner of debris.

It took on bulk as it rushed down the mountain, creating deadly lahars, torrents of mud the consistency of wet concrete, thirty feet high and traveling at forty miles per hour.

Riley stood transfixed, unable to grasp that what her eyes were seeing was reality, not special effects from an action film. Many of the scenes were overhead shots, from helicopters or high ground. In some instances, it seemed doubtful that the cameraman had survived after transmitting the last images he'd ever record.

It was utter pandemonium.

Riley felt her own problems shrink into insignificance. She experienced a wave of horror, tinged with relief, followed by pangs of guilt. This event would virtually expunge her fiasco from media attention, granting her respite.

She looked at Nate standing next to her, his face a picture of grief.

The disaster was so close and yet, at eighty-seven and a half miles, distant enough. They were safe here.

As yet untouched and unaware, Riley stared at the unfolding disaster on the screen, never suspecting how far Rainier's ripples would yet travel.

And how violently they would be rocked by it here, beyond the shadow of the mountain.

20

NATE RAN TO THE explorer, cop mode in full swing.

While he wanted nothing more than to reach Sammi and Marilyn and make sure they were safe, his responsibility was to the men under his command. The radio spit static at him as he opened the door and Rick's voice sputtered through in bits and pieces.

"...copy? We're a code four.....your status?"

"Rick, I copy. I'm a code four at Mountain Vista, heading back to you now."

"Bad idea...stay put. I'm coming...you.......partial print, got an ID...resident. Do you copy?"

"Negative. Did you say you've identified the suspect?"

"Affirmative on a suspect......Nate. I've got a name and he's there. In Mountain....."

The radio whined and popped, reverting to a steady hiss of white noise. Nate dug his cell phone from his pocket and saw the "no service" icon flickering at the top of his screen.

Tossing the phone onto the seat, he slumped against the steering wheel, staring into the distance, brain racing inside his skull.

Rick's code four indicated that things were okay at the station. For the moment, at least. A prickle of unease traced across the back of Nate's neck as he considered the rest of Rick's broken message.

He'd said there was a positive ID on the suspect, and it sounded like he believed the guy was a Mountain Vista resident.

His partner had suggested Nate stay where he was, indicating he'd make his way to the area and join him. If he'd heard and understood correctly, Nate realized his long shot with the bloody golf jacket had played out like a chip onto the green.

He tried the radio again but got only a stream of fizzing static. Returning to the Newcombe house, where the gathering crowd had grown considerably, he spotted a telephone mounted on the kitchen wall but had no luck connecting any calls.

Outside the living room, he hovered in the doorway, observing the people in the room as they clung in groups, broke apart, and shaped into new groups. Clearly, this was a popular neighborhood meeting place. Every couch and chair held an anxious body and most of the stools at the wet bar were occupied, as well.

A few free-floating groups formed near the television and the fireplace. He noticed Cappy Johanson, from the pro shop, rise to pour himself a cup of coffee from a pot at the wet bar before pulling his chair next to a couple seated together on a sofa.

The couple looked like the young, upwardly mobile type—taut, tanned, well-groomed. The man had sandy hair and wire-rimmed glasses. Smooth-faced and good looking, he had a small, perpetual smile that must keep everyone he met wondering what he was thinking.

The woman's hair was dark, forming perfect wings down each side of her exquisitely chiseled head. Her complexion was olive-toned, her eyebrows beautifully shaped and perched over dark eyes shot with golden sparks.

The strain in her posture caught Nate's attention. But as he looked around, he realized every person in the room must be feeling the stress of the catastrophe, each carrying it in their own way.

A male social butterfly circled the room. Though he appeared slightly effeminate in a lavender button-up shirt and loafers, his interest was clearly directed toward the women present. Nate caught several of his comments, flirtatious even against the backdrop of disaster, and watched as the man fluttered around Riley, settling down beside her with a coy look and a hand on her knee.

Detecting movement from the dark end of the hall, Nate watched a figure materialize like a gossamer moth. She was silvery, her long white-blonde hair brushing against bare shoulders, the boatline neck of her pale peach sweater pulled south to hug her upper arms.

Her eyes were colorless, like pools with gray-speckled rocks lining the depths. And her voice, when she spoke, was rich and smooth, rustling against his earlobe as she leaned in close.

"Excuse me, mind if I squeeze past you?"

She made the four-foot passage seem like a cramped tunnel, her hips brushing his as she slinked by, leaving a trace of throaty laughter and perfume floating in the air behind her. Breezing into the room, she drew the eye of everyone inside, accepting it as her due.

She hugged Mrs. Newcombe and stood with one hand cupped over Mr. Newcombe's shoulder, exclaiming and commiserating over Mt. Rainier's mischief. Nate sensed changes in the ambient temperature of the room, heat emanating from some directions, a decided chill from others.

The lavender butterfly's antennae quivered. Flitting off the couch, he flew into the silver dome like an enraptured idol worshipper. The smooth-faced husband shifted in his seat, turning away from his wife, and the wife's tense posture stiffened to ramrod. Cappy Johanson's voice grew loud and bantering as he turned to speak with an elderly woman in a wingback chair.

Mr. Newcombe stepped away from the silver moth woman and turned up the volume on the television.

"...in danger from lahars are being evacuated. Officials are warning people outside the evacuation zones to stay in their homes and off the roads. Do not park cars along evacuation routes."

"Thank you, Don, for that update. Viewers should be aware that power outages are expected, many roads and ferries are out of service, and channels of communication are being knocked out by the effects of the volcano. If you watched our series on Preparing for Emergencies, you should be equipped with a battery-powered radio, a week's supply of food and drinking water, and first aid materials. Above all, do not panic. We will make it through this, Seattle."

The newscaster's bright smile didn't play well against the scenes of destruction rolling on the screen behind her. Or the ribbon of disaster updates streaming across the bottom.

Nate watched the neighborhood gathering from his post in the doorway, noting expressions and behaviors, reading faces and body language. Miles away, on another plane, the volcano raged, leaving death and destruction in its path. But here, in this time and space, Nate was hunting another kind of killer.

One who could be in this very room.

21

LIKE AN ANT INCHING along a slender blade of grass, Topper steered his Jeep across the Tacoma Narrows Bridge.

He recalled how the bridge had once been known as Galloping Gertie. As a kid, he'd watched footage from the bridge's collapse in 1940, fascinated at how the structure had undulated, twisting in the wind like a child's ribbon. People abandoned their vehicles and ran to safety at the edge of the cliff before the ribbon flapped up into the wind and snapped, spilling into the water below.

Trepidation pressed down on him now as he drove over the structure. He was racing disaster, vulnerable on a narrow strand of steel and concrete suspended high over the Puget Sound.

The news came over the radio when he was halfway across.

Mt. Rainier had exploded.

The west side of her, weakened by acid-altered rock, bulging and buckling from the pressure of building magma pushing up from deep underground, had blown apart with a force a thousand times more powerful than the atomic blast at Hiroshima. Topper knew it was only the beginning of a long string of trauma.

He was vindicated.

Before he'd even left the parking lot at the Seismology lab, the radio had been trumpeting alerts, warning people away from the mountain, announcing evacuation procedures. That had been his doing.

It was only a three-hour lead, but like David Johnston, Topper had made a difference. He had mobilized thousands of people. His actions had affected the movements and welfare of half the state of Washington.

After sending the press release from Candace's computer, he'd gone home, packed a bag, and headed west, determined to stay ahead of the devastation, from whichever direction it came.

High on success, he gunned the Jeep's motor and sped across the remainder of the bridge. Candace would get the credit, initially, but the truth would come out. Public recognition was a secondary concern anyway. The heady rush surging through his veins came from the power to affect change, to move people and get them to act.

He needed gas. Passing a sign for Costco, he took the Burnham Drive exit, navigating a series of roundabouts and settling in behind a long line of cars at the pumps. This was more than just the ordinary Saturday crowd.

People waiting left their cars and walked the line or stood talking to other customers, exchanging excited, horrified talk about the volcano, shaking their heads, wiping their brows. The air held a strange current that was almost electric, fairly sizzling with an agitated energy that hummed and plucked at the nerves.

Topper pulled up to the pump and filled his tank at last. Navigating the parking lot traffic jam, he found an open space, yanked on the hand brake, and went into the store.

Inside, the lines were even longer. People pushed shopping carts loaded with food items, water, and paper products. Faces swam by in the crowd, some grim, others lit by excitement or drawn tight with worry.

Babies fussed, children darted in the aisles, bored by all the waiting, fueled by the anxiety they felt in the atmosphere. There was nothing here that Topper needed, but he joined the queue at the snack bar, edging along behind a skinny man in dungarees, with a cloth cap tucked into his back pocket and dirt under his fingernails. The name stitched onto the pocket of his grimy blue work shirt was Melvin.

Topper bought a couple slices of pizza and used a handful of napkins to swab grease off their tops. He filled his cup with a caffeinated soda and decided to take his meal on the road, putting more distance between himself and the repercussions that followed him.

He started the Jeep and headed west, driving toward an abandoned Forest Service hut tucked away in Mason County. He'd used it before, still had the key on his ring, and recalled that it held a stock of supplies.

He knew a few people in the area, too, and had played a round or two of golf at the Mountain Vista course nearby.

As he crawled along in the heavy traffic, Topper chewed pizza and marveled over the awe-inspiring power unleashed by one volcano.

22

Rick heard the news on the emergency radio.

A dull, heavy thudding started up in his chest as he thought about the wall of mud heading down the mountain. Estimated at 40 miles per hour and showing no signs of slowing, it would hit I-5 in approximately 63 minutes, destroying everything in its path, wreaking havoc with transportation and communication routes.

Rick had to move fast if he wanted to get to Nate before the deadly wave cut him off.

He grabbed his car keys, then realized they weren't his. *Oh hell.*

The station was nearly deserted. Personnel and vehicles had been dispatched to deal with the cataclysmic crises caused by Rainier. No time for coming up with plan B. He had to leave now and hightail it to Mason County.

And he'd have to do it in Nate's gimpy car.

He ran to the lot and fired up the engine, relieved to see the fuel indicator pointing to three-quarters of a tank. He gunned the motor and moved quickly out of the lot, joining traffic on the main road.

As he approached the freeway, the tangle of vehicles jockeying for position increased. With growing dismay, Rick saw the entrance ramp was clogged, cars and trucks crammed in along the entire length of it, cluttering the shoulder.

He thought about trying to cut across town but envisioned the grid of red lights and bumper to bumper traffic he'd encounter. He needed to get around the Point of Tacoma, and fast.

He racked his brain for an alternate route that might bypass the worst of the traffic, but when you're surrounded by waterways, options are limited. Travel by ferry seemed like a bad idea with a tidal wave of mud bearing down.

It had to be passage by road, and that meant I-5 and the Tacoma Narrows Bridge.

There were other ways, but none of them promised to be any better than this, and some of them would take him initially closer to Rainier. He had no wish to rush to his death. His best chance was to press forward, watching for opportunities to weave through the press of vehicles.

It took seven minutes to gain entry to the freeway, and he'd inched along for another six minutes when the coolant indicator lit up, an angry glowing red. A gap opened in the traffic, and he took it, looking for another break, and then another. Inching forward down the interstate.

Slow as it was, it was progress and he hated to give it up. He cranked on the heater and turned the fans on high to draw heat off the engine, pushing the car ahead by degrees. But when smoke began pouring from under the hood, he was forced to squeeze onto the shoulder.

He'd have to wait for the engine to cool before he could open the radiator reservoir and add fluid. Flipping on the hazards, he left the key in the on position with the fans blowing, and got out.

In the trunk, he found a pair of gloves. He put them on and opened the hood to get more air circulating around the engine.

It was maddening to be forced to wait around under these circumstances. Sweat formed on his forehead, dripping into his eyes, stinging. He swiped it away, understanding what it was to be a sitting duck.

Ten minutes ticked by, and he told himself he could afford to wait only three minutes more before he'd risk a faceful of scalding radiator fluid. When the alternative was a boiling mud flush into the Sound, cranking the cap off a hot radiator seemed a minor risk.

Due to the leak, the fluid level was low in the tank, and he thought his chances were better than even. Draping his jacket around his head and covering his hands and arms as best he could, he turned the radiator cap a quarter inch, waited for the pressure to release, and then a quarter inch more.

In this way, he removed the cap, sustaining only a minor burn on one forearm.

He added coolant and water to the tank, sending up a silent prayer that he wasn't cracking the engine block. As he finished, he noticed the traffic thinning and felt relief wash over him. A relief that faded quickly when a patrol car passed by, issuing a warning from a mounted loudspeaker.

"You are in a flow zone. A deadly mudslide is headed in this direction. Turn around and leave now. Do not delay. You are in a flow zone. A deadly..."

The message repeated. Vehicles were turning around and driving north in the southbound lanes of I-5. Rick closed the hood. The car was ready to roll.

Looking toward the Point of Tacoma, Rick saw the big turtle shell dome just around the bend. He was so close, and the road ahead had mostly cleared.

He checked his watch. If he put the pedal to the metal—and did it now—he could be on the other side before the mud thundered through.

The patrol car stopped about fifty yards north. A uniformed arm extended from the window and the officer inside gestured to Rick, giving him an emphatic wave that said to turn around and clear out.

Rick leapt into the crippled car and started the engine. He fastened the seat belt, his mind racing, weighing, deciding. Without another second to spare, he pointed the car toward the Tacoma Dome.

And pressed his foot to the floor.

23

Marie Strauss flipped through a magazine off the coffee table, pretending interest, but her attention was focused on her husband. She watched him through the curtain of hair that shadowed her face as she leaned forward over the glossy pages.

She watched Tim watching Jess.

His eyes followed the older woman around the room with hunger and longing, lingering on her bare, tanned shoulders, the restless silvery hair. Marie felt herself shrinking inside, drying out like a husk. She fought down the mocking voice telling her she didn't matter to him anymore, that she'd been replaced.

A spark rose within her, and she fed it, letting the smoldering anger inside her build.

She turned a page.

From the corner of her eye, Marie saw the good-looking man who'd been lingering in the hallway enter the room. He walked the perimeter, moving casually among the guests but speaking to no one. Jess slinked up to him, offering her hand, maintaining the contact for an inordinately long moment.

Marie watched Tim watching Jess, whose eyes were locked onto the man in the suit. Jealousy flickered in Tim's face. The flame in Marie's gut seared hot.

She wondered how far it had gone between them. And for how long.

She wished she and Tim had never come to Mountain Vista. Jess was a widow who wielded her frank interest in sex and her beautiful body like a flaming two-edged sword and posed a greater danger to the happy families of the neighborhood than the twisted stretch of Highway 3 that claimed lives every winter.

Tim used to do his internet surfing at the kitchen table, but now he took his laptop to the den after dinner and often stayed up late into the night, tapping away, ignoring her when he finally crept into bed.

Over the last three or four months, his work schedule had grown ever more demanding, and he'd spent many nights "working late." Last night he hadn't arrived home until after ten.

But Marie had been around to the office and gotten no response to her repeated knocks at the door and window. And when she'd called him this afternoon, he'd been out of the office.

During the past several weeks, Marie had worked through shock and moved into denial.

Tim was a good man, he would never behave in the horrible, debasing way her imagination suggested to her. He was simply too busy with work, under too much stress. That explained why he stayed on his computer all night and had no time for her. But the veneer of denial was starting to crack.

Giving way to rage.

24

Nate watched the silvery creature approach, aware that several sets of eyes were following her sinuous movements. She captured his hand and spoke in a low, husky voice.

"We haven't properly met. Call me Jess," she said, stroking the back of his hand with her thumb, her gray-flecked eyes appraising him with open approval.

"Happy to meet you, Jess. I'm Detective Quentin. Perhaps we could talk later?"

He reclaimed his hand and offered her an apologetic smile, making his way to where Riley sat watching him with amused eyes.

"Well and wisely done," she said as he sank beside her on the sofa. "I suppose you have to go now? There will be lots of folks needing help."

"Never a truer word, but I'll be sticking around here for a bit. Would you mind introducing me around?"

"I hardly know you, myself," Riley said. "Nate, the cop. Is that how you'd like me to put it?"

He shook his head. "Let's get a little more formal than that. How about Detective Quentin, Bellevue Police Department. Say I happened to be in the neighborhood when Rainier erupted and now, I think I should stay for a while and make sure everyone's alright. The aftermath could get pretty ugly."

Riley regarded him, a quizzical light in her eye.

"Alright, detective, I can do that."

She looked pointedly at his left hand. No ring, but a slightly whitened stripe where one used to reside. "Is there a Mrs. Quentin?"

"Aye, that would be my sainted mother," he said, in an Irish brogue.

Riley's eyebrows rose, her lips twitching with the hint of a smile.

"My ex-wife also carries the name," he admitted. "I have a daughter, too, named Samantha."

"And your mother's maiden name was...?"

"O'Malley."

"Ah, that would explain the leprechaun I just heard." She stood. "Let's get started."

She led him round on a tour through the room. He met Tim and Marie Strauss, the attractive couple on the couch, and nodded hello to Cappy Johanson.

Cappy introduced him to an elderly woman with heavily penciled eyebrows named Brenda Marsh, with the wily intent of trading him partners. He latched onto Riley, drawing her aside and speaking to her in a voice so low Nate couldn't distinguish the words, but his body language made it clear he was attracted to her.

Nate studied Riley's response while he chatted with Brenda, and decided the appeal was not mutual. He gave it five minutes, then detached himself from Brenda and regained his place at Riley's side.

She steered him toward a white-haired man with a striking, triangular head and wrinkles which formed amiable lines around vibrant blue eyes, and his wife, a well put together woman with smooth mocha skin and a serene smile.

They were Harper and Myrna Mayhew. He was a retired geologist and she, an avid gardener—an occupation, she vowed, from which she would never retire.

He shook hands with the fine-boned man in lavender, whom Riley introduced as Skillet.

"He's the best chef in the county," Riley assured him, and Nate watched the man preen under her gaze, smoothing his eyebrows with a delicately curled middle finger. "He put our little neighborhood bistro on the map and people come all the way from Seattle, sometimes, to eat his cooking."

Skillet dropped a sly wink Nate's way and pulled Riley in for a kiss on the cheek, burying his face in her hair.

"Sweeter than sugar, isn't she? Mmmmm."

The man continued holding her in his arms, humming as if they were slow dancing in an empty room. The skin of his closed eyelids was nearly translucent, like the membrane over a baby chick.

As Nate watched, the eyes opened and met his with something like a warning. Riley pulled away.

"Let me go, Skillet. I want to introduce Nate to the Dawsons."

In one corner of the room, a woman sat knitting, a long banner of yarn stretching out before her in zig-zags of green and gold.

"They're chevrons," she explained when Nate commented on the pattern. "It's an afghan for when the weather turns cold."

A girl of about fourteen sat at the woman's feet, playing with a rag doll.

"Mama made it," she said. Her features were those of a child with Down's Syndrome and she repeated the phrase, "Mama made it," any time someone looked her way.

Nate watched Riley kneel and smile into the girl's face. "Nate, this is Annette Dawson and her daughter, Wynn. The doll is named Annie."

"I'm happy to meet you ladies."

Wynn studied him soberly. "Annie's not a lady. She's a doll," she informed him.

Nate stooped and looked closely at Annie. "My goodness, you're right."

Wynn continued watching him with her wide brown eyes. "Mama made it," she said, nodding proudly.

Riley waved a hand toward two men locked in debate near the fireplace. They were making some effort to keep their voices low, but each clearly had a dog in the race and meant to flog it to the finish.

As far as Nate could determine, the dispute concerned the role of government in public school curriculum.

"That's Sandford Dawson, a red-blooded conservative, facing off against Hal Jeffries, a bit of a left-wing radical. They are currently engaged in their favorite pastime."

Mrs. Dawson continued her placid knitting. "I know it looks heated," she said, "but they've never come to blows. Sandy claims it's the best cardio-vascular workout he knows."

"Honestly," said Riley, "I don't think they could be any fonder of each other and neither will budge an inch."

"In this crazy world, there's a certain sense of security in that," Mrs. Dawson said, nodding.

Riley's eyes turned toward the entranceway and Nate followed her gaze. "Look, Teren's here."

A tall man entered the room and waved greetings to a few people but made his way directly to Riley's side. He took her arm, asking if she was okay as he smoothed back her hair. Gentle, solicitous, and a little proprietorial.

Nate fought down a prickle of irritation and returned Riley's smile as she gazed up at him.

"Detective Nathaniel Quentin, this is Teren Kirkwood, my neighbor and friend." She turned to Teren. "Nate almost caught the kid who throws plums at my windows."

"Really? They sent a detective out here for that?"

Nate ignored the remark and shook hands with the man, noting his firm grip, the healthy-looking skin and hazel eyes, the long nose that curved slightly off-center, saving him from a perfect face.

His hair and eyebrows were interspersed with sun-bleached strands, giving them a look of frosted gold. Nate dropped Teren's hand, gave him a curt nod, and drew Riley out of his grasp.

"You haven't introduced me to our hosts. I'd like to meet them."

"Of course. You'll like Frank and Millie. Come on."

She smiled at Teren, but left her arm linked with Nate's as they walked to the wet bar where the homeowners were making more coffee and setting out plates of crackers and cheese.

"Frank, Millie—I'd like you to meet Detective Nate Quentin. He's offered to stand by and help as needed. Nate, meet the Newcombes."

Frank Newcombe had the dapper, well-tanned look of a steady golfer, with neatly cut and combed graying hair and light blue eyes tucked behind folds of slightly pouchy skin.

He took Nate's hand in a firm handshake, offering a smile. When Frank released it, Millie took his hand in both of hers and patted it as if soothing a child, jingling a charm bracelet from one delicate wrist.

"Thank you, Detective. You're very kind to stay on hand."

She was a well-preserved sixtyish, with hair so dramatically dark it had to be bottle-fed. It was cut in a sleek bob and graced with a single streak of silver. Her heavily mascaraed lashes fluttered at him, bringing to mind a Disney doe. She had that kind of graceful innocence.

"And you're remarkably generous and welcoming," Nate said, gesturing to the room. "Sharing your beautiful home with so many of your neighbors. I know it means a lot for them to have a place to gather under these circumstances."

"The Newcombes also own the clubhouse down the street," Riley told him. "They are the quintessential mom and pop of the neighborhood, and we owe them a great deal."

As Millie pulled Riley into a hug, the lights flickered and guttered out. The television screens went dark and quiet, and any semblance of a party atmosphere went out of the room.

Plenty of light still spilled in through the big picture windows, but the reality of the catastrophe began to dawn. Millie placed candles out on the bar and tables, ready to light when it grew dark, and Frank rummaged up a couple of flashlights.

The guests seemed to draw together, grateful for each other's company. Nate pulled Riley aside.

"Do you have a good flashlight at home?"

"Several, in fact. Shall I get them?"

"Yes, I'll go with you."

Riley's front door was unlocked and as they entered, she hit the light switch by force of habit and gave a wry smile when it didn't produce the expected glow. Nate followed her into the living room, past the piano, to a set of stair-step bureaus made from beautiful burled wood and filled with drawers of differing sizes.

She went directly to the bottom row, third from the left, and pulled out three flashlights.

"How did you know they'd be in that drawer?" Nate asked.

She looked mystified. "Because that's the flashlight drawer."

"What I mean is, how can you keep straight what to find in which drawer? There must be a hundred drawers and no labels," he pointed out.

She shrugged. "Tape drawer," she said, pulling out a drawer filled with masking tape, scotch tape, duct tape, double-sided sticky tape.

"Glue drawer, pencil drawer, stationery drawer." Each drawer contained what she'd said it would. "Sticker drawer, clip drawer, cookie cutter drawer—"

"Okay, okay. I'm convinced you're the most organized person I've ever met."

Riley smiled, dropping her eyelashes against her ivory cheeks.

"I like drawers."

Pulling open another drawer—this one dedicated to batteries—she slotted sets of fresh AA's into the flashlights. "Ready to go back?" she asked.

"No. I want to talk to you."

He watched her go still. "I should be sitting down for this, shouldn't I?"

"Let's both sit."

They settled at each end of the leather couch. Nate heard the twittering of birds outside the window and watched the tall pines sway as he gathered his thoughts and tried to figure out how to say what he wanted to tell her.

"It's possible you're wondering why I'm here," he began.

"It's possible," she agreed.

"Under the circumstances, I think I should tell you. You could be in danger."

"You're not talking about the volcano, are you?"

Her eyes looked wary, and a furrow creased her brow. Nate found himself wanting to reach out and smooth it away.

"Correct," he said. "I'm investigating the murder of Coby Waters."

Confusion crossed her face. "You're looking for the serial killer *here?*"

"We uncovered a lead that pointed to Mountain Vista, and I think my partner verified the suspect's identity as a resident of your neighborhood."

"You *think*?"

"Radio reception was patchy and then we got cut off. I can't reach anyone by phone or radio."

"So, you didn't get a name."

"You see my problem. I'm concerned about the safety of everyone here, but I'm particularly worried about anyone with wealth or status. All the victims have been high-profile. You downplayed yourself, but several of your neighbors filled in the blanks for me. As a concert pianist—"

A harsh laugh ripped through the air between them. “You needn’t worry about me,” Riley assured him. “Any chance of wealth or status I might once have had is officially on the wane.”

“I won’t debate you on that now, but I will urge you to be on guard and stay with a group.”

She grunted. Folding her arms across her chest, she turned to the window, looking out at something he couldn’t see.

He was impressed by her equanimity. She hadn’t melted into histrionics, quailed, or screamed, and she didn’t seem aghast at the possibility that she’d been socializing with a murderer.

She half-turned, tucking one foot beneath her, and rested her arm along the back of the couch. Nate realized if he mirrored her position, their hands would touch.

“Tell me about the case,” she said.

Nate shook his head. She was a civilian, a classical musician with no expertise and no need to involve herself with sordid details. She examined him coolly, the emerald brilliance of her eyes deepening, drawing him in, and Nate felt some of the stiff resistance inside him melt.

He had a problem. He was isolated from his support system, with no clear idea of the situation he faced, and without a partner. Who knew how long till Rick would arrive?

Or if he’d arrive at all?

He broke their gaze, dropping his chin to his chest, counting the stitches in the cuff of his sleeve, and fighting his compulsion to open up to this woman he’d known for approximately three and a half hours. He counted sixteen stitches before throwing in the towel.

"I'll catch hell for this" he told her, "but I could sure use some help, and you know your neighbors."

She flinched and Nate wished he'd used more diplomacy. "I mean, you can help—"

She cut him off, her eyes glinting green. "I know what you mean. You believe someone in this neighborhood committed a string of murders and may be preparing to claim another victim."

He shifted, returning her even stare. "I'm moving forward with that possibility in mind."

"Then let me help."

He relinquished, giving her all the relevant details, disclosing how the first victim, a high-ranking Boeing Executive, had been tasered and sliced through the throat.

He told her about the altar-like structures made from sticks and stones and how they'd managed to keep that specific knowledge from the media, saying only that there were possible occult connections.

He described the swabbing of blood from the victim's wound, as if the killer wanted to absorb the life force and take it with him.

He told her about the second victim, Senator Brown, and how the details of the two cases were nearly identical. He explained how the Coby Waters death had followed suit, except that the sticks and stones hadn't been in the same meticulous arrangement.

He told her about the plastic raincoats and the dearth of DNA evidence, the absence of fingerprints except for the Mountain Vista scorecard.

He told her more than he'd ever believed he could tell a civilian and he knew—like the comfort of settling into bed after a long and trying day—that it was okay.

She was quiet when he'd finished, but he could see that she was busy behind the eyes, her fingers tapping the leather of the couch.

At length, she said, "What criteria does he use to select his victims?"

"We haven't been able to determine that, but as he chooses high-visibility targets, he may simply be looking for the limelight."

Nate watched her sifting, thinking, tapping. She grew still once more.

"I don't think that's it," she said.

25

Riley was astonished at what Nate was telling her.

The idea that she might personally know the person responsible for the brutal killings was so incredible that she felt it slide to the far side of her consciousness, to be dealt with later. What remained in focus, at the top of her thoughts, was not who, but why.

And as Nate laid out the details, a theory began to form.

She realized he was peering at her with surprised intensity and felt a flush creep into her face. She looked down, studying the leather grain, stilling her mind.

Nate shifted position, his hand reaching hers. He grabbed her fingers and gave two raps against the top of the couch, as if to shake her thoughts out into the open where he could see them.

"You've got an idea. I can tell."

"Sure, I thought of something, but what's it worth? I'm not an investigator, Nate. I have no experience or training in your field. Anything I come up with is probably unfounded and way off base."

"True," he said, letting go of her hand and leaning back. "It's not likely your untrained mind has come up with anything we haven't already considered."

His words stung. "I never said I had an untrained mind. On the contrary."

"Oh? Right," Nate said, waving his hand in a dismissive gesture. "But music is a far cry from detective work."

She knew he was goading her but couldn't help rising to the bait.

"You've heard of football players taking ballet lessons to develop balance and muscle control?" she said, putting some acid into her tone. "The same principle applies to music training. Learning and performing music develops brain skills like no other."

"I'm sure it does."

She glared. "Plenty of studies have identified links between music training and high-level cognitive abilities, such as processing and retaining information, solving problems, making decisions, thinking on your feet."

He raised an eyebrow and waited for her to go on.

"A lot of mathematicians and scientists study music because they know how it can make the brain blossom like a rose, forming synaptic connections, stretching mental capacity. My training goes way beyond flexing my fingers over a keyboard."

Nate narrowed his eyes, giving her a challenging look. "So prove it. What did you come up with?"

Clenching her hands in her lap, she said, "I see what you did there, Nate."

"Just spill it, Riley. I told you all this because I recognize you've got a fine set of mental skills. I'm short a partner and I'm asking for your help."

"I thought you were concerned about my safety, me being a big celebrity and all."

"I am concerned about your safety, and I intend to keep you at my side to protect you. And also, to pick your brain. Fair enough?"

Again, she found herself at the top of that cliff where retreat became an ugly and dangerous choice. There was nothing for it but to jump.

"Fine."

She organized her thoughts, translating them into laymen terms.

"Music is about unity and variety. It's full of patterns, woven with patterns, brimming with pattern," she began. "And then the pattern breaks."

Nate nodded. "I'm with you."

"Sometimes the pattern break is foreshadowed, hinted at, predictable. Other times it leaps up without warning, changing in surprising ways. But form is very important in music, and I've been trained to ferret out the form, the underlying structure. I've learned to identify patterns and interpret their meaning."

"Right. Not so different from my line, after all."

"Good. So you know, some patterns are obvious, others lie beneath the surface and take a little digging. Let me tell you about the patterns that came to mind as you explained the case to me."

Nate leaned forward. "Please."

"You have a Boeing executive, working for a company that makes jumbo jets and contributes hugely to the carbon footprint. Then you have Senator Brown, a conservative politician who swings way to the right on environmental issues."

"Sure, I can see a possible connection there, but how does a pot-smoking, peace-and-love-liberal, former rock star fit the picture?"

Riley hesitated. Her idea was tenuous but, in her mind, it fit.

"Did you read the *Downed Illusion* interview in *Rolling Stone*?" she asked.

Nate looked surprised. "I skimmed through it just last night."

"I read it when it came out a year ago, but I remember the interviewer saying something like this."

Lowering her voice to imitate the masculine interviewer she pictured in her imagination, Riley said, "You've been criticized by some because, even as the popularity of your band has diminished, the size of your entourage, the support group that follows you around, has actually increased. What will happen with your followers on this come-back tour?"

Putting a swagger into her voice, Riley gave what she remembered of the rock star's response. "Bigger than ever, man. My people keep the faith."

Back to the interviewer. "So, you'll be trailing trucks and buses—"

And then Coby, interrupting. "Motor coaches, RVs, Harleys, black-belching VW vans. Come one, come all. I love you, man. We're going from one end of this big, beautiful country to the other and the more, the merrier."

Nate stared at her, astonished.

"You remember that from a year ago?"

"Well, that wasn't exactly verbatim, but I memorize huge pieces of music. I'm trained to learn and retain. Coby's following could be seen as having a significant impact on the environment and his attitude about it might have struck a sour chord. To someone of a certain mind bent, that could be a crime punishable by death."

She paused. "It's possible you have a self-appointed executioner on your hands."

Nate blew out a breath, rubbing a hand over his stubbled chin. "It's a plausible theory, and one I hadn't mulled over in exactly that light."

"Except..." Riley shook her head, puzzled. "If the killer operates on that premise and lives in this community, wouldn't he have attacked one or more of the big violators living nearby? There are several to choose from."

"And that's where my training kicks in," Nate said. "Serial killers, whatever drives them, are essentially predators and generally, they don't hunt where they sleep. For various reasons, they move outside their home territory to find their victims."

A sudden thought occurred to Riley. She pushed up from the couch and began pacing across the Moroccan carpet, thinking feverishly.

"What's your pattern recognition program telling you now?" Nate asked.

"I'm afraid the pattern's about to break."

She stopped pacing and turned to face him. "What if Rainier's rumbling has driven the killer to home ground and pinned him in the area while at the same time aggravating his instinct—his need—for violence?"

Nate's brow wrinkled. "I see your point. If your theory about his being an environmental extremist is correct, the eruption may send him on a killing spree and force him to troll locally for victims."

Nate reached out a hand, pulling her back onto the sofa. Staring earnestly into her face, he said, "You suggested there are a number of potential victims nearby. Who might he target?"

Riley sat still, concentrating. Only her fingers moved, drumming on her denim-clad knees.

After a moment, she said, "Several residents in Mountain Vista and just outside the neighborhood run lavish households. They own fleets of cars and boats. Some commute to work in sea planes or amphibious aircraft. A few even use helicopters. Bill Gates owns a home not far from here. The Nordstrom's live just down the road."

She bit her lip, thinking hard. "But the man who leaps to my mind is Rico Ferguson."

"Who's Rico Ferguson?"

"He's a Scottish-Italian clothing designer with a house on an island in the Case Inlet. He lifts off to work each day in a pilot-chauffeured helicopter, rides a limousine around Seattle, and owns an amphibious plane which gets frequent use on his business trips around the country. He is famously cavalier about his lifestyle and firmly believes he's earned it by virtue of his genius and hard work."

"Do you know him personally?"

"Yes, but not well. I've attended parties in his home and met him socially on a couple of occasions, fund raisers and such."

"Okay, we'll start there. I'd like to check on him, and at least warn him to be on guard. A man like that can buy his own protection. Do you have his phone number?"

"Actually, I do."

"Good, let's go. I'll drive while you try calling."

Riley grabbed her purse and cell phone and ran after him to the Explorer, still parked on the street. As she buckled her seat belt, she peered down into the windows of the Newcombe house next door and saw her friends and neighbors, ghost-like, through the darkening glass.

Then Nate pressed the gas pedal, and they roared off into the gathering gloom.

26

RICK SPED DOWN THE empty freeway, nose aimed toward the Tacoma Dome and points west.

He rounded a gradual curve and as his vantage point opened up on the new vista, he saw a snarl of standstill vehicles sprawled across the road about a hundred yards in front of him, blocking the way.

He slowed, considering his options.

If he continued forward, would he be able to gain enough distance to clear the flow path? If he turned around, could he make it out of harm's way before the tidal wave of mud thundered across the I-5?

He had only minutes—seconds maybe—to get out of the danger zone.

The car radio squawked, sending out a high-pitched emergency signal interspersed with warnings and official announcements. He switched it off.

Glancing to his left, he saw a faint brown smudge moving in the distance amid commotion, accompanied by an uncanny rumble growing rapidly louder.

He braked, shifting into second gear. Flooring the clutch, he yanked the wheel hard to the left, pulling on the handbrake until he'd come around 180 degrees.

The car fishtailed, skidding close to the concrete median. Rick let off the handbrake and regained control, heading back the way he'd come, foot to the floor.

He pushed Nate's car as fast as it would go, disregarding the coolant indicator blinking like mad on the dashboard. As he rounded the same curve from the opposite direction, his heart sank.

A tangle of traffic stretched across the freeway, forming the other side of a giant set of deadly bookends. Afraid to look, but unable to stop himself, Rick turned his head toward Rainier.

The moving brown smudge had become a raging torrent. He was trapped.

He rode the accelerator, speeding toward the abandoned vehicles. Braking hard, he slewed to a rough stop against the bumper of a red BMW, deserted with both front doors open.

He followed the example and bailed out, barreling through the crush of empty cars and trucks on foot, working his way to the shoulder. He sprinted down the cluttered border of the freeway, weaving past vehicles left by conscientious drivers trying to keep the road clear.

He risked another look, horrified at the wall of mud bearing down with incredible speed and ferocity.

He'd thought he was running all out, but the sight produced a burst of energy beyond conscious thought. Legs pumping, leaping in desperation, he vaulted toward safety.

A hideous roar shook the air around him, like a fleet of low-flying jet planes from Boeing field, but deeper and infinitely more disturbing. The screech of metal against metal joined the cacophony as the lahar blasted over the freeway, plowing aside the marooned vehicles, tossing them like an extra-crunchy salad.

Rick was shoved forward by a laterally moving Ford which pitched and heaved toward a sturdy-looking Escalade. The two vehicles collided, locking Rick between them.

His head banged against a window, spinning from the impact and the sudden cessation of momentum. Pieces of metal and debris flew around him and something sizzling hot hit his ear, searing it. He smelled burnt hair.

He'd made it to the edge of disaster, outside the flow path. But not outside the effects of that flow. Surveying his situation, he found he was imprisoned inside a twisted metal box.

And it was raining fire.

27

Topper flowed along in the river of heavy traffic on northbound Highway 16, listening to the radio broadcast versions of the same report on every frequency.

This is an emergency evacuation message from the Law Enforcement Support Agency for Pierce County, Department of Emergency Management.

The following is not a test; I repeat this is not a test.

A debris flow has been observed coming from Mount Rainier down the Nisqually River. The size of the debris flow is unknown at this time. Anyone near the Nisqually Riverbed upstream from the Alder Reservoir could be threatened. If you are near the Nisqually Riverbed upstream from the Alder Reservoir, move to higher ground immediately.

Do not delay. Do not call 9-1-1. Move to higher ground immediately. Park your vehicles off the road areas so that others can evacuate.

I repeat, this is not a test.

A continuing ribbon of these alerts had been streaming over the radio since he'd left the parking lot at Costco. So many areas of the state had been affected by Rainier's blast that it took more than fifteen minutes for all variations, from all jurisdictions, to air before the loop started over.

Topper realized many of the service areas had already been hit, making a mockery of the radio warning.

Steering to the right, he exited the highway at Purdy. The little town was three miles and a world away from the harried bustle of Gig Harbor.

A ghost town.

Topper saw no one, the residents apparently holed up in their dens. The place was little more than a long, deserted off-ramp which passed through a non-functioning traffic light and connected to a long, deserted on-ramp back onto Route 16.

The Purdy Spit branched off at the traffic light, crossing Henderson Bay to the Key Peninsula. Topper signaled and moved into the turn lane, but shuddered to a stop as he reached the intersection.

A line of orange and white striped storm barriers lined the road, blocking the turn-off to the spit. Topper shifted into neutral and hauled up on the handbrake. Climbing out of the jeep, he passed through the barriers and peered out at the bay.

He'd watched whales play in this water, pods of orcas, amazed that they ventured this far from the open ocean. He didn't see any now.

The water level had risen, swallowing the beach, threatening to eat the road. The bay churned and seethed, full of mud and debris, heaving like a living thing intent on escaping its bounds. Topper knew the lahars must have pushed all the way to Tacoma, plunging into the Sound, carrying untold tons of mud, rock, and all the detritus gathered in passing.

He believed the effects from the wall of mud would continue to mount, breaching waterways and driving a tsunami of destruction in an ever-increasing radius. The flooding and damage would swell exponentially.

If he wanted to cross the Purdy Spit, it was now or never.

Shoving aside three of the barricades, he drove his jeep through the gap, steering along the narrow road lapped on both sides by angry waves. The jeep's tires bit into the pavement as he gained the other side and began the climb, rising above the writhing bay.

Navigating the curving lane through Wauna, he passed a solitary figure at the side of the road, the only human he'd seen since leaving the freeway. An old man, white-whiskered, with a tattered gray raincoat flapping around him.

Topper watched him shrink and then disappear in the side-view mirror.

28

THE KILLER WALKED AWAY from the Newcombe house, along the cart path and into his own driveway.

He jammed the key into the front door lock, giving it a vicious twist. He'd watched Riley with that police detective, seen how they'd driven away together. She hadn't even bothered telling anyone where she was going.

Kicking open the door, he entered the house, letting it fall shut behind him with a loud click. He stood in the front hall, silence washing against his eardrums, feeling heavy and drained, spurned by Riley and stunned by Rainier's punishing eruption in the face of everything he'd done.

A sense of betrayal, like that he'd suffered when his mother died, weakened from pneumonia and then snatched by an early cold snap in October, rose and buffeted him. Doubts niggled, biting at him, and he swatted them away like mosquitoes as he stood in the darkening hallway, remembering.

His father was a weak man. He couldn't hack living rough, off the fat of the land. Not without his wife.

They left the forest and moved to a city where the killer went to a regular school and learned regular things. His father found work as a night watchman and custodian at a funeral home, and they lived in a tiny apartment attached to the rear of the facility.

The hearses pulled right up next to their front door to unload. The killer had watched his father help carry body bags past the window as he ate his cornflakes or chicken nuggets at the kitchen table. He knew the bodies went into the embalming room on the other side of his bedroom wall.

And he knew what they did to them there.

The odor of chemicals and rot seeped through the thin plasterboard and ventilation ducts. It got into his clothes. Kids at school held their noses when he walked by.

When he got home from school, his father made him do his homework at the desk in the casket showroom, tucked between the polished walnut with pink satin inlay and the classic black lacquer.

The killer began to learn many things at school, principally that he was stupid. Some of the kids called him a moron. Others said idiot. And it was true that he didn't understand much of what the other children were up to with their textbooks and papers.

He knew how to read and could count well enough on his fingers, but the multiplication tables were beyond him, and he'd thought Andrew Jackson was a guitar player. Gaffs like these earned him scorn and ridicule, but no friends.

And just as well. He couldn't imagine bringing a friend over after school.

He made frequent use of the school library, checking out biographies of sports figures and scientists. Sometimes a mystery or a western. When he finished his homework, he was allowed to help himself to one bottle of soda from the stock in the mortuary kitchenette, kept cold and ready, in case a mourner should need refreshment.

He sat in the kitchenette with his library book, drinking his treat at the small round table with the yellow-cushioned chair. And sometimes the door to the visitation room across the hall was left open.

Sometimes, there was a body.

It felt strange at first, whenever that happened, to sit casually reading and sipping soda next to a corpse. None of the other kids at school could do anything like that.

One time, his father told him they were bringing in a toddler, a two-year old who had forced a toy into a power outlet and been electrocuted. After the tiny body had been prepared and installed in the "Serenity Room," he crept into the powder-blue parlor and gazed down at the little waxen face.

Panic gripped him, stealing his breath. He was seized by the conviction that those eyes would spring open, boring into him, hypnotizing him with a hungry intensity. Frozen, he'd stood over the dead child, fearing that if he dared look away, the boy would rise and fall upon him, small icy fingers gripping his neck, paralyzing him, draining him of life.

He stayed, rooted to the spot, until his father's footsteps in the hallway galvanized him into action and he dove behind a curtain, unwilling to be caught in this perverse act.

There were many things about the mortuary that fascinated him. He delighted in prying open the caps of the central vacuum system, watching bits of paper disappear into the maw, feeling its powerful vortex against the palm of his hand.

When his father was distracted in another part of the building, he liked to ride up and down the curving staircase in the automatic chair lift to the darkened basement, pretending he was lord of the underworld.

Sometimes a gap in the curtain of the embalming room allowed him to catch a glimpse of something chilling or gruesome, and the casket showroom at night was an ideal place for playing hide and seek.

He began to think about making a friend, but it would have to be the right kind of boy and there was no one.

Until Toby.

He shook himself from the reverie. He had done his part. He had always done his part, and still the earth shook and screamed her fury. What more could she want?

He turned and walked to the closet, removing the hidden partition, pulling out the duffel bag, preparing another plastic raincoat.

She had taught him, told him how good he was. A fine boy, she assured him. He'd always done his part.

He readied the bag and waited.

29

The air fairly hummed with tension as Riley leaned forward in her seat, peering into the night.

Her skin prickled with it as she and Nate descended the hill toward Rico Ferguson's house, and she was shocked to see how much the water in the bay had risen. Choppy, chocolate-colored waves slapped the shoreline, sending spumes shooting high into the air.

Nate activated the Explorer's wipers, clearing dirty droplets from the windshield as Riley directed him to the bridge connecting the small island to the main road. She kept trying to reach Rico by phone but couldn't get a signal.

They turned onto the approach road and rolled to a stop at an unmanned security gate made of wrought iron, limiting access to the island.

"Now what?" Nate said.

"Hold on, I was out here last month, and I think I remember the code."

Nate shook his head. "They'll change the code on a regular basis. It won't work."

"Try it anyway. Seven, four, eight, two."

Nate punched in the numbers and the gate creaked open.

"That doesn't bode well," said Nate. "If our friendly neighborhood throat slasher attended the same party—"

"He'd have the same code."

"Chilling thought, isn't it?"

"Paralyzing. It's hard for me to imagine that I've been hobnobbing with a brutal killer. Shouldn't they give off some sort of feral scent or have a wild-eyed look marking them out."

"I'm sorry to say that's not the norm. A personality organized, disciplined, and clever enough to pull off these killings would also be crafty enough to play his part well. With a certain kind of madness comes a certain degree of cunning."

"Comforting."

"We're not here to comfort, we're here to warn potential victims so they'll watch their backs."

They passed through the gate and over the narrow bridge to the far side of the island. Nate pulled into the circular driveway and parked the car.

"Stay here," he said, "and keep the door locked until I come and get you."

She watched Nate ring the doorbell, then pound on the door. He worked the doorknob, peering in through narrow windows flanking the heavy wooden entry, and drew the gun from his shoulder holster.

He set off, circling around to the back of the house, and Riley shuddered as he was swallowed by bushes and the gathering gloom. Her thoughts turned morose.

How did I get where I am? What kind of crazy course changes in my life led to this?

Not that long ago, I was a concert pianist with a promising career, a wonderful husband, an adoring son. And now I've lost it all. I'm sitting in a locked car, on a forsaken island, in the path of destruction.

And one of my friends is a murderer.

How does that happen? Is there any way to trace through the interwoven strands of decisions, repercussions, and chance events to identify the pattern, find the breaks, and discover the secret maneuverings that delivered me to this moment?

Is there any way to attach meaning, find purpose, exert control over our lives?

Or do we simply twist in the wind?

Nate rounded the far end of the house and loped back to the car. The door locks popped up and he dropped into the driver's seat with a sigh.

"No sign of a break in. They're probably off in the Bahamas or somewhere, but I can't rest easy leaving it alone."

"Why not?"

A pained expression passed over Nate's face. "Everything looks fine through the windows, except that I saw a slice of spotless white kitchen floor..." He paused. "With a single shoe lying in the middle of it."

A chill of foreboding raised the hair on the back of Riley's neck. "That does seem ominous."

"I'm going to break in. If I manage to trip an alarm and raise the police, all the better. We could use the help. Stay put."

He disappeared once more around the back of the house. Riley waited. The light turned murky, dimming perceptibly, and time stretched on so long that she was sure something terrible had happened there, out of her view.

She felt trapped. Should she venture behind the house and try to find Nate? Run for a neighbor's house? Keep waiting?

No, she couldn't bear that.

Letting herself quietly out of the car, she stood tense and still, like an animal sifting the air for danger signals. She took a few steps toward the house and froze in terror when the front door swung open.

Relief flooded over her when she saw it was Nate. He came to join her, carrying an empty laundry basket, and the look on his face was grim.

"Looks like we're late to the party," he said.

30

Rick shielded himself as best he could as debris continued to fall from the sky.

Blobs of scalding hot mud pelted down, along with burning chunks of wood, plastic, metal, cardboard, and unidentifiable bits and pieces. The mud, wicked hot when it hit, turned out to be a boon as it cooled, acting as a lubricant while Rick worked to free himself from his metal prison.

He'd been amazed to find that all his parts were present and accounted for and that he could move them, independently. What he needed now was to move them, as a unit, out of this mess.

The vehicles he was sandwiched between had smashed together in such a way that the frame of the Ford had cradled him, creating a space where he survived without damage, though he was trapped now within it, as if the car had consciously protected him and meant to keep him.

He was up to his shoulder blades in a crush of metal, plastic, and composite. He slathered the slimy mud over him, wherever he could reach, determining that his best option was to hoist himself up and out the top.

Straining to find some leverage, he inched upward bit by bit, struggling to hold each gain as he made it. It was exhausting work and took an age, the Ford groaning and screeching under him like a woman in labor.

At last, he slid free of the metal womb, and the car slumped and settled with a sigh of resignation. Rick pulled in a deep breath filled with relief and was startled to hear a baby cry.

He stumbled along the freeway, seeking the source of the forlorn bawling. A woman lay crumpled and bloody beside a minivan that had been crushed against the median. He ran to her, lifting the limp blonde hair away from her face, and felt for a pulse.

He didn't find one.

In the minivan, he found the crying baby and a sibling, sitting silent with wide, staring eyes. Both were strapped securely into child seats.

Heaven help us, what a nightmare.

Rick reached into the van and pressed down on the horn, honking out an S.O.S., repeating it several times. He thought the children were safest left in their protective seats until help arrived, but he managed to climb up into the space between the two of them.

A pacifier was clipped to the strap of the baby's carrier and Rick guided it into her mouth. She sucked at it, eyes still welling with tears. The other child, a boy, had not uttered a sound.

His eyes were unfocused and unblinking as he spiraled down, overtaken by shock. Rick took the little hands in his own and rubbed them gently, speaking in a soft voice.

"It's okay, it's okay. You'll be all right."

He repeated the words like a mantra and hoped to heaven they were true. Shouts and the sound of movement reached him where he sat. He leaned toward the open door.

"Over here!"

Emergency responders swarmed the wreckage. Two helmeted men helped Rick climb from the mangled van and attended to the children. Rick wanted to stay, to do what he could to help, but he knew he had to maintain focus on the imperative he'd given himself.

So much death, so much damage, inflicted by a volcano. If he persevered with his own mission, he might be able to prevent untold death and damage from a killer of another kind.

Surprised at how bereft he felt, he left the van and walked among the mass of broken twisted vehicles. The freeway was a hellish mess of the dead, the mourning, and those who could go either way.

An amazing number of rescue workers were on the scene and Rick was touched and humbled by their calm and compassionate demeanor. All around him, he saw courage and fortitude and felt a stab of pride for his countrymen, rallying to the occasion, pulling together.

He worked his way through the mess and found a cop who hooked him up with a buddy, who passed him on to someone else until he eventually caught a ride to his apartment. He showered, dressed, and bolted down three bowls of cereal and a slice of cold pizza while thinking about what to do next.

During his ride home, he'd confirmed his suspicions that all reasonable land and water routes to Mountain Vista were cut off. His ride had driven through a hot spot where he managed to raise a couple of bars on his cell phone and he'd briefly spoken to a friend in the media, begging him for helicopter transport.

"Forget about it, buddy. Look around, it's Armageddon. Batten down the hatches and ride out the storm. You can get back with your partner when things settle down."

"I need to get out there now. He needs backup."

"Get him some local help."

"I've tried. I can't reach anyone. I got lucky reaching you."

"Not so lucky, friend. Gotta go. Sorry."

Rick knew he was up against a crapload of difficulties. Local resources were strained beyond anything on record. He was being tested under extraordinary circumstances.

He thought about the men gauging his performance, holding him to an exceptionally high standard.

Surely, allowances would be made, a measure of slack granted him.

He finished his makeshift meal and found his Mustang in the parking lot. He drove the car slowly through downtown Seattle, stunned by the daunting desolation. It looked like a post-apocalyptic movie set—deserted, dirty sky, gray silent buildings, the streets populated only by a few wandering homeless.

The sound of his engine echoed in the steel and concrete canyon. Holding up his burner phone, he tried to find a spot with bars.

Were there any cell towers still transmitting?

The blip of a signal appeared on his screen, and he pulled over. Fingers trembling, he made the call, connecting with a person on the other end.

"I've got the name and possible location of a highly probable suspect," he reported. "I'm doing everything I can to apprehend him, but all my routes are cut off by the eruption. You understand that, right? Can you help me out?"

Silence.

"Look," Rick said, "I'm cut off from my partner and I'm dealing with circumstances out of my control."

"We cannot help you, Mr. Jimenez," came the expressionless voice. "Do it, or don't."

The line went dead, and Rick slammed his fist against the steering wheel. He'd worked years for this opportunity, sacrificing and preparing. He only had this one chance.

And Rainier had ruined it all.

31

Marie watched Jess at the wet bar, greeting, touching, spreading her poisonous charm.

The woman's husky voice and fluid movements were mesmerizing, and Marie could understand, but not absolve, the fascinated male attention she commanded. Jess glided across the room, graceful and confident, and exited into the hallway.

Marie pushed up from her chair and followed. In the kitchen, she found Jess standing on tiptoe, reaching for a box of herbal tea on a high shelf.

"Are you taller than me?" Jess asked. "Can you reach those lemon tea bags?"

Marie gave them a half-hearted swipe. "Nope."

Jess pulled a chair over from the breakfast nook, letting it screech across the floor, and climbed up. Leaning against the counter, Marie watched, arms folded over her chest, a bitter taste in her mouth.

"It's a pretty historic day, huh?" she said to Jess. "The kind where you'll always remember what you were doing when."

"Oh, absolutely."

"So," Marie pressed, tilting her head to look up at Jess. "What *were* you doing when the eruption hit?"

Jess had the box of tea in her hand and returned to floor level. She looked at Marie with a hint of knowing amusement that infuriated her.

"When the big guy blew?" she asked, smiling. "I was picking flowers."

Jess turned away. She opened a drawer and started digging through kitchen utensils.

"Really?" Marie wanted to slam the drawer shut on that slender hand, wipe the smug look from that loathsome face. "How'd that go?" she asked.

Jess closed her eyes as if savoring a memory. "It was amazing."

Opening her eyes, she fixed her mocking gaze on Marie. "What were you doing?"

Marie felt a pressure mounting within her, hot and seething, mirroring Mt. Rainier.

"Laundry," she replied through tight lips.

Jess found what she wanted in the drawer. Shaking her silver-blonde hair, she turned to leave. As she passed Marie, a single sardonic word slipped from her throat, quivering in the air between them.

"Historic."

Then she was gone.

Marie stood alone on the kitchen floor, frozen with fury.

Boiling with rage.

32

Nate tried not to dwell on what should have been happening and focused, instead, on the series of curveballs coming his way.

He fiddled with the Explorer's radio again but was unable to transmit or receive anything. He tried his cell phone, and Riley's, and the landline in the house, fruitlessly attempting to reach the local authorities.

He'd searched the house for some effective means of communication, but he was out of options and there was no telling how much time would pass before he could get someone official out here to the scene.

The sky glowered overhead, growing thick with gloom and portent. Refusing to let it affect his mood, he turned his attention to his first priority.

The crime scene.

"Alright, let's see what we've got to work with."

He forced a note of confidence into his voice as he rummaged through the items in the Explorer's trunk space. He filled the laundry basket with boxes of collection swabs, tubes, small white slider-boxes, plastic bags, paper bags, tape, and latex gloves.

"What are you doing?" Riley asked.

"Normally, we call in a team to process the site, but I think I'm on my own here."

"What can I do to help?" Riley asked.

Nate hesitated. "You know I respect your competence and I appreciate your help, but this is a fairly formal process and has to be handled a particular way. The best thing you can do for me is stay put where I know you're okay. How about the front room of the house? There are books and magazines there to keep you company."

Riley looked reluctant but agreed. On the porch, he handed her a paper coat, an elasticized hair cover, a face mask, latex gloves, and waterproof shoe covers.

"Suit up, please. Let's limit contamination of the scene as much as possible."

They pulled on the protective coverings and entered the house. Riley settled onto a plush sofa with an issue of *Architectural Digest*, giving him a little salute as he passed into the hallway.

Nate examined the controls for the security system and made a note to check the video surveillance records. The house was without electrical power now, and Nate surmised no one had been alive to switch on the generator when the power went out.

The state-of-the-art security system, taken with the absence of a break-in, squared with his theory that the killer had been known to Rico and welcomed into his home.

Nate's preliminary pass through the house had revealed three bodies and he needed, now, to fill the role of first responder, investigator, and crime scene technician. He'd found a camera in the trunk and used it to record both stills and video documentation of the three bodies and the areas between and around them.

Then he examined the scenes and made careful notes, understanding that much would hang on this initial processing of the site. Finally, he moved to the bodies, adding more notes and photographs, using a probe thermometer to determine core temperature, and recording the degree of rigor mortis and lividity. He collected anything he felt might be of possible significance.

In the kitchen, he noted that the cook had been preparing a meal. He bagged the chef's knife, stained with shreds of carrot, and every other knife in the kitchen, but he didn't think any of them would prove to be the murder weapon.

Smudged and bloody footprints tracked across the area between the kitchen and atrium where Rico's body rested. Nate photographed them carefully but doubted they'd reveal much. They were undefined and the killer had probably worn booties similar to what he and Riley were wearing.

In the atrium, he took precise photos of the altar constructed from sticks and stones before dismantling and bagging the pieces for examination by the experts.

He secured the victim's hands with paper bags, taped at the forearms, in case Rico had managed to strike at the killer and carried evidence under his fingernails.

He collected every piece of evidence he could think of, other than the bodies themselves, labeled them meticulously, and sat at the kitchen table, logging them onto a submissions sheet.

He planned to lock everything in the rear compartment of the Explorer, doing the best he could to preserve the integrity of the evidence.

His hand cramped from the hurried, continuous writing. Pausing, he took a moment to shake out the kinks and let his hand rest. Working a crime scene usually involved a team of experts and a fair amount of time. He was one man, under the gun, and he had never felt so inadequate.

Sighing, he picked up the pen and persevered.

33

THE EERIE SILENCE OF the house was getting to Riley.

She'd thumbed through the magazines and grown bored with the coffee table book detailing the history of designer labels. She stood and paced beside the floor-to-ceiling windows overlooking the inlet and wondered if, during daylight on a clear day, Mt. Rainier would be visible.

The atmosphere in the house was oppressive. She could no longer sit, and it felt like there wasn't enough air to breathe. She stepped out onto the front patio, removed her surgical draperies, and walked across the lawn to the west side of the house, drawing in great gulps of fresh air, waiting for the pent-up frustration to seep out of her.

Here, she could see the last of the sunset, deep red streaks running through fingers of rusty orange. The sky was dirty, intensifying the colors.

She stood at the water's edge, alone, vulnerable. The Puget Sound Slasher had been here. Might be here still, watching her from some vantage point, moving in for an attack.

Riley's insides roiled with some unidentifiable violent emotion. It twisted within her, turning acid in her stomach, and chewing its way up through her chest.

A few hours ago, she had watched her blood spiral down the drain, eyed a row of pill bottles, run her finger down the blade of a knife, craving an end to the relentless discontent that had become her life.

She'd given in to the feeling of senseless drifting, the niggling torment of an undefinable guilt. She had no right, now, to fear for the life she'd held so cheaply. She realized, suddenly and with surprise, that it wasn't fear, but anger that bubbled within her.

As the colors faded from the sky and gulls reeled overhead, their melancholy cries providing a plaintive backdrop, Riley stood with arms crossed, kneading her flesh, chewing her lip, trying to trace through a tangle of intertwined possibilities to identify the source of the rage juddering within her.

She faced an abundance of potential culprits.

She could blame Mt. Rainier for blowing its top on the weekend of her return to the stage, compounding the devastation of her failed performance.

She could say Nate had appeared on the scene and dragged her into this wretched mess, forcing her to engage when she really just wanted to retreat.

She could blame Teren for poking and prodding at their comfortable relationship, suggesting he wanted more from her than she could give.

If she tried, she could find fault with her agent, her sponsors, her audience, the venue, the repertoire, the price of tea in China.

She could be angry at Jim for dying in a fire. He was a firefighter, for crying out loud. There was such cruel irony in his death.

And she could be furious at him for allowing their son to die with him. She was pissed at the both of them for going off together and leaving her here.

She was irate with the teenager who threw plums at the house and the paperboy who missed the porch.

But when she followed the final twisting strand, it led straight back to her, as she'd known it must.

Hers was an elusive anger that refused to hold still for examination. She didn't know how to understand it, live with it, or conquer it. She could only acknowledge it as the cause of her failure, on stage and off, and with this acknowledgment the rising balloon of tension in her chest popped and settled down to simmer in her gut.

Riley was so absorbed in her jumbled thoughts that the sudden rush of cold water over her feet was the first sign of trouble she noticed. Looking down in dismay, she saw the waves had swallowed the beach and were creeping up the lawn.

Startled, she veered off, jogging along the shoreline, back to where the bridge jutted out to meet the mainland. The water, here, was agitated, impatient, wailing against its confinement. The bridge was minutes away from being engulfed, cutting off their exit from the island.

Riley turned and ran.

34

RICK GAVE UP ON finding police or military transport to Mountain Vista.

The situation was utter chaos. Rainier's cataclysmic disaster spread over several counties, each with its various emergency organizations covering separate, sometimes overlapping, jurisdictions and reporting to different authorities.

The situation was rife with confusion. Not only was Rick turned down; he was warned to stay out of the air space and stop bothering those trying to do their jobs.

He focused on finding a private means—someone with a plane or helicopter who would fly him out to find Nate—but he'd struck out there, as well.

He remembered thumbing through an issue of *Forbes* someone had left in the station break room and seeing an article about private helicopter owners. He searched around, found the dog-eared magazine, and culled two names of local big shots.

With all practical means of communication knocked out, he had to track them physically, actually knocking doors. He got no response from the first name on his list and was feeling pretty dismal about his chances with the second guy.

Ironically, the man's residence was in Mason County, so he had to hope to catch him on this side of the water. In his office on a Saturday.

Downtown once again, Rick parked the Mustang and started working out how to get into the high-rise commercial building. He jabbed the button outside the front door about sixteen times before he realized it wasn't transmitting a signal to the bell with the power out.

Holding his badge to the glass, he pounded and shouted, hoping for a response.

Finally, an irate fellow in a rumpled suit let him in.

"What do you want? There's no one here today. State of emergency. Hadn't you noticed?"

"You're here."

"Uh-huh." The guy ran a hand over a chin like sandpaper. He looked tired. "Yeah, well, my house was in Puyallup. I got nowhere else to go."

"Oh, man, I'm sorry. Your family...?"

"Live in Ohio. Divorced. I'm married to my work, so here I am. How can I help you?"

"I'm looking for Rico Ferguson."

The man in the rumpled suit let a breath splutter out between his lips and shook his head.

"Our boy Rico missed a meeting with an important client this afternoon, but I wouldn't worry. With things the way they are, I'm sure he's riding out the storm in comfort."

His face lit with a bright idea. "You could try his place out on the Case Inlet."

"Thanks," Rick said, not bothering to filter out the sarcasm. "I'll be sure to do that."

He returned to the Mustang and resumed his drive through the desolate city, aimless now, wandering. The silence was broken periodically by the eerie wail of a far-off siren. A light snowfall of ash brushed the windshield.

"I'm not giving up. No way."

Rick kept repeating the words to himself, but he was exhausted and out of ideas. He'd been driving without a conscious destination and found himself nearing HQ.

He decided to keep researching and digging for details on the suspect. He could sack out on the couch when he'd had enough and maybe, in the morning, new options would open up.

He parked and stepped out into the sulfurous air.

35

THE ELECTRICITY WAS STILL out when the killer made himself a cold meal, ham on rye with a dill pickle.

He took a bite, liking how the pickle crunched between his teeth. He'd never tasted a dill pickle until middle school, when the band sold them to raise funds for a trip to perform at Disneyland.

That's how he met Toby.

Toby played the clarinet. A tall, skinny boy who favored polo shirts and skipped, rather than walked. And Toby was a pickle pusher. He wanted that trip to Disneyland with a blazing passion and hit up everyone he passed in the hallways or schoolyard.

When he approached the killer, a quarter changed hands, a pickle was passed, a friendship was made.

Toby was the only one he ever brought home, the only one who seemed to understand and respect the peculiarities of the mortuary and the ways of the woods behind the funeral home where they played.

Sometimes they caught small animals, or mummified grasshoppers. He taught Toby the things his mother had taught him, the secret things, and he knew Toby would keep them safe.

That summer, a series of earth tremors plagued the area, damaging property and worrying the residents. He and Toby waited for them to subside, watching the television news with a soberness that matched that of the grownups.

When the tremors intensified and the media trumpeted warnings of doom, the boys knew what had to be done. A sense of importance, of solemn responsibility, settled upon them.

They prepared, tearing a cotton strip from the sheet they'd hidden behind a row of paint cans in the mortuary storeroom. They gathered the appropriate sticks of wood, three different kinds, and stones of the proper size and shape. They erected the altar beside a deep ravine in the forest behind the mortuary.

A squirrel would not do, not under these circumstances. They both recognized that.

The killer knew Toby understood, but still it was the hardest decision he'd ever made and when he raised the killing stone and saw the fear in Toby's eyes, he almost couldn't do it.

It hurt him, knowing that in those last seconds Toby had suffered doubt. Doubt was the worst kind of torture. The killer's job, then, had been a kindness, as well as a necessity.

He anointed the banner with the flowing blood, saving it for the Burning. Then he kissed Toby and pushed his friend—his only friend—into the ravine, watching his body bounce and slide to the bottom, where it came to rest against a large boulder.

He went home and the earth tremors stopped.

The news, instead, was about a missing boy. They found Toby the next day, the tragic victim of an accidental fall, and his body was delivered by hearse to the funeral home.

His father helped unload it.

The killer cried. He wept for days, despondent and sullen. He had never had such a friend, and never would again.

Until he met John.

36

RILEY CLAMPED DOWN ON the wave of terror spreading through her.

Sprinting across Rico Ferguson's front lawn, she made herself stop at the front door and put on the protective coverings. She understood the paramount importance of this ritual, the preservation of the crime scene.

Though she'd never been on the site of a murder, she'd watched enough television and read enough books to know about the sanctity of the scene. The sense of justice was sufficiently heavy upon her that she suppressed the impulse to run screaming through the house and proceeded, instead, with caution.

Calling out for Nate, she followed his voice to the kitchen. She stopped at a respectful distance, out of the line of sight, and modulated her voice, tamping down the panic.

"We need to go right now, Nate. The water is rising fast. It's almost over the bridge."

"I'm not finished here."

"We'll be stranded!"

"If the house is going to flood, then it's even more vital that I document everything now before the evidence is destroyed."

"If we don't get off this island, everything you've collected will flood with it."

"Debatable."

Riley clenched her fists. "There's no time for debate. Let's go!"

A pause. Then he spoke again, his voice still maddeningly calm.

"Could you come in here a minute?"

"You're joking, right?"

"Riley, I need to know if you can identify these bodies."

Unbelievable.

But again, the weight of justice pressed upon her, stamping her with a sense of responsibility. Pulling in a deep breath, she rounded the corner, steeling herself against what she was about to see. Nate took her by the elbow, walking her first to one dead face, and then the other.

Horror stole over her in a convulsing shudder. She had never seen such devastation of human life, a scene from TV, made stark and real. Nate lifted her chin, steadying her with his eyes.

"You okay?"

She swallowed and pulled her face from the tenderness of his grip, fearing his sympathy would break the last straws of her composure.

"I'm sure I've never seen the woman, but the man looks familiar. He may be Rico's butler."

"All right. There's one more, in the atrium. Can you hang in there?"

She nodded. Nate took her by the hand, leading her to the center of the house which opened onto the atrium. She'd been there before, eating canapes and chatting with guests at one of Rico's parties.

It was a beautiful space, filled with light, open to the sky, and designed to interest the eye and lift the spirit. All that had been destroyed now by the corpse sprawled at its center.

Nate stood aside, waiting silently while she gazed down at Rico. He'd been a man filled with confidence and determination. His vitality had animated his face, radiating from him.

So strange to look at him now, the sparks extinguished, his features plastic and still.

"That's Rico Ferguson," she confirmed.

Nate bowed his head. "I need to do one more thing. Will you help me?"

"The bridge, Nate."

"This won't take long, but it's important. Find a linen closet and bring me at least three sheets. White, if you can find them."

Seething with impatience, Riley ran up the stairs, flinging open door after door in the passageway. She found a closet filled with folded bed linens and towels. Grabbing an armload of white sheets, she tore back down the stairs.

"We have to move the bodies, Riley," Nate told her. "If water takes the house, they'll be disturbed."

"Moving them won't disturb them?"

"Of course, but we'll try to keep them as intact as possible. We're going to transfer each to a white sheet, which will act as an envelope, and we'll carry them upstairs where the water won't reach."

"We are about to be trapped on this island, Nate. With three dead bodies."

"Steady on, Riley. There's sure to be a boat we can use, if need be. Focus on helping me with this."

Swallowing hard, she spread a sheet next to Rico's body. They lifted him carefully onto it, trying to preserve his position as much as possible, and folded the sheet around him like a cocoon.

"Look there."

Riley pointed at an object left where Rico's body used to lie. Nate found the camera and took several photos, then lifted the item from the crushed grass with a set of tweezers. It was a brown leather tassel, the kind that might adorn a man's loafer.

"Could he have torn it off the killer's shoe and hidden it under his body?" Riley asked.

"It's not outside the realm of possibility. It certainly didn't come off the sneakers he was wearing."

Nate bagged the tassel and made a note. "Let's take him upstairs and get the other two. Chop, chop. Water's rising."

Riley shot him a poisonous look and took up the end of the sheet that wrapped Rico's feet. They carried him up to one of the bedrooms and laid him carefully on the floor before making two more trips for the other bodies.

They loaded the laundry basket with the collected evidence and stowed it, with the camera and other paraphernalia, in the rear of the Explorer.

"Let's get out of here!"

Nate drove fast down the road to the bridge, but as they crested the slight rise and saw the choppy waves slapping at the structure connecting them to the mainland, dread seized Riley by the throat.

They were too late.

37

Topper's jeep was the only car on the road.

The long strip of pavement crossed over the sparsely populated peninsula, passing through small communities and clusters of roadside concerns. Topper saw a beauty parlor, a tiny real estate office, a drive-through coffee shack, and wondered how these places stayed solvent.

Could there really be enough repeat business here to support these isolated enterprises? They seemed to him the antithesis of "location, location, location."

He was out of sight of the water now, driving west, and it appeared to be snowing. Topper knew the tiny flakes that fell were not snow, but ash. The prevailing winds would drive huge loads of ash to the east, dumping over cities like Spokane and into Idaho, probably reaching into four or five states. But here, it merely dusted down like a light snow.

That could change.

He passed a large quadrangle of grass, mostly hidden by the darkened sky, and remembered attending a medieval festival there years ago. Not far away, was a motorsports park. And there were miles of waterfront property and plenty of popular areas dedicated to water-related recreation.

He reconsidered his ideas on local free enterprise and decided the tenacious business owners might be onto something.

As he neared the Case Inlet, the road grew curvier, narrower, and inched closer to the water. Topper slowed the jeep almost to a crawl. It was too dark to see properly, but it looked as if the water had risen to an alarming level and was now licking hungrily at the road.

He'd seen hardly a living soul since crossing the spit, but he passed a car now, headed in the opposite direction. The driver flashed his brights and honked, signaling trouble ahead.

Topper rounded a curve and the road disappeared beneath a gaping hole, a crumbled mass of asphalt, chewed and swallowed by the tossing waves. He braked hard and the jeep bucked and slid, rear wheels slewing sharply on a sideways trajectory.

Unable to stop, Topper skidded toward the brink.

38

RILEY WATCHED NATE RUN out onto the bridge.

The wind had picked up and swirls of mocha-colored water surged up, splashing the rails and sliding back down in a repetitive motion that seemed intent on sucking the structure down into the murky depths.

Three sets of wooden bars ran along each side of the bridge. On the way in, they had seemed more than substantial to Riley, but now they offered her all the assurance of popsicle sticks.

Riley's hands were rigid on the dashboard as she leaned forward, peering into the shafts of light cast by the headlamps. Nate finished his survey of the bridge and returned to the car. He rolled down all the windows.

"Unfasten your seatbelt," he said.

"Are we leaving the car?"

"No."

"Then, why am I taking off my seatbelt?"

"I don't want it jamming, trapping you inside."

"What?" Riley's speeding pulse rate notched a step higher. "What are we going to do, Nate?"

"We're getting out of here."

"By boat?" Riley asked hopefully.

"Nope. Now, listen. We're driving across this bridge and it's going to hold us. But if," he held up a hand shushing her, "if we end up in the water, slide out the open window and swim for shore. Don't worry about me. Don't worry about the car."

"I don't like this."

"You don't have to like it. Let's just get through it."

Nate put the car in gear, and they entered the bridge, moving at a creep. His hands gripped the steering wheel, white with tension, his eyes staring riveted ahead. Riley's stomach shrank. She started shivering.

"Breathe, Riley. In. Out. We're okay."

She inhaled and exhaled per instruction, focusing on the feel and the sound of her breaths. A layer of stress slid away as they neared the halfway point without mishap, and she realized Nate was singing.

It was low and muttering, but it was definitely a song. And it sounded familiar.

A sudden crash shook the bridge as an enormous tree, ripped from the earth and trailing its roots, rammed against the wooden bars. A battered washing machine was tangled in the branches, stark and white against the darkness. A single gnarled bough swept over the top of the railing, reaching into their path like the tentacle of a hungry sea creature.

Riley's throat convulsed but she managed to swallow, resuming her steady pattern of breathing.

Nate briefly lost the thread of his tune, but he started up again and she joined him, recognizing the Simon and Garfunkel song. Waves sloshed over the road in front of the car as they belted out the chorus to *Bridge Over Troubled Water* and Riley tried not to think of all the things that could go wrong.

She tried to block out the episode of *Mythbusters*, the videos on *YouTube* and *TikTok* documenting similar situations with disastrous consequences. Sometimes ignorance *is* bliss.

The tree screeched against the steel supports and the dark water kicked and slapped and moaned. Nate sang, and they arrived on the far side of the bridge.

Riley felt drained, barely able to muster the strength to buckle her seatbelt when Nate demanded it. He reached over and squeezed her shoulder, and she heard him let out a long breath and knew he'd been more worried than he'd let on.

When they reached the main road, they saw that the lower end of it, which ran along the inlet, was underwater. Nate turned right, heading uphill, and they made their way back to Route 3. Parts of the road were flooded or littered with debris, and they had to stop once to clear a mass of broken timbers that had somehow ended up in the middle of the street.

They reached the highway, and Nate signaled to turn left, toward the Sheriff's department in Shelton, but Riley gasped and gripped his arm, pointing down the road to the right.

The water was over the broken center line and seemed to be clawing at the asphalt. A suckhole had formed beneath the curve of the road, pulling in trees and garbage, chewing it up and spitting it out. The remaining surface of the road was next in line.

If they didn't cross the gap now, they'd be cut off from Mountain Vista.

If they did cross the gap, they'd be cut off from the authorities.

Riley looked at Nate, saw the indecision in his face. Turning back, she watched in horror as a large chunk of earth dissolved, collapsing into the maw, shrinking their passage.

The Explorer lurched forward, racing over the narrowing road, wheels spinning and sliding on the slick, buckling pavement. They cleared the precarious ledge and Nate pulled to the inland side of the road about thirty yards ahead, where the earth appeared to be stable, and stopped the car.

He climbed out and Riley followed on shaky legs. Stopping at a safe distance, they watched the churning water eat away at the ruined foundation. The road crumbled and sank like a child's sandcastle, severing their connection to the rest of the world.

Mountain Vista had become, in every practical way, an island.

Surrounded on three sides by water and backed, on the fourth, by a high, sparsely populated ridge separating it from the Hood Canal.

Riley stood in darkness, next to a man she'd only just met, and acknowledged that they were now trapped on a virtual island.

And so, in all likelihood, was the killer.

39

By the time they returned to the Newcombe house, Nate was feeling the ragged end of a very long day.

The sky had closed in with an inky heaviness, staining his mood and draining his energy. He was exhausted, but he felt the weight of responsibility settling onto his shoulders and knew there was work yet to be done before he could rest.

He worried about Sammi and Marilyn, tortured by the thought that they might be holed up somewhere like this with Brad. A possible pedophile, according to one of the best profilers in the country.

He tried calling again but got nowhere. He fooled around with the radio for several minutes, working through spurts of static and garbled transmissions as he sent out his request for support. After a while, he gave it up and followed Riley into the Newcombe house.

The neighbors were still assembled, candles lit against the darkness, conversing in muted tones, fretful and reluctant to leave the comfort of each other's company. Nate had several concerns and he moved through the room, addressing them with Frank and Millie Newcombe and some of the other people gathered in the house.

Arrangements made, he stood beside the wet bar and whistled for attention. He thanked everyone for supporting each other and watched them respond to the authority in his voice, settling in to receive instruction.

"You all understand we have an extraordinary situation here," he began. "We're isolated, for the time being, without any practical means of communicating or traveling outside this vicinity. I have no official jurisdiction here, but I am a sworn officer of the law. As long as I find myself in the same boat with you fine people, I'm offering to help however I can."

Nate took in the nodding heads and murmured assents.

"I've spoken with the Newcombes," he continued, "and they've agreed to let us move into the clubhouse for the next few days until things straighten out and get back to normal."

"Why can't we just go home?" Marie asked and some heads in the group bobbed in agreement.

"You're certainly free to do so," Nate answered. "I only offer this as an option but let me expound some of my reasons for suggesting it."

He held up a thumb to signify his first reason. "The clubhouse is well supplied and large enough to accommodate a substantial group, on a temporary basis. There are cots and couches, a big kitchen and dining room, and an excellent chef who's indicated his willingness to help out."

A few hoots went up for Skillet and the man in lavender waved a pleased response.

Nate added a finger for reason number two. "The industrial-style doors and windows will make a better seal against the ash, should that become a problem."

He held up another finger. "Power outages will continue to be an issue and there's a good generator at the clubhouse, and gas to run it."

A fourth finger went up. "There are bathrooms with showers."

And Nate held all five fingers out as he continued. "We'd have each other's company and support and that's no small thing in a situation like this."

He waved his hand toward the older gentleman he'd met earlier in the afternoon. "Mr. Mayhew is your resident geologist, and he was around to witness the eruption of Mount St. Helens in 1980. I've spoken with him, and he heartily endorses the notion that we stick together."

Harper gave an emphatic nod and kept his eyes fastened on Nate, waiting for him to go on. Nate had debated with himself whether to mention the killings and decided it would be best to get the subject out in the open. Besides, he could lead with a bit of good news.

"I was able to reach dispatch for the Mason County Sheriff's department," he told them. "They'll be sending deputies our way, which brings me to the most compelling reason why I think we should band together and stay in a group."

Silence fell over the room. "Riley and I went out to Rico Ferguson's this evening," Nate said. "I'm sorry to report that he and two of his staff have been killed." He paused before adding, "They were murdered."

Gasps and cries flew around the room, full of astonishment and outrage. Nate held up his hand and continued.

"The last thing I want is to cause a panic and I'm not suggesting there's a maniac on the loose. All I'm saying is that there's safety in numbers. This is a good time to pull together as a community and watch each other's backs. Whether or not you decide to move to the clubhouse, I encourage you to form groups and stay together."

Dismayed chatter filled the air. Nate raised his voice to be heard over the low rumble.

"For those of you taking up the Newcombe's kind offer, I suggest you move in teams to your various houses and pack what you need for a few days. We'll settle in at the clubhouse and lock it down for the night. Let's say, by midnight. Okay, folks, thanks for listening."

Nate's pronouncement about Rico's murder left the neighbors in shock. He saw the varied reactions, the hugs and tears, clenched jaws and blank stares, that always go with a crowd of any size after such news.

Jess glided over to express her concern over the situation, and to thank him for coming to their aid.

Nate gave her half his attention while he watched Riley and Millie organize the groups, dispensing comfort and reassurance, soothing fears and handing out practical advice on what to bring to the clubhouse.

He was grateful to have such competent help. He'd exaggerated when he'd told the assembly that deputies were on the way. He had managed to reach the sheriff's dispatch but had no clear indication that his distress call had been acknowledged.

He'd heard only bursts of broken sound, interlaced with spurts of hissing static. He'd repeated his message and request for assistance several times before coming in to address the gathering of neighbors.

He hoped he hadn't lied to them.

40

Someone had scorched the coffee during their absence.

The bitter odor hung like a pall over the assembly, a subtle summary on the events of the day. Riley was dog-tired and dangerously close to tears. She couldn't scrub the image of Rico's dead face from her mind, or the thunderous sound of the ruined road as it crumbled and fell into the inlet below.

While Nate spoke, she found herself examining shoes, looking for a pair of dark brown loafers even while she hated herself for doing it.

Skillet wore loafers the color of milk chocolate, no socks. But they sported pennies, rather than tassels.

Sandy Dawson had on a pair of tasseled loafers but they were black, and both tassels were accounted for.

She found it incredible that she could be scrutinizing her neighbors for signs of a killer, yet she couldn't keep herself from peering around the room, looking at people from a new perspective.

It made her feel vulgar and afraid.

She watched Jess work the room, spreading her touch, her scent, marking her territory. She ended up near Nate, biting her lip at the news of Rico's death, her colorless eyes wide and seductive.

Riley recalled how Jim had described Jess as a cobra, saying she drew the eye, fascinating and mesmerizing her victim while she readied her fangs. Cobras, he told her, are the only snake that can actually spit their venom, and do so with remarkable accuracy, able to kill from a distance.

Riley had studied his face while he said this and he, understanding her concern, had assured her that he stayed well out of her sights.

Now, looking at Jess standing next to Nate, Riley was astonished at the little stab of jealousy she felt and chided herself. She listened as Nate wrapped up his instructions, rallying the group. As he finished speaking, Jess moved in, her voice warm and husky.

"Oh, Detective, I'm so glad you're staying with us. I'm frightened." She hugged herself, her eyes inviting Nate to join in.

Riley turned away. If Nate fell for that act, he deserved to get bit. She teamed up with Millie to organize the groups. As they worked, Teren came and stood at her elbow.

"Good grief, Riley," he said. "That must have been awful for you. Why on earth did you go to Rico Ferguson's with Detective Quentin?"

"He wanted someone who knew Rico, to introduce them. I never thought we'd find...what we found."

"Of course not, but he had no business bringing you along on such a dangerous task. I would've gone with him."

"I know, Teren. I appreciate that."

He paused. "I guess I meant why did you go to Rico's at all?"

A disquieting feather brushed down Riley's spine and she found she didn't want to discuss her ideas about the crimes with anyone, not even Teren. She shrugged.

"He said he wanted to speak with Rico and asked if I'd go along to make the introduction."

They were interrupted by Nate who asked Teren if he would join Skillet, Jess, and Brenda Marsh on an expedition to pack overnight bags before heading to the clubhouse.

"You're really taking this "safety in numbers" thing to extremes," remarked Teren.

"I see nothing extreme in this approach," Nate said. "It's common sense and the mundane nature of the task is calming. It takes a person from thinking about a monster to thinking about a toothbrush."

"Ooh, clever," Jess said.

Nearly everyone had decided to make the move to the clubhouse, craving the comfort of company in the face of disaster. After Teren's group left, Nate pulled Riley to the sofa and lowered her onto it.

"Rest for a minute. I need some advice."

Riley yawned and stretched. "Okay, but if I sit here too long, I'm liable to fall asleep." She pulled her feet up under her and waited for him to continue.

"We can't accommodate the entire neighborhood at the clubhouse and we're not going to extend a general invitation. But is there anyone you recommend we should bring in? People who are particularly vulnerable? The elderly or the sick?"

"Now you're making me feel like a bad neighbor. I don't really know that many people outside of the ones you've already met."

"That doesn't make you a bad neighbor, it makes you typical, in that regard. I wouldn't expect you to know everyone."

"Millie invited a couple of families with small children and an elderly couple from around the corner."

"Okay, good." He hesitated. "We could use a doctor. Any doctors living in Mountain Vista?"

"Dr. Hunt. But he's spending a couple weeks in Tahiti and Dr. Bradley passed away in June. Hmmm. We have a veterinarian, Dr. Summerton."

"That'll do. Let's go get him."

"Her. Dr. Debra Summerton."

"Alright, let's go see if we can persuade her to join our gathering."

41

The jeep was down for the count.

Topper rubbed his sore arms, dazed and marveling at how close he'd come to going airborne into the bay. The jeep's wheels had continued their sweep, skimming the yawning chasm formed by the broken road. The tires had pitched him into a steep ditch, embedding the jeep with its rear end sticking up like a stink bug's.

He climbed around precariously within its slanting confines, gathering his pack and as many supplies as he could comfortably carry. He'd be hiking on foot the rest of the way.

But not tonight.

He'd been bustling since early morning, and he was beat. He had a sleeping bag, a rope, and a tarp. With those, he could fashion a shelter for the night. He wanted solitude and hoped to avoid running into anyone as he climbed up the steep verge and into the forest above.

It had been a banner day. A day for the great and terrible. It's rare that a volcanologist gets to actually witness a history-making eruption and live to tell about it. He would drink a toast to David just as soon as he could get his hands on a beer.

Marking out a spot level enough for his purpose, he went about clearing rocks and fallen branches. He constructed a simple tent, using the tarp and two trees, aided by the beam of his flashlight.

He ate a can of cold pork and beans, relieved himself behind a clump of bushes, and crawled into the sleeping bag, listening to the breeze in the branches, smelling the resinous pine.

He smiled.

Drowsing under the rustling tarp, he thought about his day's work, his ruse to activate evacuation procedures and the mad scramble it had engendered. He had made a real difference.

Then he remembered Jack's tale of the man who tried to escape death by fleeing. His last conscious thought as he drifted off to sleep was that the angel of death had kept a full appointment schedule that day.

How many, running away, had met him face to face?

42

The clubhouse, with its many windows, was lit like a beacon in the darkness of the neighborhood.

The generator cranked out a steady stream of power and by the time Riley and Nate arrived with Dr. Deb, Frank and Millie Newcombe had things well under way. They'd set up cots in meeting rooms A and B, where most of the families were bedding down, and distributed pillows and blankets among the couches in the lounge.

Before everyone went to bed, they gathered in the dining room so Frank could dispense some basic instruction as to drinking water, the use of the toilets and showers, power conservation, and meal arrangements. Riley was drooping, fighting the yawns, when the peace of the room was split by an abrupt and deafening siren, complete with revolving red lights.

"And that," said Frank, "is just a fraction of what this baby can do."

He held a cylindrical contraption in his hand, and a pleased look on his face. "It is also a high-powered lantern, a flasher, and has a built-in bullhorn," he said, demonstrating each feature.

"We have four of them," he added, "and I'll place them throughout the clubhouse. If anyone needs to raise the alarm, you know how to do it."

The crowd dispersed and Riley was relieved to see how well everyone was settling down. She was exhausted and wanted only to sink into something soft and go to sleep.

Overhead lights went off, giving way to cozier lamplight. Riley said goodnight to Nate, who was bedding down on a cot near the main door in the glassed-in lobby. She knew he would act as a sort of quasi-sentry.

Moving quietly, she entered the lounge and surveyed her options for sleeping arrangements. The area was walled by glass, with sliding doors opening out onto the wrap-around deck that backed the bistro and hung out over the trout pond.

The adjacent wall was taken up by built-in bookshelves on either side of a stone-bordered fireplace. Centered along the third wall was a shiny, ebony grand piano which Riley had used to accompany sessions of Christmas caroling and for her student recitals. The sight of it was like probing a wound and she avoided looking at it as she chose a sofa next to the glass.

She saw that Brenda Marsh had claimed a spot in one corner and lay propped against a pillow, reading glasses perched on her nose, an open book on her lap. She peered into the distance, a thoughtful expression on her face.

"What are you reading?" Riley asked.

Brenda shook herself from her reverie and glanced at the page. "A voice was heard upon the high places," she read. "Weeping and supplications of the children of Israel: for they have perverted their way, and they have forgotten the Lord their God." She paused, lifting her chin. "Jeremiah, chapter three, verse twenty-one."

Jess spoke up from her couch in the center of the room. "Jeremiah was all about gloom and doom, wasn't he?"

She pulled a brush through her long, silvery hair, maybe counting the strokes. One hundred every night, volcano notwithstanding.

"Jeremiah prophesied," Brenda said. "He spoke truth. If there's gloom and doom, it's because we choose it."

"Nobody *chooses* doom."

Brenda uttered a cackle, her penciled eyebrows arching, her face looking sinister in the shadows of the room. "You deceive yourself. Every day you choose it."

Jess's hand stopped midstroke. She sent Brenda a look filled with acid. "You self-righteous b—"

Riley broke in. "I think Brenda is making a general statement, saying that we all make mistakes, do things that bring unhappiness upon us."

Brenda gave an elaborate shrug and Jess looked skeptical but continued with the brushing in sullen silence. Brenda switched off her lamp and settled down under a blanket, turning her back to the room.

Soon, all the lights were off, and Riley adjusted the pillow under her head as her muscles loosened and relaxed. Her thoughts drifted and she pushed them away from Rico's house, directing them down a more pleasant avenue.

She thought about Nate.

A light sleep overtook her, and she drowsed for a time, but came out of it when something roused her. Propping up on an elbow, she listened. The night had become silent. A gentle, rhythmic snore came from Brenda's corner but that wouldn't have been enough to wake her.

It was something else.

Settling back onto the pillow, she tried to slip back into unconsciousness but simply couldn't let go enough to fall asleep. A tiny visual disturbance in her left eye began spinning like a kaleidoscope, growing gradually larger. She sat up, groaning at this unfailing precursor to a migraine.

She hadn't brought her migraine medication. Hadn't even thought about it. She got them so rarely, but when they came, if she didn't dose up right away, she'd be incapacitated for an entire day. Or longer.

This was not a good time to be laid low. She must get that medicine, and now.

She moved softly through the lounge, passing Jess's couch, noting that it was occupied only by a crumpled blanket. Should she wake someone to accompany her? No, she hated to do that, and she was a grown woman, independent and responsible for her own safety.

As she tiptoed into the widening area near the staircase, she heard a furtive rustling, two murmuring voices, and realized she was passing two people involved in a passionate clinch. She guessed the woman was Jess, but the man could have been anyone. It seemed to Riley that she cast out her lure pretty indiscriminately.

The couple seemed not to notice her passing and she crept on, into the lobby.

It was empty. Nate was nowhere in sight.

A glaze of misery settled over Riley, hardening into a thin shell. So what if the man under the stairs with Jess was Nate? It shouldn't have surprised her. Nate was free to do as he wished, and she had no reason to doubt that he'd snap up the bait like any other man.

She slipped out the door and let it lock behind her, hoping someone would be there to let her in when she returned.

There was a half-moon, but the sky was clouded, dimming the moonlight. Riley hadn't stopped to find a flashlight, but her house was only two doors down and across the street. She knew the neighborhood well, even by moonlight. She regularly jogged the three-mile route that circled the lake and, with her erratic schedule, had done it in the dark, aided by a headlamp, many times.

She found her front walk and let herself in the door, reflexively hitting the light switch. The house remained in sooty blackness as she felt her way to the stair-step drawers, counting three down and two over. Opening a drawer that contained butane wands, she lit one of the candles from the dining room table and carried it into the kitchen.

She found the box of Zomig and placed a lozenge on her tongue, letting the fast-acting medication dissolve. Tucking a blister pack with two more tablets into her pocket, she took a couple of deep breaths, willing the medicine to go to work, and blew out the candle.

Enticed by the thought of crawling into her own comfortable and familiar bed, she moved down the hallway but nixed the idea when she realized that might cause a fuss and worry when the others discovered her missing from her couch.

Sighing, she returned to the front door and closed it gently behind her. Moving with instinctive stealthiness, she kept to the bushes, stopping frequently to survey the terrain. Now that her migraine had been allayed, her concern over the killer took the forefront once again.

She crept past her own front yard and into the fringe of trees across the street. Movement caught her eye, and she froze, watching a shadowy figure down by the lake.

The clouds had thinned, intensifying the moonlight. A chill passed over Riley as she watched the man walk to the clubhouse and climb the stairs to a dining deck over the pond, an extension of the bistro.

A hard-muscled arm snaked around from behind her, pinioning her arms as a hand covered her mouth, stifling the scream that shot up from her throat.

"It's me, don't make a noise."

Riley shuddered as Nate dropped his arms and stepped back. Whirling, she whispered, "Dang it, Nate! Way to scare a girl to death."

"Sorry. You shouldn't be out here, Riley. What are you doing?"

"I forgot my medication and it couldn't wait until tomorrow. Who's the creeper?" she asked, pointing toward the figure outside the clubhouse.

"It's Mr. Johanson. I've been following him for the last half hour, trying to decide what he's up to."

"Is he the killer?"

"I don't know. Could be," Nate said. "Or maybe he just forgot his medication."

Exhausted as she was, the comment irritated, stirring Riley's temper. She stalked past Nate and out into the moonlight. He caught up, taking her by the elbow.

"I'll walk you back."

Riley jerked her arm free. "I can get there under my own power."

"Sure, but you might need these." He jingled the keys to the clubhouse doors.

"If Cappy can get in, so can I."

"Good point," said Nate. "Let's go find out how he did it."

Riley resigned herself to following him and they went up the stairs to the deck, which wrapped around three sides of the dining room and extended along the length of the lounge. Slider doors stood at three separate entrances.

All were locked.

"He probably left one of these open and locked it after him when he turned in for the night," said Riley.

"Undoubtedly. Let's go around through the front door."

They entered and Nate secured the door behind them.

"Goodnight, Riley," he said. "Go get some sleep."

"I intend to. See you in the morning."

This time, when she snuggled beneath the blanket, Riley barely had time for a single thought before winking into oblivion. The solitary thought crossing her mind was that Nate couldn't have been the man under the stairs with Jess.

She slept like a baby.

43

Sunday morning. But there would be no sleeping in, no leisurely perusal of the morning paper, and no church today.

Nate sighed. The truth is, he didn't always make it to church, even on an ordinary Sunday. He meant to repent.

In the meantime, he turned his attention to Cappy Johanson, determined to pin him down and get some answers. But the man avoided his eyes and dodged his queries.

"It's a simple question," Nate repeated. "What were you doing skulking around the neighborhood last night?"

"None of your damn business." Cappy glowered at Nate and attempted to move past him into the dining room.

"Still, I'd like to know," Nate persisted.

"And I'd like a million dollars," Cappy snapped. "If you're offering me an even trade then we've got something to talk about."

"Come on, Cappy. Just come clean. You'll feel the better for it."

Cappy rolled his eyes. "I forgot something at home," he said.

"I didn't see you carrying anything when you came back."

"I wasn't killing anyone, if that's what you're suggesting," Cappy whined in an aggrieved voice. "Stop hassling me."

Before he could pursue the matter, there was a bellow and a loud clatter from the kitchen. Alarmed, Nate ran past the tables, pushing open the kitchen door to find copper pots swaying on an overhead rack and Skillet waving a knife at a distinguished-looking older gentleman who was backing away with a look of surprised distaste.

"Whoa," said Nate. "What's the deal, Skillet?"

"Mr. Snowden says he's hungry."

The chef hurled the words out, loaded with heat. "He wants some breakfast."

The gentleman turned a mild face to Nate, looking mystified. "I got up this morning and found I've nothing in the house to eat, so I came here. I'm used to having my meals prepared, you see."

"Oh, yes," said Skillet, his lip curled in a snarl. "He's used to having his meals prepared, but he's never considered me good enough to prepare them. I've been trying for months to get him in here to sample my creations, but he made it quite clear that my little bistro is beneath him." Skillet pointed the knife toward the exit. "So, he can get the hell out."

Nate turned to Mr. Snowden. "Sir, if you'll take a seat in the dining room, we'll see about getting you some breakfast."

Mr. Snowden raised an eyebrow and left the kitchen. Nate leaned against the counter and crossed his arms. "What's the rest of the story?"

An angry sizzle arose from an overheated pan as Skillet emptied a board full of chopped vegetables into it, swirling and tossing them with passionate intensity.

"You ever been to Le Poisson D'Or?" he asked, naming a fine restaurant in Seattle. Nate shook his head.

"How about Die Wolke Zimmer? No? These are two top-drawer restaurants owned by Mr. Snowden. I had hopes of becoming a chef in one or the other establishment. Hell, half the reason I moved to this neighborhood is so I could impress the chief there with my cooking, but he never even gave me a chance. Wouldn't deign to dirty his mouth at my bistro, so he can damn well starve for it now."

Skillet cracked a dozen eggs into a stainless-steel bowl, whipping them with punishing vigor. Nate waited until the thwack of whisk against steel dropped to a decent decibel level.

"Seems to me this is your golden opportunity," he said. "Serve the man."

"Hell, no. He snubbed me and publicly embarrassed me. Tell him to go home and pop open a jar of caviar."

"You know, Skillet, if you handle this right, you could have him eating out of your hand. Literally. I'd think twice before throwing away this chance."

Skillet's whisk came to a halt. Nate pictured the wheels turning inside the man's head. Presumably, he was starting to appreciate the power hand he'd been dealt.

Only, how would he play it?

A sly look passed over his face. "Yeah, okay. Tell Mr. Snowden I'd be delighted to serve him."

"Will do," said Nate. "You need any help in here?"

"I could use some help, but not from you," Skillet said, appraising Nate and finding him wanting. "Send someone in here with some experience."

Nate rounded up Mrs. Dawson and Dr. Deb for kitchen duty and stepped into the lounge, hoping to find Riley. She was absent.

A bank of bookshelves lined the back wall of the lounge and Nate pulled out a random volume and surveyed the title, *The First Global Revolution.* He flipped it open and read a passage that someone had underlined in red pencil:

"*It would seem that men and women need a common motivation, namely a common adversary, to organize and act together; in the vacuum, such motivations seem to have ceased to exist—or have yet to be found.*"

Idly, Nate turned over a page or two and read another underlined passage that seemed to follow from the first:

"*In searching for a new enemy to unite us, we came up with the idea that pollution, the threat of global warming, water shortages, famine, and the like would fit the bill.... All these dangers are caused by human intervention.*"

This was followed by a passage with a double underline: "*The real enemy, then, is humanity itself.*"

Nate looked inside the front cover and found an *Ex Libris* sticker with the name *Amanda Horton* written in a large, cursive hand. He placed the book back on the shelf and pulled out another, titled *If I Were An Animal.* He found a highlighted passage which read:

"*If I were reincarnated, I would wish to return as a killer virus to lower human population levels.*" This one also belonged to Amanda Horton. Or had, at one time.

He perused a third book, skimming through a collection of writings by Sir Francis Galton, stopping to reread a heavily highlighted paragraph:

"What nature does blindly, slowly, and ruthlessly, man may do providentially, quickly, and kindly. As it lies within his power, so it becomes his duty to work in that direction."

There was a hand-written notation in the margin:

Human weeding and eugenics.

Nate's stomach turned queasy. He felt as if he had lifted a stone and come face to face with a writhing mass of maggots feeding on something rotten.

These books propagated the wide-scale extermination of human beings. Someone had collected and studied these volumes. For what purpose? Did Ms. Horton support these ideas or seek to combat them?

Tucked among these books, Nate saw a volume covered in purple-blossomed fabric. He was interested to note that it was a personal journal and was filled with the same handwriting with which Amanda Horton had claimed ownership of her books.

He examined the pages, reading many passages on a continuing theme:

"Christianity is on the outs. The rising religion embraces a new center of control, combined with Gaia worship, and we will prevail!"

Also: *"The hope is that people will willingly submit to sterilization to save our Earth. If they don't, we must resort to other methods."*

Nate turned the page and found a paragraph bemoaning the critics who refuted these views:

"The ignorant accuse us of using environmentalism as a ruse, a means to establish a world Utopia for the elite who see themselves as gods ruling over the many. This offends me. We are saving the world."

Nate wondered if Amanda Horton had any connection to the Mountain Vista resident whom Rick had identified as a suspect. If Riley was correct in her theory, then in Ms. Horton he may have found a kindred spirit.

Shouts boomed out from the kitchen, signaling that breakfast was ready. Nate selected some of the slimmer pamphlets, including copies of the *Earth Charter* and *Agenda 21*, and stuffed them in his jacket pocket.

He caught the scent of soap and turned as Riley entered the room, running her fingers through towel-damp hair.

"You hungry?" he said.

"When Skillet cooks, I'm always hungry."

"That good, huh?"

"Just wait."

44

Riley sighed with pleasure, marveling over the perfection of the omelet, butter-kissed and golden, bursting with crisp vegetables and the sharp tang of some cheese she couldn't identify. She forked into a fruit salad, enjoying the gorgeous array of colors spritzed with fresh-squeezed grapefruit juice and shredded peppermint leaves.

"I was short on time, so just muffins today," Skillet said. "Maybe rolls or pastries tomorrow. If we're still here."

"The muffins are great," Riley assured him, savoring a bite of blueberry and streusel. "Thanks so much, Skillet. This is fantastic."

Murmurings of agreement rose around the room. Riley noticed Skillet shooting furtive glances at Mr. Snowden, who ate with apparent vigor, and wondered what prompted the trace of smug satisfaction on the chef's face.

The meal was served buffet style. The clubhouse and bistro had attained the air of a country house full of guests, rather than a restaurant and meeting place. She shared her table with Skillet and Teren, and they lingered over hot cups of coffee or tea until Nate rose and reminded everyone to stay in groups throughout the day.

He'd eaten with the Mayhew's, but now took the fourth chair at Riley's table.

"I see that Riley's endorsement of you is justified," he said to Skillet. "Fabulous meal, thanks."

"Glad you enjoyed it. What are you doing today to earn your keep?" Skillet asked, a hint of asperity threading his voice.

"I'm going to patrol the neighborhood and try to determine if there's anyone who needs help."

"What about this killer fellow? How do you plan to track him down, detective?"

"Let me worry about that. Just focus on lunch."

"Nothing to focus on," Skillet said. "You all can deal with the sandwich fixings and carrot sticks. I'm not doing lunch. I'll be busy all morning with dinner prep and after lunch I'm taking some down time."

"Good," said Riley. "I'll help, if you like."

Nate held up a hand. "I need you first."

She looked at him, eyebrow raised, waiting for him to continue.

"I'd appreciate it if you came with me on my rounds through the neighborhood."

He turned to Teren. "The Newcombes need some help with a few things, Teren. Would you be willing to check in with them?"

Teren looked a little miffed at being directed around by the new guy, but he covered it with grace. Nodding, he rose from the table and left the room.

Riley went with Nate to the parking lot. She noticed that he checked to make sure the rear compartment of the Explorer was locked tight and hadn't been tampered with. They rolled slowly through the streets of the neighborhood, looking for obvious signs of distress or anything out of place.

Riley watched Nate from the corner of her eye, interested in his attentive behavior but not wanting to stare. His eyes scanned the yards, the doors and windows, the spaces between the houses. After a complete circuit throughout, Nate pulled the car into a driveway, and they started knocking on doors.

Many of the houses were unoccupied, owned by summer vacationers, and Riley marveled how the sound of their knocking sounded different, echoing against empty walls and hardwood floors when there was no living soul inside to respond.

After rapping at the door of a house on the fringes of the neighborhood, they were met by an elderly woman wearing a lace kerchief and sensible shoes. She peered out, studying their faces and looking vaguely disappointed.

"Good morning, ma'am," Nate said, showing his identification, "I'm Detective Quentin. Everything okay here?"

Her face crumpled. "I'm fine. My cats is all fine. But there's no electricity and my phone is busted. I'm worried about my grandson. He lives in Kent and he's coming over for Sunday supper."

Nate gave her a cheerful smile. "I'm sure he's okay, ma'am, so don't fret when he doesn't show up. All the roads are closed. He'll be staying home and so should you." He paused. "Do you need anything?"

Her eyes wandered around the doorstep as if mentally searching her cupboards. "Well, no. I got plenty of canned food and a kerosene lamp. Only thing is, I'm worried about my grandson."

Nate stepped back a little, making room for Riley. She came forward and took the woman's hand, patting it, making direct eye contact. "What's your grandson's name?"

"His name is Daniel. He's a good boy. He'll be coming for Sunday supper."

Nate and Riley had checked the name on the mailbox before walking up the drive. Riley said, "Are you Mrs. Ransome?"

"Yes, Mabel Ransome."

"Mrs. Ransome, Daniel won't be coming for supper today, but don't let that worry you. He's staying safely at home. The roads are closed, people are staying in their houses. And so should you. Okay? Do you understand?"

Riley watched Mabel Ransome's watery blue eyes focus, could almost see clarity take hold. The woman nodded.

"Yes, I understand. Me and the cats'll stay here safe." She gave a decisive nod. "Daniel can come next Sunday."

"That's right," said Nate. "Stay safe, Mrs. Ransome."

They waved and left, moving to the next house on the block. It was a contemporary model, gray with white trim, stone accents, and a stylish colonial red metal roof. Riley laughed as they approached.

"We're at the home of the infamous red roof."

Nate stopped and surveyed the house. "What makes it infamous?"

"It caused a furor in the neighborhood when they put a metal roof on their house. And a red one, at that!"

"Really? Metal's the way to go now, isn't it?"

"Traditionally, only cedar shake or tile was acceptable, and the covenants prohibited the use of other roofing materials. Architectural shingle edged a way in, but metal was far too avante-garde. The homeowners had to go before the board to plead their case and one disgruntled neighbor showed up to complain, wanting the roof torn off and replaced to match what everyone else had."

"You're kidding. Was the covenant written during the Elizabethan era?"

"Close. 1965."

"Ah. What happened?"

"The owners collected signatures from a hundred of our more forward-thinking neighbors and as you can see, they kept the roof. I think it's lovely."

"And," Nate added, "it won't need replacing until the next century. One and done—a freedom worth fighting for."

No one answered their knock, and Riley hoped the inhabitants of the red-roofed house were enjoying a European vacation or ski weekend in Colorado. Somewhere safe and far away. She and Nate continued to the next house on the block.

The land parcels were generous, with enough room between to give them a bit of a walk, but not enough to make it worth driving to each house. They parked in a central location and hit eight or nine houses, then got in the car and moved to the next section.

Riley estimated about a hundred houses in the neighborhood and several belonged to those who were already apprised of the situation and had moved to the clubhouse. They fell into a rhythm.

"So, how'd you become a concert pianist?" asked Nate.

"I was born into it. My grandfather was Zach Riley. He played jazz piano during the Big Band era. He married a musician and they had little musician children, one of which was my mother, who married a musician, and then there was me. I learned music the same way I learned to walk or talk. I can't imagine being anything else."

"You never wanted to break out of that mold?"

"Well, for a while I wanted to go to law school. But I was in my rebellious early teens. I also pierced my ears and streaked my hair purple."

"You wild mustang."

Riley laughed. "Then, when I was fifteen, I won the Bachauer Gold medal and signed my first recording contract. I was hooked."

"Did your parents pressure you to succeed?"

"The pressure to succeed has always been tremendous, but not directly applied by my parents. Just a result of my heritage."

"Interesting. Tell me more."

"Both my parents played, of course, and we had that beautiful old Bechstein. I gravitated toward it, and I met so many people who helped me along the path. I studied in Washington D.C. and then in Spain and London."

Nate stopped in their walk between houses. "But you married a fireman. How'd that happen?"

Riley gave him a grim smile. "It happened as a result of the monumental curve ball we call 9-11. The events of that day made a huge impact on a lot of people and you can include me in that. I lost friends and contacts that day and in 2002, I performed at a series of charity fundraisers in support of victims and their families."

"Ah, and that's when fate stepped in."

"Right. I met a handsome firefighter by the name of James Forte and, as I think I mentioned, I became intrigued with the name and then by the man, himself. We married a year later."

"How was your career at that point?"

"It was really taking off, so we were often apart, both traveling. He was involved in training events and speaking engagements and I with my tours and recording. He loved his job and allowed me to love mine."

"And then you had a son?"

"Yes, Tanner."

"Did that change things?"

"Of course. I slowed down a little and we moved here, to Mountain Vista, so that Jim could take a position with the Tacoma Fire Department, and I could focus more on composing and learning a series of new concert pieces."

They were walking very slowly now, lingering on the asphalt road.

"We wanted to live someplace serene and rural, but not too isolated, so this seemed like the ticket."

"But the fire...it wasn't in your house here?"

"No." Riley hugged herself, feeling a little chilled in the weak sunlight.

Nate removed his jacket and draped it around her shoulders. "We can talk about something else," he said.

Riley shook her head. They stood beside a stretch of fairway and Riley gazed across the manicured grass, her eyes focused inward, seeing something else entirely.

"It was almost Christmas, and I was on a holiday tour in the Midwest. Jim and Tanner came out and rented an apartment so we could spend time together. My schedule kept me out late and it was nearly two o'clock in the morning when I arrived at the apartment. I was shocked to see it surrounded by police and firetrucks. I couldn't believe what happened, it all seemed so unreal."

"That's awful, Riley. I'm so sorry."

She didn't speak right away, her thoughts spooling across time and distance. Finally, she said, "The police are not satisfied the fire was an accident."

"What?"

"There was never enough evidence to make a case for arson, but they suspected it."

"Was anyone else killed?"

"Yes, two neighbors died, as well."

"Oh, hell." Nate walked in agitated little circles, his jaw clenched tight.

"I haven't been able to perform properly ever since," Riley told him.

Nate stopped in front of her, taking her hands, squeezing them gently in his own. "That's a lot of grief to deal with, Riley. It takes time."

"Yes. A lot of grief… and guilt."

"What do you have to feel guilty about?"

Riley's eyes went back in time again, reviewing the awful moments. "I wish I knew," she whispered.

Nate wrapped her in a gentle hug. "Come on, let's go back. It's almost lunchtime."

They returned to the Explorer and Riley tossed Nate's jacket onto the backseat. They crossed the bridge, but Nate passed the clubhouse and kept driving.

"Where are we going?"

"I've got a feeling."

"Ah, the scientific method."

Nate laughed. "I noticed a side road along the back edge of the neighborhood. We haven't talked to anyone there yet and that's the direction Cappy came from last night."

They parked the car and covered the circuit of houses on the cul-de-sac. Three times their summons went unanswered. Twice, the homeowners had nothing to report.

The last door opened, and they were looking down the barrel of a shotgun wielded by a tall man wearing low-slung jeans and a belt buckle that looked liable to pull them off his hips.

"Whoa," Nate said, waving his police ID. "We just have a few questions."

"Sorry, officer. I'm a bit jumpy after last night." The rifle retreated.

"What happened last night?"

"Someone tried to break in here. I figure the sound of my pump-action scared 'em off."

"What time was this?"

The man thought about it. "I'd say between midnight and one."

"Are you Mr. Calloway?"

"That's me."

"Did you get a look at anybody, Mr. Calloway?"

"Nope. Slept on the couch there," he bobbed his head toward the front room, "with one hand on my gun, but never heard nothing more."

Nate handed him a card. "I'm staying over at the clubhouse. If you think of anything else I should know, will you come by?"

"Will do." The man gave a two-fingered salute and closed the door.

45

LUNCH WAS A DO-IT-YOURSELF project.

Nate entered the kitchen to see all the components laid out on the big stainless-steel counter—deli meats and cheeses, a container of chicken salad, lettuce, pickles, tomatoes, a selection of breads, chips, fruit, and carrot sticks. He assembled a sandwich and grabbed a canned soda, joining the others in the dining room.

Power to the neighborhood had not been restored and to save gas, the lights were switched off during daylight hours. The weak sunlight glow coming through the windows cast the room in gray and Nate sensed its occupants were fighting that enervating effect with a forced jollity.

He sat and munched, listening to the bantering conversation. When it hit a lull, he swallowed and leaned forward.

"Who's Amanda Horton?" he asked.

A brief silence followed before Cappy cleared his throat and spoke up. "She was a real sweet gal, lived in the neighborhood. On the far side of the lake."

"She's gone, then?"

Another pause.

"Yes, she's gone," said Brenda.

"She was well-liked?"

"I'll say." Cappy tipped his chair back and winked. "Teren and Skillet liked her especially well."

That evoked a round of titters and a smiling blush from Skillet. Teren's face was stony, arms crossed over his chest. Skillet returned Cappy's fire.

"Johanson spent a good bit of time with her, too, but he did it on the sly." He slid his tongue across his lips, letting his eyelids drop to half-mast.

"Nothing sly about it," Cappy defended. "She was a good friend and a nice woman."

"Although she could be a bit of a Nazi when it came to recycling," Myrna Mayhew said. "Forget to put your green bin out and she'd land on you like a ton of bricks."

"She was an environmentalist wacko, and no mistake," Harper Mayhew agreed.

"She was passionate about a lot of things," said Skillet. "I can attest to that."

More titters.

"What happened to her?" Nate asked.

The tittering stopped and Teren spoke into the silence. "She got drunk and drowned in her own bathtub."

"Oh," said Nate. "I'm sorry to hear that." He sensed an undercurrent in the quiet that followed. Mr. Dawson was the first to offer an explanation for their unease.

"Amanda would have said we brought this volcano on ourselves—as a result of greenhouse gasses, or something."

"And she'd have had a point. The earth is becoming more volatile, thanks to global warming and climate change," said Skillet.

Harper grunted and shook his head. "If you think there's anything you can do about it, you're being facile, buying into the popular philosophy. It's bunk," said their resident geologist. "Man is incredibly puny in the face of the earth's might. Nothing we do, or neglect to do, can significantly affect the workings of the earth." He paused. "It's how we treat each other that really matters."

"Now that's a crock!" Skillet half stood, then calmed himself and resumed his seat. "It does make a difference how we treat the earth."

"Oh, I agree," said Harper. "It matters very much how we treat the earth, but only in terms of our stewardship over it. We must, of course, care for the earth because that is how responsible human beings behave. But the environmental movement goes way overboard, pushing extreme tactics that serve only a political function and have no real bearing on the environment."

Cappy decided to stick his two cents in. "So, you think it's okay to dump toxic waste in our oceans or bury it where it can leach into the soil?"

"I think nothing of the sort!"

Harper's voice rose, rumbling like thunder as he continued to voice his opinion. "I do not advocate for pollution or mindlessly stripping away our resources, or doing anything that will lead to our own destruction. But I believe in an all-powerful God who created this world in which we live, and the earth will roll on, under God's power, for as long as He deems fit."

He finished speaking and sat with his hands clenched in front of him on the table. A small silence followed his speech and Myrna smiled at him, covering one of his fists with her hand and giving it a squeeze.

"What do you think, Brenda?" she asked, turning to the woman. "Are we contributing to the deterioration of the environment by our actions, or failure to act?"

Nate understood that Brenda was an avid reader of the Bible and he expected that she would subscribe to Harp's theory of the puny man, but she surprised him.

"Absolutely," she said. "Without a doubt. Our actions and behaviors are indeed driving climate change and causing an escalation in natural catastrophes. But it's got nothing to do with forgetting to put out the green bin or flushing the toilet too many times."

She gazed across the room, as if reading the writing on the wall. "The prophets have written. They saw our time and knew that the earth would be plagued by these things. They gave warning repeatedly."

She lifted her chin and went on. "We have brought this on ourselves—not because we use the wrong kind of light bulbs or drive gas-powered cars. We are in these dire circumstances because we have turned away from our God, forgotten his goodness, spurned his blessings, and incurred his wrath."

A general cacophony broke out, with debate on both sides. Nate saw Skillet get up and head toward the kitchen. They made eye contact and Skillet motioned with his head for Nate to join him. The door swung shut behind them, dimming the argument in the dining room.

"I made dessert," Skillet said. "It might just be enough to shut them up. Help me serve it."

"I thought I wasn't good enough for kitchen duty."

"Oh, get over yourself."

Skillet had made individual trifles, citrus-spritzed berries and kiwi layered with a creamy concoction and fudgy chocolate cake.

"Beautiful," Nate commented.

"I hope Mr. Snowden likes it," Skillet said with a wicked smile.

"What are you up to, Skillet?"

"Just trying to impress the big guy."

They loaded trays and delivered the goods. Like a miracle, dipping spoons and appreciative murmurings replaced the heated argument and tempers damped to glowing embers, an uneasy peace settling over the company.

Skillet presented Mr. Snowden a double portion, delivered with a flourish.

"Specialty of the House."

Snowden seemed hesitant to try it. He picked up his spoon, then set it down again.

"No?" mewed Skillet. "Very well." He retrieved the dessert, setting it on his tray, and turned away.

"Wait," Snowden called. "I'd like to have it, please."

Skillet made a big production of replacing the trifle in front of his finicky customer. The man wielded his spoon with defiance. He tasted a mouthful and downed the rest of the dessert with growing ardor. Skillet stood by with a satisfied smirk.

Nate hoped he had not created a monster.

He left the dining room and wandered into the lounge. Riley sat silently on the piano bench, head bowed, hands in her lap. She looked wretchedly bereft.

Nate wanted to reach out, to touch her somehow, put his hands on her shoulders or kiss the top of her head. But he cringed at the thought of her bristling or shrinking from him, afraid that she might.

Instead, he stood at her side. "Will you give me a lesson?" he asked, aiming to distract her from her morose thoughts.

The look she shot him said she knew what he was up to, but she slid over, and he joined her on the bench.

"Do you play at all?"

He demonstrated the extent of his prowess with a two-fingered version of *Hot Cross Buns.*

She laughed and Nate felt her come into her element, warming to the opportunity he'd given her.

"All right, I think we can improve significantly on that with one quick lesson." A crafty smile curled the corners of her mouth. "We're going to play an improvisational duet," she told him.

"We are?"

Riley gave an emphatic nod. "Indeed, we are. But there are three rules you must agree to obey."

She raised her eyebrow, and he nodded his acceptance.

"Rule number one—keep to the black keys. Play anything you like, as long as it's on the black keys. Got it?

"I think I can handle that."

"Okay. Rule number two—listen. Use your ears. Listen to the sounds as we make them and form an opinion about what you hear. Is it harmonious, or does it make your skin crawl?"

Nate harbored a strong suspicion that his skin was going to crawl at the discordant jangle he expected to make, but he nodded and said, "What's rule number three?"

"The third rule is that I want you to relax, have fun, and don't be afraid. Just get in there with both hands and play. You get what I mean? Play. Are you ready?"

Nate felt foolish. He looked around and saw they were not entirely alone in the room.

Riley locked eyes with him and pulled his attention back to the keyboard. "Nate, we're here together, you and I, at the piano. And we're about to do something significant. Grasp this moment."

He swallowed and nodded.

"Let's do this," he said.

Riley began, rolling out with a saucy Habanera beat. Nate felt the spicy undertones of her part but didn't know how to complement it. He sat with one finger poised over the keyboard.

"Come on in, the water's fine," Riley assured him.

He touched a key, made a plunk. It sounded okay, so he twiddled around a bit, adding another finger to the ensemble.

"Both hands," Riley reminded, giving him a little nudge with her elbow. He sighed and brought his left hand to the keyboard.

It felt awkward at first, but he soon understood the reason for rule number two. Listening, he realized it didn't sound half bad. He relaxed and found himself falling into the rhythm of Riley's playing.

"Are you hearing this?" she asked.

He was. It was amazing, really.

He sensed her picking up the volume and the tempo and he responded, keeping pace with her, letting the tones roll out from under his fingers.

Together, they built to a crescendo—a big, full sound—and Nate felt his heartbeat quicken as he played beside Riley, feeling the pulse of the music. After a romp on the keys that left him tingling, they dialed it back and Nate sensed the end coming. He played his last notes in unison with Riley's, and it was over.

Applause burst out behind them, and Nate turned, surprised and pleased. He nodded his head in a modest bow towards their little audience and laughed.

"You see?" Riley said. "You didn't know you could do that, did you?"

"Truly, I never saw it coming."

Riley gave him a radiant smile. "Let's talk about why we did it."

"Because it was spectacular fun!"

Riley laughed. "It was," she agreed, "but there are reasons beyond mere fun. I like to do that with a new student because it illustrates something so important."

She paused. Her cheeks were still pink with pleasure, but her eyes had grown solemn.

"Music is about relationships," she explained. "One note by itself—" she played a key on the piano—"doesn't mean a whole lot. Not until it's put into context with other pitches, in a rhythmic structure."

She played a fragment of *Moonlight Sonata*. "That's when it really becomes music."

She turned to Nate, her green eyes bright. "What we did worked so well because the black keys are all related to each other. They're like a family. They're tied together in a special relationship called a pentatonic scale, and that's why they work well together."

Nate nodded his understanding.

"When I teach," Riley said, "I emphasize the *relationships* in the music. I really believe that understanding and fostering those relationships deepens the meaning and the pleasure we get from creating and enjoying music."

Nate heard the passion in her voice, saw the earnest look in her eyes, and he believed it too.

"Madame Musician," he said, "you amaze me."

46

AFTER THE LAST OF the lunch crowd wandered off, Riley returned to the kitchen and helped Skillet square things away.

She admired his efficiency and the way he kept things organized and spotlessly clean. Listening to his chattering with half an ear, she let her mind linger over the duet she'd played with Nate. They had moved well together, and she wished she could summon that same easy confidence at will, unhampered by fear and guilt.

This thought tarnished her memory of the duet and she pushed away, mentally, from the piano and began churning over Rico's murder and the attempted break-in down the street. Were they related? Had it been Cappy?

And why was Nate asking about Amanda Horton?

Riley was hunkered down in front of a corner cabinet putting away a stack of paper plates when she realized the kitchen had gone suddenly silent. She backed out of her position and turned to find Skillet obstructing her exit from the corner niche.

He stood with one hand anchored to the sideboard and the other to the center island, like blue-veined cordons. It was exactly the kind of teasing move that Skillet was known for, but Riley felt a frisson prickle the back of her scalp.

"Nate warned us to stay in groups of three," he said, "but here we are, just the two of us." He spoke in a caressing tone, his eyes capturing hers.

For an instant, Riley was frightened, but she shook her head and forced a laugh, pushing against his arm to get out. The arm wrapped around her, its wiry strength bringing her close, turning her into him and holding her there where she could feel the beat of his heart.

"I knew him," Skillet whispered, his breath hot against her ear. "The rock star. He used to frequent my restaurant and give his compliments to the chef. Sometimes he'd buy me a drink after dinner."

He paused, and Riley counted three beats of his heart before he said, "We spent some time together, Coby and I."

His breath feathered against her neck, sending a shiver through her. Riley bit down on the whimper rising into her throat.

"I heard what was done to him." Skillet tightened his grip on her. "Terrible things."

Suddenly, he spun Riley away from his chest and let her go, leaving her gasping and dizzy. His voice rose several decibels. "Only someone mentally unhinged would do such things."

He grabbed a meat cleaver from the woodblock and punctuated his words with a Jack Nicholson pose, waiting for her to laugh or slap his face. Pure Skillet tactics.

Riley knew he thrived on shock value, loved to curry attention with over-the-top antics. But before she could choose how to respond, Skillet dropped the act. And the cleaver.

He moved his hands over the butts of the knives protruding from the woodblock, then turned and searched the kitchen with frantic eyes, all teasing gone out of them.

"Oh hell," he said. "One of my knives is missing."

47

Every sound echoed in the gloomy restroom as Marie left the stall and stepped to the sink to wash her hands.

The taps were covered with plastic bags as a reminder. Nate had warned that they should conserve water because it was probably fed by gravity from a storage tank during a power outage and the situation could last for days.

He also said the water treatment system might be compromised and not to drink from the tap. They'd filled buckets and pots and gallon jugs to use in the toilets if it came to that.

She blew out a sigh. This just gets better and better.

Dispensing hand sanitizer, she squinted into the mirror as she smoothed it over her hands. The shadows in the room cast strange shapes into the hollows of her face, but even in the muted light she could see the emerging wrinkles. No doubt about it, she was past her youth, her looks were sliding.

What did Tim see when he looked at her? A face he could love forever, or had he stopped loving her already?

The flame inside her, ignited by Jess's outrageous behavior and her own doubts, had dwindled to a simmer during the last hours. But now she felt it flare again, searing her stomach. She left the bathroom.

Most of the group was still assembled in the dining room, lingering over coffee and the last of Skillet's mouthwatering trifle. Marie stood at the threshold, listening to the murmur of conversation, riding its ebb and flow like a gentle surf, her eyes searching the low-lit dining room.

Neither Tim nor Jess was present.

Marie wanted to ask if anyone had seen where they went, but she knew she wouldn't be able to make her voice sound normal, wouldn't be able to fool anyone that everything was okay. She couldn't bear the looks of scorn or pity they might turn on her.

Deciding not to draw attention to her marital difficulties, she twisted away and started a systematic search through the clubhouse.

Meeting room C was in the basement, a dank-smelling room used only as a last resort. No one had chosen to set up camp in its far reaches and to access it, you had to go through a vestibule. Marie pulled open the outer door and it let out a screech like a sack full of angry cats.

No longer able to count on the element of surprise, she crossed the vestibule and yanked open the door to the meeting room. Jess whirled to meet her, wisps of silver hair floating out from her face as if she were a mermaid under water. Dust motes floating on the air around her twinkled like stars.

She was alone.

"What are you doing down here?" asked Marie.

Jess swung an arm toward the long wall of the L-shaped room. "Not that it's any business of yours, but I'm finding the local history very interesting. I didn't know all this was down here."

Marie looked at the series of framed photos, plaques, and mementos. They were dry and dusty, black and white images from the past.

"Doesn't strike me as your sort of thing."

"You talk like you think you know something."

"Don't I?" She paused. "Where's Tim?"

"I have no idea."

Marie stared at the heavy exterior door leading outside, the only other exit from the room. Had Tim slipped out that way? Had there been time?

She looked back at her rival and felt herself shrinking, some part of her vital essence evaporating into the shadows. Struggling to get control of her quivering vocal cords, she sorted mentally through all the accusations, threats, and insults she wanted to hurl at the odious woman standing before her.

Turning, she fled the room without saying a word.

48

THE KILLER ZIPPED OPEN the duffle bag with a savage yank, his hands shaking, heart pumping.

A sprawl of houses adorned the two short ends of the long narrow lake and spread along its eastern flank, but the west side of the lake was mostly forest land. A paved trail ran its length, just wide enough to serve as a cart path for those who lived on the far side to access the golf course. A few narrow trails led off the cart path into a stand of trees beside the lake or up into the hills above Mountain Vista.

The killer knelt in the little knot of trees fringing the lake. From his duffle, he pulled the stones and strips of wood he'd gathered earlier, laying out the pieces as he'd done so many times before.

He began assembling them, positioning the three types of wood, interspersing them with the stones in the prescribed manner. He took a deep breath and let it out slowly, calming himself, allowing her voice to enter his head, listening for her instructions.

That smarter-than-thou geologist had made his choice so easy. The self-righteous pedant with his scientific numbers and theories, acting as if he had an inkling of an understanding about the Earth and her needs and demands.

Still, she trembled. Still, her wrath vented, scorching hot from the depths of her soul. He needed no television or radio or internet to tell him this. She whispered it to him.

She loved him.

He drew the knife from the bag, inspecting it in the weak sunlight. He'd taken it from the kitchen just before lunch, slipping it up his sleeve and walking casually past the storage closet. Stopping to chat with the Dawsons, he circled back after they moved on and slipped, unseen, into the closet.

Squeezing behind the stacks of folded chairs, he reached the spot where he'd stashed the duffle, adding the knife to his collection of items.

It had been easy.

Shifting the knife in his hand, he liked how it felt. A carving knife with a good heft, it fit well enough into an old sheath he'd taken from home. He tested it, running his thumb down the blade, feeling the razor edge, but with a pressure so light and teasing that it merely split the top layer of skin and drew no blood.

A good chef keeps his knives sharp.

He studied the altar, frowning. Something wasn't right. In his agitation, he'd miscounted. It was a foolish mistake and he berated himself while he corrected the error.

There. Now it looked right. Now it was perfect.

Slipping the knife back into the sheath, he turned and started for the clubhouse.

49

Myrna Mayhew wanted to go home.

She had work to do and gardening to keep up with. The vegetable patch needed to be put to bed for the winter and she had about a hundred bulbs that needed planting before the first frost hit.

She wanted to forget about the volcano, forget about the murders, and go on with life, as usual.

Mr. Rico Ferguson hadn't even lived in the neighborhood. He had a fancy island house and now the road between here and there had been washed away. There was no reason to think that whoever had killed him and his staff was in Mountain Vista.

If you killed someone, didn't it make sense to get as far away as possible? The killer was long gone.

But Harp insisted that they move into the clubhouse and stick with the group. She knew he felt some sort of responsibility for the assembly of neighbors, but she didn't understand why. Harp was a funny man, stubborn and often ornery, but she loved him with a fierceness that gripped her heart.

He'd married her back in the day when interracial marriages were frowned upon and he'd never let her feel, for one moment, that he ever regretted it. Even when times were hard. He came to her, now, as she stood on the deck of the clubhouse, overlooking the trout pond.

"Myrna, my dear, let's take a walk."

"What about staying with the group? We're not supposed to go anywhere alone."

He drew her close and planted a kiss on top of her head. "We won't be alone. I'll be with you, and you'll be with me."

"We could do that at home."

She saw that he'd tasted the tartness in her tone. The wrinkles came out on his forehead. "I'm sorry, my dear. I'm sure we'll be able to go back in a day or two."

She gave him a hard look and he shrugged in apology. "Maybe three or four."

Myrna rolled her eyes and took his hand, tucking her arm beneath his. "Where are we going on this walk?"

"I want to observe the water level in the lake and see how much the sediment has stirred. This is a momentous event and even from this distance, there is a lot to take note of. I want to compare what I see here with what I remember from Mount St. Helens."

They navigated the wooden stairs of the deck and struck off across the road toward the lake. Walking out onto the swimming dock, Harp stooped to touch the water, rubbing grit between his fingers.

"Let's go around on the far side," he said. "Just a little way up the path. I want to observe the color of the runoff into the lake."

They walked along the grassy shore until the blackberry bushes grew too thick and they had to keep to the paved cart path. As they rounded the bend into the western side of the lake, they heard a shout.

Squinting, Myrna peered ahead and saw a man near the small glade of trees that graced that stretch of shoreline. As they drew nearer, she recognized him. He beckoned to them from the trees, an excited smile on his face.

"I found some ash deposits on the tree branches," he called out as they rounded the last curve in the path. "I thought you might be interested to see them, Harper."

Harp quickened his step and Myrna felt the eagerness in him. He had such a lively interest in anything to do with nature. She found it deeply endearing. He was like a child, a clever and curious child.

They followed their neighbor into the trees and Harp stepped forward to see more clearly where he was pointing. The man was behind him, now, and he took something from his pocket and held it out toward Harp.

Myrna saw two wires spring forth and bury themselves in her husband's back. She froze in shock. Reeling, she drew breath to scream, but before she could make a sound, the killer raised a stone from the ground and brought it smashing down toward her head.

Myrna's world went black.

50

HIGHWAY 3, ONCE LIVELY and thriving, stretched out now like a severed tentacle.

Topper's boots against the blacktop made clapping noises, the slow applause of a one-man audience as he progressed down the deserted motorway. Soon he'd reach the old service road that wound up behind Mountain Vista. His destination—the abandoned ranger hut—was up on the ridge that backed the neighborhood, separating it from the Hood Canal.

He'd woken in the pale light of morning to a blank slate, unable to remember where he was or how he'd arrived there. Then he'd heard the sound of a woodpecker scrounging up breakfast and the pieces flew together, reminding him of the previous day's turbulent events.

Staring up at the tarp, watching it ripple in the breeze, he'd fingered the slippery pine needles beneath his sleeping bag and known it was time to pack up and move on.

He ate two granola bars and downed half a bottle of water, stashing the rest in his backpack. The sun filtered down through fir trees and maples, diffused by their leaves into a green mist as he disassembled his tent and laced up his boots. Shouldering the pack, he set off to find the highway.

He walked the lonely piece of the severed artery for an hour and a half before coming upon the turn-off for the service road. As he rounded the first bend, losing sight of the highway, he thought he heard a car pass by on the road behind him. But it might only have been the trees, sighing in the wind.

The sun had reached its zenith and was now starting down the other half of the sky. Topper followed it, keeping it just a little to his right, until the forest closed over him again.

He came to the locked gate which closed the road off to unauthorized personnel. The padlock was rusty and disused, suggesting it had been a long time since anyone had ventured to drive beyond the gate. He vaulted it and kept going.

At length, he reached the footpath that led down a rocky pass to the lake. Should he follow it down to Mountain Vista and find out how the neighborhood was handling the disaster? He thought about the residents, many of them pampered and unprepared for rough times. He knew there would be much he could do there.

After a moment's consideration, he decided to press on. Right now, he needed solitude, a quiet period in which to think and recharge. After that, perhaps he would hike down into the neighborhood and meet up with some people.

He left the road and set off through the trees, using his internal compass and his memory of the area to find the hut. He took care through the underbrush, watching for poison ivy and bear traps.

The air was scented with pine, and he drew in a deep breath, cleansing his lungs. The trees thinned and soon gave way to a clearing where the dark brown hut sat, a little crookedly, beside a stand of alders. A mass of early fall leaves, orange and gold, had blown against the foot of the structure, adorning it like a cake frosting border.

Topper climbed the sagging front steps to the porch. They stretched and creaked under his boots with the shriek of tortured nails clinging to decaying wood.

Dropping his pack to the dust-laden floor of the porch, he stepped up to the half-rotted doormat. His key scraped in the keyhole, but the knob turned, and he let himself into the musty interior.

The small hut had no electricity or running water, but once he got the grimy windows open, there was adequate light for now and butane lamps for later.

This would be a good place to rest and reflect. Topper started to think about lunch.

51

Myrna swam up, out of the dark abyss.

Light pressed against her eyelids, causing star bursts of tremendous pain. Her eyes were closed, but the horrific scene played repeatedly across the stage of her consciousness. The two wires thrusting out, Harp going down, the rock plunging toward her head, blocking out the sun.

Blocking out the sun.

Harp!

Forcing her eyes open, Myrna saw a blur of muted colors and waves of nausea engulfed her throat, nearly causing her to retch. She made herself focus on the place where Harp went down. In the shadows, she could see him, drenched in darkness, his lifeblood spilled around him.

Myrna bit back a sob. The killer was there, looming over Harp. He moved in a strange, trance-like dance, circling a pile of sticks and stones, murmuring something she couldn't hear properly or understand.

She knew that Harp was gone from the earth, that it would be a while before she saw him again. In a better place. She imagined him beside her, plucking at her elbow, urging her to move herself, to get away.

There was nothing she could do for Harp, not here and not now. But she could take the most important part of him with her, keep it safe within her.

The killer continued his eerie movements, absorbed in his profane ceremony. Slowly, and with the utmost caution, Myrna eased herself up, bracing against the dizziness. She knew she must avoid catching his eye and forced herself to maintain small movements until she could reach the cover of the trees.

Once there, she moved as quickly as she dared and, without thinking, headed for home.

The house she had shared with Harp was the fourth one on the far side of the lake, closer than heading back to the clubhouse. She tried to feed herself hope that having the home field advantage in a game of stealth would save her, but she could not fasten upon a scenario in which the killer would not find and eliminate her.

He was committed to that outcome. She had seen him, and she would tell.

Glancing behind her in an ecstasy of terror, Myrna ran with frantic and erratic steps. As she neared the driveway, she thought she heard a howl of fury in the distance behind her. A burst of adrenaline pushed her up the steps and she fumbled the spare key from the secret panel Harp had built under the windowsill.

As the panel slid open, her mind cleared like clouds blown by the wind, leaving a shining blue sky. She knew where to go.

It had been years, decades even, since she'd thought about it. The children had loved that secret hiding place, a niche within a niche. In the space underneath the stairs, Harp had fashioned a playroom for Sandra and Kelly and, to their delight, it included a hidden room.

He had not known, when he built that secret place, that it would be her refuge. That it might save her life.

Sternly, she took hold of herself. No time now for tears. She let herself in, locking the door behind her.

Acting on instinct, she grabbed a pillow and an afghan from the couch as she sped by. Taking care to leave no trace of her passage, she entered the room under the stairs and secreted herself in the tiny hidden room, working to steady her breathing, wrapping the blanket around her to stave off the onset of shock.

Several minutes ticked by and then, in the quiet, she heard the tinkle of glass as someone broke a window and entered the house.

52

Rick had put in six years as a Navy SEAL.

He knew his way around the water in hazardous conditions and could drive a boat like he was born to it. He'd spent hours walking the marina, pondering the possibilities. Wrinkling his nose against the odoriferous cocktail of ozone, sulfur, and hot mud, he looked out over the debris-strewn water.

The lahars had dumped tons of mud, rock, and garbage into the Sound, dislodging whole trees, bridges, and lumberyards full of logs. Travel by boat would be a suicide mission and he knew it, but he had been trained to succeed at all costs and he was running out of options.

His biggest problem now was that he didn't own a boat and no one he'd spoken with was willing to loan him theirs. Not surprising.

He was contemplating theft when another thought occurred to him. It was clear that his best hope of getting from point A to point B was by air. He had to keep pushing in that direction. He wondered if the journalist who'd written the piece in Forbes had spoken with any local helicopter owners who hadn't made the final edit. Perhaps there were sources as yet untapped.

It was a long shot but seemed a better bet than stealing a boat and trying to work it through a passage of water choked with obstructions.

He spent a tedious ninety minutes tracking down the journalist's address and was relieved to find that Chris Bardot lived just six miles from the station. By midafternoon, he was pulling into the man's driveway.

Walking to the front door, Rick surveyed the row of houses tucked behind semi-scruffy lawns. A tangle of hula hoops and beach balls graced one side of the Bardot front porch, topped by a pair of roller skates, the adjustable kind that fit over a child's shoes. By the size, Rick gauged the kid would be about nine years old.

He pressed the doorbell and waited.

After a minute with no response, he kicked himself when he realized that, once again, he was ringing an electric bell with no electricity. He knocked and waited an interval, then knocked again, peering through the elongated window that flanked the front door. The house appeared empty.

"Can I help you?"

The voice behind him sounded peeved and Rick turned to face a giant of a man. He was Tongan, or perhaps Samoan, his long black hair pulled into a ponytail, meaty fists resting on substantial hips.

"I'm looking for Chris Bardot. Is that you?"

The man studied him through narrowed eyes. "Are you a cop?"

"Yes," Rick admitted.

The giant face split in a huge grin. "Then join the party."

He placed a ham-sized arm around Rick's shoulders and escorted him to a backyard two houses down.

"Sorry for the rude greeting. We've had some run-ins with prowlers, people looking to loot empty houses. I'm Lou, by the way. I'm married to a cop, Alessandra. Bothell City PD. You'll love her."

Rick caught the smell of barbecuing meat as they neared the yard and he realized he was famished. Three or four families were gathered there, and a picnic table was laden with bags of chips, cold beans, and warm beverages.

"We got no cooking power inside, so it's all barbecue, all the time," Lou told him.

Rick accepted a paper plate and the invitation to load it up. He took a bite of burger and chewed while Lou steered him to a man in a lawn chair.

"This is Chris Bardot," he said. "Chris, this is the guy who was snooping around your house. He's a cop."

"Really?"

The journalist leaned forward, extending a hand. They shook and Rick lowered himself onto a rickety-looking lawn chair. It lurched, protesting, then decided to take his weight.

"What brings you here?" Chris asked.

"I'm hoping you can give me some information."

The journalist regarded him with a cold eye. "Usually, it's me pumping the cops for information. From them, I've learned a whole lot of ways to say take a hike."

"Please," Rick said. "I hope you won't send me packing. This is a matter of life and death."

"Yeah, I've tried that one a time or two, but it generally gets me nowhere."

"Look, Chris, I get it. I apologize for any short shrift my fellow officers have dealt you in the past, but I could really use your help. Is there any way I can get you on my side?"

The journalist hesitated, a doubtful expression crossing his face. A sudden ripping sound tore through the air and one of the threadbare straps on Rick's lawn chair gave way. His hind end fell through and the whole contraption collapsed, dumping him onto the lawn.

Hoots of laughter broke out and Chris stood, pulling Rick to his feet.

"I think you just did it."

An hour later, when Rick left the backyard barbecue, he had a full belly and a name with a reachable address.

53

Nate pushed open the vestibule door and Riley cringed, hands pressed over her ears.

"That needs about a gallon of WD-40," she said, following him through to Meeting Room C. They searched the L-shaped chamber for Skillet's missing knife, even removing and looking behind each framed picture and document on the walls.

Helpless frustration mounted in Nate's chest. The basement meeting room was the final spot on their list of places to search, but the knife remained unaccounted for. He understood the dire implications.

Inventing an errand for Riley, he sent her upstairs where the others were gathered. He needed a moment alone to process, to work through the mess in his head.

A bolt of tension grew along the base of his neck, splitting to stab just behind his ears with an unbearable tightness that radiated pain through his skull. He'd learned that a hot bath or a massage could relieve the pressure, but he had time for neither.

Closing his eyes, he kneaded the back of his neck, trying to relax, trying to think.

"Detective Quentin?"

He dragged his eyelids open and saw Brenda Marsh standing in front of him, hands clasped in a supplicating gesture.

"I'm sorry to disturb you," she said, "but I saw the Mayhews go off by themselves. That was over an hour ago and they haven't returned. I'm getting worried."

And with good reason.

Aloud he said, "Which way did they go?"

"They set off around the far side of the lake."

"All right, thanks. I'll check it out."

Nate let himself out the basement exit and circled the building to the parking lot and the Explorer. He grabbed his jacket off the back seat, spilling the pamphlets he'd taken from Amanda Horton's bookshelf onto the floor.

Ignoring them, he checked his gun and holster and pulled a metal box from under the seat. It contained ammunition magazines, and he shoved a backup into his jacket pocket and went looking for Riley.

He found her in Meeting Room A, visiting with Annette Dawson and her daughter, Wynn. Nate greeted them and stole Riley away, guiding her into the empty corridor.

"We've got a situation," he told her. "It's possible the Mayhews have run into trouble. I'm going out to investigate."

"I'm going with you."

"No need. I'm sure they've simply gone for a walk. I'll find them and route them back here."

"I'm going with you."

"Riley—"

"Unless you intend to cuff me to the railing, I'm going out to look for them. I can go with you, or head out on my own."

Nate felt a spike of heat rise within him, quelled by a shiver of apprehension. "You sure know how to pinch a guy. Let's go then."

"Give me one second," said Riley.

He watched her disappear into the dining room, returning a moment later with one of Frank's fancy siren gadgets. He nodded his approval, and they left the clubhouse and crunched down the gravel walk to the road over the bridge.

Nate turned and led the way down to the lakeside path, sweeping his eyes slowly across the terrain, putting out his feelers for anything off-kilter.

It was only mid-afternoon, but the sky was tinged gray, making it feel like dusk, and the air had an almost metallic tang to it. He spat on the ground.

"Tastes bad, doesn't it?" Riley said.

Nate looked to the east. "Yep, and I'm afraid it's getting worse."

"Brenda quoted me a scripture today, something about the east wind bringing destruction."

"It's unusual for us to get an east wind, but it seems like the weather is all over the place now. Anything could happen."

They walked in silence until they reached the end of the blackberry bushes and the path curved around the long side of the lake.

"Why would they go down here?" Riley said. "Harp knew better."

We may never know.

Nate kept the dismal thought to himself and pointed out the trail branching off to the left. "What's down there?"

"Just a small grove of fir trees and a couple of benches."

"Let's take a look."

As they neared the fringe of woodland, they heard the yip-yip of a coyote and saw the creature slink out from among the trees and run off up the hill. Nate stopped and put out a hand to break Riley's stride.

"Wait here a moment," he said, drawing his weapon. "Yell out if you see anything."

He had a bad feeling about what he might find, and his feet didn't want to take him into the trees. But he forced them forward, stepping over fallen deadwood, peering into the shadows.

Nate had seen a lot of dead people, but mostly they were complete strangers to him. He'd eaten breakfast with the Mayhews only hours ago and was growing to like and respect the man and his wife. He grimaced as dry leaves crackled under his feet, dreading what instinct told him he was going to see among the moss-covered pines.

A heaviness fell over him when he caught sight of the blood-spattered altar of sticks and stones and Harper Mayhew's lifeless body. It hit him like a blow to the gut. He swallowed several times, trying to make the rising lump go back down, but it stayed in his throat, an aching mass.

He looked for Myrna, quickly searching the piles of leaves, behind benches and rotting logs. Where was she? Could she have escaped or had the killer taken her?

He returned to Riley.

"Sound the alarm," he said.

54

Myrna curled in a fetal position, silent tears wetting her cheeks, ears straining to catch the sounds of the intruder.

She'd heard him moving through the house, opening closets and cupboards, pushing around pieces of furniture. It seemed hours since he'd broken into her home, invading the space she and Harp had created together.

An age since he had killed her husband and shattered her future.

Footsteps sounded in the corridor, moving down the hallway. Slow, deliberate. When the killer spoke, her heart spasmed in her chest and she pressed her lips together to stifle a gasp.

"Myrna, are you listening? You have no idea how much I regret this. Harp was an old fool, but you—you are a gem."

The footsteps stopped. He was just outside the door, now. He had not yet searched the room under the stairs. It was the only part of the house remaining to him.

"Don't be frightened, Myrna. I always make it quick and painless. Suffering is not the point. I do it to take away the suffering. Can you understand that, Myrna? I have done so much to stop the suffering."

A silence followed that lengthened into minutes, pulling at Myrna's nerves, stretching them taut. He was waiting. Waiting for her to give herself away.

Or was he expecting her to come to him, to present herself willingly, head bowed, the sacrificial lamb?

Myrna felt the urge to scream. He was a madman. She squeezed her eyes and mouth shut and sent up a beseeching prayer.

The click sounded loud in the silence of the house as the door to the playroom opened with a sorrowful wheeze.

55

THE KILLER STEPPED INTO the room under the stairs.

It was dank and musty, as if it hadn't been used for a long time. In the dim illumination that spilled in from the kitchen window, he saw a pink plastic stove, a set of tiny cooking pans and utensils strewn over the dusty surface.

To the left, a large dollhouse dominated a child-sized table flanked by child-sized chairs. This was a playroom, designed for little girls.

Carpet scraps blanketed the floor, remnants from three different sources. Princess posters were tacked to the walls and an aquamarine dream catcher hung from the ceiling, its iridescent feathers stirring gently in the wake of his motion.

He pivoted slowly, taking in the whole space. She must be here.

His gaze fell upon the corner beyond the doll's house, piled with stuffed animals. A woman could hide beneath those.

Advancing slowly, he listened to the sound of his own breath in the confined space. Reaching the mound of stuffed toys, he lifted a Teddy bear and inspected it. The bear wore spectacles, lending him an air of intelligence.

The killer tossed it aside and reached for a monkey, then dug both hands into the pile, pushing to the bottom, feeling for flesh.

He'd made a mess but hadn't found his quarry. Where was the woman? What had he overlooked? There was nowhere left to search but the walls.

He looked at the far end of the room. He took a step toward it, then flinched when a burst of noise sounded from the direction of the lake. One of Frank Newcombe's sirens.

They'd found Harp.

The strident racket continued, and the killer realized all able-bodied men would respond to the call. If he didn't, it would look suspicious.

Casting his eye once more around the room, he set his jaw and moved to the door. Myrna had gone to ground somewhere, and he could only hope she would die there from the head wound he'd given her.

It had worked for Toby.

56

RILEY'S FEET FELT HEAVY.

She'd been lifting and putting them down, scouring the neighborhood in search of Myrna, for nearly two hours. Fighting the despair that settled over her by degrees and seemed to sink into her shoes until she could barely raise her feet, she pushed herself to keep going.

Nate had divided them into groups of three to comb for Myrna, keeping one group to guard the perimeter of the crime scene while he once more documented and gathered evidence. He told Riley that he'd try again to radio the sheriff, but she felt no great optimism about the results.

The sky was beginning to darken, matching her mood. She was teamed with Teren and Dr. Deb. They'd searched through their sector of the neighborhood twice and found no trace of Myrna.

"I say we head back to the clubhouse for a drink," said Teren. "It seems pretty clear she's not in our section of the grid."

Dr. Deb stopped walking. "We've got to find that woman," she said, shading her eyes against the setting sun while she scanned the nearby houses.

"We will find her," Teren assured. "But right now, we need a little refreshment and a rest."

As they trudged down the road that ran along the eastern shore of the lake, a figure appeared on the intersecting road, walking toward them. Riley was startled to recognize Rebecca, one of her piano students who lived in the neighborhood. The girl had a load of books under her arm and Riley remembered they had scheduled a make-up lesson for today.

That had been a lifetime ago.

Everything had changed. The earth was tipped on its axis, pigs might be flying, and into this surreal atmosphere walked this expectant student, toting a book bag.

"I'm late for a piano lesson," Riley told Deb and Teren. "I'll catch up with you later."

"You're kidding," said Teren.

Riley gestured to the student now waiting on the front steps of her house. "In a world where everything is falling apart" she said, "this girl shows up with confidence and the expectation that she can go on. I've got to respect that kind of courage."

"I'm coming with you then," Teren said. The clubhouse sat another thirty yards up the road, in sight of Riley's house. He turned to Dr. Deb. "You'll be okay?"

Riley thought the veterinarian's nod held a trace of annoyance, but she agreed. Riley and Teren veered off and approached Rebecca.

"I'm sorry," Riley said. "With all that's been going on, I forgot about our lesson."

"Can we still do it?"

Riley had taken Rebecca on as a student four months ago when the twelve-year-old had arrived on her doorstep, clutching a trembling folder of sheet music.

"I'd like to audition for you."

Riley had been taken aback. "I'm sorry," she said. "I'm not accepting any new students right now."

The girl's quivering increased but her chin rose, and her topaz-colored eyes flashed.

"I'm Rebecca," she announced, "and I'm going to be the best student you ever taught."

Riley's heart and curiosity were caught in equal measure. She invited the girl in, and they sat at the kitchen table, drinking iced peppermint tea and getting to know one another.

At length, they moved into the living room and Rebecca took her place at the piano and played a Kabalevsky Toccatina and one of the Clementi Sonatinas from Opus 36. She clearly had talent but needed help in developing her phrasing and technique.

The girl's earnest-eyed plea hooked Riley and her new student worked hard to fulfill her prediction, eager to learn and willing to listen. Riley had enjoyed every moment of their lessons together.

Rebecca stood now, waiting for Riley's answer to her question, her eyes imploring, jaw firm.

"I don't see why we can't have our lesson," Riley said, rallying to the determination radiating from this girl on her porch. "There's still enough daylight to see by."

She let them into the house and Teren wandered discreetly into the kitchen as Riley led Rebecca to the piano. The girl was progressing quickly through all the major scales on the circle of fifths and Riley demonstrated the fingering for a D-flat major scale, marveling at the girl's instant comprehension.

"I'm starting to get what you mean when you talk about how my hand fits the keyboard. When you position your hand the right way, the keys you need are right under your fingers."

"Exactly. Once you figure out an effective fingering strategy, you can achieve flow. It's almost like dancing, the way your fingers move when they're strong and conditioned and you follow a good working strategy. Feels great, doesn't it?"

Rebecca's hands flowed up and down the keyboard and she turned to Riley with a delighted grin. "It feels fantastic."

They worked through a Scarlatti sonata and Riley demonstrated an exercise using a legato touch in one hand while simultaneously executing a crisp staccato in the other. Rebecca was chagrined at her failure to perform it perfectly, but Riley assured her she'd master it, with practice.

To finish the lesson, she reviewed some chord theory and introduced C.P.E. Bach's Solfeggietto, pointing out how the patterns are established and repeated in various keys and registers. Rebecca looked doubtful.

"I feel the order in the music," she said, "but I can't always see the patterns. Sometimes, it's just a flurry of notes."

Riley rose from the bench and went to her music cabinet. On the wall above, there was a set of framed art that appeared to be abstract collections of brightly colored dots. She took one down and handed it to Rebecca.

"What do you see?"

Rebecca studied the print. "I see a lot of tiny splotches of color. What am I missing?"

"Do you see any light reflecting off the picture? Okay, good. Focus on that point of light but keep your eyes relaxed. Don't be shocked when the image starts to firm up. Just go with it."

Rebecca gave her a mystified look, but obediently gazed at the artwork, her eyes taking on a far-away glaze as she stared down at the collage of apparently random dots. After two minutes of silence, she looked up, embarrassed.

"I'm sorry. I don't know what I should be seeing. It's just dots on a page."

"Shhh...relax and keep looking. Be patient with yourself. Learning how to look at something a different way takes time."

The girl took a deep breath and focused down on the picture again. Riley watched, perceiving the moment when the image began to swim into view. She saw Rebecca lose it, and struggle to get it back.

A look of wonder and satisfaction spread over the girl's face.

"It's the Statue of Liberty! So bright and sharp I could almost touch it."

Excited, she popped up from the bench and went to examine the other framed pictures, gazing into each with the same technique and exclaiming over the images that emerged.

"So cool," she said, "but what's it got to do with music?"

Riley smiled. "Sheet music is just dots on a page," she said. "Until you know how to look at it properly. Once you figure out how to see the big picture, it opens up worlds you didn't even know existed. My aim is to teach you how to see the big picture, how to open up some of those doors. It is, as you say, very cool."

Rebecca uttered a little trill of laughter. "Awesome," she agreed.

"For now, work on your C-minor chord inversions, along with the rest of the assignment I wrote in your folder. Mr. Kirkwood and I will walk you home."

During their walk, Teren and Rebecca debated the merits of algebra while Riley's mind wandered. Something flickered at the back of her consciousness, pulling at her attention like that point of light reflecting off the mass of dots.

An image waited there, fuzzy and obscure, but Riley sensed it was somehow vitally important for her to see it clearly. It wouldn't happen easily, though. Every time it began to come into focus, her mind shied away and the picture faded to black.

Someday that difficult picture would come to light, and she'd have to look at it, acknowledge it, deal with it. She thought it might be someday soon.

Rebecca ran up the brick path to her front door and her mother waved from the bay window that jutted out over a bed of asters just coming into bloom. Riley returned the wave, admiring this glimpse of normality in a world gone haywire. Candles burned in the windowsill, a warm glow of innocence in the gathering dark.

These people didn't know, they were unaware of the killer in their midst. Riley prayed it might remain so.

As they turned to retrace their steps, Teren put an arm around her shoulder, letting it rest there.

"I should eavesdrop on your piano lessons more often. Damn, you're a fine teacher."

Riley smiled. "I love teaching most days anyway, but that girl makes it a genuine pleasure."

He let his arm drop and they walked a beat or two in silence. When he spoke again, his voice held a husky, intimate tone.

"What's bothering you, Riley?"

She let out a snort. "That's a peculiar question. I just destroyed my career, my life's work is down the tubes. Mt. Rainier erupted, killing a hefty number of people, and we have no idea how many or what's really going on because we're cut off from the rest of the world, without power or means of communication."

Teren opened his mouth, but she swept on, cutting him off. "I haven't even got to the good part yet. We have a serial killer rampaging the neighborhood, picking off victims one by one. So, what could possibly be bothering me?"

Teren's face never lost its look of calm gravity as he listened to her rant. She looked away, pressing her lips together, trying to staunch the restless irritation which tore at her.

"Despite that impressive line-up," Teren said, "I think there's something else, underneath it all. Something utterly fundamental."

He gripped her chin with gentle fingers and turned her face, studying the lines and planes of it. "Guilt," he said. "You're feeling guilty over something."

She slapped his hand away. "Okay, doctor, what is it then?"

"The one thing you didn't mention."

Riley felt the heat on her simmering emotions flare up a notch. If she didn't get a handle on this, she was going to blow.

"I surmise you're referring to my dead husband and my dead son."

"I am indeed."

His unruffled composure infuriated her, and she struggled to keep her voice in check. "Oh, sure, yes, because I feel so much better when I bring them to mind."

Misery swirled over her, dampening the anger. "What do you want me to talk about? Shall we discuss how if they hadn't come out to be with me, they wouldn't have burned with the apartment?"

He said nothing, but the look he turned on her was gentle.

"Well, Teren, it's taken me a hell of a long time, but I think I've pretty much worked through that. Maybe we should hash out how I should have been there with them. It should have been me. But again, I've more or less made my peace with survivor's guilt."

She paused, walking in agitated silence, then let out a groan. "It's the uncertainty, not knowing what really happened. Was the fire deliberate? And if so, who caused it and why."

"That's part of it."

"Part of it? What's the rest of it?"

"That's what you need to figure out."

The flame in her gut flared up again. "You know, Teren, you're really pissing me off."

"That's okay, be pissed at me if it makes you feel better. Just don't get careless."

He stopped, swinging her to face him. "Please, Riley, be vigilant. Don't go off alone and don't trust anyone. Not even the detective, and especially not Skillet."

She broke away from him and crunched up the gravel drive to the clubhouse, angry enough to take a swipe at anyone who stood in her way. But beneath the anger lay the guilt and a layer of something else.

Fear.

57

NATE WATCHED WITH RELIEF as Riley and Teren entered the clubhouse, though he was less happy to note Riley's flaming cheeks and flashing eyes.

Everyone else was already assembled in the dining room, eating dinner, and he beckoned to them, drawing them close.

"Did you find Mrs. Mayhew?" Teren asked.

"Not yet," said Nate, "but I was able to process the scene and we moved Harper's body to a secure location where the coyotes won't get him."

Riley shuddered and Nate saw that she was struggling to calm herself. "Come on in and sit down. You need to get some dinner in you. Skillet's cooking," he added, with a grin.

Riley offered him a taut smile that stopped short of her eyes. She was showing strain and Nate worried. She'd been out there, alone with Teren, and that raised a host of issues in his mind.

After they'd served themselves at the buffet-style sideboard and found a seat, Nate used a spoon against his water glass to get everyone's attention.

"We all feel the loss of Harper Mayhew and I want to thank you for the hard work you've put in today. Skillet," he bowed his head toward the chef, "is feeding us well and many of you put in some hours this afternoon helping me and searching for Mrs. Mayhew."

There were a few murmurs of acknowledgment, but most heads were bent and silent as people concentrated their dwindling energy on chewing their dinners.

"I'd like to restate my advice that you stay together in groups of at least three. We'll have to—"

"You think one of us did it," Brenda interrupted. She dropped her fork onto her plate, producing a metallic clang that vibrated in the silence of the room. Head swiveling, she took in the assembly before continuing in an aggrieved tone. "You're suggesting the murderer is here, in this room."

Nate shook his head. "I didn't say that, but I won't discount the possibility. Right now, it's imperative that we find Myrna."

"Oh, my word!" Mrs. Dawson rose from her seat, a hand pressed against her chest. "Myrna can identify the killer."

"If she's still alive," someone shouted.

A mild uproar rippled through the room, but Nate used his butter knife like a gavel and took back the floor.

"It's true that I'm hoping Myrna can tell us who attacked Harper," he admitted. "But it's by no means certain that the killer is known to any of you. It could be an outsider whose escape route has been cut off, someone who's hiding within the confines of the neighborhood."

He held up his arms, shushing the flurry of alarmed voices. "The point is, we don't know, and our best precaution is to stick together."

Dr. Deb stood and cleared her throat. "I'm concerned about Myrna's medical condition. We don't know what kind of injuries she may have sustained. I don't think we can wait until morning to mount another search."

"I agree," Nate said. "I hope no one will accuse me of being sexist when I suggest that the women and children stay here with the doors locked, while the men go out in groups."

No one argued, but there was a palpable tension in the air as Nate organized the teams and gave instructions. Riley walked with him to the glassed-in lobby. She seemed more subdued now, and he wanted to wrap his arms around her, soak up some human contact, feel the beat of her heart.

Instead, he took her by the hand. "Stay inside," he told her. "And keep all the entrances locked."

She looked up at him, forehead pinched, eyes filled with worry. "Nate, do you think Myrna's still alive?"

He blew out a pent-up breath. "I believe there's a good chance she escaped somehow. We've searched pretty hard and haven't found a body and this killer has never bothered to hide his handiwork before."

He paused. "I think she's hiding."

"Nate, if the killer finds her first—"

"Not going to happen."

She nodded. He squeezed her hand and stepped away, slipping out the door to join his group. The lock clicked as the door shut behind him and he spun around to give Riley a final wave.

As his team moved off into the darkness, he turned back to see her standing against the glass, an aureole of light radiating from her auburn hair like a halo.

58

Rick drove fast toward the address Chris Bardot had given him.

There was little traffic on the road, but he had to backtrack twice when he encountered bridges that were washed out or closed off and the delay was maddening. The merest sliver of an orange sun remained on the horizon and the darkness was almost tangible, a live thing which might brush you with its wing.

He turned off the highway and entered a winding side street. He rounded a bend, his headlights catching two deer as they bounded along beside the road before veering off into the forest. Hitting one would have seriously hampered his night's mission, and he proceeded with caution, pulling up at last between two brick pillars spanned by a wrought iron gate.

He pressed the intercom button and got dead silence.

Giving the instrument panel a belligerent smack, he began entering codes at random into the keypad. He'd come a long way for it to end like this. He got no click, no ping, no response.

Backing the Mustang away from the gate, he parked on the shoulder, idling the engine while he considered his options. He was about to switch off the car and jump the fence when he heard the rising pitch of a vehicle approaching at fast speed.

He realized it came, not from down the road on which he sat, but from behind the property line. As he watched, the gates swung open, barely in time to allow clearance for the black Jaguar which burst through them, fishtailing on the sharp turn out of the driveway.

The tires skidded, leaving half a pound of rubber, then bit the pavement and the car was gone.

If he'd stopped to think about it, things might have turned out differently, but there was no time for deliberation. His foot worked the gas pedal, and he was through the closing gates and barreling down the driveway before conscious consideration caught up.

Slowing the car, he tried to make his heartbeat follow suit. He was trespassing, but he'd been stretching the law all day and wasn't beyond breaking it outright, if need be.

This was one fight he wasn't backing down from.

The drive passed through woodland, but soon the trees thinned and gave way to a vast, close-clipped lawn. Another deer loomed out of the darkness and Rick nudged the brake, slowing to a crawl.

It wasn't a deer, and it wasn't alone.

A veritable herd of creatures swarmed him, forcing the car to a halt, creating a barrier between him and the house.

He'd been captured by a phalanx of llamas.

59

RILEY WAS SO WEARY her knees wobbled, threatening to buckle with each step.

She paused, watching the overhead lights wink out as Millie turned off switches to save power. A few lamps burned, one in the lobby and one in the lounge, but the intervening darkness seemed thick and menacing.

Jess came around the corner from the lounge, moving with her customary grace, lamplight reflecting from her silvery hair.

"Riley, you look done in. I'm making you a cup of tea."

She took Riley's arm and guided her through the shadowy dining room to the kitchen. Riley sank into a chair at the kitchen desk and watched Jess move around Skillet's well-ordered domain, filling a kettle, sniffing tea bags, pulling two cups from the shelf.

"I think Chamomile would be best."

Riley was too tired to reply, and it wouldn't have mattered, anyway. Jess was the sort of woman who decided what she wanted and made no bones about getting it. It was an admirable quality and Riley gave the woman points for candor, if not for moral rectitude.

Despite the steady confidence she displayed in her own sex appeal, Riley sensed a vulnerability, the hunger to connect with another person while remaining unfulfilled by that connection. In her present state of exhaustion, what she felt for Jess was gratitude, tinged with pity.

Jess set a steaming cup on the desk blotter and a warm, fragrant cloud enveloped Riley. The muscles at the base of her neck loosened as some of her surface tension dissolved.

"How did you happen upon the good-looking detective?" Jess asked.

The rising vapor from her cup drifted in front of her face, distorting her features. Riley felt the measure of her gratitude diminish and she glared at Jess.

"Down, girl," the woman said, catching the drift. "I'm just making conversation. I'll keep my paws off your policeman."

"He's not my policeman."

"Then why the dirty look?"

Riley waved away the question and tested the tea, finding it still too hot to drink.

"I'm going to miss Rico," Jess said. "He gave some great parties." She paused and blew across the top of her cup. "Who do you think killed him?"

Riley realized how much she'd evaded that question in her own mind. Who, indeed? Someone in her group of friends and acquaintances? Or a maniac lurking on the fringes?

"I really have no idea," she said. "And I'm too tired to process anything right now. It's been a rough weekend."

"To put it lightly."

The tea reached perfection and Riley sipped, feeling the tightness in her chest relax a bit as warmth spread over her. Jess finished with her cup and washed it out in the sink, tipping it in the drainer to dry.

"I'm for bed."

"Don't wait for me," Riley said. "I just want to sit here and veg for a moment."

"You sure?"

Riley nodded.

"Okay, then. Goodnight."

The kitchen door swung shut behind her, *thub-thubbing* until it settled into inertia. Riley finished her own tea and sat staring into the cup, trying to divine meaning from the tiny shreds of chamomile that lay at the bottom.

She was on her way to the counter when a horrific scream ripped the air, and she nearly dropped her cup and saucer. Dumping them in the sink, she ran through the darkened dining area.

As she reached the corridor outside the lounge, a shadowy figure rushed for her, driving an elbow into her stomach. She went down, gasping, and the attacker fled through the lobby and out the front door, disappearing into the night.

Riley writhed on the floor, unable to draw breath. She had to get up, had to get help. Even in the darkness, she had seen the knife.

And the blood.

Crawling to the lounge, she used a sofa to pull herself upright. A whimper rose in the silence of the room and Riley scrambled around the sofa and stared down at Jess, curled in a ball on the floor.

Her silver hair streaked with red.

60

THE HERD OF LLAMAS closed in on the Mustang, encapsulating Rick in a virtual tin can.

He pushed open the driver-side door, hoping to scare them off and create a path for his exit, but they were having none of it. The hairy mob crowded in, forcing the door closed.

Rick hastily withdrew and sat for a moment, bemused by the unexpected scene. Beyond the llamas, a flock of matted wandering sheep filled the yard with a mournful, bleating racket. The llamas peered at him balefully, clearly blaming him for disturbing the peace.

He counted eight cream colored, long-necked creatures and at least half a dozen dark brown counterparts. Each treated him to a contemptuous stare. Rick locked eyes and leaned heavily on the horn. The llamas startled, side-stepping away from the car, ungainly, their heads bobbing on slender necks.

Three seconds later, they surged back.

One inquisitive beast swiped a tongue over the dusty window, leaving a slimy track. Rick returned to the horn and pounded out a chorus of *La Bamba*. Through the forest of necks, he saw a woman wading through the woolly pack. Her long, golden hair was burnished by the security lights, creating a halo effect, and she was moving fast.

She gave a signal and the animals retreated, holding a perimeter about ten yards out.

Before Rick could unfold himself from the seat, the woman wrenched the door from his grasp and planted herself where the llamas had vacated, eyes smoldering.

No angel, this one.

A single word exploded from her compressed lips. "What?"

Rick stared. His mind went blank. It had been a long day.

"Sorry," he mumbled. "My mistake."

Clearly, this was not Robert Baines. Presumably, Robert Baines had been in the speeding get-away car that had nearly clipped him at the gate. And who could blame him?

He reached for the car door, wanting to swing it shut and be on his way.

"Oh, no you don't."

The angry woman hip-butted the door so that it strained at its hinges, gaping open like a wound. Her arms remained crossed over her chest, eyes flinty, cheeks flamed.

"Let's do this," she challenged. "I want to see you try putting lipstick on this pig."

Rick realized he'd walked into the middle of some kind of mess. "I think you were expecting someone else," he said. "I'll come back another time."

She'd taken in a breath, ready to lambaste him, and she expelled it in a huff. Some of the sparks left her eyes. "You're not working for my husband," she said, her tone flat.

"No, I'm not. But if your husband is Robert Baines, that's who I'm looking for."

She laughed, a harsh, broken sound. "My *husband*," she said, putting bitter emphasis on the word, "just left. I'm surprised he didn't run you down. He was flying like a bat out of hell."

"Oh, that guy. Missed me by mere inches."

She darted him a hostile look and he kept his face ruler straight. "Sorry I wasted your time. I'll get out of your hair now."

He made another move for the car door, but she didn't budge.

"What do you want with Robert?"

"It's a long story, and it doesn't matter. I'm gonna call it a day."

She stood, braced hard, cold as a January pond. Then she moved half out of his way, releasing the door. "Care for a drink?"

"Mrs. Baines, I really should go."

A shadow moved across her face and was gone. He considered. What are the chances she could help him? She hardly seemed in a position to influence her husband in a positive direction.

Still, he could use a drink.

They walked together across the yard. It seemed the llamas had forgiven him, or more likely, forgotten him. Their complacent gazes followed their mistress, and the frantic bleating of the sheep had diminished to the occasional sleepy comment.

The ranch house had a wide veranda and cedar boxes planted with bronze chrysanthemums. The smell of mulch hung in the crisp air and floating over it like a faint melody, Rick caught a whiff of expensive perfume.

"So, what's with the llamas."

Her face opened up with a genuine smile. "They make great guard dogs, don't they?"

"Can't argue with that."

"They nanny the sheep, too." She threw open the front door and walked in, expecting him to follow. "Watch your step," she said.

Rick's foot crunched over something brittle. Too late.

He looked down where his shoe had pulverized broken crockery. Shards and splinters lay scattered through the entryway, and he counted fragments from at least three different sets. No respecter of plates, this girl.

"Never mind," she said. "Just step around the mess and come into the great room."

She poured him a drink, without regard to his preferences, and motioned him onto a fawn-colored leather couch.

"I hope you'll forgive my behavior. I was...upset."

She mixed a drink for herself and sank into a matching chair. "So, what's your story? I know a soul in need when I see one. I'm not a bad sort, despite appearances."

Rick realized a sudden desire to air his predicament, to lay off some frustration on another human being. But he was reluctant to become ensnared in this woman's affairs as would surely happen if he let down his guard. He kept his peace and drained his glass, rising to go.

She raised an eyebrow, waving him back to his chair. "Vent with abandon, sir," she said, seeming to understand his quandary. "I won't require tit for tat."

Stepping to the sideboard, she returned with the decanter, splashing another round of amber liquid into his tumbler.

Two refills later, the dam broke.

Rick left out few details and found her to be a good listener, drawing him out and setting him at ease. He ended by recounting his visit to the journalist who'd written the article in *Forbes*.

"He told me if anyone could get me where I need to go, it was Bobby Baines, and he gave me this address. I hope you don't mind."

Snapping his empty glass down on the rosewood table at his elbow, he poised to rise. "I'm afraid Bobby was my last hope."

She swirled her drink, regarding its depths with a solemn eye, then shifted her gaze to his.

"You're looking at a classic good news/bad news situation here," she told him. "The good news is, *I'm* Bobbi Baines and I am one hell of a pilot."

Surprise rippled over Rick, and he felt stupid for assuming Bobby was a man.

"The bad news," Bobbi continued, "is that the sort of operation you're talking about, aside from the extreme peril, would tear up an engine, virtually killing the helicopter. No one wants to subject their bird to that."

Rick absorbed the dismal pronouncement and wondered if he was too drunk to drive. It was time to go. He gathered his feet under him and pushed up from the chair.

Bobbi Baines took a swallow from her glass and raised a finger for attention.

"You're gonna want to stick around for the capper, stranger," she said. "More good news—it's not my helicopter. It belongs to that rat bastard I married."

She raised her glass. "When do we leave?"

61

From a hundred yards back, Nate could see that something was wrong.

Light shone from every window of the clubhouse and figures were moving in the glass-walled lobby, though he was too far away to make out any details. He brought his trot up to a gallop and Teren and Sandy matched him step for step.

They arrived and Riley met them at the door.

"No one's been killed," she said, her voice calm, hands moving in gentle, soothing motions. "Jess was attacked, and her arm was cut."

Nate's breath caught in his throat, relief flooding over him.

"Dr. Deb has stitched the wound and Jess is going to be fine," Riley continued. "The doctor gave her a sedative, though, and she's down for the count. You'll have to save your questions for tomorrow. Any trace of Myrna?"

"Nothing. Tell me what happened here."

"I'll tell you all I can but first, there's something I better show you."

She started away, but he grabbed her by the elbow.

"Wait just a moment."

He dispatched Teren and Sandy to check that all points of entry into the facility were secure and to search the building for anything suspicious. Then he followed Riley to the lounge.

The center of the room had been cleared, the oriental carpet rolled up against the piano bench to expose the bare floor. A figure had been drawn on the planks of hardwood with a grease pencil. A pentagram. The center of the greased-in lines was smeared with blood.

Nate used his cell phone to photograph the scene, then he led Riley to the dining room, and they sat at a table while she told him all that had happened. As she finished, Teren and Sandy returned and reported in.

"All doors and windows are secure, and we found no signs of forced entry," Sandy said.

"Everyone is present and accounted for," added Teren, "except for the last group of searchers. That would be Skillet, Cappy, and Frank."

"Alright, thanks. I don't know how he got in, but Riley says she definitely saw him leave by the front door."

"What did he look like?" asked Teren.

"I hate to sound like your typical eye-witness dope, but it was dark, and it all happened so fast. All I can say is that he wore jeans and a black hoodie pulled down over most of his face."

"How tall?" asked Nate.

"He didn't tower over me, but then he was sort of crouched down, hiding his face."

Teren pulled a chair up to their table. "This points to an outsider, doesn't it, detective? All the men in our group were watching each other's backs out there, while someone was hiding in here, waiting for a chance to strike."

"I don't know," said Nate. "I didn't have eyes on you the entire time we were out. Sometimes you circled one way, and I went another and we lost sight of each other for a time."

Teren's jaw dropped, then snapped shut, hard. Nate knew he'd upset the man, but he wasn't ready to draw any definite conclusions about the pool of suspects.

"Not long enough for me to come back here and carve up Jess," Teren retorted.

"No," said Nate. "I wasn't accusing you. I'm just saying that none of us have a clear-cut alibi. I'm sure it's the same with the other searchers. We weren't holding hands out there. It's possible someone could have slipped back here for a quick attack to make it appear as if an outsider did it."

"Or an outsider did it." Teren's tone was belligerent.

"There is that possibility," Nate conceded.

"Now what?" said Riley.

"Tomorrow, we find Mrs. Mayhew," Nate said, "alive and squawking."

62

The morning air had the gentle bite of early autumn, crisping the multi-colored leaves that fluttered against the evergreens in gorgeous array.

A slightly smoky aroma hung in the air, reminding Riley of a camping trip with Jim and Tanner. She remembered how it had felt stepping out of the tent in the early morning to the smell of wood ash, tree sap, and Jim cooking breakfast over the fire.

An ache settled into her throat, and she plodded on with grim determination. The driving thought that they must find Myrna became the controlling idea in her head, and she allowed it to push everything else aside.

They were out, searching in force this morning. Her group included Skillet and Marie. They worked down one side of the street while Nate, Teren, and Cappy covered the opposite side, combing through the yards, checking bushes and outbuildings, knocking on doors. The water level had risen even further and there were several spots where they had to squelch through, muddying shoes and soaking socks.

Riley's group finished searching the Rupert property, which was bordered by a hedge separating it from the Krueger's next door. Skillet leaped across the grassy drainage ditch and disappeared into the next yard. Riley tried to follow him over, but her shoes slipped on the wet grass, and she went down hard, with a little cry.

Both Nate and Teren rushed to her aid from across the street.

"I gotcha," Nate said, pulling her to her feet.

Teren crossed to her other side and put a supportive hand under her elbow. "You okay?" he asked.

"She's okay," said Nate.

Riley thought his confident tone was meant to minimize her embarrassment and move them past the moment, but Teren took exception to it.

"I think Riley can speak for herself," he said acidly.

"No doubt. I'm just—"

"She might have twisted an ankle or, worse yet, a wrist. You don't—"

Riley shook them both off of her. "I'm fine."

Skillet stepped in and linked arms with Riley on one side and Marie on the other.

"Ladies," he said, "let's continue our search and let these two fight it out amongst themselves."

A sullen tension hung in the air as they moved off.

"Crazy thing, that attack on Jess last night, right?" Skillet said, steering them to another subject.

"It was frightening," Riley agreed. "Jess is pretty shook up."

"I'm glad she got cut," Marie said. Lifting her chin, she sent Riley a challenging look. "She deserves a good scare and a small portion of the pain she deals out."

"That's harsh, Marie."

"Easy for you to say. You don't have a husband at stake. You've seen her operate. She's poison."

Riley clamped her lips together.

"That's enough, Marie," Skillet said.

"I hate her. I wish the guy had killed her."

Riley listened to the venomous intensity in her voice, alarmed. "Please stop, Marie," she pleaded.

"Oh, I'm just getting started. Do you have any idea what it's like to work hard to make a family and then have it all go up in smoke? Do you?"

Riley gasped, cut to the core and shocked at the woman's complete lack of consideration. Skillet raised a hand as if to smack her.

"Shut the hell up," he said. "If anyone knows what it's like..."

His voice trailed off and Marie fell silent, her fists clenched at her sides, eyes hot and narrowed, an indication of the fury and indignation still cooking inside her. Turning on her heel, she stalked off into the trees.

"She takes the prize for crass and moronic," Skillet said. He peered at her. "You all right, sweetheart?"

It had grown very still. They were in a cul-de-sac of unoccupied houses, surrounded by woodland. Nate's group had finished and moved on to the next block.

"We shouldn't have let her go off by herself," Riley said. "There's still a killer out there."

"No killer in his right mind would attack that woman now. She'd make him eat his knife."

"I think it's pretty clear the killer hasn't been in his right mind for quite some time."

"Good point."

A cool breeze rushed through the pines, making them whisper and sending a chill down Riley's spine. She looked at Skillet. He wore his bedroom eyes, and a smile came and went on his lips, like the flicker of a candle.

She realized how alone they were.

63

Myrna felt like she'd been eating sand.

Her mouth was dry, her skin coated with a layer of gritty dust from sprawling on the dirty floor. For ages, she'd been too scared to move, had simply curled beneath the afghan, shivering, swimming in and out of consciousness.

But now she had to acknowledge that dehydration would do the killer's work for him if she didn't get some fluids in her soon.

She'd lost blood from the head wound, but it had clotted into a filthy mat on the side of her head. Raising herself to a kneeling position, she groped in the dark for a handhold. Her head reeled and a wave of nausea squeezed her stomach. She leaned over and vomited.

When the spasm passed, she steadied herself and drew a deep breath, listening for sounds of movement outside her hiding place, the creak of a floorboard or tap of a shoe that might indicate a presence.

It was silent. Grunting with effort, she pulled herself up and clung to the wall until the dizziness passed.

She winced at the squeal the door made as she pushed it open. Stepping into the children's playroom, her feet found the clutter of stuffed animals tossed there by the killer. They plagued her, tangling with her shoes as she plodded across to the kitchen, and she fought to keep panic from taking hold.

She sagged in the doorway, a tremulous mass of nerves, and knew she needed help. She had to get to Dr. Deb but right now, just getting to the kitchen sink seemed a task beyond doing.

Grasping a wooden chair for support, she pushed it ahead of her then hobbled to catch up, inching her way across the room. That worked fine except it was achingly slow and the chair sent out a screech with each shove, as if voicing the screams she kept locked inside.

After an eternity of push and shuffle, the sink was in reach and she worked the faucet, scooping handfuls of water into her mouth and over her blood-encrusted face and hair.

Thirst sated, she looked with longing at the chair. Its seat pulled her like a magnet, but she understood that if she sat now, that's where they'd find her, frozen and defeated. Dead.

Were they looking for her? They must know she held a vital piece of information. They might even have been in the house searching for her while she was unconscious. She imagined the detective would have divided the neighbors into search teams, and she calculated her odds at about ten to one that if she ventured forth, the good guys would find her before the killer did.

Fair enough.

The chair was too unwieldy for the journey she had to make. Casting her eyes around the kitchen, she drew the broom from its nook beside the refrigerator. It would have to do for a cane. Turning it bristle side up, she used it to make her way to the front door, slipping once or twice on the smooth tiles.

At the door, she paused to catch her breath and plan her next move. The door had a small window, a square of cloudy yellow glass held closed with a simple peg latch.

When the girls were small, they pretended the house was a castle and they'd climb on a stool and peep through the tiny window in the large, wooden door. She remembered how they'd deepen their voices, imitating authoritative command and shout, 'Hark, who goes there?' and then ruin the effect by giggling.

A pang of sorrow shot through her. Harp was gone and oh, how she missed him. The girls would be devastated when she told them, and she strengthened at the thought. She must be the one to tell them. To hear it from a stranger would be worse, would mean both parents dead.

She must survive this ordeal. She must come through for her girls.

Easing open the little window, she peered out at the vista it afforded. By the light, Myrna judged it to be near noon and as her eyes adjusted to the glare, she caught the movement of figures in the distance. She squinted, refocusing, and realized she was looking straight out.

At the killer.

She backed away from the window, pushing it shut with a shaking hand. Bracing herself in the corner behind the door, she stood and waited, violent tremors racking her body.

One minute passed, then two. She drew in several long, deep breaths, calming herself, her eyes glued to the little window in the door, telling herself it would not move.

But as she watched, a hand pushed it inward.

A voice spoke her name.

64

Riley climbed the front steps of Myrna's porch and saw that the little window in the door was open a crack.

They'd searched the house last night, and again first thing this morning. It seemed the most logical place for Myrna to take refuge. They'd found one of the windowpanes in the back door broken and knew someone had shattered it to gain entry to the house.

Maybe Myrna, caught without her house key.

Or maybe the killer.

Either way, their systematic searching yielded zip.

But the little window had been latched when they left the house. Riley was sure of it. Pushing at the square of yellow glass, she called Myrna's name.

From behind the door, she heard a gasp and a sob, followed by the sound of wood on wood, and the doorknob turned. Riley pushed the door open and saw Myrna, bent at the waist and clinging to an upended broomstick with both hands, an ugly, crusted wound on her head.

Her violent trembling was enough to set the straws of the broom vibrating as she sank slowly to the floor. Riley shouted for help, rushing forward to ease her down.

"That man," said Myrna, her voice a harsh rasp. She pointed out the door. "That man killed my Harp."

Riley twisted around to see Nate bounding up the porch steps, followed by Teren and Cappy.

"Which man?" she asked Myrna, but the woman only stared, wrapped in fear, unable to speak.

Skillet came through the back door, approaching from the hallway. "You found her," he said.

Myrna's face jolted at the sound of his voice, and she gave a whimper, eyes rolling as her head thrashed from side to side. She jerked in a final spasm of terror and went limp in Riley's arms.

"We've got to get her to the doctor," Nate said.

"It might be better to bring Deb here," Teren countered. "I can stay with her while you run for the doc."

Nate shook his head. "Riley, find a sturdy blanket. Quickly."

She tore up the staircase with a sense of deja vu. Would she be forever raiding linen closets at Nate's command? The first door she reached was a bedroom. She ripped the comforter off the bed and returned to Myrna's side.

"That'll do," Nate said, fashioning a makeshift stretcher. He and Cappy carried Myrna back to the clubhouse and Riley followed with Teren. Skillet, the fastest of them, ran ahead to prepare the way.

When they arrived, Dr. Deb met them at the door and motioned them through to the dining room where she'd requisitioned a table. Mrs. Dawson stood in as her assistant as she examined Myrna and washed and dressed the head wound. Nate pulled Riley aside.

"I'm going to set up a cot in the club treasurer's office," he told her. "We'll put Myrna in there, behind a locked door, and set a watch over her, two guards at a time so that she is never left alone with any one person. Will you and Frank take the first watch?"

Riley nodded and started off to look for Frank, but Nate caught her arm and pulled her close. He held her for a moment and Riley felt the warmth of him, sensing there was a lot he wanted to say. But when he spoke, he said only one thing.

"When she regains consciousness, we need a name."

65

THE KILLER WATCHED THEM transport the Mayhew woman into the Treasurer's office.

He saw Riley follow, carrying a blanket and pillow, her lovely face pinched with worry. She and Frank Newcombe would stand guard, and after their turn, another team would take over. There was no way he could get to Myrna now and once she woke up, she'd point him out.

He had to see to it that she never woke up.

His Adidas cross-trainers were wet and muddy after trudging through the swampy neighborhood. He left the dining room and walked to the door of the lobby, squelching with each step. His feet were cold, and he felt a blister forming under his left big toe. It was time to change shoes.

Letting himself out the door, he walked down the street and around the corner to his house. He paused on the front porch to pull off the wet shoes and socks, leaving them to dry beside the welcome mat. After entering the house, he went to the garage for a flashlight and climbed the stairs to the master bedroom where he shined the beam around the walk-in closet.

A false wall in the closet hid the space where he kept his duffel and accoutrements. He ignored it. He wouldn't be needing those things for Myrna. The situation called for different methods.

More like what he'd done with Amanda Horton.

His shoe shelf was neatly ordered with footwear housed in the original boxes. A shoe-shine kit rested next to a case of accessories—pads, inserts, replacement parts. A narrow, three-tiered chest of drawers held an assortment of socks. The illumination from the flashlight was just adequate for him to see his way, and he wedged it between two stacks of sweaters on an upper shelf and pulled a pair of loafers from their box, slipping them on.

The left shoe was missing a tassel.

He froze, focusing, reflecting hard on his recent activities. Where had he lost the tassel?

At the Ferguson's? He recalled how Rico had made a feeble grab for his foot. At the time, he'd double-checked to ensure that his shoes were well covered, protected by the elasticized booties.

He judged that the tassel could have fallen off at any number of locations, and if it had been dislodged at the Ferguson residence, it would have been contained by the protective cover and disposed of with the rest of it.

The killer mulled through it again and gave a nod, dismissing his anxieties over the tassel. He had more immediate concerns.

Switching his clothing needs to automatic pilot, he focused his brain instead on his plans for Myrna.

66

Rick scanned the shelves of the supply shed, picking out the items Bobbi wanted.

He was high on a ladder, pulling down blankets, when the lights flickered and went out. Electricity to the property had been intermittent all day, but sunlight filtered in through dust-streaked windows, sufficient for him to finish his task. Climbing down the ladder, he shouldered the pack and returned to the house, threading his way through the wandering sheep, avoiding the llamas.

As he entered Bobbi's study, she pulled off her headset, turning to him with a dejected shrug.

"I managed to get through, but the FAA denied every flight plan I submitted. The second the mountain erupted, they put up a TFR—that's a Temporary Flight Restriction—covering a hundred nautical miles. The air is choked with rescue operations, and they want all civilians grounded. Conditions are hazardous and communication is a hellish mess."

She let out a long yawn, stretching her arms to the ceiling. "I even called an old buddy in the Flight Service Station in Seattle to get us cleared in as an emergency supply ship, with no joy. I pulled every string I had, but no one wants to sign off on this."

Bobbi slouched in the chair, closed her eyes, and rubbed her palms in a circular motion against her temples. Rick felt a pang. The lady didn't need him complicating her life, but she'd put out the welcome mat and now that he had his foot in the door, he might as well cross the threshold.

They'd stayed up late into the night, considering contingencies and writing up plans. An hour or two before dawn, he'd crashed, grabbing a few winks on her living room couch. Now, he studied her face, drawn and tired, but he sensed untapped reserves in her and felt just ruthless enough to dig for them.

"Outline our options," he challenged her.

She opened one eye and gave him a look, letting it drop shut again. "You're an officer of the law," she reminded. "We're out of legal alternatives."

"Humor me. Field me a less-than-legal suggestion."

Bobbi bit her lip and looked away. A minute ticked by.

"I know you're cooking up something," Rick prompted. "What is it?"

"Well...we could do a scud run."

"I'm not sure what that means."

"It means we'd have to go NOE, flying Nap Of the Earth, the entire time. Staying under the main volcano plume cloud in Golf air space, flying at treetop level, making sure to stay out of SeaTac's radar. And heaven help us if we punch in."

"Punch in?"

"The helicopter's not equipped with IFR, so if I inadvertently go to instrument meteorological conditions, we'll have to radio in to SeaTac so they can vector us back to VMC."

"I didn't follow all of that. Just bottom-line it for me."

"Best case—provided we can make radio contact—I lose my license. Worst case," she paused, "we die."

"Okay," Rick said. "Other than death and going outside the law, any other drawbacks I should know about?"

"Flying Golf is actually legal, under certain conditions."

Bobbi paused, then blew out a breath that ruffled her blonde bangs. "But none of those conditions apply in our situation," she admitted. "It's damn deadly and difficult. Are you ready to risk your life to get that information to your partner? Wait a day or two and you can probably reach him by phone."

Rick winced. "There's more to this than I can divulge, but I promise you innocent lives are at stake. I can't just sit tight, but I see no reason for you to put yourself in danger. I'll find another way."

"You don't think *I* care about innocent lives? Besides, I've got a helicopter to demolish, and I can't think of a better way to do it."

Rick sent her a grateful smile. "Have you done this scudding before?" he asked.

"Scud running, sure. In Afghanistan, it's the only way to fly. We do this, and I promise it's the coolest flight you'll ever take. By the time we touch down, you'll have the seat cushion sucked so far up your butt you'll need a crowbar to pull it out."

Rick raised his eyebrow to show he was impressed.

"Of course, here," she continued, "the hazards are a bit different."

"What kind of hazards are we talking about?"

"We need visibility and that, as you've observed, is less than optimal. We'll be flying low where there are lots of obstacles. The biggest problem will be trying not to floss our teeth with a big old set of Alphas."

"And in plain English that means...?"

"Staying out of the power lines. We'll have to rely on daylight, as the wires are near impossible to spot in the dark. We'll be flying by TV and radio towers taller than a thousand feet with guy wires that stick out about 800 feet on each side, creating an invisible net in the sky."

"At least no one will be gunning for us," Rick reminded her.

"A point in our favor. But these towers of which I speak, are butt ugly. So a lot of effort goes into making them blend into the environment. Easier on the eyes, but cold comfort if you smack into one at eighty knots."

"You're just full of comforting thoughts."

"Hey, you asked the question. With Rainier knocking out the juice, the tower lighting systems are likely to be down, making them more difficult to spot. And to cap it off, cell phone towers are deliberately constructed to be just under the height for reporting and marking on aeronautical maps, so the sectionals will be of limited use in that regard."

"Sectionals are maps?" Rick asked.

"Correct."

He sighed. "Anything else you want to bring to my attention?"

"One last hazard does come to mind," Bobbi confessed. "The air is full of ash which will choke our engine, causing it to stall."

She twirled her finger in a fast descent, a charades version of crash and burn. "We'll most likely fall to our deaths."

Rick paced, thinking about the case, imagining what might be happening in Mountain Vista and considering the consequences if he sat on the sidelines while Nate wrapped up the case without him. He had to get there, but this was insane.

He turned to Bobbi and cracked a grin. "So," he said, "what's stopping us?"

"Not me. We're burning daylight."

She jumped up, grabbing hold of the pack and an armful of supplies. Rick gripped her arms, the smile erased from his face.

"I give you full points for pluck," he said, shaking her gently, "but this is no joke. We do this, it may be the last thing we do. Are you willing to accept that?"

Bobbi raised her chin, a flash of heat in her eyes. "It won't be the first time I've had to answer that question and I'm betting it won't be the last. Let's get off the ground."

67

THE KILLER STOOD OVER Myrna's cot.

He watched her chest rise and fall, waiting for his chance with the pillow, wishing Sandy Dawson would drink his coffee and fall asleep. He'd prepared the coffee with care, dissolving a number of crushed Lunesta tablets into it before pouring it into a thermos.

"I brought the coffee supply," he said to Sandy as Nate ushered in the two of them to replace Riley and Frank Newcombe.

Sandy acknowledged this with a nod. "Very kind of you."

The killer looked down into Myrna's sleeping face, counting the beats of her heart by the faint throb at the hollow of her throat. She wouldn't even struggle when he held the pillow over her face, not like Amanda had struggled.

He thought about that last evening with Amanda. She'd been so bright and wonderful, speaking with such eloquence about the beauty and majesty of the earth and condemning with derision those who denigrated her.

They spoke together of their common convictions, and he'd been so convinced she shared his dedication.

They sat on colored cushions on Amanda's living room floor, sharing a bottle of wine. And then another. After that, they progressed to single malt Scotch and he found himself telling her about Toby, how they'd worked and learned together in the forest behind the funeral home.

He told her about the earth tremors and how he and Toby had done what was necessary.

"He was the only boyhood friend I ever had," he admitted. "It was hard losing him like that, but what hurt most was the doubt I saw in his eyes at the very last. Toby lost the faith."

Real pain had speared through him as he relived that moment. "That was the hardest thing."

"Good Gaia," she said, staring into his eyes. "That's the saddest thing I've ever heard. You poor kid."

He remembered her nose turning red at the tip, and she'd cried, tears tracing her wine-flushed cheeks. A part of him found that thrilling. He told her more about the things he'd done, but he saw the wariness creep into her eyes, stamping out the spark of sympathy until there was only a cold reflection of the doubt he'd seen in Toby.

He'd been wrong about her. She didn't share his convictions. Her dedication was lip service only.

He remembered the stab of regret that tore into him, the brief flame of anger at the earth's hungry demand, taking everyone he'd ever cared about.

In reality, it had been the alcohol that killed her.

It had loosened his tongue, and it affected Amanda by slowing her reflexes so that he was able to press his arms against her neck, choking her out. She fell limp against him, and he dragged her up the stairs, listening to the rhythmic thump of her heels against the risers.

Filling her marble-trimmed tub, he'd poured in a capful of bubble bath and undressed her. The water roused her as he eased her down into the tub, and she fought him to the end.

He remembered weeping as he held her under, dodging her thrashing arms, watching suds splash over the edge of the tub. He'd cried tears for Amanda, as she had given tears for him. He thought he'd learned something from that.

He'd never tell Riley a thing.

He looked at Sandy Dawson. The man sat wedged into a corner of the gray leather couch, reading from a tablet. He needed only to lean his head back and go to sleep. And then, quietly, gently, the killer would apply the pillow to Myrna. Done right, there'd be no way to prove she hadn't simply succumbed to her injuries.

After that, he'd pour himself a cup of coffee and join Sandy on the couch. When Nate brought the next team of watchers, he'd find two sleeping men and a dead woman.

Not many people had a key to this office. No one would be able to say with certainty what had happened.

"Would you like me to pour you some coffee?" the killer asked. "You're looking a little sleepy."

"No thanks. I'm fine, but you go ahead."

The thermos rested, untouched, on the desk, almost buzzing with unfulfilled purpose. The killer rose from the desk chair and walked to the window. He stood looking out, not seeing a thing. His mind was turned inward, communing with the earth as nearly as he could while clothed and behind walls.

She was in agony. He felt it, and it grieved him.

Time passed and he glanced at his watch. Riley's team had put in four hours, but there was no guarantee he'd be granted an equivalent period. This had to happen now.

He screwed the cap off the thermos and poured out a cup of coffee, feeling its warmth against his hand.

"Here you go," he said, handing the cup to Sandy.

Sandy waved away the offering. "I thought everyone in the neighborhood knew this about me, but perhaps you don't," he said. "I'm a Mormon. I don't drink coffee. It's kind of you to offer, but it's all yours, buddy."

Clamping down on the anger rising in his chest, the killer retreated to the desk chair to reconnoiter. He hadn't thought much about plan B and time was running short. Perhaps he could throttle the man, stage a choking incident.

Ridiculous.

He had a pocketknife. Could he use it on Mr. Dawson and then Myrna, jimmy the window, give himself a slash or two, then cry for help? He couldn't imagine Nate buying this scenario.

Why couldn't the blasted woman just die?

He heard a key in the lock. The door opened and Nate walked in, followed by Dr. Deb and the guy who was always squaring off against Sandy Dawson.

"Hey, Hal." Sandy greeted him with an anticipatory grin.

"No time for a debate just now, Sandy," Nate said. "I'm calling a meeting in the dining room, and I need everybody there. These two have already been briefed and they'll take the watch from here."

The killer watched Hal Jeffries take his place behind the desk. Dr. Deb approached her patient, and the killer caught a last glimpse of Myrna's chest, rising and falling, before the door shut and locked.

Signaling the end of opportunity.

68

"We're losing the daylight."

Bobbi's voice piped through the headset he wore and Rick nodded. She sounded on edge, and he couldn't blame her.

Every hoop they'd had to jump through before they could get the Bell 206 JetRanger off the ground had taken longer than planned and the sun was low on the horizon when they'd finally lifted off.

Rick strained his eyes, looking out through the windscreen and the chin bubble. It was his job to spot trouble, and he was sure his hair had turned white from sheer tension. Ash-laden mist swirled in the air, further darkening the sky and limiting visibility.

The thin-stretched wires were impossible to pick out in the gloomy atmosphere. Bobbi taught him to watch for the poles, instead, and keep her just above the tops of them, though she often had to dip below for better visibility.

Rick understood Bobbi was running on fury aimed at her husband. She was mad as a nest full of hornets and that was driving this mission for her. He was happy to take it however it might come, but fury was a fickle and unsustainable force.

At some point, he might have to provide support of another kind.

He peered to his right. The ashen shimmer shifted, seeming to evaporate and a utility pole materialized like a ghost.

"Pull up, pull up!" he shouted.

Bobbi adjusted the controls, and they skimmed up over the array of high tension wires and leveled out. Rick released his breath in a long sigh and gave her a shaky thumbs up.

"You're doing good, soldier," she told him. "Just keep your eyes peeled."

"I hate that expression."

"My apologies. Glue your face to the windscreen and goggle like your life depends on it."

The helicopter edged along through the dirty air, sucking it in and spitting it out. Below them, Rick could make out green, mounded treetops.

Lots of them.

They were over forest land now, so there were fewer wires to watch out for. Plenty of other hazards, though. He kept his head on a slow swivel, scrutinizing the smudgy sky on the other side of the glass.

Ten minutes of smooth flying and the vibration and hum of the machine, teamed with inadequate sleep, tugged at Rick's eyelids.

Remain vigilant. Remain vigilant. It was his mantra.

And then, his lullaby.

His chin touched his chest and he jerked awake, shaking himself, scanning the sky.

He saw Bobbi flick the plastic covering on the fuel gauge and was astonished to see that the needle rested on dead empty.

"Cripes!" he shouted, his heart leaping. "Are we out of gas?"

Bobbi waggled her head, and he watched the indicator swing up to full and drop to the halfway mark.

"What's that about?"

"The guy who manned the pump told me one of their seals failed and there might be water in the fuel. Looks like he was right. We'll have to drain it when we land."

Rick returned his gaze to the dismal sky and the monotonous drone of the engine settled into his bones. They were in a dream world. Drifting clouds of mist and ash danced before him. Surreal. Sleep inducing.

He fought it, but at length his head dipped again, and he drifted.

The sputtering of the engine snapped him into awareness. Opening his eyes, he swung them at Bobbi, heart slamming in his chest. She tapped the instrument panel, pointing out a lit indicator.

"Our EBF, that's Engine Barrier Filter, is impending a clog. Engine's cutting out. Add that to the bad fuel and we're done for today."

He detected no trace of panic in her voice, but that did nothing to slow the racing of his own heart. He stared out of their little, defenseless bubble, eyes wide.

"Nothing like a hard-core adrenaline rush to wake you up. Am I right?" she chided.

A wave of heat washed over Rick's face, lighting a spark of anger. At himself, at the situation, at the volcano still spewing ash.

"Better find us a clearing where we can land," she instructed.

Responding to the clear command in her voice, he marshaled his resolve, peering out through the windscreen. Below, he saw only treetops. An endless carpet of them.

"I got nothing over here," he reported.

"And a whole lot of the same on this side," Bobbi said. "Hang on."

She worked the controls and the helicopter rose with a shudder.

"What are you doing?" Rick asked, alarmed.

"Trimming the rotors up to get all the power I can before we lose the engine. Buy us a little time and maybe something will open up down there."

They continued to climb, and the ash layer grew thicker. Rick's stomach churned.

"The higher they are, the harder they fall," he said.

"*Au contraire*. The higher we get, the more room I have to maneuver. As long as the rotor turns, I can fly this baby, engine or no."

Every vestige of sleep had fled. Rick focused his attention down and ahead, determined to find a break in the trees.

Pockets of ash appeared and dispersed, alternately raising and dashing his hopes. His stress meter peaked when the engine coughed and breathed its last.

They fell through the sky.

"Brace up, soldier," Bobbi ordered. "We're not dead yet."

Without the engine, the noise level dropped dramatically, and Rick heard confidence in her voice. He watched her thrust the collective to the full down position. The muffled stutter of the rotors whirred through the silence and their rate of descent slowed.

"Feel that?" she asked. "The air through the rotor system has changed direction."

She spoke as if giving instruction, demonstrating for a class. He studied her face. It was creased in concentration.

"Eyes front," she reprimanded. He returned his attention to the treetops but stole one glance back at her. She was smiling.

And then he spotted it.

“I got something,” he said, pointing.

“Roger that.” She seemed to attack the sky with relish, tweaking pedals and levers, directing the helicopter to the tiny clearing.

“We’re going to do an autorotation landing with zero ground run,” she told him. “Powered by the engine, the rotor pulls the air down and out. Without power, we have to use the air under us to turn the rotor. Like a pinwheel.”

They seemed to float above the trees, drifting into place, and then suddenly everything shifted into high speed and the ground zoomed up to meet them. Bobbi flared the aircraft, lifting its nose, and they dropped into the opening in the tall trees and landed with a bump.

“Oh damn,” she said. “I think we squat the skids.”

Rick gulped air and realized he’d been holding his breath. He wiped his sweaty palms over his jeans and sent a prayer heavenward.

Bobbi inspected him.

“If you get out and kiss the ground, I swear I’ll sock you in the face,” she said.

69

"It's more important than ever that we band together."

Nate let his eyes rove across the faces in the room. "We are dealing," he added, "with a well-organized and clever killer."

They'd finished with dinner and several of the residents had pitched in to clean up until Nate pulled the kitchen crew back to the dining room, telling them to wrap it up later. As a result, Skillet was eyeing him with distinct disfavor.

Teren had reverted to the stony glare he so often reserved for Nate, and Sandy sat at a table across from his wife, their hands clasped, drawing strength from one another. Wynn sat beside them, feeding her doll with a plastic spoon.

"I believe the killer acts to serve a cause," Nate continued. "He is committed to an ideal and will go to any length to sustain and protect that ideal."

He hesitated. "I'm not entirely certain what that ideal is, but I believe it runs somewhere along the lines of Earth worship."

He caught Riley's eye, noticing the tension in her shoulders, the dark shadows in the hollows of her face.

"Harper Mayhew dared to challenge those ideals," he went on, "and that may be why the killer singled him out. I believe Myrna witnessed his death and knows the identity of his killer. When she regains consciousness, we'll know it too."

He looked out over the group. "That puts every one of us in a dangerous position."

Nate saw several heads dip in acknowledgment. He began a slow walk between the tables, hoping to impress the import of his message on each person present.

"Besides being clever and possibly very lucky, our killer's got guts. He's brazen enough to operate right under our noses, so I will emphasize, again, how vital it is that you stick together in groups so that he cannot isolate anyone. Groups of at least three."

Nate completed his walk among the tables and as he turned to retrace his steps, his eye fell upon Brenda. She had her Bible open on her lap, her finger running slowly down the columns of scripture as she read.

"The frequency of these murders," he finished, "seems to correspond with the violence of the volcano, so folks, we are on red alert."

Skillet spoke up from his corner near the kitchen.

"Ho, there, boss. Are you going to address the elephant in the room?"

Nate stopped, scanning the group, taking in each face, the expressions and body language, hoping for an indicator, a clue that would mark one of them out. He saw nothing outside of what he'd already established as each person's baseline behavior.

"I believe Skillet is referring to the fact that the killer is right here, a member of your community."

"No, he isn't," Frank said, standing as the heat poured out of him. "A killer can never be a part of any community. He cuts himself off from humanity. He may walk among us, but he is not one of us."

He looked around the room, eyes smoldering, jaw clenched into rock-hard angles under his cheek.

Annette Dawson spoke up and there was grief in her voice. "Excepting you, Detective, I've known everyone in this room for a good long while. I can't believe any one of my neighbors is a murderer."

Nate acknowledged her with a grave nod. "I understand your sentiment, but I do believe it. What's more, we'll soon know who it is, and that man will go to prison."

"That man is already in prison," Frank spoke again. "When a man commits murder, he isolates himself from the rest of us. He creates a distance, becomes a different creature in a prison of his own making. He is not one of us."

"That may be," Nate agreed. "But that self-made prison doesn't stop him from killing again and again. What he needs is concrete and bars and I intend to see that he gets it."

There followed a period of subdued murmuring and Wynn Dawson started to cry with a hoarse, forlorn sobbing that squeezed at Nate's heart. A new layer of gloom was settling over the company, sinking them into dejection, and he cast about for some way to raise the morale.

Making his way toward Riley, he noted the exhausted droop of her head. Even her hair looked tired, its vibrant color muted, the bounce gone out of it.

He didn't know if he was about to boost her up or thrust her down to that level of hell that she put herself through in connection with her art. Sitting beside her, he smoothed back a curtain of hair so that he could see her face.

"Will you play for us?" he asked, seeing the quick stab of dread that darted across her eyes.

"Please, Riley. We need you."

70

Other than the hiccuping sobs from Wynn Dawson, the room was silent.

Riley sensed the many faces looking her way but saw only Nate's. His eyes echoed the appeal he'd voiced. Could he know the impossible burden he'd just placed on her?

The despair in the room was palpable, drawing her down with the rest of them. She was broken, her wings gummed with the gluey weight of the undefined guilt she struggled against, rendering her powerless to lift the heavy pall.

Nate took her hands in his and began gently kneading them, willing them to life. She felt strength emanating from him like a low hum from a live wire, and the face of her intrepid student, Rebecca, swam into view in her mind.

The student's determination to press forward under the attack of daunting forces had impressed and fortified her, going a long way toward restoring her equilibrium. The power of music was real and potent.

And it was in her hands.

Music was her story, the way she portrayed the big pictures of life to the world. It was how she communicated who she was and what she was about, how she shared her visions and hope for the future. Music was her sentinel and her herald. Her gift.

She could do this.

Though she'd risen to her feet, she couldn't feel the ground beneath her, and she arrived at the piano bench with no thought of the mechanics that took her there. Music and the moment worked within her, and her fingers were on the keys, spilling out the chaotic tones of Mendelssohn's Agitation, feeling the release of expression.

As she moved into the aching melancholy of Blumenfeld's Berceuse, the flowing notes of the midsection brought tears to her eyes, bathing and soothing them. Beneath her fingers, the music built to an almost unbearable loveliness that seemed to mirror the power of love, even amid ruin and decay.

Riley felt determination solidifying within her. Rachmaninoff came next, the militant maneuvers of the Prelude in Opus 23, No. 5, building, firming, and triumphant, with the heart-tugging arpeggios halfway through that never failed to bring goosebumps to her arms and a wrench to her heart.

It lived in her, the music. The travails of their plight had not killed it. It sang forth, flowing out of her with fervor and meaning.

She transitioned into the playful doctor gradus ad parnassum and it streamed from her fingers like trills of laughter, lifting her so that she felt the smile on her lips. Gliding up and down the keyboard like a child in the sunshine, her mind fetched a picture of Jim, his cherished face, eyes crinkled against the slanting light.

She skittered to a stop.

Shaken and blank, she sat trembling as a sheet of desolation descended, enveloping her, locking down the music. She felt the shock in the room, the awkward silence.

And the pity.

Springing from the bench, she stumbled for the door. From the corner of her eye, she saw Nate leap forward to intercept her, but Teren grabbed his arm, holding him back with a grim look and the shake of his head.

And then, she was out the door and into the night.

71

Rick watched the flickering light of the campfire play against Bobbi's features.

Now that the tension of the day had eased, he saw the close-held misery that owned her face. Rooting through his pack, he found the fragment of china he'd kept for her. She slumped on a downed tree trunk, staring into the shifting flames, and he settled down beside her, placing the package in her hands.

"What's this?"

Bobbi folded back the wadded tissues he'd used to encase the broken piece of plate. She stared down at the shard of hand-painted pottery, running her finger over the glossy surface. Several minutes passed before she spoke, her voice sounding creaky and close to tears.

"We bought this at the medina in Asilah, a village in Morocco."

Again, she traced over the pattern of the plate and uttered a harsh laugh. "I was so happy playing the newlywed. Foolish and deceived, as it turns out, but during that time in Morocco, I was so blissfully in love."

"What happened?" Rick asked, his voice soft against the crackling of the campfire.

After their hasty landing, they'd climbed out of the helicopter into a gathering dark beneath the tall pines. There was nothing else to do but gather firewood, eat a simple meal, and sit as they were now, warming their hands around tin mugs of coffee.

At the end of a long pause, Bobbi said, "I opened Pandora's Box."

Rick leaned forward and poked at the fire, stirring up a mass of sparks. He said nothing.

"I met Robert in Iraq," Bobbi explained. "Where he was born. His parents still live there, but he embraced western culture, Americanized his name and started an import business. He became very successful."

She tipped her face away from him, but not before he caught the spasm of pain crossing its darkened planes.

"He's a charming and persuasive man," she continued. "Not handsome. Never handsome, but startling to look upon. Compelling and maddeningly attractive. I fell, like head meets guillotine."

Rick saw that her hand still gripped the rough fragment of Moroccan pottery. A smear of blood stood out against the paint and her face looked cruel in the firelight.

"He's a strange man. A mixture of ancient and modern. He had a mystique which drew me and which I refused to examine too closely. I was willingly blind, in a way, so I bought and paid for my troubles."

She stopped and bit her lip, looking away.

"Buyer's remorse?" Rick asked.

She expelled a pent-up breath. "In spades."

She tipped her head to the sky and Rick saw the rapid pulse beating in her throat.

"I flew helicopters for the Army. I loved the rush, the unpredictability of it. But Robert..."

She stopped speaking and turned her face away from the firelight. She was silent for a long moment and Rick expected to hear a sob in her voice when she resumed. He was startled, instead, by the dusty dry syllables which followed.

"I twisted myself inside out for Robert. We married and I put in for a transfer stateside, looking to settle, do the domestic tour, you know? I ended up at Joint Base Lewis McChord for a while and then I left the Army and started up that sheep ranch."

She paused, changing position on their log bench. "Robert is always traveling. He's got an import business. It made sense and I didn't question it." Her voice was bitter. "I should have."

A beat passed, filled only by the sputtering of the fire.

"But no, I was happy enough and busy enough that I didn't give it much thought. I have a couple of ranch hands keeping me company and enough baby lambs to keep my bottle-feeding whims at bay. We own horses and I love to ride. I've got a beautiful house, plenty of land, enough money and then some. Life is good, right?"

She ran agitated hands through her hair.

"So, why did I open the box?"

Rick was surprised. "You're talking about a literal box, aren't you?" he asked.

"I am."

She bolted up from the log and paced beside the fire.

"We have an enormous walk-in closet. Right at the back of it there's a shelf, empty except for the box. It's a lock box, about the size of a toaster oven, and covered in red silk, traced with gold. Beautiful. Robert called it Pandora's Box and warned me never to open it. A joke,

I thought, right? Surely a joke. But I respected his privacy, and I left the box alone."

"Until...?"

She sank back onto the makeshift bench and buried her face in her hands.

"It's so stupid. So unbelievably absurd. I watched something on TV, one of those unsolved mystery type programs. An American woman snooped in some of her husband's papers and found out she was married to a mobster. That started me wondering what was in the box."

Lifting her face, she wrinkled her nose and stared imploringly at Rick.

"What if Robert was a sleeper agent for some terrorist organization? What if his import business was a cover for moving drugs or weapons? I couldn't banish those thoughts from my mind."

"Did you find proof of anything like that?"

"Oh, I found proof of his illegal activities," she said bitterly, "but it's nothing so earth moving as all that."

Straightening her spine, she captured his gaze. "Robert is a bigamist," she announced. "He has a wife in New Jersey and, I suspect, one or more in Iraq. I'm not even his first wife, so in the eyes of the law, we were never married. I was nothing but his harem girl."

Her eyes had turned stony, but they held a sheen, reflected in the firelight.

"The thing that really burns me is how easy I made it for him." She let out an infuriated growl. "I was so cheaply had."

Rick shifted in his seat, the rough bark of the tree biting into his flank. He didn't know how to field this one. He'd been prepared to commiserate with her over clandestine crime of some sort.

But not this sort.

The sting of her lover's betrayal shimmered in her eyes and his impulse was to do something. Fix it, or at least reciprocate and allay the hurt by revealing his own messy quandary.

The temptation was strong. She'd opened herself, given him a piece of her private pain. But the road he'd started down was a solitary one, paved with loneliness and the emptiness of closed doors.

A chill wind rustled through the pines. Rick stood.

"It sounds like the ruin of one small helicopter won't put paid to his account," he said, pouring the remains of his coffee onto the fire. He hesitated, regretful.

"Goodnight, Bobbi."

Crossing to the other side of the dying flames, he climbed into his sleeping bag and pulled it up to his chin. Eyes shut tight, he tried to ignore the silence radiating across the gap between them like a siren.

72

On the grass beside the lake, Riley sat hunched and miserable, her knees hugged to her chest.

The ball of ice in her stomach sent chills shivering through her, amplified by the cool breeze of the night. She clenched her fists, fighting the darkness looming, hovering to take her down.

For so long, she'd been running from these phantom thoughts and images, the unfocused dots of Jim's portrait. She'd kept herself busy, filling her days and nights with music and rehearsals and preparations.

Now, in the ash of her ruined world, it was time to stop and let it come into clarity.

His face materialized before her, sharpening in intensity until every detail was visible; his irises, a precise gray-blue flecked with green; the slight folds on either side of his mouth, laugh lines; the shadowed stubble that bloomed on his strong jaw at the end of the day; his dark hair, slightly curling over his high brow, both artless and beautiful.

For two years, she had been too frightened to host this clear image, banishing the full essence of her dead husband, allowing him only into the periphery of her mind. He and Tanner were ghostly shadows she'd been unable to face head-on.

Now she looked him in the eye.

What did she need to say to him? She longed to ask his forgiveness, but for what, precisely?

She'd puzzled it out, discarding the survivor's guilt. She accepted that the fire had not been her fault. That wasn't what haunted her.

A glimpse of the real, hidden reason flashed, like a fish jumping in a pond, sending out ripples. The ripples radiated through the coils of her brain, creating patterns until the picture solidified and she steeled herself, resisted pushing it away, and looked into the harsh face of regret.

She'd used Jim.

She had loved the idea of him, her fortress, her Forte, the man who held down the fort so she could play. She'd used him as so many men have used women, as a token figure.

She had a husband and a son, an ideal little family. He was handsome, a heroic figure as a firefighter. He made a great foil and looked good in her media kit, the three of them posing for photo ops and publicity engagements.

Soaked in bitterness, she rocked on the dewy grass, trying on this brand of guilt, feeling its snug, pinching fit and knowing it was too late. Nothing she did now could change it.

The ball of ice inside her grew heavier and colder. This burden, this blockage within her, is what stopped her fingers at the piano. How could she ever melt it? She didn't deserve to play, and she could never win his forgiveness, never make it right.

But she *had* genuinely loved him, too. She knew that. Her choice to marry him, build a family with him, was never calculated, never weighed like that in conscious terms.

A moan escaped her lips, and she bit down on it, facing another facet of her remorse. Despite how close they were, she'd never quite broken through his walls, nor let him completely inside her own. She'd held back from making that honest, unguarded connection.

And now it was too late.

Now, just as she was grasping how that connection was what mattered most.

And Tanner. Dear, treasured Tanner. She'd loved him with an almost aching tenderness, but again from a certain distance, never wholly dissolving the blockade around her heart.

Why had she allowed this, letting these barriers stand until it was everlastingly too late?

Music was about relationships. She knew this. She'd said it hundreds of times to students, in lectures and lessons, in conversations to herself.

How had she not understood it was true of life, as well?

She had treated Jim as a symbol, and he should have been so much more. Tanner, too. They were gone, her chance was over. That could never be changed.

Fierce regret knifed through her. The moonlight reflecting off the lake shimmered, dancing with the dark, blurring before her stinging eyes. Despair and recrimination clutched at her, and she let the sobs come, let them wrench and carry away some of the tension she'd held onto with such intensity.

But they could never wash away her guilt.

She was broken.

73

Nate watched Riley from his stance in a clutch of trees beside the lake.

He felt like a rat, spying on her through what was clearly a private moment, but he refused to leave her unprotected and defenseless while a killer walked among them.

Teren had pulled him back from following her as she fled the piano. They both understood that what she was going through needed to be done alone.

So, he kept his distance as he watched her back.

She looked small and forlorn, a huddled figure in the moonlight, misery written in the sag of her shoulders. He wanted to run to her, hold her, help her banish the demon of her despair. Instead, he planted his feet and locked his jaw.

For a long moment she sat, folded into herself, still and silent. And then, he watched in powerless agony while Riley rocked in the rhythm of grief, snatches of desolation reaching him where he stood, as if torn off and floating in the sooty air.

Time passed, and Riley grew still again, a brooding silence settling over her, so thick he felt its twining tendrils from his place among the dark-shadowed pines.

At last, she stood, and he cast about for the best course of action. Should he go out to meet her, walk her back to safety, offer some words of comfort or support? Or was it better to fade into the trees and pretend he was never there?

And there were other questions he had to consider: should he voice his suspicions about the killer's identity and present his proofs, or save that for a less sensitive moment?

Should he let her see how she was beginning to affect him, let her know she was becoming more to him than a sounding board and neighborhood liaison?

Feeling for the bar of chocolate in his jacket pocket, he decided on a compromise.

He walked to meet her under the moonlight, pulling her into a long and wordless hug. In silence, they returned to the quiet clubhouse, and he imagined she knew all the things he wanted to say.

In the end, he simply handed her the candy he'd pilfered from the kitchen.

"Life is full of sweet things, Riley" he whispered. "And you deserve the best of them."

Brushing his lips against her forehead, he retreated to his cot beside the entrance, knowing exhaustion would put him deep under in a matter of moments.

But he feared what the morning might bring.

74

Someone was squeezing her shoulder.

Riley flinched and pushed against the grasping hand, pulling herself upright on the couch, the blanket sliding off over the slippery leather surface. The room was dim, lit only by the gray-tinged sky outside the window, and she couldn't see the face which loomed beside her, though the willowy silver hair gave it away.

"Shhh." Jess brushed a cold hand against Riley's mouth. "Come with me."

Her head felt heavy, full of cotton, and she glanced at the luminous hands of her watch, realizing she'd only managed two and a half hours of sleep after an eternity of restless tossing. She allowed Jess to pull her from the couch and lead her into the corridor.

She looked to the left, where Nate's cot was swallowed in darkness, but Jess pulled her to the right, weaving between the tables in the dining room until they reached the kitchen. There was a flicker and then light flooded the room as the door *thubbed* shut behind them.

Riley shielded her eyes, squinting as they got used to the full brilliance. Jess tugged at her elbow, guiding her into the chair at the kitchen desk.

"We need to talk," she whispered, urgency in her voice.

Riley blinked her eyes, trying to clear the sleep from them as she watched Jess fill a kettle and put it on to boil.

"What's up?"

Jess pulled a stool from the chopping bar and brought it close to Riley's chair. She leaned forward, keeping her voice low, her breath tickling Riley's cheek.

"Some of us were talking last night and we came to a frightening conclusion."

"Only one?"

Jess ignored the sarcasm. "Several, actually."

Her gray-specked eyes darted around the room, lingering on the door with its high, little window. She looked scared.

"We all know each other pretty well," she said, making a circular gesture meant to take in the neighborhood. She paused and fastened her earnest gaze on Riley. "But we don't know Nate."

A pulsing shock ran through Riley, bringing her fully awake. "You're not suggesting—"

Jess laid a cold finger against her lips. "Shhh." She nodded. "I am suggesting that but hear me out. What if he's not who he says he is?"

She began ticking points off on her fingers. "First, we checked the glove box in the Explorer. It is a registered law enforcement vehicle, but the driver ID lists an unfamiliar name and photo, which led us to wonder—what became of that guy?"

Riley opened her mouth, but Jess squeezed her shoulder, silencing her as she rushed on.

"Second, Nate claims to have contacted the Sheriff's department, but if that's true, why has no one shown up? Did you actually hear him speak to someone on the radio?"

Riley shook her head.

"I thought not. We tried the radio and got nothing but static."

She held up another finger. "He just happens to be in the neighborhood when this whole thing goes down. How long have you known him, Riley?"

Riley's stomach felt hollow, and she offered no answer.

"We know from news accounts where the first victims were found. Isn't that where Nate came from? He was there, Riley, where those people were murdered."

Jess paused, taking Riley's hand. "And now he's here and more people have died."

Riley pulled her hand away and shook her head, breaking out of Jess's intense gaze.

"No," she said, standing. "I don't believe it. That's ridiculous. Nate is here because he's investigating those deaths. The trail led him here."

"Did it? Three high-profile murders on the other side of the Sound, and someone from our little neighborhood is their best suspect? Think about it, Riley. Does that seem likely?"

"I would know if it was Nate. I'd be able to tell."

Jess blocked the way out. "Would you? If it's not Nate, then it's someone else in this group. Who is it, Riley? Which one of our friends is a butcher?"

The room was airless. Riley couldn't breathe. She had to get out.

Pushing past Jess, she butted through the kitchen door, leaving it swinging. In the darkened dining room, she stumbled against a table, sending its legs screeching across the floor like nails on a chalkboard. Recoiling, she moved at a more cautious pace, gaining the corridor where Nate slept.

The killer could not be Nate.

Though the sleep fuzz had left her brain, forcing such an idea through a logical thought process was proving difficult. Her mind and emotions had taken such a pummeling in recent days that she didn't trust herself to think straight. She needed some distance. She wanted to go home.

But could she get out the door without waking Nate?

She stared toward Nate's cot, limned in pearly light from the windows. Jess had not followed her, and the early morning silence was complete. She took a step forward and then froze.

The cot creaked as the sleeping figure stirred, turning toward her. She couldn't see well enough to tell if his eyes were still closed or staring right at her. Shivering, she retreated to the staircase, treading its steps into the basement.

Meeting Room C, she remembered, had an exterior door. Padding softly along the hallway, she used the wall to guide her to the exit. Reaching the door to the vestibule, she paused, recalling the horrendous shriek it had made when Nate pushed it open during their search for the missing knife.

She drew a deep breath and gave the door a gentle nudge. It swung open, smooth and silent. Someone had oiled the hinges.

Someone who wanted to come and go without signaling his movements.

Her scalp prickled and she bolted through the vestibule, stumbling across the meeting room floor, stubbing her toe against the wooden podium. Ignoring the pain, she fumbled with the heavy door handle and let herself out into the chill of dawn.

It was dark.

Darker than it should have been, and the wind had shifted, coming from the east, bringing ash and destruction like the scripture said. As Nate had predicted.

Riley felt raw, exposed. To the elements and to her doubts. Circling the parking lot, she tried the door to the Explorer, surprised and disturbed to find it swinging open under her hand. How had Jess and her contingent managed to unlock it? Had the evidence locker in the trunk also been violated?

Climbing inside the Explorer, Riley pulled the door to a gentle close and sat still, listening to her own harried breathing. She concentrated on taking deep, even breaths, attaining a steady rhythm before reaching into the glove box and removing the leatherette folder of documents.

Squinting in the dim light, she noted the name of the official driver. Enrique Jimenez. His handsome Latino face gazed out from the ID card, exuding life and authority, hailing from a time before the world turned upside down.

Where was he now, and why was Nate driving his car?

She would ask him. The explanation was sure to be simple and logical. She refused to believe Nate was the killer. There could be reasonable explanations for all of Jess's arguments and Riley's gut told her to trust him.

She turned on the two-way radio and listened to the static. She had never heard anything but hissing and crackling from it, but she had believed Nate when he told her he'd reached the Mason County dispatch.

That was two days ago.

If he'd told the truth, why had no deputies arrived? What was the reasonable explanation for that?

Racked by chills that had little to do with the cool of morning, Riley sat, thinking. The seat beneath her, cold at first, gradually accepted her body heat and shared it back again, creating a warm cocoon. Overcome with exhaustion, she drowsed.

Shaking herself awake, Riley blinked, focusing her eyes on the interior of the car. The light had strengthened with the rising sun, and she examined the passenger seat, noting scuffs of mud on the floormat and inside of the door.

She might have made those marks herself in their mad dash from Rico's island, but there was something off about the smudges on the door handle. Leaning closer, she inspected the smears.

Blood.

She had been dirty and muddy, but she didn't think she'd had blood on her hands.

A thick, dull thudding started up in her eardrums and she felt heat spreading across her face. Unbidden, a nasty thought rose in her mind. She didn't want to give it space to grow, but it took hold, prying into her stress-numbed brain.

Had Nate murdered Rico, and the members of his household staff, and then "processed" the scene to taint the evidence? With communications down, he'd had the field to himself. She had been the only one there to witness his actions.

No. She could not support this theory. It was crazy.

She turned to exit the car, but a flash of color caught her eye. Peering into the back seat, she stretched out a hand and retrieved one of the glossy papers scattered there.

It was a pamphlet. She opened it and read a highlighted section entitled, *The Human Problem*:

The Earth is infested with human parasites. She cries for our help. Those of us who love her consider it not only our duty, but our high calling, to do what we can to defend her. Those who hate her are pests, destroying the environment, and must be exterminated.

Riley closed the pamphlet, feeling sick. Why did Nate possess such propaganda? Was he studying it in order to track down an insidious killer?

Or did he follow its tenets?

Who was he really?

She wanted to believe she knew, but three trauma-packed days was no basis for such an evaluation.

Her face cooled, a pervasive chill feathering down her spine. No, she couldn't believe Nate was a murderer, but she couldn't afford to deny the indications that he might be.

That any of them might be.

She was isolated, on her own. The best hope for their little group was to bring in outside help.

And she would have to be the one to bring it.

75

The killer pulled the cotton strip, stained with Mayhew's blood, from his pack and let it flutter in the breeze against his naked thighs.

He'd struck the fire, igniting the char cloth with the first sparks off the flint, sending out a prayer of fervent thanks. A chill hung in the early morning air, and he hurried, knowing he had to get back before he was missed.

He watched the strip burn on the altar fire, diminishing into a curl of cinders.

By blood and by fire.

He spoke the words, working through the prescribed movements, pressing himself into the pliant earth.

He finished the ritual as the sun's watery light rose on the day, bringing with it a fringe of ash, singed bits of detritus drifting in the sky like fool's confetti.

He thought of Riley, her beautiful face glowing and alive. She was dear to him. By all that was wonderful, she was exceedingly dear to him.

And that made him afraid.

She must take care. She was spending too much time with the meddling detective. The killer was taking steps to deal with that, spreading doubts, tipping off a few key people, turning them against the cop.

Soon Riley would hear it, too.

He wanted to get her alone, to talk to her. He'd guard his tongue, make sure he didn't tell her too much, but he needed to share with her a portion of his anxiety, feel the touch of her understanding hand.

Today. He would talk to her today.

Dressing in haste, he raked a hand through his hair and started for the clubhouse.

It was time to get ready for breakfast.

76

A FINE LAYER OF ash coated the small windows in the garage doors, making it too dark for Riley to find what she needed.

The garage had been Jim's turf, and his organizing skills were not on a par with hers. She'd planned to clean out the area, pitch the junk, and bring order to the space, but it felt too much like scrubbing him out and so she'd left it.

She vaguely remembered seeing a large, square flashlight on the corner workbench and she made her way there, moving her hands over the objects until she found what she wanted. Switching it on, she watched a feeble beam poke a finger of light into the gloom. Making a mental note to visit the battery drawer upstairs before setting out, she ran the light beam over the storage shelves.

Seizing upon an old backpack, she dumped its contents onto the concrete floor. After rummaging through the garage, she filled the pack with two bottles of water, a package of dust masks and a pair of goggles, a plastic rain poncho, a waterproofed box of matches, a skein of twine, and a Swiss Army knife.

Pushing aside some of the clutter on the shelf, she shone the light toward its nether regions and found a few more useful items. She added a lightweight tarp, an emergency flare, and a small metal box containing a dart gun and three small tranquilizer darts.

Jim had used the dart kit once, during a forest fire. To subdue wild animals escaping from the blaze.

Such a thing might prove valuable.

Letting herself into the house, she climbed the stairs from the garage level to the kitchen. After replacing the flashlight battery, she raided the pantry, throwing in foil packets of tuna, a handful of energy bars, and a package of peanut butter crackers.

In the bedroom, she changed into jeans and a hooded sweatshirt, pulling on a pair of sturdy boots and tucking her hair under a charcoal-gray beanie. She tossed a couple pairs of clean socks and underwear into the bag and zipped it shut.

It was time to move.

Skirting the clubhouse, she kept to the trees, not wanting to be seen or detained. She located the dirt track leading up to the ridge and followed it past a sagging, abandoned barn and into the thickening forest.

She made good time, moving at a steady jog, keeping her breathing even and untroubled. She had never made this hike but knew that the Hood Canal lay on the other side of the ridge. On past occasions, she'd driven the long way around, taking Highway 3 to where it meets the 106, and turning left to follow the south shore of the canal.

This was her first time going up and over on foot.

The dirt path twisted through thick trees and vegetation, becoming more rutted and muddy with each turn. Riley kept to the edge of it, treading closer to the needle-covered verge. At length, she arrived at the padlocked gate which blocked public access to the unpaved road.

The railroad track ran past here. Riley reasoned that if she followed the tracks, they'd eventually lead her to a community, provided they hadn't been washed away by flooding. The tracks were solid, easy to walk along, and the prospect was tempting. She wouldn't get lost if she followed the train route.

But the tracks meandered, keeping mostly to the low rises, making it the long way round and she didn't really know where they'd lead. Heading straight up and over the ridge would surely take her to the clumps of houses she'd seen during her drives along the canal. It was a shorter distance but covered more rugged terrain.

And she might get lost.

Shrugging off the backpack, Riley opened a bottle of water. She took three or four swallows, weighing the alternatives. The sky seemed to blacken before her, and tiny bits of ash swirled in the atmosphere, choking out the sunlight.

She recapped the water bottle and dropped the pack over the fence. Taking care not to snag her clothing, she climbed the wooden gate and shouldered the pack, setting off up the hill.

Behind her, the sturdy iron tracks wound away into the distance.

77

NATE STIRRED ON HIS cot, swimming up to consciousness.

He heard the faint rustlings of people moving past, trying not to wake him, and the light of morning pressed against his eyelids. Opening them, he sat up and groaned.

His eyes felt rough and full of gravel, the bane of the sleep-deprived. Swinging his legs over the side of the cot, he stood and stretched, then headed for the bathroom.

A quick shower and a swipe with the toothbrush, and he was ready for breakfast. In the dining room, he looked for Riley, hoping the light of day had washed away last night's dejection, but he didn't see her.

He ate bacon-studded scrambled eggs and a cinnamon roll, calling down a blessing on Skillet's head. Chatting with Cappy and the Dawsons, he finished his meal with a swig of orange juice and cast his gaze over the dining room. Still no Riley.

In the kitchen, he quizzed Skillet and Jess, but they offered no useful insights. He did a full sweep of the building, fighting the growing apprehension that threatened to envelope him.

Looking in on Myrna, he learned there was still no change in her condition. Dr. Deb was with her, and Brenda Marsh dozed on the sofa, clutching her Bible like a Teddy bear.

"It's about time for a changing of the guard," he told the veterinarian. "Who's next on the roster?"

"Mrs. Dawson and Marie."

"I saw them finishing up breakfast. They should be here soon, and you can go eat one of Skillet's famous cinnamon rolls."

She nodded, her face pale and weary. Nate sighed and rubbed at his eyes, moving his hands down over the sandpaper surface of his jaw.

"I've looked everywhere, but I can't find Riley," he told the doctor.

Deb darted a glance at him, then dropped her gaze.

"What?" he asked. "Do you know where she is?"

The doctor thinned her lips and lifted her shoulders in an apologetic shrug.

"Doc, if you know, you've got to tell me. She could be in danger."

"We're all in danger, Nate. Riley came in early this morning to see if Myrna was awake. She's upset, tired of feeling trapped and helpless."

Nate's breakfast did a slow turn in his stomach, sinking like a weight.

"What did she do?" he demanded. "Where is she?"

"She asked me not to tell anyone."

Nate pressed his hands together, working to stay calm, and pointed them at the vet. "I need to know where she is," he said, in a careful, even tone.

The doctor studied him. He watched a delicate tendril of color wash over her face. She bit her lip and sighed.

"All right. She went for help. I think she was going up over the ridge, headed for the fringe of houses along the canal." She gave him a faint smile. "But you don't need to worry over her, detective. Teren was in here just ten minutes ago, pumping me for the same information. He went to catch up with her. He'll take care of her."

"Oh, hell," Nate growled, bolting for the door.

He turned and jabbed a hand toward Myrna's cot. "Guard that woman," he commanded. "I want her talking by the time I get back."

78

A BEAM OF SUNLIGHT striped Rick's face.

The palisade formed by the towering pines blocked the early rays that should have woken him, and it was after eight o'clock when he stirred and stretched. Rolling up his sleeping bag, he poured a cup of coffee from the tin pot on a hot rock by the fire. Bobbi was tinkering with the helicopter.

He stood alongside and watched her rotate and remove the fasteners from the air duct.

"G'morning," he said.

"Yep," she said curtly, as if he'd offered an observation instead of a greeting.

Rick watched the fasteners come off, counting sixteen as he heard them clink into a tin plate. He said nothing. The filter element resisted as she tried to lift it out, and he moved to help her.

"I got it," she snapped.

Turning to face him, she folded her arms across her chest. "Why don't you cook breakfast," she said, dismissing him.

He stood a moment longer, then shrugged and retreated to the box of supplies. He found a small carton of eggs and broke four of them into a cup, seasoning them with salt and pepper. He scrambled them in the mess kit skillet, all the while keeping an eye on Bobbi as she tapped the element to dislodge the ashes and dirt.

He caught the single vicious swear word that sprang from her lips and understood there was a problem. Approaching cautiously, he asked, "Anything I can help with?"

She stood and sighed, swiping a hand across her brow and leaving a smudge of dirt.

"Our chances for an early start are shot to hell," she said. "There's water in the fuel tank, which will take time to bleed out. And the air filter is filthy."

"I thought a dirty filter is a good filter. Smaller holes, better filtration."

"Sure," Bobbi agreed. "To a point."

Raising an eyebrow, she added, "We're well past that point. I'm used to banging out dirty filters in the dry desert air. Works great. But this is fine, gritty ash and moisture. Caked mud."

She grimaced, staring down at the grimy filter element. "We'll let the sun take a crack at it," she said. "See what that does for us."

They ate the eggs and peeled some tangerines. Bobbi's mood passed from irritation to despondency and Rick began to worry. Rage was the driving force behind her participation in this wild scheme. It was fury that animated her, spawned her recklessness, kept her going.

If she lost that drive, would he lose his last shot at reaching Nate?

He writhed inside, hated himself for thinking like this, but then he considered what was at stake and how deep they were already in it.

Feeling like a cad, he reflected on the wound she carried and thought about poking it with a stick.

He rose. "I'll clean up," he said, gathering the dishes. There was no water for washing so he packed them, dirty, back in the box and used a small cup of drinking water to brush his teeth and splash his face.

Bobbi had moved her sleeping bag to a sunny patch and lay stretched out next to the air filter, eyes closed. He unrolled his own bag and claimed a corner of the sun-splayed clearing.

The faint chattering and chirping of the woodland floated around them. An occasional buzzing of bee or fly, the rustling and creaking of moss-covered trees. As the sun strengthened, it pulled forth the sweet smell of warming grasses, pine needles, and forest berries.

Rick spoke into the air, almost to himself. "This is crazy, what we're doing. Maybe we should just hike out of here. You could still go home to your lambs, patch things up with your husband."

She shot up like he'd prodded her with a hot fork.

"Oh, he'll need patching when I'm finished with him," she assured him. "But there's not enough bandaging and stitching in the world to bind me to him now."

Her eyes were hard and narrowed, her lips pressed together in a grim line. "We're not married," she said. "We never were."

Pulling in a deep breath, she cast Rick a scathing look. "I know what you're doing," she said, her voice as bitter as the unsugared dregs of coffee he'd just finished. "And there's no need. I'll run this helicopter into the ground if I have to, but I'll get you where you're going."

With a final poisonous glare, she settled back onto her sleeping bag and turned her face to the sky, closing her eyes.

"You can count on it."

79

Frank Newcombe felt the weight of responsibility settling ever more heavily upon him.

He and Millie had offered a refuge for their friends, but in doing so they sheltered a killer, as well. That was more than they'd bargained for.

A lot more.

Finishing his circuit of the building, he saw that the exterior door from Meeting Room C leaned slightly ajar. He also noticed that someone had sprayed a mess of WD-40 on the hinges of the vestibule. He pulled the exterior exit shut, listening for the solid click of the latch, and made sure it was locked.

Riley had gone haring off, and both Teren and Nate were on her trail. Frank knew he'd lost positive control of the situation. He felt their little group teetering on the edge, three degrees from flying apart, and it stoked his heartburn.

Fumbling a roll of Tums from his pocket, he chewed a couple, staring around him, running the numbers through his head. They had enough gasoline for the generator to last about a day and a half more. Food supplies were low and they'd have to start rationing the drinking water. He'd organize a group to salvage resources from their homes later today.

He climbed the stairs to the upper level and stood on the deck outside the dining room. The air was thickening, becoming choked with ash. It was starting to accumulate on the roofs of houses, swirling and sticking in the corners where any two surfaces came together.

They would have to wear masks and carry flashlights at this rate. He went back inside, closing the door behind him, and watched the ash particles dance like dirty snowflakes against the plate glass windows.

Millie came to meet him, her face pale, smudges of mascara darkening the skin under her eyes.

"Frank," she said, her voice subdued, "we're down to two rolls of toilet paper and the last of our hand sanitizer."

She swayed on her feet, and he wrapped his arms around her, pulling her close. She murmured against his chest.

"I thought we'd be back in our homes by now, with power and order restored. I don't know how much longer—"

Loud pounding reverberated from the lobby door. Frank looked up to see two uniformed sheriff's deputies peering in through the glass. A flood of relief washed over him, and he ran to let them in.

"Hell's bells boys. You sure took your time," Frank said, showing his frustration.

The man in front gave him a hard look. "Your Mountain Vista is an island paradise," he said. "You have no conception of the difficulties we encountered getting here." The man offered his hand. "I'm Chief Deputy Randall Steadman and this is Detective Frost."

Frank dipped his head. "I'm sorry. I'm wound a little tight right now. We're just about tapped out here. Frank Newcombe," he said, shaking the chief's hand.

"Dispatch got your distress call, but the message was garbled," Steadman told him. "Am I to understand you're dealing with a murder?"

"And then some," Frank nodded. He opened his mouth to explain, but the chief held up a hand.

"I see you're running a generator and you've got things well in hand. We've been working our way to you since yesterday afternoon. Any chance we could discuss this over breakfast and a cup of coffee?"

Millie gasped, her face contrite. "Of course, I'm so sorry. Please come into the dining room and I'll make sure we've got a pot on."

She led the way and got them settled at a table before disappearing into the kitchen. Frank rubbed a hand over his stubbled face.

"That's Millie, my wife," he said. "Sorry I didn't introduce you. I'm a bit rattled."

He took a deep breath, feeling like a man preparing for an underwater swim. "You know the killer the media is calling the Puget Sound Slasher?" he asked. "We believe our little 'island paradise' is harboring the bastard."

Chief Steadman's craggy face remained steady, but the eyebrows shot up on his partner's forehead. As Frank explained the events since the eruption, the junior deputy beat out an excited tattoo on the table each time the story upped a notch until his chief placed a large palm over his fingers, stilling them.

Millie delivered breakfast to the table, and the deputies chewed and swallowed Skillet's superb cooking without the appreciation it deserved, their attention focused on Frank's unfolding story.

As he wrapped up by telling how Riley had set off on her own and how two of his best men were going after her, Mrs. Dawson swept into the room and stared at the group seated at the table, her eyes huge and black against the pallor of her face.

"Myrna's awake," she said. "And you'll want to hear what she has to say."

80

Riley walked to the rhythm of her breath as it rose and fell against the dust mask.

She wore goggles, too, but the ashfall continued to thicken, coming now in shifting clouds that cut her visibility, disorienting her so that she lost contact with the narrow dirt path. She wandered through forest, using the slope of the land to direct her toward the top of the ridge.

Struggling to keep her breathing steady, she fought against the flower of panic blooming inside her chest. The uneven ground beneath her feet was rife with obstacles, crumbling with loose stones and slippery pine needles. She crept with care.

Reaching a sea of ferns and underbrush that stretched the length of her sight, she waded into it, knee-deep, wishing now that she'd kept to the railroad tracks. She strained her eyes, peering into the deepening gloom, moving forward with slow cautious steps.

She lifted a foot and froze, startled by the flurry of wings as a group of soot-colored birds flew past. They melted into the darkness like chocolate shavings on a griddle and Riley looked down, directly into the jagged metal jaws of a bear trap.

One more step, and she'd have been in it—broken, bloodied, snared. She knew such traps were outlawed, but so was cooking meth, and there was plenty of that going on up in these hills.

She found a stout branch and pushed it into the gaping mouth of the trap, wincing at the resounding snap of the metal teeth as it crunched down, shattering the wood. Shivering, she picked her way carefully out of the underbrush and paused to lean against a tree, catching her breath, rallying her courage.

The air felt peculiar, as if flattened under a blanket, the natural noises of the forest muted by the pall of ash in the atmosphere. With the volcano's effects impairing her vision and hearing, Riley carried a burden of vulnerability that threatened to shred the dregs of her determination.

A sudden longing to be back at the clubhouse, surrounded by friends and neighbors, hit her hard, breaking her stride. The urge was so strong it made her chest ache. Only the notion that one person among those friends and neighbors must be a killer steadied her aim.

Pressing her lips together, she soldiered on, working uphill, each step slow and deliberate. As she climbed, one sound made its ceaseless way around her, a familiar summertime hum.

She was surrounded by cricket song.

Remembering Teren's explanation about the last-of-summer crickets, their desperate and hopeful mating calls and their early warning system, she was comforted, though their chirping sounded hollow in the ash-laden sky. The only other noises she detected were generated by her own feet in their interaction with twigs, stones, and pine needles.

She began to feel she could do this, that she could make it up and over the ridge and summon support. She pictured the sprawl of houses along the Hood Canal. She would knock on doors until she got someone who offered to help.

She imagined being brought inside and coddled, warmed and fed by the good lady of the house while her man gathered a party for the return trip. She was so caught up in the vision that she nearly missed the alarm.

The crickets had gone silent.

Riley froze, straining her ears and eyes for some clue to the danger. Her skin felt electric, charged with high-frequency tension. Ash fog shrouded the trees, thicker than night, and she couldn't see more than a yard or two in any direction.

Listening intently, she heard the faint crackling of footsteps, downward and to the left. Dropping into a crouch, she held her breath and waited.

Seconds of silence ticked by. The smell of wet earth and crumpled pine needles rose to envelop her, tickling her nasal passages, sending tiny shock waves to the back of her skull with the urge to sneeze. Gritting her teeth, she pressed a hand against her nose, which only sharpened the sensation. Her eyes streamed as she screwed them shut, fighting the histamine surge.

The sounds of someone approaching grew closer and more definite. As suddenly as it had begun, the compulsion to sneeze faded and Riley sent up a prayer of thanks. She controlled her breath, keeping it shallow and soundless, ignoring the moisture stinging her cheeks. She stilled her muscles and waited.

"Riley?"

The voice was stealthy, so soft it was almost swallowed by the ash-padded air. "Riley, are you there?"

It was Nate.

A finger of ice traced down her spine.

Why didn't he just call out? Why did he speak in that eerie furtive way? It was creepy.

He whispered her name again and she didn't dare move, except to hunker lower in the clump of ferns. The clouds of ash hid her, but they shifted and swirled, opening and closing holes in the vista like a maniacal game of whack-a-mole.

She waited, hardly daring to breathe, her ears aching with the effort to hear his location. A twig snapped further to the left, and her head swiveled in that direction.

As she watched, the ash thinned, leaving a window for her to peer through, and there he was, only fifteen yards distant.

If he turned his head, they'd be face to face.

She fought the impulse to run to him, feel his strong arms around her, to no longer be alone in this mad escapade. Surely, she could trust her intuition that marked him as a good man and a friend.

But what if she was wrong?

She stared, agonized, her muscles taut and frozen, uncertain what to do and fearing the intensity of her gaze would draw his own, like a magnet. His face looked rapt, his eyes focused forward, up the slope.

As she watched, he took another step upridge, moving with stealth. She caught the tiny movement as his head began to rotate in her direction, and bit down on a scream.

With startling suddenness, another sound tore through the soupy air, sending a streak of lightning down the back of Riley's neck. It was the snarl of a wildcat, and as Nate's head jerked toward it and away from her, she broke from her frozen pose.

And ran.

81

The cry of the cougar sent an electric zing through Nate's body, raising the hairs on the back of his neck and cranking up his heart rate.

As he turned to face the noise, he heard the sound of footsteps behind him, rushing away down the hill, and this scared him more than the mountain lion's nasty snarl had. He prayed the big cat wouldn't take off in pursuit.

If that was Riley running, the cougar would consider her prey. It could overtake and bring her down in seconds.

He shouted to draw the wildcat's attention. Unzipping his jacket, he grabbed the corner hems and raised his arms over his head, waving them slowly, trying to look as big and scary as possible. Through the mist of ash, the cougar slunk into sight, its golden coat gliding in sinuous waves over its well-muscled shoulders.

They made eye contact and Nate intensified his gaze. He'd won staring contests with cats before, but this was the one that counted.

"I'm the alpha here," he told the animal. "Face it and go home. No lunch for kitty."

He spoke in a loud, growling voice, meant to establish his dominance. He wished he'd thought to grab some throwing stones before the cat spotted him. He didn't dare stoop for them now.

Bellowing out a series of shouts and grunts, he continued waving his arms with the jacket stretched between them, standing his ground. The mountain lion took a step back, showing uncertainty. Nate began his own gradual retreat, working to increase the distance between them.

"I'm not worth it, buddy," he roared. "All gristle and bone. Go on home, now. Scat, cat!"

The cougar replied with a resentful grumble, but turned and disappeared upridge, swallowed by the wall of ash and fog. Nate sighed in relief.

He waited two or three minutes, maintaining his dominating stance in case the cat should return. Then, dropping his arms, he started off in the opposite direction, working diagonally down the hill, following where he thought those running footsteps had gone.

He had to find Riley.

Whatever had possessed her to take off alone like this? As much as he wanted to know, a more burning question occupied his mind.

What if Teren found her first?

He thought Teren might be in love with Riley. But he'd also begun to suspect that Teren was not mentally sound. He had no solid evidence, but Nate believed Teren was the killer he sought and that he operated under a code, the nature of which was a mystery, full of rules a sane person could never understand.

Teren was on this mountain, searching for Riley.

What would he do with her when he found her?

Nate picked up his pace. Riley respected and trusted Teren. She would be slow to suspect her friend and she would be at his mercy. He fought the gorge that rose in his throat at the thought.

In the ashen gloom, the labyrinthine forest where pine needles slicked over tracks and traces, it would be difficult to find Riley. But that difficulty would affect Teren, as well.

"Riley," he called out, pitching his voice deliberately low so that it only carried into the immediate vicinity. He didn't want to broadcast his location, or Riley's. He didn't want Teren anywhere near her.

"Riley, please," he pleaded. "If you can hear me, let me help you. Please don't do this alone."

He stood, listening, hoping, but heard only silence. If those running footsteps had been Riley's, she'd disappeared, her passage shrouded in ash.

82

Riley ran downhill because it was easier.

She hated to lose the progress she'd made toward the top of the ridge, but her first thought was to put distance between herself and her pursuer, be it Nate or a wild mountain creature. She kept to a roughly diagonal path, planning to work her way upward again once she was sure she'd shaken off anyone—or anything—trying to follow.

Slipping and scrambling among the trees, she pulled in desperate breaths, harsh gasps that were almost sobs as she scraped her palms along the rough bark of the pines she used to steady herself. The curtain of ash veiled the way before her so that she had no way of knowing what lay ahead and she tried to slow her reckless pace.

Her legs felt outside her control, flailing beneath her in a desperate attempt to keep her upright. Her foot hit a patch of crumbling soil sheeted over with pine needles, and she slid down a jagged chute, landing with a hard thump on her backside. The wind shot out of her lungs in a swift, surprising blow, leaving her writhing and breathless.

She lay in a crumpled heap, working to suck air into her lungs and deafened by the wheeze of her own panicked gasping. She struggled to get it under control, and when her respirations fell into an even rhythm and she could hear beyond herself, she tested body parts to ensure they still worked.

With the panic held at bay, a flood of other considerations surged through her, and she was surprised to realize that chief among them was regret, cutting at her with sharp, raw strokes.

Oh, Nate.

Though she'd given in to Jess's reasoned argument and the circumstantial evidence which corroborated it, Riley could not bring herself to believe that Nate was their killer. She wanted, instead, to embrace the feelings of comfort and companionship, the reawakening of hope, that stirred within her when they were together.

If her instinct to trust him was wrong, how could she rely on any of her feelings? If her inner compass was that skewed, she could do nothing but founder.

That thought pressed her down, weighing her to the ground, eroding her determination to cross the ridge and bring help. Clouds of ash and mist swirled over her head, but as she lay staring up, she caught glimpses of branches above her, intertwining, needles interspersing with needles, learning to lean on and draw strength from one another.

Would she never learn the things she was so adept at teaching others?

Pushing up from the dirt, she brushed loose soil and leaves from her backside and stood like a deer in hunting season, sensors alive to danger. She worked her way laterally along the ridge until she reached a clump of spruce and fir trees too thick for her to push past.

Turning right, she followed them uphill until the mass thinned enough for her to break through. Vines and low-hanging branches sprang into her path, and she brushed them away, pushing through the growth to the clearing ahead.

As she stepped into the open area amid the trees, the clouds of ash shifted, and she saw the dark form of a lone man turning to meet her.

It was Teren.

83

Topper cringed at the screech his spoon made across the tin plate of his mess kit.

Despite the annoying sound, he continued scooping up mouthfuls, needing every drop of nourishment from the can of beef stew he'd heated. Isolated in the abandoned hut and with digital communications down, he had no way of knowing how bad conditions had gotten, or how long they'd last.

His watch told him it was nearing noon, but the sky spoke of dusk, laden with clouds of ash which darkened the little cabin, throwing deep shadows into its corners.

He sensed death in the air, and thought about Jack's mythical figure, so diligent in keeping his appointments no matter how far his clients ranged.

Candace's face shimmered and solidified in his mind's eye, and he wondered how she fared. He knew he was finished at the lab, that there'd be no going back. He'd thrown his Hail Mary and run the other way. He'd started a wave that got people moving. He had made a difference.

But if those he'd moved were marked for death, death would find them.

Had he done all he could? Would he be remembered like David was, as a hero?

Or would his name be lost in obscurity, buried under the mass of trauma caused by the eruption?

No, not that. Whether people deemed him angel or demon, he would be remembered as someone who had done something in the face of disaster.

The question remained—had he done enough?

He had friends in Mountain Vista who might need his help. He'd had this respite alone, to contemplate and recharge. Perhaps it was time to get back into the mix of human frailty.

He found a box of stale toaster pastries in an otherwise empty cupboard and ate a packet without benefit of toaster. The 'real fruit' filling had dried to a paste, sticking to his teeth, cloying and overly sweet.

After dessert, he used a paper towel and hand sanitizer to wipe out the mess kit, and reassembled it, tightening the wingnut that held it together. He checked the rest of his gear, making sure he had everything organized, then settled onto the cot.

Staring at the cobwebbed ceiling, he began planning his next move.

84

Riley watched Teren's face twist, appearing half relieved, half exasperated.

He held out his arms and she ran into their embrace, a rush of affection washing over her, weakening her knees. His warmth enveloped her, and she realized how cold and isolated she'd felt until this moment.

Why had she thought she must do this alone? Teren had proven his friendship, offering her unfailing support over the two years since the deaths of Jim and Tanner.

"What were you thinking, Riley?" he scolded. "There's no shortage of danger out here. If you had to leave, why didn't you take me with you?"

His voice was full of reproach, and she avoided his eyes, knowing the pain she'd see there.

"I'm sorry, Teren. I've been so frightened and confused. Jess woke me this morning and told me a group of them have started investigating Nate."

"I know. I was in that group."

He took her hand and led her to a cluster of large rocks rising from the forest floor. "Let's sit and rest, let you catch your breath. Then we can decide where to go from here."

He brushed the dried needles from a bench-like stone and Riley sat, grateful for a moment to relax and release the tension that pulsed through her.

Teren remained standing. She watched his eyes sweeping the tree line, on the alert, and when they came around to rest on her, she was surprised to see they were hard as the stone she sat on. Deadly serious, with a stirring of anger.

"You could have been killed out here, Riley," he said. "What possessed you to do something so stupid?"

His words stung, rousing a tinge of resentment. "I was scared. I checked the Explorer and saw the driver ID that's not Nate's. And the pamphlets, and the—"

"The blood on the door handle? Yeah, I saw it, too. What we should have done was overpower the guy in his sleep and lock him in the storeroom. I just wasn't sure."

"Exactly. I wasn't sure about anything. We're too close to this to see things clearly, so I went for outside help."

She shifted on her stone bench so she could meet his gaze, show her sincerity.

"I figured I could clear this ridge and find someone on the other side who had no connection to this business. And once the idea entered my head, I couldn't get it out. I went into flight mode and here I am."

"Well, you scared the hell out of me," Teren snapped. "You should have stopped to think about the conclusions people would jump to when they found you missing. Do you have any idea the worry you caused?"

"I told Dr. Deb."

Teren gave a dismissive grunt and they fell into silence. Riley watched the little glints of light that poked down from the ashy sky like tiny miracles.

"I saw him," she said. "He's out here, looking for me."

"Nate?"

"Yeah."

A weight like a heavy stone sank and settled in her chest. Why did she feel like a traitor?

She'd known Nate for less than a week, hardly enough time to establish a solid foundation of trust. She owed him nothing.

She stared down into her lap and past it, to her hiking boots. At least she'd taken the time to put on decent footwear. She noticed Teren had taken off to find her, inappropriately shod in a pair of loafers.

Tasseled loafers.

A sharp needle of ice gave one quick thrust through her heart and was gone.

The notion was ridiculous, but her gaze focused on his right foot, planted there beside her own booted feet, tassel and all. His left leg was bent at the knee with the foot resting on a low rock, hidden from her view by a mass of ferns.

How could she even entertain the thought that the shoe might be missing a tassel? It was silly, but she couldn't stop herself from staring at the clump of ferns as if she could burn through them with the intensity of her scrutiny.

"What's wrong, Riley?" Teren asked. "You have such a horrified look on your face."

"Is there any reason I shouldn't have? After everything that's happened?"

Leaning in, he drew her head against him, cradling it, stroking her hair. "I'm so sorry, kid," he said.

She willed herself to relax, not wanting him to feel the bowstring tension in her neck. "We'd better get going if we're to make it over the ridge before dark," she pointed out.

"True enough," he agreed, releasing her.

Dread crept over Riley. Now she would see, and part of her didn't want to know.

He pushed back from the rock, bringing his left foot down, next to his right, and Riley felt giddy with relief.

Of course, both shoes had their tassels.

She stared down at the brown loafers with a foolish grin.

"You sure you're up to this?" Teren asked. "You seem a bit dazed."

"No, I'm fine. I feel much better now. Really."

He led the way and once more, Riley was pointed uphill. There was no discernible trail, and they picked a path through the trees and underbrush, pulling themselves up crumbling channels where the earth had eroded under runnels formed by the frequent rains.

The swirling ash continued to limit their field of vision, and Riley labored along behind Teren, watching his mud-encrusted loafers, placing her feet in the places he'd established before her.

The heavy air continued to flatten the sounds of the forest, brushing an oppressive glaze over the silence of their progress. Riley felt dull and uneasy as she followed in Teren's footsteps.

Some faction inside her reared uneasily, fighting to be acknowledged while the rest of her, the part that couldn't bear to face any more horrors, quelled the rebel voice.

Even so, the constellation of dots in her mind was pulling together into an ever more coherent and definitive shape.

They reached a place where the land leveled out, picking up a fragment of a trail where they could walk more easily. Riley had shared her packet of dust masks, and they chuffed along, their panting breath amplified by the filtering fibers strapped across the bottom half of their faces.

After walking for some time, Teren stopped and turned to face her. He wasn't wearing goggles, and his eyes were raw and red, the skin around them streaked with soot, as he met her gaze.

"Something's bothering you, Riley," he said. "What is it?"

His voice held a hard edge that shocked Riley, sending a wave of apprehension over her, washing her mind blank.

"You keep staring at my shoes," he added. "Is there something wrong with them?"

The big picture bloomed like fireworks in her brain, and she saw it, the thing that part of her hadn't wanted to know. The tassel was there, but it was the wrong color, a darker shade of brown, as if it hadn't weathered along with the rest of the shoe.

As if it was a replacement for one that had been lost.

Fear fluttered through her, and she hugged herself, feeling so cold.

"No, nothing's wrong," she insisted. "I'm just trying to follow your footprints, step where you step."

His eyes shone like flint, and she struggled to hold steady as they probed into her, sullen and resentful. Dropping his gaze to his own feet, he examined his shoes and Riley felt sick, as if her stomach were turning inside out.

Dreading what might happen next, she was shocked to hear an eerie giggle ripple up from Teren's bent head, warped by the mask that covered his mouth. Riley felt as if someone had squeezed a spongeful of ice water over her.

Teren raised his head, gleeful as a child caught in a prank. He pulled the mask from his face and sang, his voice high and child-like.

"A tissel, a tassel, a green and yellow rascal."

Grinning, he said, "Don't fret over my tassel, Riley."

The grin dropped from his face and his voice rose to a snarl, eyes glinting redly at her against the darkening sky.

"We've got bigger things to worry about."

85

Rick watched Bobbi inspect the helicopter.

The sun had crossed the overhead position by the time the filter was dry enough for Bobbi to dislodge the worst of the buildup and reinstall it. The sky was darkening again as the wind shifted, bringing another crop of ash, and he sensed her impatience to get in the air.

"Good enough," she announced. "Let's ride."

They climbed into the cockpit, buckled up, and donned the Davie Clark headsets and sunglasses. Bobbi hit a switch, initiating the starting sequence, working the throttle to moderate the fuel.

A large cloud of black smoke puffed out, enveloping the machine, and the high pitch of the turbine engine whined into life, accompanied by the whir of the rotor.

"Well, that's alright, then," Bobbi said. "I was afraid I might fry the engine, but we're good."

She turned to face him. "There's no telling how far we'll get before the engine chokes down again. All yesterday's hazards still apply, and new troubles are always a possibility, so I'll turn your words and aim them right back at you."

She smirked, and Rick saw his twin reflection in the lenses of her shades.

"This is crazy," she mimicked. "We could just hike out of here and go home. You could patch things up with your superiors and get back to business as usual."

"Okay," Rick complained, "now you're just trying to make me sound like an idiot."

"No effort required," she assured him. "Our lives are back on the line, officer. So," she said, waiting for his answer, "are we doing this?"

Rick stared at her, then lifted his finger and pointed it upward with a twirling motion. "Let's go."

Bobbi turned forward and initiated the takeoff. As they rose slowly, the right side of the helicopter seemed to sag. Rick watched the slender trunks of the pines taper as they neared the treetops and suddenly they were tipping, pivoting to the right.

"Damn!" Bobbi shouted. "We're caught on something. We're gonna roll."

"Pull us out!"

"I'm fighting it," Bobbi said with a growl, "but something's resisting me. There's nothing I can do if we exceed the critical angle." Her face beneath the flight goggles was white. "Find out what's holding us!"

Unstrapping, Rick twisted in his seat, his wild stare rocketing back and forth, searching for some way to help the situation. His brain registered something that didn't make sense.

A tree sprouted through the floor of the passenger cabin. A fraction of a second slid by before he realized a slender sapling had pierced the skin of the helicopter when they'd landed the night before, running along the inside of the cabin, camouflaged in such a way that neither he nor Bobbi had noted the invasion.

He allowed himself no time to think, no time to acknowledge fear. Rolling open the door, he climbed out onto the skid, gripping the overhead handle with desperate strength. Peering up at the roof of the JetRanger, he saw the top of the tree poking through.

Its lateral branches, though fragile, were enough to catch and throw the helicopter off balance, creating a pivot point. Bobbi was struggling to level it out, but the tree was pulling against her.

He couldn't reach it from the skid, had to scramble up to stand on the threshold. The outward angle of the helicopter worked against him, and he had to cling, like an insect, to anything he could get his hands on.

Staring back at the ground, he saw they were low enough that a fall might not kill him. He pictured himself in a wheelchair, in a white-sheeted bed with a feeding tube. He swallowed and pulled himself up, reaching for the protruding tree.

The whir of the blades terrified him. He feared coming too close and losing a hand. Or a head. He took a breath, banished these thoughts, and twined his fingers around the top of the sapling, stripping the branches away.

One.

Two.

When the third branch came away, releasing them from their tether, the JetRanger sprang into the air, swiveling and banking violently.

Rick lost his grip, and his balance. Teetering, arms pinwheeling in the open air, Rick felt the knife edge of disaster open up beneath him.

As he began to fall.

86

Riley ran.

Once again, she was barreling downhill, stumbling and scraping along, the hair on the back of her neck raised like antennae, sensing the terrifying presence behind her.

He was insane. How had she never seen it?

Teren was dangerously ill. She'd been friends with a killer, alone with him, taking comfort from him, confiding in him. For two years.

Part of her must have known.

"Riley!" His voice came from behind, but it was impossible to tell how close. "Slow down, Riley. You'll hurt yourself."

She slid down a hill of pine needles, grasping at branches to keep herself upright, nearly taking a tumble. She prayed she wouldn't sprain an ankle.

"Riley, stop. I want to help you."

She imagined his breath, hot on her neck as he closed the distance between them. Her hair streamed out behind her as she ran, providing an easy way for him to grab her and bring her to a halt.

Driven by panic, she flew along the forest floor, heedless of the loose stones and uneven ground beneath her feet. She remembered that he was wearing slick-soled loafers, unfit for this terrain. She had an advantage, and she would need it.

"Riley!"

She was now certain he was falling behind, and a spurt of renewed energy buoyed her up. Skittering down a steep slope, she fell, sprawling, at the bottom. Something whirred over her head, close enough that she felt the stir of its passing. She looked up to see the haft of a knife quivering in the trunk of a tree a yard in front of her face.

Dismayed, sickened, she scrambled up and ran on.

"Wait, Riley," Teren called after her. "I have to get my knife."

She did not wait. The sounds of his pursuit faded behind her and she finally put some distance between them. She'd been running on pure instinct. No thought, no reason, had entered into it.

But now she had to think, she had to reason out where to go, what to do. As soon as he freed his knife from the tree, he'd be on her again. How could she evade him?

The cloudy ashfall made it difficult to see far ahead. She could use this to her advantage. It distorted noises, as well, and she hoped that it would swallow the slight sounds she made as she slowed and shifted, moving in a lateral direction.

She found a billow of underbrush and took cover. Even with the benefit of the better shoe, she could not outrun him for long. Stealth was her best hope.

She quieted her breathing and crouched low, hidden by trees and the lush growth of ferns. Straining her ears, she heard only random sounds, creaks or sighs that could come from anywhere and mean anything.

She almost screamed when his voice floated suddenly out of the ashen mist, far too close to give her any comfort.

"A tissel, a tassel, a green and yellow rascal."

He paused, as if waiting for her to chime in, and a pleading note came into his voice.

"Don't be a rascal, Riley. Come out."

His tone had grown child-like again, thin and high. Riley had an unnerving notion that if the mist cleared, she'd see a young boy standing, like a fawn in the forest, sweet-faced with clear, open eyes. She shivered, staring toward the sound of his voice, and prayed the curtain of mist would hold.

"I got my knife," he said, and she could hear the pleased smile in the inflection of his words. "I'm glad it didn't hit you, Riley. It shouldn't be that way. It's best across the throat, but I wasn't ready," he complained. "You didn't let me get ready."

He was pouting now, and Riley cringed, sensing the coming change, the cycling pattern of his madness. When he spoke again, his voice smoldered, underlaid with coals of rage.

"I have to get ready, Riley. She needs me. Don't you understand?" The volume of his voice rose with each word, ending in a crescendo that clawed through the clouds of ash. Riley cowered, desperate to remain hidden.

She heard the crunch of a pinecone under his foot, and then another as he moved away and his voice dropped into a lower register.

"Toby understood," he said. "And John. It's what we do, Riley. It's what we've always done."

He laughed, a ragged titter that hung in the mist for an eerie moment. "Don't you get it, Riley? It's an honor. Such an honor to be chosen."

Riley swallowed hard, fighting a wave of dizziness, pressing her hands together to keep them from shaking so hard that he'd surely hear them, as he must hear the pounding of her heart.

He spoke again, a little more distant, another layer of ash coming between them.

"In the more enlightened cultures, the sacrificed are recognized as heroes. They draw lots for the honor. The people weave crowns of flowers for them and observe the ceremonial ritual with diligence. The hero gives his life with great pleasure.

"I've been selfish, Riley. I wanted to keep you for myself, and she is angry with me. I tried to appease her with others, but it's no good. We both know it."

A chill finger traced down Riley's spine as he announced, "It will be your privilege, a coveted honor, to die for her."

His voice was soothing and rhythmic, the simple chant of a dedicated disciple. "I know you can hear me. Come Riley, come to me now. Let's do this together."

He sounded so persuasive, and heaven help her—the lull of his voice, the misty mountainside, her utter exhaustion--all the elements combined to make it undeniably hypnotic. She could almost understand the draw felt by the ancient victims, the promise of glory, the end of pain.

"By blood and by fire, Riley. That's how I will honor you. I swear it."

In that moment, a fierce suspicion rose up from the scattered dots in Riley's mind, coalescing into a terrifyingly cohesive picture.

The questions surrounding the fire that killed Jim and Tanner. Teren's compassionate support of her in the rawness of her widowhood. A look of arch satisfaction she'd once caught on his face and wondered about.

These things came crashing together with such vehemence that she nearly cried out. How long had Teren been meddling in the inner workings of her life? How much damage had he done?

The questions burned with such intensity that she had to grind her teeth together to keep from screaming them out.

Hot tears stained her cheeks as she cowered under the ferns, but an idea for escape came to her. She waited for him to speak again, giving away his position, then she sprang away, tearing downhill.

Heading for the lake.

87

Rick fell.

He sensed himself sinking backwards by inexorable slow-motion increments as the blades of the helicopter blatted above him, drowning out the hammering knell in his chest. Time suspended, ticking out its moments at long stretches as his arms wheeled, cleaving the air in a demented backstroke.

It crossed his mind that he would land on his head.

The helicopter swerved toward him and in that instant, his flailing hand reconnected with something solid and time snapped back into place. He grabbed on with a sob, groping for the opening, clutching solid metal with shaking hands.

Pulling himself back into his seat, he slammed the door and sat shuddering, barely able to take in what had just occurred. The bird continued its wild flight, jerking this way and that, and he braced himself in place while he struggled to catch his breath.

"Whoo hoo!" Bobbi crowed. "Feel the blood pumping now."

She turned to Rick, and he was amazed to see a delighted grin spreading across her face. His own face felt frozen and a wave of nausea spasmed through him, settling in his belly. He fought the urge to vomit.

Bobbi spared him another look before focusing on the sky ahead.

"Belt up, soldier," she said. "And keep it in your shirt."

"What?"

"If you're going to barf in my bird, do it inside your own shirt."

He considered. "It's not your bird."

Her eyebrows shot up and her smile widened. "Good point. Spew at will, then."

He laughed and she joined him. It felt good. The near disaster had cleared the air, erasing the tension between them. She got control of the helicopter, and he resumed his post as lookout.

"You know," he said, "if a lot of people toss their cookies with you at the controls, you might want to consider the implications."

"Wise guy. It's happened once, and once only."

As the helicopter skimmed over the tops of the tall pines below, she told him about that one time.

"During training we were informed that we had two choices if we had to puke. Down our own shirt or keep it in our mouth. So, this once, I was transporting a couple of recruits and we hit some turbulence, what we call yanking and banking."

"Is that what you call it? I think I just made its acquaintance back there."

Bobbi grinned again. "Well, it got pretty choppy," she continued, "and I handed down the rule. One guy said sure thing. The other guy couldn't speak. He had his mouth full."

Rick grimaced. "Ugh."

"Oh yeah. Another ten minutes and we touched down. This guy got off and spit out a mouthful of fillings onto the tarmac. The acid in the vomit had dissolved the cement in his dental work and he lost every last one of them."

"You're kidding me!" Pausing, he said, "I'm curious. Why'd you give me just the one option?"

She gave him a sideways glance. "I only met you yesterday. I don't know the state of your dental work, but I figured if the acid burned away your chest hair, you'd live through it."

Rick laughed, thumping the front of his shirt. "No mere stomach acid could eat through this manly thatch."

They fell into companionable silence and Rick looked out over the canopy of treetops stretching away for miles, his thoughts returning to Nate.

What was going on down there? Had Nate crossed paths yet with the killer?

88

Riley sprinted through the forest.

Low-hanging branches whipped at her. The thorny stems of wild blackberry bushes plucked at her sleeves and pant legs, slowing her down, adding to her terror.

A coat of ash filmed her goggles, and she swiped her hand across them, managing only to smear the grime. The sound of crashing pursuit behind her spurred her forward so that it seemed her feet hardly touched the ground.

Soon, she'd reach the lake.

A wild plan raced over the synapses of her frantic brain. It was frail, but it was something, and to make it work, she needed to gain a few minutes of lead time. With all the lateral traveling she'd done, she calculated that she would emerge from the forest at the far end of the narrow lake. The clubhouse sat across the water at the opposite point. Once she hit the path that circled the lake, it was a mile and a half run to reach her refuge.

Or she could paddle a straight shot down the lake.

If she was correct in judging the lay of the land, her pell-mell flight down the ridge would bring her out near the boat yard where Teren housed his two kayaks. If she got there first, with enough lead time, she could take the sea kayak.

If Teren tried to follow, he'd be stuck with the broader, slower recreational model, minus the oars. She'd take the double-headed paddle and toss it in the lake. It was a slim hope, but nothing else sprang to mind, so she clung to it.

She could no longer hear Teren behind her but had no way of knowing how far back he'd dropped. Now that she had an objective, it gave wings to her feet. She broke through the tree line and saw that she was only two houses down from the boat yard.

And no sign of Teren.

After the soft rustlings of pine needles, the pounding of her hiking boots on the asphalt path seemed shockingly loud, telegraphing her location. She moved onto the softer verge and then onto the hard-packed dirt outside the gate to the boat yard.

The green metal gate was unlocked. Riley remembered that Teren's kayaks were secured only by a bungee-corded tarp and thanked heaven for the carefree and trusting ways of the neighborhood.

The gate screeched and dragged as she pushed it open, and she cringed. She'd just announced her presence and she could go through with her plan or scrap it and take off in a new direction.

But there was no time for thinking out a well-ordered strategy. She squeezed through the opening in the gate and flew to the tarp-covered kayaks.

The bungee cords resisted the panicked yanking of her fingers, but she managed to release them, pushing off the tarp and dragging the narrow, red sea kayak off the wooden pallet. She made sure the oar was there, then heaved the other kayak's paddle as far as she could into the lake.

As she shoved the boat down to the water, the eerie wail of the rusty gate screeched behind her. Alarm zapped through her, and she scrambled into the kayak, pushing off with the oar and paddling like a windmill.

Thirty yards out, she paused to look back, but the screen of ash left nothing to be seen.

She dipped and worked the paddle, nose pointed toward the center of the lake, but the limited visibility was disorienting. Without reference points, how would she know if she was heading in a straight line? How could she be sure she was even going in the right direction?

She stopped moving and cocked her head, listening for the slap of paddles or any indication that Teren had entered the lake behind her. She heard only the caw of a crow passing through the ashen mist above her head.

She'd have to maneuver the kayak closer to shore where she could see the houses that lined the contour of the lake. She paddled for several long minutes, pulling to the right, without seeing anything beyond the prow of the kayak.

Just as she thought she might have entered the Twilight Zone, the faint outline of a house materialized. Just a shimmer at first, then clarifying into something solid. Beside it, another house loomed, and Riley understood where she was.

Again, she stopped to listen for sounds of pursuit. Tiny, gentle waves lapped the nearby shore, but she heard no rhythmic paddling. There was something, though, some sound she couldn't identify. A kind of electric hum.

No motorized boats were allowed on the lake, and she was pretty sure the boat yard harbored no such craft. It was difficult to distinguish where the sound was coming from and as she drifted closer to shore, the hairs on the back of her neck rose in a prickling wave.

The volume increased suddenly, as if an obstacle had been removed, and around the corner of the nearest house, a golf cart bobbed into view.

It bounced over the manicured lawn and gained the path that ran along the shore of the lake. She was close enough to look into Teren's eyes as he sat at the wheel. They were flat and hard, matching the granite planes of his jaw.

The path circled the lake entirely. He could dog her the whole way, and he'd never let her reach the clubhouse.

If he lost sight of her, he'd cover that end of the lake, cutting her off. If she shouted, would someone hear her?

Would it matter?

They could play cat and mouse until one of them ran out of juice, or she could just cut and run, heading for the opposite shore and banking that he couldn't get clear around the two long sides of the lake before she could cover the short radius and disappear into the forested ridge once again.

Opting for Plan B, she turned the kayak and dug in with the paddle.

89

Frank stood over his helplessly sobbing wife.

The name Myrna spoke when she roused from her comatose state had shocked them all. Teren was a respected member of their community, and Millie had adored him. It was near impossible to absorb the thought that he was the killer who'd terrorized their camp and murdered a string of innocents.

He rested his hand on Millie's shoulder. Her bones felt fragile under his fingers and a flash of anger speared through him. He wanted to do something, take some kind of constructive action against the evil that had permeated the shelter he'd provided for his wife, for their friends.

He gave Millie a gentle squeeze and kissed the top of her head, then went to find Chief Deputy Steadman. He was in the dining room, staked out at a table with a map and his two-way radio, neither of which seemed to be doing him much good.

"Two of our people are still out there, Sheriff," Frank said. "With the killer, and unaware of his identity. What's the plan?"

"We're going to pull together an old-fashioned posse. I'll leave Detective Frost here to cover home base. You and I will comb the ridge. Can you gather three or four men to go with us?"

"Give me ten minutes."

Cappy was pacing the deck outside the lounge, ready as a snapping turtle. Sandy Dawson hugged his wife and daughter, strapped a sheathed hunting knife to his belt, and gave a salute. Frank found Tim and Marie Strauss outside the vestibule in the basement, engaged in a seething argument.

"Sorry to interrupt, Marie," he said, "but I need your husband."

"Get in line," she said, turning hot eyes on him.

"Whatever you need from me," Tim said, "I'm in."

He shook off Marie's clutching hand and walked away without a backward glance.

As they climbed the stairs, Frank said, "Look, Tim, we're heading out on a search for a killer. We don't know what might happen out there. Do you really want those to be the last words Marie ever hears from you?"

Tim shrugged, but his face was tinged with shame.

Frank sighed and stopped at the top of the stairs. "Go on back," he said. "I'll wait but make it snappy."

As he watched Tim trudge back down the stairway, he considered including Hal Jeffries in their party, but hesitated. He'd never known Hal and Sandy to resist debating politics, and he didn't want to risk any distractions, however good-natured their arguments might be.

He was also concerned about thinning the home base contingency, so when Tim reappeared, it was just the five of them who left the clubhouse ten minutes later, heading up around the lake.

Into the ash-shrouded forest and the dark looming ridge beyond.

90

RILEY PADDLED WITH ABANDON, digging at the water's surface, harsh breath ripping from her throat.

The distance she had to cover was far shorter than Teren's, but his golf cart would travel faster and spare him physical exertion while she was wearing herself out. There were no docks on this forested stretch of the lake shore, and the water was murky, dotted with submerged and broken tree trunks.

She watched out for them, looming beneath the surface like surly ghosts, and her progress slowed as she was forced to steer a path between them. A creaking groan broke through the rhythmic slapping of her oars as the kayak scraped over the splinters of a water-logged tree, tendrils like fingers grasping at the boat, bringing it to a halt.

With a sob, Riley braced an oar against one of the stumps and pushed off. A shriek of protest sounded as the tree relinquished its hold and the kayak glided forward. Weak with relief and exhaustion, Riley aimed for a stretch of bank overhung with willowy branches, hoping she could use them to pull herself from the boat without taking a swim.

The sour smell of marshland was overpowering as she paddled among the husks of dried and broken cattails. She maneuvered the kayak under the shelter of the mossy trees, the mass of limbs providing handholds and concealing the boat. Riley scrambled from the cockpit with a minimum of splashing and rubbed her hands dry on her grubby jeans.

Crossing over the cart path, she wasted no time in attacking the uphill climb. Too frantic to bother seeking a trail, she barreled upward with a desperate need to lose herself among the bushes and trees. She noted the absence of the golf cart's drone, but took no comfort from it, never doubting that Teren would be close behind.

With luck, he wouldn't find the kayak beneath the drooping tree branches she'd used to pull herself to shore. Without that indicator, he might not be able to locate her entry point into the woods.

Riley's chest began to ache, and she realized she'd long ago lost the dust mask screening out the worst of the ash. She found a level piece of ground and stopped, pulling a water bottle from her pack. Her hands shook, and she felt too weak to unscrew the cap.

Moaning, fighting tears, she steeled herself and pried open the bottle. She gulped some of the water and felt the coolness of it spread through her chest, clearing it, calming her a little. She fitted a fresh dust mask across her mouth and nose and as she replaced the package, her fingers brushed hard metal.

The dart gun case.

She pulled out the metal box, popped the clip that held it closed, and examined the contents. A rough schematic was pasted into the lid of the box, showing how to load and operate the gun. Three darts, essentially syringes filled with some sort of sedating agent, rested in slots among the foam padding.

Each was tipped with a large-gauge hypodermic needle. A tuft of fibrous material fluffed out on the tail end so that each dart resembled a sleeker, more lethal badminton shuttlecock.

The kit included a dose of antidote in an injector like an EpiPen. Following the schematic, she loaded a tranq dart into the barrel of the gun. Tossing the case back into her pack, she shouldered it and resumed her uphill march, careful to hold the gun pointed away from herself as she climbed.

The smell of wood smoke reached her before she broke through into a small clearing. A battered hut leaned in the middle of the leaf-strewn circle of alder and pine, a thin stream of dark-gray smoke streaking up from the chimney, dissipating into the ashen sky.

An overwhelming surge of relief flooded over Riley, and she took a few running steps toward the cabin, then stopped. The impulse to throw herself on the mercy of a stranger was strong, but she realized the result might be disastrous.

If Teren traced her this far, the obvious hiding place would be this hut, and it was no fortress. It would likely offer little defense against a determined intruder, and the inhabitant was an innocent.

She thought of Myrna, whose only crime was being on the sideline when Teren attacked. Riley didn't want to involve a bystander when their chances of surviving were so small. Her only weapon was the dart gun, and who knew how effective that would be? What were the odds the cabin's occupant would have a rifle?

Weighing her options, she decided to press on over the ridge where she counted on finding safety in numbers.

She struck off, away from the cabin, and continued her climb. The mist of ash distorted both sound and vision as it wafted in the air, and a blanket of eerie silence hung over the forest. Riley felt a lull and thought of studies she'd read about deprivation chambers, the claim that floating in a medium devoid of sensory stimuli provided a release from stress and pain.

She suddenly understood the appeal, thinking how marvelous it would be to simply lie down on a bed of needles and let her troubles fade into the fog. The idea held an alarmingly hypnotic attraction. Riley shook her head to clear the notion and forced herself to plod on.

Her back ached under the weight of the pack, and she stopped to shift it off her shoulders and take another swallow of water. Somewhere, a twig snapped, and Riley froze, unable to tell if her own foot had done it, or someone else's.

With startling swiftness, a flurry of black birds broke cover and flew to the sky, nearly scaring a scream from her. As she stood gazing after them, a strong arm looped around her from behind, pulling her against a warm body.

Teren.

His breath feathered against her ear in soothing tones. "Don't be afraid, Riley. I'll protect you. You won't be needing this."

He yanked the dart gun from her fingers and hurled it yards away where it disappeared into a clump of underbrush.

"I've been watching over you for a long time, Riley," he crooned. "You can count on me. I know what's best."

She struggled against him, trying to gain a position where she could kick at his shins or stomp down on his foot.

"Did you know what's best when you murdered Harp Mayhew?"

He laid a gentle kiss against the shell of her ear.

"I never murdered anyone, Riley," he said, his voice soft and earnest. "I offered up a sacrifice, and I acted in our best interest."

She shuddered, swallowing hard to keep from retching.

"And now you're planning to kill me, too."

He stiffened. "I never wanted that, Riley. To extinguish your flame just as you're reaching your zenith distresses me more than you know."

He paused, his voice strengthening with conviction. "But she requires it, and as much as I will miss you, dear Riley, I must obey."

Riley still held the pack, and she worked her hand into it, fumbling for any kind of weapon. She hoped to find the Swiss army knife, but it evaded her hand. She needed to keep him in this expansive mood, giving her a chance to think, to form a plan.

"Who is *she*?"

"She?" His tone was surprised. "Why, Mother, of course. The mother of us all."

Riley's hand found the clasp on the metal case, and she worked to manipulate it, but it was slick, and her fingers kept sliding off.

"My mother and your mother are not the same," she said.

"Oh, but they are, Riley. Undoubtedly, they are."

The catch flew open, and Riley hoped she wouldn't encounter the needle end of a tranquilizer dart. Her fingers felt the fluff of a fletching and closed around it, taking it into her fist.

"What mother are you referring to?"

Teren's voice hardened. "Can you really be so ignorant, Riley? No wonder she's displeased."

He tightened his grip on her, as with a wayward child. "The Earth, Riley. I speak of Mother Earth."

Swinging her arm forward, Riley jabbed back with all her might, driving the dart deep into Teren's thigh. He screamed and fell back, letting her go.

Riley ran.

91

Topper stared into the fireplace, mesmerized by the whispering rustle and pop.

The flame was finished, and all that remained was a wisp of charred log and the lambent coals beneath it. He was debating himself over putting another log on, when the sound of pounding footsteps invaded the sagging porch of the hut.

Turning, he watched the knob twist and the door fly open. A wild female figure burst into the room, and he gaped at the mass of red-gold hair streaking back from a face covered by goggles and a sooty dust mask. The woman panted, making frantic motions in the air with shaking hands.

Pulling the mask from her face, she gasped, "Please help me. I'm sorry to break in like this, but I need your help."

Topper jumped up from his stool. "Of course."

The woman was distraught, and Topper wondered which of the many hazards brought by Rainier's eruption had put her in such a state. He tried guiding her to a chair, but she gripped his arm and pulled him toward the door.

"A man tried to kill me," she sputtered. "I've injured him, but I don't know how long he'll be incapacitated. We must go for help."

Topper resisted her pull. "Hold on," he said. This was not a hazard he'd anticipated. "Explain what you're talking about."

The woman fixed him with a pleading stare, but he stood firm. "I'm not going anywhere until I understand the situation."

She bit her lip, clearly unhappy about the delay, but began talking. Topper gathered the injured man was known to her, and that she believed he'd been intent on killing her, though she gave no reason for such a dubious action.

"I managed to stab him with a tranquilizer dart," she finished, "but I don't know how long that will last."

"What kind of agent did you use?" Topper asked.

She stared at him, lines of consternation forming on her brow. "I have no idea. I just grabbed what I could get my hands on."

"Let me see the case."

"For the love of Pete," she cried, "what does it matter?"

"Drug and dosage matters," Topper said.

With a strangled cry, she dropped her pack to the cabin floor and knelt beside it. Rummaging through, she seized a metal case and tossed it to him. He surveyed the contents, then snapped it shut and tucked it under his arm.

"All right. Let's go."

She bolted out the door and he followed. At the edge of the clearing, she waited for him to catch up.

"Which way?" he asked.

She looked confused. "I was headed up and over the ridge. There are people down there who can help."

"No, I mean which direction to the man you hurt?"

Her eyes widened and a flush spread up from her neck. Before she could tear into him again, Topper explained.

"I think it's best we know what we're dealing with. If he's dead, or if he's already up and moving."

She pressed her lips into a thin, disapproving line but led him in a northerly direction. Less than five minutes brought them to where a man lay sprawled in a churned-up patch of dirt and pine needles.

Topper gently nudged the body but got no response. Kneeling, he felt for a pulse, then ran his hands over the man's legs and arms, checking for weapons.

The woman stood well back, twisting her hands together, a worried moan escaping her lips at regular intervals, almost like a chant.

"Is he dead?" she asked.

"Nope."

"Deep under?"

Topper shrugged and stooped to brush the hair off the man's forehead and lift an eyelid to peer at the bloodshot orb beneath.

"So it appears."

He dropped to a knee and opened the metal case. Seizing the pre-loaded injector with the antidote, he plunged it into the man's thigh.

"What are you doing?" the woman shrieked.

"You have an appointment this afternoon," Topper told her. "I'm helping you keep it."

92

Riley was stunned.

The accumulation of stress, shock, and physical exhaustion dropped over her like a tangling net, trapping her in a nightmare from which there was no waking. She needed to move, to get away from these horrid men, but her feet wouldn't respond to the urgent message she sent out.

Her heart boomed in her chest, pushing out sickening waves of hot fear that washed through her extremities with an electric tingle. She watched the man from the cabin drop the spent injector into the case. He pressed his hand to Teren's neck, monitoring his pulse, and turned calm eyes in her direction.

His calculating expression broke through her malaise, acting as a spur. In one motion, she shed the pack from her shoulders and bolted uphill with a lurching gait as her feet slipped, then regained traction.

Sobs broke from her throat, and she grabbed onto them, using them as a woman in labor uses her utterances to muster strength. Pressing upward, she snatched at bushes and branches, heedless of the cuts and scrapes they carved into her hands.

She tossed a frantic glance over her shoulder and felt a surge of panic. The man behind her leapt and scrambled like an agile leprechaun, a determined gleam in his eye, lips stretched in a rictus of a smile.

Riley ran, her heart sinking, pulling her to the ground even as her eyes rose to the heavens, pleading, praying to be caught up, plucked out of the grasp of this demonic pursuer.

He hit her like a Peterbilt on a Yugo, sending her sprawling and coming down on top of her, pinning her to the pine needles.

He stretched over her, squeezing the breath from her body, and Riley's head swam in a darkening sea. As she neared total blackout, he rolled off her and she half-sat, gulping in lungfuls of air.

Before she could fully catch her breath, he swung a fist into the side of her head, knocking her flat and sending a burst of pain and white-hot light through her skull, like a brief glimpse of a Fourth of July sparkler.

Yanking her from the ground, he dragged her back in Teren's direction, his hands digging painfully into her armpits.

Teren was still prone, but moaning and stirring as he swam back to consciousness. Riley's captor kept one vise-like hand clamped on her forearm while he rooted through her opened pack with the other. Discovering the skein of twine, he pushed her face down to the ground and used it to bind her hands behind her back.

Riley struggled against him but achieved nothing beyond badly chafed wrists. "Who are you? Why are you doing this?"

He was slow to answer, waiting until he'd finished his task before rising with a grunt and giving her bottom a hard slap that stung through the denim.

"Let's save that for Teren to divulge."

A chill trickled over Riley's scalp like a sluice of ice water.

He knew Teren?

Turning her head away, she bit her lip and lay staring into a thicket of trees. The stranger placed one large hand atop her skull and twisted her head back toward Teren.

"Watch him," he commanded. "He'll be coming around any minute now."

Riley watched, her eyes burning with ash and fatigue, as Teren twitched and murmured. A shiver rippled through her, raising gooseflesh on her arms.

He had been her friend, beside her in her grief, and all this time, a murderer. He'd killed Harp and Rico, Rico's cook and butler, those people in Seattle. How many more?

As she wondered, a snippet of conversation from the clubhouse flitted across her mind. She remembered Teren's face as Nate asked about Amanda Horton. Teren had been Amanda's friend, also, and now she was dead. A lot of people Teren knew were dead.

He had known Jim and Tanner.

Like so many painful realities, she must have been pushing this thought from her brain for some time, not wanting to know, not being *capable* of knowing while keeping her sanity.

But she was entrenched on a journey of discovery, however unwillingly, and she had to face it now, the hard hand of a stranger forcing her to look, and to listen.

When Teren wakes up, I will know. But how can I bear it?

Teren let out a shuddering sigh. Riley stared into his face, the papery eyelids shut but flickering. A sickening dread crept over her, and she desperately wanted to look away, but the hand cradling the top of her cranium prevented her, tightening like iron bands when she tried.

She closed her eyes and was seized with instant panic. That was worse. She swallowed a sob and steeled herself, fastening her gaze on those blue-veined eyelids, and waited.

No birds twittered among the branches of trees. No living thing outside their circle hummed life into the day. Only the wind soughing gently through pine needles and Teren's sonorous breathing made a backdrop to the silence.

Riley watched Teren's chest rise and fall, counting the inhalations. When she reached sixty-three, she heard the hitch in his breath, and a groan.

Teren opened his eyes.

93

NATE TRUDGED ALONG A roughly defined trail, his feet growing heavier with each step.

For three hours he'd combed the wooded ridge above Mountain Vista without encountering a sign of another human being. He saw a lot of small woodland animals and sensed there were larger marauders skulking around, though he hadn't seen any since the mountain lion.

His chest felt tight, his eyes burned, and his tongue was furred over with ash and thirst. He sank to the ground and took a few swigs from the canteen on his belt.

An oppressive dimness hung in the sky. Lead-colored vapors of ash and mist hovered like a miasma, dampening his hopes, pulling him down like the deadly poppy field in The Wizard of Oz.

He poured a trickle of water over his face and rubbed the ash from his eyes.

What an insane situation. His thoughts went to his daughter, Sammi, and his ex-wife. He prayed they were safe.

And Rick? How had he fared through the eruption and its aftermath? It rankled Nate that he could do nothing to help. Not them, not Riley, not even himself.

Enough with the pity parade.

He pushed up and stood, straining his ears. A faint rustling to his left caught his attention and he took a tentative step toward the sound, pausing again to listen.

There was definitely something moving in the brambles and trees about twenty yards off. Something stealthy.

He took another careful step, watching to avoid twigs and pinecones that would crunch underfoot. Creeping slowly, he lifted vines and branches out of his way, peering forward for a glimpse of his quarry.

He stopped, no longer able to hear the sounds of movement ahead. Had he been too slow, or had the noises been only a product of stress and imagination? He stood frozen, holding his breath, listening hard.

The flesh on the backs of his arms prickled and crawled, responding to some dire frequency in the air, and a phantom chill raised the hairs along the back of his head.

As he poised, listening, a high scream tore through the ash-laced sky, thick with terror and pain, a series of high-pitched wailings laden with doom. A zing of fear raced down Nate's spine as he sprang forward, snapping open his holster as he ran.

He crashed through the underbrush, following the agonized screaming, and broke upon a small clearing in time to catch the merest glimpse of some creature disappearing into the woods. He'd interrupted the woodland dinner hour and saved a lucky animal from the menu.

What was it? Rabbit? Raccoon? He'd heard there were a lot of animals that produced an eerily human-like scream under duress.

The devastation from Mt. Rainier had hit the wild as hard as it had the civilized. Flooding had reduced the available dry land and Nate reflected there was bound to be an abundance of predators and prey taking refuge on the high ground, increasing the concentration of wildlife on the ridge.

He felt weak with relief. The screaming had sounded like a woman, but it hadn't been Riley.

The relief flickered out as a new stab of fear galvanized him. He had to find her. Their tame and domestic world had turned upside down and peril lay in every direction, pressing in.

His heart squeezed in his chest. Riley was out here alone.

Or, worse yet, with Teren.

94

Riley's throat ached.

She could barely swallow around the lump of fear and regret that lodged there, throbbing. She had been so close to escape, and now her plight was worse than ever, with two captors.

She sat on the ground, hands still bound behind her back and the twine pinched and irritated her skin. Teren knelt beside her, stroking her cheek with the back of his hand. His eyes, tender and wet, searched her face.

"Riley, darling Riley. I wish you could be happy about this. We're part of something far bigger than ourselves. Something momentous."

She looked away, hardening her jaw.

"You've suffered so much," he said. "But all that sorrow and heartache has nourished and stretched your artist's soul, Riley. You have gone from merely bright to brilliant like the sun."

As if he'd set a lit match to a trail of oil, a hot tongue of rage ripped through Riley. Her chest heaved as she struggled to control the roar threatening to break out of her.

She kept her head turned, unwilling to share even a glance with this man who'd deceived her, taken her family, broken her heart.

Teren placed a firm hand under her chin and brought her face around. Jerking her head free from his grasp, Riley sank her teeth into his thumb, grinding down.

He pulled away, cursing, wiping his bleeding thumb against his brown leather jacket. She watched him, tasting his blood, thinking she could tear his throat out with her teeth if he gave her the opportunity.

The stranger from the cabin sat lounging against a tree, his legs stretched before him, crossed at the ankles. He munched on peanut butter crackers he'd pilfered from her pack and seemed to be enjoying the show.

"Are you going to let her get away with that, big guy?"

"Stay out of it, John."

"Suit yourself."

He shrugged, taking another bite, and shot Riley a grin. Teren squatted down to her level, looking into her eyes without touching her.

"You're upset, and I can understand that. For you, things are happening too fast to fathom. But I've been waiting a long time for this, Riley. Waiting and preparing."

"Killing my husband and son, was that part of your preparation?"

She held his gaze now, determined at last not to run from the truth. A tinge of burgundy spread over Teren's cheeks and his eyes turned dark as if a cloud had crossed the sun.

Dipping his head in a bow of acknowledgment, he said, "Now you know, Riley. Now you know. Does it change anything?"

She stared at him, incredulous. "Why?" she screamed. The rope of fire blazed within her, twisting and snapping. "Why did you do it?"

"If you still don't get it, I don't know how I can explain it to you in the time we have left."

The man called John rose from his pine needle resting place.

"Keep her quiet," he said. "I'll be right back."

As John melted into the woods, a spike of desperate hope flashed through Riley. He'd seen or heard something that alarmed him.

Was help nearby?

Throwing back her head, she wailed like a siren. Teren was on her instantly, one hand clapped over her mouth, the other at the back of her neck, holding her head like a vise. She struggled uselessly against him, straining the muscles in her neck until she thought they would tear apart.

John came back, at a run. He stuffed a dirty rag into her mouth and secured it in place with a dust mask, tightening the rubber fastener against her cheek with a vindictive snap.

"We got company coming," said John. "They're a quarter mile down the ridge yet, probably making for the ranger shack. I'll go head them off. You take the woman that way," he said, pointing northwest, "and finish what you started."

Riley's heart swelled with hope as she watched John sprint away toward the south, the rhythmic *pfutt, pfutt* of his hiking boots fading into the forest.

They were out looking for her, and they were close.

Teren zipped and shouldered her pack, smoothing pine needles, erasing the signs of their presence here. He pulled her up and into his arms and she stiffened to show she wanted no part of him. He held her for a moment, stroking her hair, whispering against her ear, but she did not thaw.

Stepping back, he said, “Let’s go.”

Voice gone cold, his iron hand tugging her by the upper arm, Teren led her away from the spot where she’d come so close to defeating him. He led her away from help.

And away from hope.

95

"There's an old ranger's hut up the hill a piece," said Frank.

Chief Steadman nodded. "I've been there a time or two, hiking in from the canal side to make sure no one's turned it into a meth lab. We'll check it out."

Their little group pressed up the ridge, spread into a rough V-shape, looking and listening for any signs of Riley, Nate, or Teren. The air swirled with mist and ash, coating their skin and clothing with a grimy film.

The woods were quiet, the thudding of their boots strangely without resonance, as if the sounds were being sucked into a vacuum before they could leave an impression on the ear.

Frank tasted grit and spat, trying to clear it from his tongue. He felt nauseated, the ham sandwich and barbecue-flavored potato chips he'd eaten for lunch threatening a return appearance. How much of it was caused by the noxious air, and how much by his anxiety for Riley, was an equation that would remain forever unsolved.

The bottoms of his feet ached and throbbed. His plantar fasciitis was plainly along for the ride, but he pushed the pain aside, focusing on the terrain, on finding Riley.

The tall, tapering trunks of pine and fir thinned as they approached the clearing. A man in ragged jeans and a green-checked flannel shirt sat on the porch steps of the weathered and leaning hut.

His face was full of hollows, cheekbones jutting like carved stone. He had a knife in his hand and used it to whittle a Y-shaped stick that might be destined for a slingshot. He rose to his feet when he saw them, walking forward to shake their hands.

"I'm so glad to see you guys. It's getting kind of creepy up here, all on my own."

Chief Steadman nodded toward the hut. "That's Forest Service property."

The man looked startled, then bobbed his head in conciliation.

"Oh, I know. I know. I'll clear out and no harm done. I was driving to my aunt's house, over in Union, but the roads were washed out. I tried to hike over the ridge, but when I came across this little cabin I thought no one would blame me for taking a rest. Under the circumstances."

He still held the knife, and Frank noticed it was a KA-BAR, new-looking, without scratch or blemish. The guy's dirty blond hair stuck up in awkward patches and his teeth were slightly bucked, giving him the look of a hapless, underfed guinea pig.

He offered an apologetic smile and Chief Steadman let the subject drop, bringing up a new one.

"Have you seen anyone else up here? A woman, perhaps?"

"Oh yes, about half an hour ago. I called to her, but she ignored me."

"Which direction was she headed?

"That a-way." He gestured up the ridge to the southwest.

"And she was alone?"

"I didn't see anyone else with her."

Frank watched the chief, unable to read anything from his impassive face. The lawman reached for the canteen at his belt and took a pull, wiping his mouth with the back of his hand.

"All right, we'll be moving on. Take care you leave that facility the way you found it," he warned, indicating the ranger's hut. He gave the man a final nod and walked to the southwest tree line. Frank and the rest of the men followed.

"Our best bet for finding Teren is to find Ms. Forte," the chief said. "The man says she went this way and I've got nothing but my gut to tell me otherwise."

He paused, and Frank saw the muscles of his jaw tighten. "Let's fan out a little, but stay in shouting distance."

Frank felt as if he carried a lead ball in his stomach. The chief seemed to doubt the woodcarving stranger's word, but who could make sense of anything anymore? In the space of a few short days his civilized existence had morphed into something surreal and barely recognizable as his.

He crunched forward over a bed of crackling sticks and struck into the woods, spacing himself from the next guy, straining his eyes and ears for any trace of Riley's presence.

He was *not* going to lose his best neighbor.

96

THE MAN KNOWN AS Topper continued to whittle.

A light breeze lifted the hair off his forehead, stirring eddies of ash as he watched the posse of men spread out over the deepening shadows of the ridge, pressing off in the wrong direction.

He smiled. He got such a kick out of messing with people, making them do things. Crazy things. Stupid things.

Evil things.

It had been fun manipulating Candace, reeling her in like a fish, making her hot to please him and then watching her thrash on the line, pouting with those lush red lips and giving him the cold shoulder when she felt spurned.

She was so predictable. Fun, but not much of a challenge.

What a rush, though, when he'd moved the governor and the press with his 'impassioned pleas for public safety.' On his word, thousands of people had fled in panic. Some had managed to escape, but many had been caught, one way or another, keeping their appointment with Death.

He had been sorely tempted to stick around and enjoy the pandemonium, but wisdom dictated his removal to a safer clime. Even from a distance, it was a delight.

Rainier had unleashed an unprecedented cataclysmic event. But he'd beaten her to the punch, mobilizing a giant wave of humanity, making them dance to his tune. That's what he had so admired about David Johnston.

He'd moved the masses.

As a child, John Harrigan had been glued to the television coverage of Mount St. Helen's eruption, fascinated by how David had used scientific and persuasive means to impel the movement of so many. He'd convinced them to leave their homes, their cities and towns, and run, chased by fear.

That kind of potency thrilled him.

He had modeled his own rise on David's example and earned the nickname Topper because of his eagerness to climb to the peak of any mountain. He exulted in the feeling of power it gave him, but it wasn't as intense as the elation he experienced from snuffing out life.

John had never directly killed anyone. Never been the one to wield the knife or the gun, never put his hands around a woman's neck and squeezed, though he had no compunction about doing so.

He derived his greatest satisfaction from goading and manipulating others to do his will.

Of course, Teren didn't need much pushing. He'd been killing people under his own steam for decades and it was gratifying to inspire him and watch him work.

Teren had been choosing random folk, the low-hanging fruit, for his sacrificial knife. It was John who ramped up the stakes by suggesting he hand-pick select members of society, the ones whose deaths would really stir the pot.

John had been there, standing by, when Teren sliced open Michael Gagnon's throat, emptying the life from Boeing's big cheese, taking him from animated one moment, to inert in the next.

That had been their first joint effort. John had been along for Senator Brown's demise, as well. And he had watched, hidden in the trees, when Teren killed the rock star.

After that, they had parted ways.

They were both focused on Mt. Rainier, but their respective goals regarding the volcano were too diverse. After John achieved his aim of scrambling the population of western Washington, he had headed for Mountain Vista, figuring it would put him out of harm's way while possibly reuniting him with Teren for a little post-eruption fantasy fulfillment.

It seems Teren had been busy without him, and now there was the woman. He sensed Teren was ambivalent about killing her, blowing hot and cold.

He may have to do this one himself.

He wondered if he'd feel the same power pulsing through him like an ecstasy high when he slipped the blade into her. Would removing the middleman heighten the experience? Or dilute the thrill?

The question kindled his curiosity.

Setting his face to the north, he ascended the ridge, moving toward Teren and Riley. Toward an exercise in first-hand execution.

He needed to christen his new knife anyway.

97

RILEY STUMBLED ON LOOSENED stones, falling to her knees, tasting bitter blood from her bitten tongue.

Teren pulled her to her feet, taking the opportunity to whisper endearments in her ear. The man was chillingly deranged, treating her like the love of his life one moment, preparing to slit her throat the next.

She shuddered, realizing that, to him, this was consistent behavior. How had his madness escaped her notice for so long? He had always appeared so rational, so sympathetic and ready to help.

In his mind, he had been helping all along.

He prodded her forward, then clutched her arm and froze. A familiar sound had them both staring into the sky as a wavering, distorted whir filtered through the pine needles, sending a bright spear of hope through Riley.

A helicopter.

More help was arriving.

Teren lowered her to the ground. Standing over her, he pulled his knife from the sheath at his belt. Riley braced herself for the stroke of pain, the blow of death, but he only used it to strip some of the small, spindly branches from the surrounding oak and fir.

"This isn't the right way, Riley. This is not how it should be done."

His voice was full of sorrow, his face a mask of grief. She watched him gather and arrange sticks and stones to form a sort of pyramid and realized he was building an altar.

She hoped his attention might be so focused on his preparations that she could squirm to her feet and escape, but it was too long and awkward a process with her arms still bound behind her. Every time she began, he looked at her sharply, infusing her with the hopelessness of her situation.

He finished constructing the altar and turned to her, drawing the knife once again from its sheath. Kneeling beside her, he stroked her hair, pushing it away from her face.

Riley locked eyes with him. If they had come to their final moment, she intended to be fully present, holding him accountable for what he did to her.

Her heart pulsed madly, and the blood felt hot in her veins. Teren's eyes, as they looked into hers, were tender. His hand, touching her face, caressing her cheek, pleading with her to understand, was gentle.

"My mother taught me," he explained. "She understood the ways of the Earth, and I learned from her how to alleviate the danger, how to appease her wrath."

She saw the muscles in his arm tighten as his hand gripped the knife. He slipped it between her wrists and cut the twine, freeing her hands. And then, in an instant, the blade was against her throat, ready to slice.

"The world has forgotten. They desecrate the Earth, using her, stripping her, raping her."

His voice was harsh, and the edge of the knife was tight enough against her neck to draw blood. She felt it dripping into the collar of her shirt.

"I will honor you, Riley, and she will accept my sacrifice."

His face crumpled and his eyes turned wet. He lifted his head and shouted to the sky. "I always do my part!"

The man from the cabin stepped out from the trees.

"Yes, you do," he said, his voice both consoling and encouraging. "You do, Teren. So do it now. The time is ripe."

Teren's eyes swung back to Riley's, and he lowered his face, kissing her hard on the mouth. His chin was like a stone, grinding against the softness of her lips, tearing at their tenderness.

She felt anger in him, and it sparked with her own. She tossed her head to separate herself from him, and the knife at her throat sliced a bit deeper. It stung, and she felt more blood, slick and warm, sliding down her neck.

"She's waiting, Teren," the detestable stranger warned. "Don't disappoint."

The man's voice had grown mocking and he came to stand beside them. Riley felt the power he wielded and hated him. She turned bitter eyes on him, but Teren forced her face back to his.

"Never mind him, Riley. Look at me. You are a hero."

He spoke like a proud parent, bolstering a child's confidence. "I salute you as one of the honored few who've given everything. You've earned praise and glory in my eyes, and in the eyes of—"

His eyes flew wide as he broke off and fell forward against her. Riley stared down at the knife protruding from his back, at the crimson stain blooming like an opening rose, soaking the fabric of his cotton shirt and dripping to the earth.

The man from the cabin smiled. “What a mind-sapping windbag.”

He gazed down at his blood-smeared hands, a look of wonder and pleased discovery on his face.

Riley recognized opportunity.

She pushed free of Teren’s body and ran for the trees.

98

Rick stared down through the helicopter's globe-like windshield, marveling at the devastation caused by the eruption.

Bobbi was following the waterway now, tracing along a finger of the Puget Sound. Rick swallowed hard, surprised to see that even this far out, there was massive flooding.

Through patches of ash, he saw logjams of trees piled into the crevices of the inlet. Debris of every description floated or lodged in the chocolate brown, foamy flow. Bridges had been torn off their pilings, huge bites of road lost to the voracious stream. Communications towers leaned or slumped in the morass, wires severed and splayed.

He had done the right thing. He'd pulled out all the stops. He was going to make it.

"We're close now," he told Bobbi, pointing northwest. "Somewhere in there is where we'll want to land."

She nodded. "Find us a spot."

Above the place where the water formed a bay, Rick picked out the fairways and greens of the Mountain Vista golf course and the house-lined lanes threading among them. The approach road to the neighborhood had been washed away in large chunks, but the interior roads appeared to be undamaged.

In the heart of the clustered houses, beside the lake, he saw the clubhouse parking lot.

Perfect.

"Put us down right there," he said, pointing.

Bobbi was already heading toward the square of asphalt when the engine began to choke and sputter. Rick looked at the fuel gauge and then at Bobbi.

"No malfunction this time," she said. "We've got just enough to see us to the target."

Rick's view of the parking lot clarified as it grew nearer, and he could make out the type and color of the few vehicles parked along one edge. The white lines defining the separate spaces solidified.

They were nearly there.

As they glided in low, the helicopter suddenly pulled out of trim, veering and bucking like a rodeo show horse. Rick braced himself in his seat. His gaze flew to Bobbi's face, and he was dismayed to see her frowning in surprise as she adjusted the controls and continued forward.

A sound like an angry buzzsaw burst at them from behind. The helicopter jerked and began to rotate.

"Shoot," Bobbi shouted. "Tail rotor must have hit something."

They spun crazily over the pavement, dipping and swaying in dizzying circles.

"We need speed," Bobbi yelled.

She accelerated and gained some control as they zoomed away from the parking lot and rose again into the sky.

"How do we get down?" Rick asked.

Bobbi had recovered some of her normal spunk, though her face was still pale. She grinned.

"It'll have to be a run-on landing. Like an airplane," she shouted.

Rick stared down at the eighteenth fairway. It extended along beside the clubhouse about a hundred and fifty yards, curved slightly, and continued for another fifty yards before reaching the green. A par three.

"Gonna be one heck of a divot," Rick said.

As Bobbi sent the helicopter higher, maneuvering to make the approach, the engine spluttered again. Bobbi bit her lip, a look of dogged determination gleaming in her eyes.

"I gotta somehow coax forty knots out of this thing," she said, "or we're just a chunk of metal falling out of the sky."

Rick looked down and saw several tiny people gathering at the edge of the parking lot. They waved or shaded their eyes, peering up at the spectacle. Rick hoped the helicopter wouldn't give them much of a show.

Sorry to disappoint, folks, but we're gonna put her down nice and easy.

Rick's stomach sank as they descended fast, skimming the trees at the edge of the tee-off area.

"Oh yeah, baby," Bobbi said, her voice full of elation. Rick felt a small bump and a bounce, followed by a more pronounced thud as the skids made solid contact with the ground.

They glided along the fairway like a kid on a sled. The slick grass did little to slow their advance as they skied toward the looming pines on the other side of the green.

Rick kept his eye on the little flag marking the cup. They plowed over it, a precision shot, and cannonballed into the trees.

The body of the helicopter bulldozed a phalanx of reedy bushes, sliding between tree trunks, the blades splintering apart as they met the sturdy pines. With a resounding *smack,* the nose of the aircraft smashed into a solid trunk, and they came to a stop.

Rick's ears buzzed, driving all other sounds from his head. He was deaf.

He watched Bobbi remove her helmet and make speaking motions with her mouth. Bits of chopped up branches and pine needles showered down in a silent rain, cascading off the spider-web fractured glass bowl of the windscreen.

He shook himself, valsalva-ed his ears, and let out a huge yawn. His hearing returned.

"You alright, soldier?" Bobbi asked.

Her voice was like music, a sweet and beautiful sound. He took her face in his hands and kissed her, full on the lips.

She let it linger for a long moment but pulled away at the sound of running people approaching the wreckage.

"Smart decision kissing me," she said. "You know, if you had kissed the ground—"

"Right. I remember. A punch in the face."

She laughed and squeezed his hand. "Not the smoothest landing I've ever made, but we're in one piece."

"Even my dental work and chest hair survived intact."

Bobbi raised an eyebrow. "I may have to verify that, soldier," she warned.

Rick grinned as the rescue team arrived.

"I'll look forward to it."

99

Riley tore through the pines, slipping, scrambling.

Frantic.

Moss-covered tree trunks stretching to the sky, carpet of ash-frosted ferns, rugged stones and crumbling earth. All became part of a nightmare she couldn't escape.

Distorted by her terror, they took on monstrous proportions and sinister intent, grasping at her, towering over her, aiding in her demise.

A sense of finality seeped cold into her veins, and she knew at last her time had come. This insidious man would not hesitate to kill her. Her long battle on the ridge was drawing to a close and she would die without honor, without victory of any sort.

She ran, no longer caring whether it was uphill or down, east or west, the thudding of her feet matching the frenzied beat of her heart.

The sky, thickened by ash and the falling dusk, was a heavy blanket impeding her progress, causing her to stumble over brambles and roots. Gray light filtered down through long-needled branches like a dim glow from a grimy bulb, illuminating just enough to keep her from running headlong into the looming trunks.

Without looking back, Riley gauged how far behind he was by the sound of his thrashing through the brush. She was a good span ahead.

But he was gaining on her.

A dark shape materialized in front of her, a form in motion, and she was stunned into stillness when she recognized it as a bear cub. A baby bear meant mama was close by, and likely to be fiercely protective.

One way or another, Riley seemed destined to meet death on the mountain tonight.

Her hesitation cost her the lead and the man called John was nearly on her now. Galvanized, she sprang away from the cub and mustered all her energy for a desperate sprint, but gasped in pain as John snatched her by the hair.

He swung her against him, and she slammed hard into his chest, expecting to feel the sharp, severing sting as he drove the knife into her. But he had no blade.

Instead, she felt a harrowing shiver spear through her as he spoke into her ear.

"Teren was a purist for blood and fire. He adhered to a stringent method whenever he could."

Riley clamped down on the whimper rising in her throat.

"But me, I'm a beginner at the hands-on stuff, Riley," he explained. "My knife didn't want to let loose from Teren's ribs, but as it happens, I'm open to experimentation."

His hands closed around her neck.

"A knife in the back was quick and efficient, a good way to end Teren. But squeezing the life out of you while I look into your eyes—that sounds more my style."

His lips curved in a smirk of pleasure as his hands tightened on her throat, thumbs pressing against her windpipe, cutting off her breath.

His eyes, so dark, so dilated, locked onto hers and she couldn't look away.

He seemed to be pulling the life from her, sucking it into himself through those ravenous eyes. She struggled, but he was fueled by passion and a wiry strength, and she made little headway.

Her limbs felt heavy, filled with sand like an hourglass that has reached the end. Darkness pushed in at the edges of her vision and she let her eyes fall shut.

He shook her viciously. "Look at me!"

Her eyes fluttered open, and she cut her gaze to where she'd seen the cub. It was still there.

He followed her line of sight, and his hands went slack, shock loosening his grip. Thrusting an elbow into his belly, Riley pushed away from him, clambering three steps toward freedom before he clasped her upper arm with a hand like an iron band, keeping her a prisoner.

A sudden angry roar shook the ashen sky.

Mama was on the scene, standing upright and bellowing her displeasure. A spike of terror speared down through Riley's scalp, sending out waves of agonizing fear.

Bits and pieces of her life flashed through her feverish brain—not her whole life, as convention holds, but snippets. Her father teaching her Minuet in G as her feet swung below the piano bench, his large hand, tanned and agile on the keyboard beside her small one.

Her mother, hair tied back in a crimson scarf, running to launch a kite into the sky, laughing with delight, the sprinkle of freckles across her cheeks standing out against her flushed skin.

Her son, Tanner, wrapped in a periwinkle blue blanket and handed to her moments after delivery, still warm from her womb, tiny, wrinkled, and red, the most beautiful creature she'd ever seen.

Jim, dropping her off at the airport for another tour, his face twisted with an expression she'd read as equal parts regret and irritation as they'd kissed goodbye and she watched him drive away, not meeting her gaze in the rear-view mirror.

These images passed through her fevered brain in a split second, followed by the incongruous memory, decades old, of a camp song about a bear in tennis shoes.

What course of action should she seize upon? Should she try to climb a tree? Run?

She'd once read a book where someone escaped a bear by running downhill because bears can't run well on a downgrade. Something about their hind legs.

But no, now she remembered learning that was a fallacy.

What to do?

The man, John, stood transfixed, staring at the she-bear towering over her young. He'd frozen, his hand around her arm like an ice-bound vise, spreading despair through her veins.

As hope and energy drained from her, a new image flashed on the screen of her memory. Teren, beside a backdrop of moss-draped branches, bracing his paddle against the gentle current, teaching her about crickets.

Sometimes, when danger threatens, it's best to be still. Like the crickets.

Teren had done so much harm in her life. It would take years to realize the extent of the damage. But he had given her this nugget, and it came when she needed it.

Be still.

John let out a harsh, rasping wheeze. Letting go of her arm, he shoved her toward the outraged bear and shot away, running downhill, disappearing into the forest, the sound of his footfalls like the thump of a battleground tom-tom.

Riley froze, keeping her head down to avoid eye contact, watching from under the fringe of her hair. Mama bear fell to all fours, sniffing at her child, pacing in a fit of nervous pique.

Alarm gripped Riley and she wanted to wipe her mind clear of it, certain the bear would smell her fear. She stood frozen, not even breathing, willing her heartbeat to quiet, the rush of blood through vein and artery to slow into silence.

The she-bear let out an irritated growl and the hair on Riley's arms rose and tingled, sending a tremor through her body. Continuing to roar, the bear reared up again, complaining to the sky.

Riley felt the earth tremble as the bear's heavy front paws dropped onto the forest floor a scant ten yards from where she crouched. The angry mama snorted and shook her woolly head, then took off in a loping run, following John's scent.

Riley melted in a heap of relief. A violent shaking afflicted her legs so that she could barely move, but she had to put some distance between herself and the cub.

Once again, she set her face up the ridge, feeling a kinship with the Greek King Sisyphus. Sucking in a deep and tremulous breath, she steeled herself to persevere.

Forcing her way forward, she wound along a rough trail through the birch and pine. A minute passed and then, from far downhill and hovering on the misty air, she heard a tattered human cry, drawn-out and eerie against the hush of the darkened forest.

Riley stopped moving and strained her ears, listening for more sounds of the distant clash. But there was nothing.

Deep weariness suffused her, touched with sorrow and loneliness. She was spent. She wanted nothing more than to sink onto the needle-covered ground and sleep for a week. She settled for leaning against a tree to catch her breath.

Teren had taught her about the crickets, and that knowledge had saved her life. There was wisdom in the silence of crickets, a safeguard from danger.

But another wisdom, just as profound, was woven into the crickets' song.

They sang to the end, hopeful of finding a mate, of making a connection, of leaving a legacy. They reached out with their music and, in the end, their need to connect surpassed their fear, their urge to remain silent.

They bestowed their night song—a nocturne—and with a strange cadence quivering in her chest, Riley realized this might be hers.

Her nocturne in ashes.

The rough bark of the pine left its impression in the palm of her hand. Riley shifted her position, leaning her back against the sturdy tree.

She stood for a long moment, swaying gently with the rhythm of the soaring pine. Breathing in. Breathing out. Savoring the stillness and peace. She stood waiting in the silence of the gathering dark.

Until the crickets began to sing.

100

RICK WINCED AS DR. Deb probed his ribcage, her fingers waking the sleeping pain and making it dance to the beat of his heart.

"Sorry about that," she said. She'd patched a cut on his face and given him some aspirin for the headache, but there was little she could do about the ribs.

"You'll be sore for a couple of days, but I think it's just bruising. Nothing broken."

He thanked the veterinarian and eased back into his shirt, fastening the buttons as he joined Bobbi at a table in the dining room. She was nursing a cup of coffee and a bandaged wrist. Beneath the table, her foot rested on a stool, ice packed around the swollen ankle.

He gave her a rueful grimace. They'd been knocked around a bit, but they'd both been lucky, sustaining only minor injuries from the chopper's demise.

"Congratulations," he said. "You set out to destroy a helicopter and I think no one could argue that you did a bang-up job."

She smiled, but Rick thought he saw a twinge of regret in her eyes.

"What about you?" she asked. "You made it to your destination."

"Yes," he sighed, "but no closer to my goal. I still haven't found my partner or the suspect."

Rick had been disappointed to find that the vital piece of information he'd worked so hard to deliver was redundant by the time he arrived. Teren was old news.

"So, what are you going to do about it?" Bobbi challenged.

Rick sagged, slumping in the chair, rubbing at his burning eyes. He desperately wanted to slide to the floor and saw some logs.

"I'm going to get a bite to eat, drink about six cups of coffee, and head for the hills."

Bobbi saluted him with her eyes. "Good for you."

Rick rose from the table, intent on finding some food. As he approached the kitchen, a woman came through the swinging door, carrying a pot of coffee and a plate of bread.

"You go on and sit down," she said, waving him back to the table. "I'll find something for the both of you to eat. I'm Millie," she told them, placing the bread on the table and filling Rick's coffee cup. "My husband, Frank, is out with the Chief Deputy, looking for our Riley."

Rick frowned, his inner radar stirring. "I thought they were after Teren Kirkwood, the man responsible for the murders."

Millie's face crumpled and the hand holding the coffeepot trembled, creating a storm of dark liquid inside the bulbous glass. Bobbi scooted over and patted the bench seat.

"Sit down, Millie. All of this must have been very distressing."

Millie sank to the cushioned bench, relinquishing the near-empty coffeepot. She pulled a cloth napkin from underneath a place setting and dabbed at her eyes, bleeding the last of her mascara onto the pristine linen.

"I'm so terrified for Riley. None of us ever suspected Teren and I think she's really fond of him. She won't be on her guard if he finds her."

Rick's heartbeat quickened. He was under the impression the suspect had fled up the ridge and that Nate and the Sheriff's posse were in pursuit. This was the first he'd heard about a woman in the mix.

"Who's Riley?" he asked. "And will you explain what she's doing out there?"

Millie nodded, but needed a moment before she could speak.

"Riley's the sweetest girl, our neighbor, and a fabulous concert pianist. She's a widow, been going through a real rough patch."

She paused, patting the napkin to her eyes once more. "She was helping Detective Quentin with his investigation, but when it started to look like *he* was the murderer—"

Rick choked on a sip of coffee. He coughed and wiped his mouth, staring at her. "You thought *Nate* was the killer?"

"Well, *I* never did," Millie assured him. "But some people started saying he wasn't who he claimed to be and since he was the only stranger among us..." She gave an apologetic shrug.

"I can guess who started that rumor," said Bobbi.

"Yes, well, it must have been Teren," Millie agreed, "but we all thought he was such a nice man. People listened to him."

"So, what happened with Riley," Rick asked.

"She took off early this morning, when it was still dark. She told Dr. Deb she was going up over the ridge to bring help we could trust. When Teren found out, he went after her."

Rick finished his coffee and pushed the cup aside. "And Nate went after Teren?"

"Of course, but I think his real concern was finding Riley. I knew he suspected Teren, though I couldn't believe it at the time. He was frantic to find Riley before Teren did."

Rick stood, snatching a slice of bread from the basket. "Scratch my dinner order," he said. "I'm heading out now."

He checked his weapon and took the dust mask and flashlight Millie offered. The sun was lowering in the sky, leaving him with about an hour and a half of daylight. Skirting the lake at a near run, he tried to determine the best point to break and head uphill. He passed a trail opening, but instinct kept him on the lakeside path.

His attention was focused on the ground rising on his right flank and he almost missed the patch of scarlet peeking from a mass of willowy overhanging branches at the edge of the lake. A quick investigation revealed a deserted sea kayak. The water-slicked seat and broken twigs above told him it had not been long abandoned.

Following the signs from the boat to the edge of the sloping forest, he found his entry point.

Scanning the terrain, he picked up the spoor, noting overturned rocks and spindly branches stripped of leaves, suggesting they'd been used as handholds by a desperate climber.

The angle of his ascent leveled off a bit as he tracked the signs of passage, winding through moss-coated tree trunks and low-lying ferns.

He was late to the party, and it gnawed at him. He needed to make up some time. The evening breeze rustled through, stirring the ash beams which floated on the air, carrying a curiously chemical odor.

Rick grunted in frustration as he reflected on the completely botched situation.

Cal had told him he had one shot at this, one chance to convince the board he had what it takes. And he trusted Cal to give it to him straight.

They had trained together as SEALs and Rick would have sworn Cal meant it all those years ago when he said the SEALs were the highest and the best and he was in it for the long haul. Rick had been buoyed by those words, and then disillusioned when Cal left the team after only four years and joined the police force.

Cal's performance with the cops was nearly legendary, and Rick's reaction went from disillusionment to dismay when Cal next left the force and disappeared.

Nearly two years passed with no word from his best buddy and then one day he showed up and invited Rick out for tacos.

Cal was cautious in his conversation over chips and salsa, but by the time their fish tacos were served, Rick had formed the distinct impression he was working for a very low-profile, well-placed private organization that fights crime and injustice around the globe.

Over bowls of deep-fried ice cream, Rick told Cal he wanted in.

"Oh, you don't pick them, they pick you," Cal said.

"So, what do I do?"

Cal simply gave him a look that said figure it out.

"Okay, I get it. I follow your lead. I get all the training and experience I can out of the SEALs, follow that up with investigative training on the police force, and then what?"

"Make it to detective. They'll be watching and take it from there."

They had been watching.

They took it from there by placing a phone call, telling him it was time for the test. A cold, disembodied voice informed him that his first case as homicide detective would determine his future.

The higher profile, the better.

He was on trial, and Rick had been elated to land the Puget Sound Slasher case, certain he could shine and prove his worth. He'd been pumped and confident, ready to go.

And then Rainier blew her top.

Unbelievable timing.

Rick pushed through the forest underbrush, remaining vigilant for meaningful signs. Half an hour passed, and the sky had grown dusky when something ahead caught his eye.

Almost transparent, it gave a feeble glint in the waning light, barely noticeable. Rick squatted, identifying it as a cellophane wrapper that had contained peanut butter crackers, recently discarded. He remembered how U.S. troops in Vietnam had been easily tracked by the trail of Kool-Aid packages they left behind.

Americans and their litter.

He rose and continued forward. The raucous call of a crow rang out, answered by more cries and the fluttering of wings. Rick stooped under an arch of low-hanging branches and entered an opening among the tall pines.

In the clearing, black birds congregated in a flurry of activity, ripping into a fresh kill. Even in the gathering dark, Rick could see it was a human body.

He ran forward, shouting and waving his arms to scatter the scavengers. They fell back into the tree line, but lingered there, resentful and watching.

The handle of a knife jutted from the prone man's back. Rick turned the body on its side, checking for any signs of life, but the guy was truly dead. Rick looked at the face and his breath caught in his throat.

Fumbling the flashlight from his pocket, he switched it on and shone it over the dead man, focusing the beam on his face. He stared for a long while, comparing it to his memory of the photo driver's license in the Slasher case file.

A grim feeling of satisfaction settled over him.

He'd found his man.

101

Nate saw the pale handkerchief materialize in the middle distance before him.

No longer pristine white, it fluttered where he'd tied it onto the stub of a branch early that morning, marking the start of his search grid. This was the third time he'd encountered it as he'd circled back in his fruitless combing over the ridge.

He fought a sense of deepening gloom. It claimed the forest, and it claimed his soul.

He'd heard the stuttering sound of a helicopter and knew help was coming, but that had been more than an hour ago and still he'd seen no one. Should he have gone back to the clubhouse to reconnoiter with the new arrivals?

No, he needed to find Riley and with every passing moment he felt it more urgently. What could she have been thinking to head out on her own like that? This mountain was rife with hazards. A dozen different tragedies might have befallen her out here.

If she'd made it over the ridge, she was safe, and might even have been the one to summon the helicopter crew. But his gut told him she was still out here, exposed and in danger.

He needed to find Teren, too, and he hoped to heaven they weren't together. Nate wished he had his partner to help cover the area. He'd made a mistake allowing Rick to go off on his own, but he'd wanted to give the rookie detective some space and see what he'd do with it.

He'd chosen Rick to help him with this case because he saw grit and determination there, and because he'd gotten a hefty nudge from the boss. Nate wasn't the only one who had eyes on Rick.

Someone was fast-tracking him.

He passed under the handkerchief, suppressing a groan as he started another round of searching. He struck off in a different direction, hoping the variation would bring a better result.

The light had dwindled to a matte gray, giving everything a flat look and a feeling of unreality, as if it were nothing but a set on a darkened stage. Night noises provided a gentle soundtrack, evening breeze and cricket song.

Nate stopped, pulling the mask from his face. He cupped his hands around his mouth and barked out a shout.

"Riley!"

It was hopeless. He drew a deep breath.

"Riiileeeeey!"

"I'm here, Nate!"

He almost yelped in surprise. Her voice sounded so near. He stumbled toward it, and she appeared out of the misty pines, running to him.

He wrapped himself around her and held on, absorbing her trembling, overwhelmed by the relief that swept through him. And then another voice cut through the woods, reinforcing Nate's quivering sensation of unreality.

"Is that you, Nate?"

Rick?

Nate watched his partner step into view. Riley grinned up at him, delight dancing in her eyes.

"I've brought company." she said.

Nate was stunned. Two minutes ago, he'd been missing them both and in despair over the shambles he'd made of everything. And now...

"Now," he told them, "we just need to catch up with our suspect. The man's name is—"

"Teren Kirkwood?" Rick interrupted. "Yeah, that's what I risked life, limb, and liberty getting out here to tell you."

So, the kid *was* good.

"He's killed a lot of people, Rick. We can't let him get away."

"He's not going anywhere," Rick assured. "I can take you to him now, if there's anything left to see. This place is crawling with predators out for a meal."

Nate gave a fervent nod.

"Yeah, tell me about it."

102

RICK CHOSE THE RESTAURANT but hadn't realized he'd need a reservation.

Chico's had come up in the world since he'd last met there with Cal, and the place was packed, tray-laden servers threading their way through a maze of noisy tables, trailing the seductive scent of hot grease and cilantro.

The buzz of conversation competed with piped-in Mariachi and cheers from the football fans gathered in the bar. Rick watched the hostess seat a table of twelve, passing menus and fielding questions, the smile never slipping from the broad planes of her pleasant face.

As she returned to her station, he stepped forward to meet her.

"What are the chances you've got a quiet table hidden somewhere?"

"You maybe heard about the snowball in hell? How many in your party?"

"There will be three of us."

She consulted a seating chart. "I can put you in D," she gestured to a distant alcove, "but there's a birthday party going on in there and it won't be quiet. Or you can sit in the bar."

Rick shook his head. "Don't you have a private room?"

She regarded him, head cocked. Rick gave her a hopeful smile.

"No one is booked in the banquet room tonight," she told him.

"I'll take it."

"It seats thirty-six and there's a two-hundred dollar minimum."

Rick winced. It had to be Chico's, and it had to be tonight. He rejected the thought of doing it anywhere else, feeling the compelling tug of tradition.

"Do you take Visa?"

She led him up a stairway to a room with a large central table and a few satellite booths with seating for four. Television monitors were mounted in two of the corners and Rick chose a smaller table under one of the TV sets.

"Do you have a remote for that?" he asked, indicating the TV.

She found it for him, took his drink order, and left. Rick thumbed a button and turned on the TV, scanning for a news station, keeping the volume low.

Nate and Riley wouldn't arrive for another fifteen minutes, and he liked to stay on top of the fallout from the volcano. Two weeks had passed since the eruption, and chaos still reigned, though Seattle and the surrounding areas were rallying with determined cheer.

Rick had spent much of that time at an isolated island training center. With Cal.

He'd been whisked there soon after his reunion with Nate, leaving his partner to wrap up the details of the case. They'd had little time to compare notes and share their separate experiences.

That was the reason for tonight's dinner date.

When he'd found Teren's body, Rick knew he'd have problems keeping predators away long enough to get a crime scene unit out there. The battery on his cell phone lasted just long enough for him to take several photos in the waning light, doing his best to document the scene, and fearing it wouldn't be enough.

As he scribbled notes on a pocket pad, he heard someone passing through the underbrush and tensed. Was it Teren's killer? A knife in the back didn't exactly square with self-defense. He didn't know who'd killed the man, or why.

Rick had crept into the tree line, crouching low and straining his eyes to see who was passing. He was surprised to discern the figure of a woman and knew it must be the Riley he'd been hearing so much about.

He tried not to alarm her as he stepped out from the trees and introduced himself. Frightened at first, she rallied well and told him what had happened with Teren and John. While they were talking, they heard Nate's shout.

During the hours that followed, Rick learned a lot more about Riley. He'd been so intrigued that he told Cal about her during their long debriefing, and Cal had followed up with several phone calls to Nate.

After that, those higher up the food chain than Cal had taken the ball.

The hostess brought his Samuel Adams, trailing Nate and Riley behind her. Rick rose and clasped hands with Nate, giving Riley a big grin.

"Enjoy your vacation?" asked Nate. "Way to shuffle off and leave me with all the paperwork."

"Hey, I did my share of paperwork on the front end, remember? Is it true you never found the guy?"

Nate shook his head. "Mama bear must have swallowed him whole."

"And we still don't even know who he is?"

Riley scooted onto the bench seat, making room for Nate. "Teren called him John," she said. "I met with a sketch artist, so we have a likeness."

"But so far, no good leads on identity, and he's still at large." Nate said.

Riley raised her hands in exasperation. Turning to Rick, she said, "Nate's left me hanging in suspense about what's going on. Some bullpucky about not discussing an open case."

A grimace passed over Nate's face. "I'm sorry, Riley. I'll come clean tonight. I promise."

He leaned forward, fixing a gaze on Rick that left no doubt he was in supervisor mode. "But before I do," he said, "I want to hear more about your process at the beginning, Rick. How did you settle on Teren as the suspect?"

Rick cleared his throat. "Sure, I'll happily reveal my genius. After you took off to follow up on the jacket—"

"Which you thought was a dead-end," Nate reminded.

"Don't rub it in, man. That still smarts."

Rick swallowed a mouthful of beer. "I got lucky," he said. "The crime techs performed a miracle. They were able to raise a print off a rock, and that gave me a name. Then all hell broke loose, and I couldn't get out of town, so I used the time to find out all I could about Teren Kirkwood."

Leaning back, Rick watched his two friends, enjoying their expectant faces, drawing out the suspense.

"He taught for a while at UDub in Tacoma," he told them. "I found a case folder from the campus police reporting how a student had filed a complaint against Professor Kirkwood, claiming that he acted 'weird' and was inappropriately enthusiastic about a rash of animal sacrifices that had been found on and near the campus."

"Ugh," Riley said. "That sounds like Teren."

Rick nodded. "Teren was investigated, but there was nothing to substantiate the complaint, and it was dismissed. The report suggested the kid had a beef with the professor because he was pulling a D in the course."

"A reasonable conclusion," Nate admitted. "If there was nothing else to go on."

"The person, or persons, responsible for killing the animals," Rick continued, "was never apprehended. That perked up my antennae."

The waiter arrived to take their orders. As he left, Nate picked up the thread.

"I've been able to piece together some background," he said. "Let me give you a picture of Teren's psychological profile. He was born to a hippie couple who lived off the land in grand nomadic style, occasionally picking up citations for vagrancy or loitering."

"Teren came from hippies?" Riley asked, shaking her head. "I thought I knew the man."

"From what I can tell, the family roamed mostly through Colorado and New Mexico, camping in a tent and worshiping nature. The mother in particular was an earth worshipper. Who knows what kind of whacked-out stuff she taught the poor kid."

Nate's face took on a pained look. "She died when he was eleven, taken by pneumonia during a cold snap."

Riley shuddered, and Rick noticed two lines furrowing her forehead.

"His mother warped him, gave him a kind of brain damage," she said, her voice low and forlorn. "I can't believe I knew him for two years and never saw the madness in him."

"He hid it well," Nate said, giving her shoulders a brief squeeze. "After the mother died, dad took a job as janitor and night watchman for a funeral home, and they lived on the premises. That's a morbid place to bring up a child, and no doubt Teren witnessed a lot of things a young boy just shouldn't see."

"He was smart, though," Rick said. "By the time he reached college, he'd learned to excel within the academic framework and gained the respect of his peers."

"What about his wife and child?" Riley asked. "He told me they died in a forest fire."

"That's true," said Rick. "According to the information I uncovered, Teren's wife and his daughter were the only human casualties in a small wildfire that spread through a forest near Snow Lake. But here's what I find interesting—"

He broke off to finish his beer and gather his thoughts. "The news coverage on the fire was scanty, due to the fact the media were busy elsewhere, covering a series of natural disasters. That was a particularly vicious hurricane season and there was a big earthquake in Peru."

Riley gasped, her eyes widening. "Are you insinuating what I think you are?"

The look in her eyes went from incredulous to haunted. Rick almost felt the energy drain from her as she drooped in her seat.

"There's no way to prove it now," he said. "But it's definitely suggestive."

Riley's head bent low over the table. When she lifted it, her eyes were hard and brilliant, like petrified fire.

"He killed *my* family," she said. "I don't find it difficult to believe he murdered his own."

Nate put his hand over her clenched fists on the tabletop. No one spoke.

Rick felt the truth in what she said, and wondered how many more deaths should be laid to Teren's account. Nate's next words echoed his thoughts.

"The man certainly spread havoc and misery. Hal Jeffries suffered an overdose when he drank too many cups of spiked coffee intended for Sandy Dawson while he and Teren stood watch over Myrna. Teren was desperate to keep Myrna from waking up and blowing his beautiful cover."

"Is Hal all right?" Rick asked.

"It looks like he'll pull through, but he was comatose for long enough to give his wife a real scare."

Riley smiled. "Actually, I can report in on Hal's current condition. I was at the Newcombe's last night and Hal and Sandy were back at it, sniping and cannonballing each other with political fodder. He's all back to normal."

"Glad to hear it," Nate said. "But there's one thing we've been blaming Teren for of which he is innocent."

"What's that?" asked Riley.

"Marie Strauss came forward and admitted she was the one who attacked Jess, claimed she only wanted to frighten her. She was angry and jealous, thought her husband was having an affair with the woman."

"Wasn't he?"

Nate shrugged. "I talked to them a couple days ago. They're trying to work it out."

"So that's why there was a pentagram symbol on the floor," said Riley. "Marie was trying to follow the Slasher's MO, only she didn't know the details. The media only released that there were occult elements involved, without specifying what they were."

"Right," said Nate.

Rick caught the aroma of fried onions and peppers as the door opened and their dinners arrived, a sizzling plate heaped with steak fajitas for Nate, fish tacos for him and Riley.

Nate loaded up a tortilla and used it to gesture at Riley.

"The experts analyzed the evidence you helped me collect off the island. To my mind, it confirmed Teren as the perpetrator, but it's a good thing we didn't have to take it to court. He was a hell of a careful killer."

Riley blew on a forkful of steaming rice, her face mournful. "Did you ever find out what Cappy Johanson was up to with his late-night skulking around?" she asked.

"We did. He was looting the neighbors. We found a load of valuables in his basement, pilfered from houses in the neighborhood. Charges are pending."

"Oh dear," said Riley. "And we're losing Skillet. Do you want to hear how he completed his revenge on our big shot, Mr. Snowden?"

"Of course."

"Snowden fell in love with Skillet's cooking and hired him to head up the kitchen at his German restaurant in Seattle."

"Fantastic!" Nate said. "But I'm not sure I'd call that revenge."

"Oh, here's the revenge part," Riley continued. "Skillet made it a condition of his acceptance that Snowden must address him at all times as 'Chef.'"

"So?"

"In German, '*Chef*' means 'the boss.'"

Nate laughed.

"And..." Riley paused to wipe her mouth with a napkin. "If Snowden makes him angry, Skillet says he'll give him a gift."

"Doesn't sound like a bad deal."

"No, except that in German, *Gift* means poison."

"Ah! Well played, Skillet. I trust he won't actually poison the old man."

"Probably not," Riley agreed, taking another bite of her taco. "But then, there's the whole thing with the sheriff, and Frank's broken leg."

"Oh, this sounds interesting," Rick said.

"I thought so too," Riley agreed, "but I'm beginning to wonder if I'll ever hear the story behind it. When I asked Frank how it happened, he pasted a wicked grin on his face and said he wouldn't talk about it 'til he cleared it with you," she said, narrowing her eyes at Nate.

Nate took a huge bite out of a fajita-laden tortilla and made a big show of chewing slowly.

"Come on, Nate," she pleaded. "Tell us what happened. Frank's awfully pleased with himself for being part of the posse, but as far as I can tell, it's unjustified. The villain escaped."

Nate raised his eyebrows. "Yes," he said. "And no."

Riley slapped her hand down on the table, sending a fork skittering.

"Aaaarrr! You men *so* exasperate me! What happened with the sheriff?"

Nate opened his mouth to speak, but a sudden flash of movement on the television screen caught Rick's eye. Grabbing the remote, he cranked up the volume.

"*...uncovered a curious angle on the governor's evacuation order that got thousands moving before Rainier erupted. It appears the press release which prompted the governor's actions was unauthorized, leaked to the media by this man, John Harrigan.*"

A photograph of a man with unruly tufts of blond hair appeared on the screen, his brown eyes uncrinkled by the faint smile that touched his lips.

"*Harrigan, a volcanologist associated with the Seismology...*"

Riley shot from her seat, bumping the table as she stood. Rick watched the color drain from her face, her eyes rapt, glued to the TV.

"That's him," she said. "That's the man who killed Teren."

Nate studied the man's image. "Are you sure?"

Riley speared him with her gaze. "Absolutely."

Pulling the phone from his pocket, Nate rose and paced the room, speaking in low tones. Rick watched, lost in his own thoughts. They centered on Riley, and on recent conversations he'd had with powerful men regarding her unique talents.

He saw she was still staring at the screen as Nate threw some bills on the table.

"I've got to go," he said. "Rick, will you make sure Riley gets home safe?"

"You bet."

Turning to Riley, Nate said, "Good job on the ID, Riley. We're on this."

Rick collected the bills off the table and held them out to Nate. "Dinner's on me."

Nate waved him away and fled the room. Rick watched the door swing shut behind him as Riley sank back onto the cushioned bench seat.

"Well done, indeed, Riley," Rick said, reaching across to Nate's plate. "Now I can steal the man's tortillas with impunity."

She looked shell-shocked, and his attempt at humor slid past, unnoticed. He gripped her hand, squeezing it, rubbing some warmth into her cold fingers.

"Drink some water, Riley Forte," he prompted, "and pull yourself together. There's something we need to discuss."

103

The curtain opened.

Riley stepped onto the stage and bowed to the audience, heart fluttering in her chest as she smiled past the hot, beaming lights. Turning toward the piano, she drew a shaky breath and stepped out on what was always the longest walk, the distance stretching out in front of her across the polished stage.

Holding all the possibilities of triumph.

And disaster.

This time, she felt something new in that walk. Her gift, the music within her, gave her power. It emanated from her in waves of energy and sheer, potent emotion of a sort she couldn't help but communicate to her audience.

In days past, she had wielded that power as a separator, in some way holding herself aloof, even from those she loved best. She had allowed her fear to make those most vital connections more symbolic than real.

And this had been her shame.

The wasted opportunities, the moments of reaching out and almost touching, but always drawing back, keeping herself apart. She'd been too gutless and too self-centered.

An image formed in her head, the memory of tree branches, crossed and intertwining. Up on the ridge, running foolishly from Nate, she had slipped on crumbling soil and gone sliding down a jagged chute to land with a hard thump on her backside, knocking the wind out of her.

As she lay struggling to catch her breath, she had stared up at the network of boughs overhead, their needles interspersing, leaning on one another as the clouds of ash and mist swirled around them.

The image was sharp and clear in her mind, stamped with meaning. She held it as a talisman, a token of her determination to stretch, to connect, and use her talent for something outside herself.

She sat, adjusted the bench, and centered her focus on the opening chords of Chopin's Fantasie Impromptu. She'd had only a few short weeks to prepare for this performance and had opted to follow the program from her disastrous comeback concert, gritting her teeth and climbing back on the horse.

She struck the opening chord, letting it resonate, floating on the air like a burst of thunder. Then her fingers started moving and she was lost in the music, swept away by passion and emotion, and by the joy of sharing it. She rode the wave into the final stretch.

Exhilaration filled her as she reached the crowning piece in the evening's program—the Beethoven Sonata which had been her stumbling block. Her hands felt nimble, her mind sure and steady.

She could do this.

She produced the solemn tones of the opening *"Grave"* from *"Sonata Pathetique."* It had always seemed to her like a musical conversation, an interchange between sweet supplication and stormy rebuke. As the clean lines penned by Beethoven emerged from the piano,

Riley's heart sang. She was surprised and delighted to discover that she had no desire to flee.

She finished to unanimous applause. Bowing her pleasure and gratitude for the evening, she wished Jim and Tanner could be there in the audience, giving her another chance to be the wife and mother she should have been. Another chance to let them reach and touch her.

A brief stab of pain ratcheted through her, but she let it go. She was working through her guilt, in all its emanations. The power it held over her to defeat and paralyze was waning, and tonight it was low enough to stomp on. She felt light, almost floating as she gave herself grace to rise from her shortcomings and try again.

Though every hand clapped, the applause sounded thin in the immensity of the auditorium. There were only twelve people in attendance. This concert was 'invitation only' and twelve constituted a full house. She walked down to meet them.

Nate clasped his hands and raised them over his head in a victory salute, his grin so big it nearly reached his ears. He grabbed a sheaf of yellow roses, tipped with a red blush.

"Bravo! You were incredible!"

She flushed, relief and bliss flooding over her.

"I did it," she said, nodding. "I'm so happy—ecstatic—that I didn't crash and burn."

"I am mightily impressed by you, lady."

He pulled her into a massive hug and whispered into her ear. "And so glad I met you."

Rick stepped close.

"Okay, you two, break it up. Riley," he said, squeezing her shoulder, "you were terrific."

He handed her another bouquet, white roses interspersed with blossoms of scarlet.

"The red ones," he told her, "are nasturtiums. They stand for victory in battle. And," he waggled his eyebrows, "you can eat them. Beauty plus functionality. Reminds me of someone I know."

Riley's eyes grew watery, and she shook her head, determined not to cry. She put her arms around both men, hugging them to her.

"Thank you so much for sharing this experience with me."

Pulling in a deep breath, she let it out in a shaky laugh. "This audience may be small, but I don't think I've ever felt the pressure of performance like I did tonight. Rick," she said, shaking her head at him, "you really know how to put a girl through the wringer."

"Tell me about it," said Bobbi, joining the group. She wore a flame-orange gown that brought out the shine in her eyes. Embracing Riley, she said, "That was the best concert I've attended all year."

"And the only one?" Riley smiled.

"Not by a long shot."

The remaining nine audience members stood in a loose knot near a side exit, conversing in low tones. Riley glanced at them, an anxious lump forming in her throat as she saw the way they were studying her.

As she and Rick had finished their fish tacos at Chico's, he'd told her what he'd been doing since they'd met on the ridge, divulging how and where he'd been spending his time.

"The people I'm working with are quite anxious to meet you. They're extraordinarily interested in a talented lady who can think on her feet and analyze patterns at a glance."

"There's nothing unique about my ability to do that."

"I suspect you're wrong about that. Plus, Riley, you've got a built-in beautiful cover. And it's not just your skin I'm talking about. A concert pianist can open a lot of doors."

They'd stayed talking until Chico's put up the 'CLOSED' sign and kicked them out the door.

"If you're agreeable," Rick had said as they climbed into his car for the ride home, "I'll arrange a meet.

"I *have* been thinking about expanding my repertoire."

"They put me through one hell of an audition," he warned her. "And you'll get one too. In your case, a concert."

And here she was, three and a half weeks later, giving the show of her life.

Riley met Rick's gaze as he offered his elbow. She swallowed around the lump in her throat and wrapped her hand around his arm.

"Are you ready?" he asked.

She nodded.

"Let's go meet the future."

Thank you so much for reading

Nocturne In Ashes

YOU'LL FIND MORE SUSPENSE AND EXCITEMENT

AS RILEY'S STORY CONTINUES

IN THE SEQUEL

Staccato Passage

And don't miss out on more of the story...

find out why Chief Steadman and his deputy took three days

to arrive at the clubhouse in the exciting paraquel,

Steadman's Blind

Thank you for reading *Nocturne in Ashes.*

If you enjoyed the book, I would love for you to leave a review to help other readers find and enjoy it, too. Thank you so much for taking the time to make that happen.

Visit my book page at Paraquel Press for more suspense-packed stories or scan the QR code to check out more Joslyn Chase books.

Start Reading

DISCOVER THE THRILL OF CHASE!

ALSO, DON'T FORGET TO sign up and join the growing group of readers who've discovered the thrill of Chase! You'll get *No Rest: 14 Tales of Chilling Suspense,* as well as VIP access to updates and bonuses.

Visit joslynchase.com to get started or simply scan the QR code.

Get The Ebook

Thanks again, and hope to see you around!

Author's Notes

Idea and Inspiration

For as long as I can remember, I have loved stories that give me a chill and a tingle, that keep me in a terror of trepidation over what to believe and who to trust. That element of psychological suspense, often coupled with physical peril, is the hallmark of my favorite type of book or movie.

One of my best-loved old-school authors is Mary Stewart. So many of her novels carry that delicious brand of tension. Decades ago, I read one of her books, *Wildfire At Midnight,* and though I later forgot many of the specifics of the story, it contains a scene implanted so vividly in my memory that I will never forget the prickles up my spine and the lip-biting, unbearably tense anticipation of one particular scene from that book.

When I arrived at the time in my life where I could begin to write the stories simmering on the back burners of my mind, that scene is the first that sprang to mind. I wanted to write a story that could produce that same kind of exhilarating suspense, with a scene modeled after that one.

Mary Stewart's *Wildfire at Midnight* is set on the island of Skye in the Scottish Hebrides. The elements which make it so compelling include the fact that it's an isolated island, shrouded in an all-encompassing mist which hampers visibility and distorts sound, and there is a killer among the company.

The scene I so admire involves the heroine fleeing in a panic through a thick fog and running straight into a bog where she must freeze and remain still or give herself away by the quaking ground. The other side of the coin, of course, is that she can tell by the quivering earth, when someone is approaching her, but she cannot see who it is.

To heighten the tension, she suspects her lover might be the killer and she doesn't know who, if anyone, she can trust. Intense.

Of course, I didn't want to copy Ms. Stewart's book, but I wanted to capture the same quality of tone and situation. Where could I set my story to create an isolated situation? A boat, a plane, a spaceship, a speeding train or bus? They've all been done. Frankly, most everything's been done, so what's a writer to do?

Islands have certainly been done, but what if I could put a twist on my island that hasn't been done, or at least not overdone. I've never heard of another story with exactly the setup I've written here.

Although I lived in Germany when I wrote the bulk of this story, I'm from the Puget Sound area. A major part of the landscape in that corner of the world is the majestic Mt. Rainier, and that got me thinking. I did some research and unearthed some pretty scary stuff. Mt. Rainier, an active volcano, is primed to blow. It's not a matter of *if*, only a question of *how soon.*

I discovered that Rainier's western flank, the one aimed in my direction, has been weakened over many centuries due to sulphuric acid mixed with rain and snow, seeping through the rock, altering it into a clay-like substance. When she blows, that will be the most likely outlet, and the results are predicted to be beyond devastating, the most destructive natural disaster in the history of the United States.

I constructed a scenario where this happens, and the displacement of water in the Puget Sound and its appendages is so great, as a result of the massive lahars, that even my distant perch in Mason County is affected. Surrounded by water as we are, we frequently deal with flooding, even without such a disaster as this.

With these conditions in place, I could set my story in a fictional version of my own neighborhood, transforming it into a virtual island.

Anyone who lives in my neighborhood and reads this book will recognize the area but let me stress that Mountain Vista and its surroundings are fictional, based loosely on an existing locale. I took many liberties with the setting and covered everything over with a thick layer of my own imagination.

In addition, all the characters, except the scientist David Johnston, are completely fictional. To reiterate a statement from the copyright page:

This book is a work of fiction. The characters, incidents, and dialogue are drawn from the author's imagination and are not to be construed as real. Any resemblance to actual events or persons, living or dead, is fictionalized or coincidental.

In addition to the element of isolation, the thick fog that obstructed the heroine's vision in Mary Stewart's book is the other component that made the scene so chillingly effective. I read many accounts during my research of ashfall obscuring vision and disorienting people, acting much like a thick fog. And there it was—my answer.

The eruption of Mt. Rainier could isolate my characters in an island-like environment and shroud them in a disorienting curtain of falling ash, thus creating a similar atmosphere in which to set my story.

That scene, where Riley crouches in the shifting ashfall while Nate creeps by, whispering her name, is the kernel of the novel, the idea that started it all. The rest of the story unfolded from there.

Riley Forte

I studied classical piano and taught private lessons for over twenty years. Becoming a concert pianist was never my aim—I don't have the temperament or the technique for it—but I can go there in my imagination. For years, I have thought about creating a character, a concert pianist who can move freely to venues around the world as a cover for investigating various crimes or suspicious circumstances.

That's how Riley was born.

Riley learned her style of teaching from me. I took the lesson scenes straight from the way I teach my own students. I almost always play an improvisational duet with a new student at our first lesson together, and it's almost always a joyous eye-opener.

I do have the framed pictures which I use to illustrate the point that printed music is just dots on paper to the untrained eye, but when you correctly and identify the shapes and patterns, the big picture emerges and radically changes what you see, infusing it with life, meaning, and interest beyond expectation. They are lots of fun.

I gave Riley a famous jazz pianist grandfather, Zach Riley, for whom she was named. She grew up immersed in music, bred to it. So, when she met James Forte, she knew she'd marry him. It was just too perfect to be sheer coincidence.

As a result, I think she always held him at a slight distance, not wanting to mar the perfection of his image, promising herself that someday she'd do the work to let him in and really connect with him on the deepest, most intimate level.

When he died before she took that chance, it devastated her, flooding her with a guilt she couldn't identify. The guilt and sorrow stymied her, paralyzing her ability to perform. Her career stalled until she could pinpoint the cause and quality of that guilt and take steps to form real connections with the people in her life, however messy that might get.

Mt. Rainier

Once I decided on a volcanic disaster to provide the setting I needed, I watched a TV documentary on the History Channel to gather information and get some idea of the scope I was dealing with. It was called *Mega Disasters, Season 1, Episode 4, American Volcano.*

This was absolutely terrifying to watch, and fascinating at the same time. The scenario it presented of Rainier's potential for damage made my incredible idea seem quite plausible. This is where I first learned about the altered rock on the western flank, weakened by centuries of sluicing in sulfuric acid. This is where I first learned about lahars, how fast and ferocious they are and the devastation they cause.

I also read *In The Path of Destruction,* by Richard Waitt. The book is a pretty comprehensive coverage of the Mount St. Helens eruption. This is where I first learned of David Johnston and his heroic efforts to warn the public and save lives.

Until I read this book, I had no idea of the political machinations working behind such an event. It made for interesting reading, and I was tempted to use more of it in the novel but didn't want to pull readers in the wrong direction, placing too much focus on a side story, albeit a fascinating one.

Riley is the heart of the book.

I visited some fun and informative websites. The United States Geological Survey (USGS) has pages of information about the volcanic hazards at Mt. Rainier. Another good site to visit is geology.com.

In the first edition of *Nocturne in Ashes,* I included links, but the internet changes so constantly that almost none of them were still active when I produced this second edition. Rather than links, I'll point you in some basic directions if you're interested in digging deeper.

Mt. Rainier *will* erupt with devastating consequences. It's only a question of how soon. Everyone who lives in the shadow of an active volcano should be aware of the hazards and prepare for a possible eruption. Visit the sites I mentioned above for more information about volcanic eruptions and spend some time preparing your family for emergencies of any kind. I've included a few good places to go for information:

The Red Cross

The Epicenter

FEMA

USGS Volcano Hazards Program

The Survival Mom

SurvivalBlog

And, specific to Mason County, Washington, a couple of emergency management divisions got together and created an . The guide covers the hazards most likely to hit the area and details how to protect your family, home, and neighborhood.

What's the deal with the Sheriff's story?

Do you share Riley's curiosity about how Frank broke his leg and what the Sheriff's deputies had to do with that?

Don't get exasperated. Get ready to quench that curiosity. You'll find that story—and a whole lot more—in Steadman's Blind.

So often when I'm reading a book, I'll wonder how the same story would look seen through the eyes of a different character. This kind of thing fascinates me no end. Every story should be presented from the point of view of the character best suited to tell the story, but I like to think about different perspectives.

My original outline for the book included two subplots which I ended up cutting out. The book was running too long, with too many characters, and I didn't want to pull focus away from the main storyline.

One of the subplots involved sheriff's deputy, Randall Steadman, and his partner, Cory Frost, who responded to Nate's call for help but took three days to arrive.

Theirs is a whole other story that intertwines in a couple of places with Riley's adventure. I hated cutting it out because these characters became real to me, and I enjoyed getting to know them. I had a lot of fun putting their adventure together and it's an exciting story that really wanted to be told.

So, I devised a plan which allowed me to indulge my passion for looking through another set of eyes. I cast about for a word to call it—a story that runs alongside another story. Not a prequel, or a sequel, but something like a paraquel—a parallel story. I thought I was quite clever with that, but it turns out I'm not the first one to think of it.

At any rate, that's how Steadman's Blind sprang to life. I think you'll enjoy following Chief Deputy Steadman's story and seeing how it weaves back and forth through Riley's. Don't miss *Steadman's Blind!*

Also, be sure to sign up for my readers' group to get VIP access to bonuses and updates.

How will the story continue?

Riley Forte faces off against a lethal criminal mastermind in *Staccato Passage*, the white-knuckle sequel to *Nocturne in Ashes.*

Recruited by an elite, under-the-radar security firm, Riley trains to go undercover at an ultra-secret spy academy in the heart of Bavaria. Upon her arrival, a shocking revelation shatters her confidence, making the struggle to stay atop the learning curve more challenging than she ever imagined.

Dogged by intrigue, treachery, and the mounting threat of terrorism, can Riley acquire the skills she needs to survive spy school and stop a disaster that could rock the world?

If you're a fan of Jeffery Deaver, Nelson DeMille, or David Baldacci, you won't want to miss this wild ride! Grab your copy and clear your schedule—the thrills don't stop until the very last page.

Sample from Staccato Passage

PROLOGUE

Mid-morning.

The sun shone golden on the wide spread of evergreens seven thousand feet below, gilding and lifting them like jewels from dusty velvet, making the lush pools of shadow sink in contrast. Purring vibrations from the sturdy little four-seat Sundowner filled the cabin, muffled by the headset she wore, and the woman at the controls smiled, remembering the days when she had to drop a quarter into a motel bed to get that kind of relaxation.

To the east, the waters of the Atlantic Ocean sparkled deep blue, edged by a rind of white Brazilian beaches along the coast. She glanced at her companion in the seat beside her and gestured toward the distant expanse.

Speaking into the headset mic, she said, "Maybe we can go sailing this afternoon."

He gave her a look, waggled his head. "I'd prefer a leisurely lunch and a nap."

She laughed. "Oh ye of little adventure."

"Little adventure?" Leaning close, he sent her an air kiss. "Just being with you is the adventure of a lifetime."

She gave his knee a squeeze and checked the gauges. Everything looked fine. Everything was—

Bang!

The plane shuddered and bucked with a sickening shriek of metal.

The explosion had come from the engine compartment, and it sent a plume of greasy black smoke billowing across the Sundowner's wrap-around windshield, shrouding visibility, throwing a dark cloud over the little plane.

The woman pilot screamed, then clamped her teeth together, holding tight to the yoke. The smoke blew off, leaving behind a grimy film and enough light for her to see the control panel.

All zeroes.

The needle on every gauge lay flat at the bottom of its range.

She tore off her headset and heard the last thing she wanted to hear.

Silence.

The engine was gone.

Next to her, the man had gone sickly pale. He said nothing, but his lips worked soundlessly and his hands dug into his thighs, the knuckles white as bone.

Fumes crept into the cabin, choking and nauseating. The woman stared out at the thick, endless field of tiny, distant pines and eucalyptus, approaching too fast. Relentless.

She gripped the yoke, pulling up, willing the plane to rally and rise. But the controls that had always felt so responsive, so alive under her fingers, now felt cold and dead.

Wings, and the dynamics of flight, kept them aloft. For now.

Despite that knowledge and her experience, she wrestled the panicky notion that they were dead and falling like a brick in the sky. Going down hard and fast.

She fought to keep the nose up, to force the plane into a long, slow turn, buying time. She needed a break. A meadow, a clearing, something to aim for.

There was nothing.

With a desperate burst of hope, she tried starting the engine again.

No use.

The woman tried feathering the controls, straining to eke some altitude out of the plane, slowing its descent.

Nothing responded. Nothing worked.

Heart booming, she peered out the windshield. The looming pines still appeared tiny, but they were close enough now to see stony projections, stark cliffs and diamond-hard rock formations thrusting up between them.

The woman blinked. Sweat dripped into her eyes, stinging.

Beside her, the man let out a series of strangled sobs. She heard frantic breaths—harsh and wheezing—and realized they were her own. She swallowed hard, struggling for control, but felt the fight seeping out of her like air from a spent balloon.

With shaking hands, she activated the GPS emergency beacon and tried the radio.

Static.

It didn't matter. None of it mattered anymore.

The trees grew large, a black sea reaching up to swallow the broken Sundowner.

FROM HIS VANTAGE POINT at the top of the highest hill, John Harrigan watched the plane go down.

He followed its decline with his binoculars, noting with interest how the wings sheared off as it hit the inexorable wall of Brazilian forest and how abruptly it came to rest against a jagged crest of rock.

The day was fine, almost too hot for his taste. Screwing the cap off a thermos, he took a long draught of cold water, feeling the chill trace through his chest, tasting the slight metallic tang.

His radio hissed and he picked up.

"The charge went off exactly as planned," Haagen told him. "And she activated the GPS beacon."

"Good," John said. "Move in, and have the ambulance standing by. I'll meet you at the hospital."

He didn't hurry as he hiked back to the road where his car waited. Rescue operations took time. His people would have to traverse difficult territory to retrieve the plane crash victims. He could afford to linger.

The heat of the day brought out the smell of pine resin, heavy in the dry air of the Rio Grande do Sul. Not so much different from the forests around Seattle where he'd grown up.

Where he'd blossomed.

The woodlands were full of tiny sounds—insects, birds, an occasional rustling breeze. As he trekked through the carpet of pine needles, John heard another sound, a sort of frenzied sniffling. He slowed his steps, approaching cautiously. He'd once met a bear cub in the Washington woods, and that hadn't turned out well.

The noise came from a small deer, a young doe, caught in a jumble of vines. The creature stamped her hind feet as John came near, eyes wide and roving with fear. John watched her struggle, all alone in the big, bad forest.

Coming closer, he saw the doe's front hooves had become entangled in a trailing mass of vines. A slice of the knife could free the creature.

Reaching for his pocketknife, John opened the Damascus steel blade. Slowly, carefully, he stepped nearer, speaking soothingly, reassuringly. The deer snorted, rearing back, trying frantically to get away before he reached her.

He laid a hand gently on her neck, feeling the pulse beat beneath his palm, her life in his hands. He waited until she went still, until her heartbeat matched his own. Then he leaned in and made a swift cut.

The animal was free.

He watched her bound away, clumsy in her haste, the sound of her flurried escape reaching him for whole seconds after she'd disappeared from view. He knelt in the dirt, touching the place where she'd been. A thrill shuddered through him.

Rising to his feet, he folded the knife. Sun-dappled leaves quivered in the eucalyptus breeze as he tucked it back into his pocket.

He walked on.

At the hospital, John watched the ambulance arrive, saw his men jump out and wheel in two gurneys, each carrying a sheet-swathed figure. He met Haagen in the corridor and they rode the elevator down to the basement together.

"Did she make it?" John asked.

"She's hurt bad, but I think she'll recover." Haagen lifted the sheet off the body on the gurney. The woman pilot lay still and cold, traces of fear frozen on her face. She was dead.

"Good," John said, offering a grim smile. "Let's get her into surgery."

In the basement, they were met by another of John's men, dressed as a morgue attendant. He stood beside a third gurney with another sheet-covered form. This one sedated but breathing.

The man swapped gurneys with Haagen. Without a word, the attendant began wheeling the DOA crash victims to the morgue.

John watched him for a moment, then returned to the elevator, followed by Haagen steering the newly-acquired gurney. Upstairs, the eminent Dr. Daniel Bernardo awaited their arrival. He was prepped for surgery and John had supplied the nurses and an anesthesiologist.

A discreet team he could trust.

Dr. Bernardo didn't know the name of his patient. Nor did he want to. He understood that the less he knew, the greater his chances of survival.

John was confident the good doctor would keep silent, a silence guaranteed by the continued wellbeing of his wife and three daughters.

In addition, the money he was being paid would provide critical funding for his medical school to stay open, giving hope to the poor people of his home region.

John knew very well how to find the beating pulse, how to wield a knife.

And precisely when.

The operating theater allowed him to watch from above as Dr. Bernardo raised the scalpel and made his first cut, working from a photograph on the table beside him. They had discussed the changes he would make to the ears, the cheekbones, the shape of the chin.

The skilled surgeon would create a new woman, fashioned in the likeness of the expired pilot. And John would use her. He'd mentor her.

He would teach her how to fly.

CHAPTER 1

A hundred feet off the ground, Riley clung to a narrow crevice of rock.

Heart pounding against the sun-heated stone, she wedged her hand into a crack running vertically along its rough surface. The fleshy part of her palm lodged in the constricted space, allowing her to pull herself another twelve or thirteen inches up the cliff. With her knee angled outward, she found a place to cram her toe sideways into the crack and turned her foot, pushing upward, increasing her progress.

Careful not to look down, knowing how dizzy, how shaky, that made her feel, she concentrated on the stretch ahead. But squinting upward, she saw an endless expanse of sheer rock, broken only by the jagged crack. No end in sight.

A wave of nausea washed over her. The energy reserve she'd tried so hard to foster drained away as if someone had pulled a plug.

She couldn't move.

Her legs trembled uncontrollably and her hands ached. Sweat poured down from her hairline, bringing the taste of salt and coconut sunscreen but she didn't dare lift a hand to wipe it clear.

"My foot's stuck!" she shouted, feeling the rise of panic.

Far below, her partner, Christopher Neville, held her lifeline, belaying her. "Rotate your knee, Riley," he called. "Reverse the movement."

His steady voice calmed her. Pulling in a shuddering breath, Riley angled her knee, returning her foot to its sideways position. With a jiggle, she pulled her shoe free but lost her balance. Gasping, she thrust her hand deeper into the crack and felt the pressure of her weight pulling against her wrist and palm.

It hurt.

Gritting her teeth, she jammed her foot back into the crack. "Why are we doing this, Chris?"

She heard the petulance in her voice, but felt it justified. Why had he brought her here? Chris was a friend, and a fellow concert pianist.

Except, his career was blossoming, growing, whereas hers...

Pushing the sour thought aside, Riley yelled, "What are we supposed to be gaining from this? You value your hands as much as I do."

His voice floated up to her and she heard the smile in his words. "Exhilaration! Inspiration! As needful to feed our souls as to school our fingers, Riley. Your playing will be the better for it. I promise."

"Not if I snap them off in this horrid crack," she muttered.

A shadow flitted by on her right, a bird making a clacking sound. It perched somewhere out of her range of vision and continued to scold.

"Are you done?" Chris asked.

Riley lifted her chin, straining her eyes against the sun, looking again for the top of the climb. Still not seeing it.

She closed her eyes and swallowed hard, thinking of Jim. Thinking of Tanner.

She still missed them so much.

The image of a face shimmered across her mind—the man who'd taken her husband and child from her—and she let it come. It was a rare moment when she allowed herself to think about him. He had been her friend, taking care of her, encouraging her. He'd taught her to kayak, told her the secret of crickets.

And betrayed every trust she'd ever placed in him.

He was dead now too, but the shadow of evil under which he'd crouched still loomed. It was still out there.

Riley moved her head, rubbing her face against her sleeve, trying to wipe away the sweat stinging her eyes. She raised her chin again, but the top of her climb had not materialized. It was no clearer to her now.

Dragging in a deep breath, she shouted down to Chris. "No! I'm moving on."

Reaching above her, she jammed a hand into the crack and turned her thumb, securing her grasp. She levered herself up, hand over hand, moving her feet up by intervals. Determined. Single-minded. Making progress.

And then, for a fraction of a second, she failed to keep the exhaustion at bay, letting it shatter her concentration, sap her energy. She wavered and her foot skidded down the rock, losing its purchase. She gasped as her hand slipped from the crevice, flailing and finding nothing.

She fell.

Her stomach lurched as she swung back and spun in the air, held by the rope and safe enough, but with the crush of defeat washing over her.

Shaking, exhausted, she finished her descent and slumped in the shade cast by the towering rock, working to catch her breath.

"You did good, Riley," Chris said, passing her a water bottle. "It's better than the gym, right? A lot more fun."

She gulped the water, still blessedly cool in the insulated flask. "I'll reserve judgment on that for now. Maybe I'll feel better in hindsight."

"Of course you will. I know you, Riley."

Did he? Did she even know herself? It felt like she'd lost everything she'd ever fought to keep. Was there really any point in looking for something new?

A crescendo of chords jangled from the bag beside her. Even out here, in the thin air of the Cascades, her phone picked up a signal. She saw who was calling and answered, feeling the stir of curiosity.

"Riley, it's Devin Wright."

Wright was the founder and CEO of Olivero Security, a firm providing private protection and investigative services to clients around the world. He'd been angling to recruit Riley for the better part of a year and she'd finally signed on, making it official.

"I know we talked about sending you out to the academy in June," he said, "but..."

He paused, and Riley pictured him running his hands through the thinning hair on top of his head as she'd seen him do on previous occasions.

"Things are happening, Riley. I don't know how closely you've been watching the news." A beat passed. She said nothing. "We're moving your training forward. You leave day after tomorrow."

The stirring curiosity in her gut churned into anxiety. "What? So soon?"

"My secretary will email your instructions and travel itinerary."

Riley's tongue felt thick in her throat. "I don't know what—"

"Riley," Wright interrupted her. "You are important to us. To our mission and the values we hold dear."

She said nothing.

"I wouldn't be calling you to come in early like this," he continued, "if I didn't feel some urgency." A pause. "You can do this."

Her chest felt tight, making it hard to draw breath. Inside her stomach, something moved, slow and greasy. She felt sick with trepidation, and another sensation she couldn't identify.

She thought it might be excitement.

She gripped the phone in her chalky hand, pressing it against the side of her face.

"Yes, sir," she said.

She ended the call and took several steps back from the cliff, moving on uneven ground tufted with scrubby brush. Shading her eyes, she looked up. From here, she could see the top of the rocky precipice.

From here, it looked reachable.

A surge of nervous energy rushed through her as she packed her climbing gear into a canvas duffle, making her feel light-headed and anxious to get home.

"That's it for today," she told Chris. "I've got to get going."

CHAPTER 2

Rush hour traffic in Seattle.

Rick hated being on the road at this time of day. The fumes, the noise, the stop and go.

Whenever he could, he avoided the snarl of vehicles vying for pavement, their erratic movements sometimes unpredictable and downright foolish. He hated the squeeze, the feeling of being hemmed in.

He had good reason.

Barely seven months ago he'd been literally sandwiched between two cars on this stretch of freeway, trapped in a crushed metal cage during the worst disaster Seattle had ever seen. The memory of it left him feeling queasy.

Gritting his teeth, he pressed on, watching for his exit and taking it with a sigh of relief. Watery sunlight spilled down from the eastern sky, painting a stripe across the newspaper on the seat beside him. The paper was folded to reveal a news story on page two.

The article wasn't surprising. Little surprised Rick when it came to the news of the day. Murder, arson, terrorism. Kidnapping, sex trafficking, conspiracies. All of it was too prevalent, too disheartening.

But something about the owner of a local jewelry chain being arrested for homicide and selling stolen merchandise disturbed him beyond the usual. It was the part where the reporter had interviewed the man's nephew.

"I guess I never really knew him," the nephew said. "I haven't seen him in years, but I wouldn't have believed he'd do something like this."

A common enough sentiment among friends and family of apprehended wrong-doers, but in this instance it touched an ominous chord at the back of Rick's mind, not letting go.

He turned off on a side road, following its shaded curves beneath towering evergreens. He was always amazed by how quickly the feel could go from urban congestion to rustic tranquility in the outlying areas of the city.

Olivero Security, a private, high-end and under-the-radar investigative firm, had its headquarters in a tucked away spot, giving it the ambiance of a mountain retreat. Rick enjoyed the effect—found it somehow both calming and energizing—and he relished the work he did for the firm.

It made him feel effective and useful in the world.

The complex spread out over a dozen acres and included three main structures joined by breezeways and several outbuildings. The muted gray exteriors with forest green trim blended well into the landscape, giving the place a harmonious feel while still maintaining a business-like impression.

To the outside world, the company simply ran a crack team of private investigators and bodyguards. To those who knew, Olivero's scope encompassed so much more and ran so much deeper.

Rick pulled his Mustang in next to a copper-colored Mini and set the parking brake. Scooping up his messenger bag, he shoved the newspaper inside and hustled for the building's entrance, breathing in the pine-scented air.

Inside, he headed straight for Devin Wright's office. Wright was the founder and chief executive officer of Olivero Security. He'd poured everything he had—money, time, energy, integrity, personal commitment—into the company, and was rightly proud of what he'd built, ever vigilant to safeguard it.

More than a full-time job.

"Right on time, Rick," Wright greeted him. "Let's get started."

The chief's face was grim, almost gray beneath the sparse hair at his temples. Rick took a seat at the conference table between a large, well-tanned man and a diminutive woman in a green dress. The woman, a top-notch analyst named Sophie Alvarez, had a copy of the morning paper on the table in front of her. It lay open at the same article Rick had flagged.

Wright paced the room, hands folded together beneath his chin. "I have some startling news," he announced. Halting, he pivoted, pinning the assorted group around the table with his eyes. "Hugh Jenkins turned up yesterday."

Rick took in the gasps and raised eyebrows, but he didn't know anything about Hugh Jenkins.

"Alive?" someone asked.

Wright dropped into his chair at the head of the table. "Barely."

Directing his attention to Rick, the newbie of the group, he explained. "Hugh Jenkins is an agent we sent undercover in Argentina a few years back. He disappeared, presumed dead."

Turning back to the table at large, he said, "Hugh showed up at one of our safe houses in Costa Rica. My man there, James Holloway, tells me he was sick, exhausted. He'd been kept in a sort of prison camp and subjected to hard labor. Somehow, he managed to escape."

"Is he okay?" asked Daniel Escobar, the man at Rick's side, one of the best IT investigative specialists in the country. Wright didn't answer his question directly.

"Holloway said Hugh could barely talk, but he had some incredible things to say. A lot of it he picked up in the prison camp—"

"Of dubious validity, then," Daniel stated.

"But disturbing nonetheless," Wright continued. "Anyone here ever seen the movie *The Princess Bride?*"

Everyone had.

"Anyone here ever heard of a criminal puppet master called The Cincher?"

Frederick Yates, head of the Personnel Department, snorted. "Cincher is a myth, chief."

Nods around the table agreed with him.

"So I always thought as well," Wright said. "I may be re-evaluating that position. According to Hugh, The Cincher leads an international criminal syndicate called The Knot. And according to Hugh, it's a position of power passed down from one mastermind to the next, much like the Dread Pirate Roberts in *The Princess Bride.*"

Rick looked around at the group. Most faces held skepticism or even scorn. He thought his own face must look the same. It was an improbable idea.

Ramona Reed adjusted her glasses, looking doubtfully at Wright over their rims.

"Sounds far-fetched, Devin."

A former DARPA scientist, she headed up the Research and Development arm of the company. She wore her graying, thick blonde hair piled haphazardly atop her head, secured by a pencil. Every time Rick saw her he had to fight an urge to pull out the pencil and watch the hair tumble down around her shoulders.

"I would concur," Wright said. "Except that someone killed Hugh to keep him from saying anything more."

A small, shocked silence fell over the room.

"What happened?" Sophie asked.

"Hugh told Holloway about Cincher and The Knot, said they were involved in coordinated attacks around the world—targeted robberies, terrorist actions, orchestrations of rioting and looting. A tangled network of powerful, well-funded mischief makers."

Wright gestured to the newspaper in front of Sophie Alvarez. "I wonder if you've been thinking what I've been thinking. Hugh suggested part of The Knot organization specializes in placing imposters in key positions by secretly replacing players with their own people."

"Creepy," Ramona said. "Like *Invasion of the Body Snatchers.*"

"A bit like that maybe, but before Holloway could get any details, he was called away for an important phone call."

"Oh no," Daniel said. "I see where this is going."

"Yes," Wright confirmed. "It was a ploy. When Holloway returned, Hugh was choking on his own tongue."

"How did it happen?" Rick asked.

"I spoke to a witness who saw a nurse bring Hugh a cup of tea. A few sips into it, Hugh was dead and the nurse had disappeared."

"Damn." Daniel slumped back in his chair. "We need more information." He pointed to the newspaper. "What's the deal?"

"It may be nothing," Sophie said.

"It probably *is* nothing," Rick piped up. "But I had the same idea when I read the story. A jewelry store owner arrested for homicide and trafficking in stolen merchandise. The jeweler had no close friends or family. The report quotes a nephew hadn't seen the man in years, but swears he acted out of character."

"Almost as if it wasn't even the same guy," Sophie agreed.

"I highly doubt this jeweler has anything to do with The Knot," Wright said. "But it caught my attention as the *kind* of situation we need to be thinking about—where key people can be subbed out for doubles and no one the wiser. Apparently, it's worked before for The Knot, and if it ain't broke..."

"It's a sinister idea," Ramona said. She turned to Frederick. "I'm very sorry to hear about Hugh. I know he was a particular friend of yours."

"Yes, from way back. I recruited him."

Rick was used to seeing Frederick brimming with vitality, always smiling and full of bonhomie. The man now looked like a popped paper bag, wrinkled and flat.

"That's all, everyone," Wright said. "I just wanted to pass on Hugh's information. He paid a high cost to get it to us."

Murmured agreement rippled around the room as people rose to leave.

"Rick?" Chief Wright motioned him back into his chair. "I'd like you to stay."

When the room had emptied, Wright closed the door and pulled a chair close to Rick, leaning forward, hands clasped, elbows on knees. He grimaced.

"I had some of my operatives in Europe dig a little deeper on this Cincher thing. It appears there may be some truth to this Dread Pirate Roberts type of passage. They're saying a new guy has recently taken command. By all accounts, a more brutal and innovative leader than his predecessor."

Rick shifted in his seat. Bad news, of course, but it didn't explain why Wright was telling him, specifically. The chief paused, something delicate and unsaid suspended in the air between them. Rick wished he'd just take a breath and say it.

"There's some indication that Cincher could be the man we know as John Harrigan."

Now Rick wished he hadn't said it.

"Are you going to tell Riley?" he asked.

Riley Forte was not only a good friend, but Rick had been the one to recruit her. Like Frederick had recruited Hugh Jenkins.

"I'm sending her to the academy in Bavaria tomorrow. I haven't decided whether or not to tell her our suspicions about Cincher. That's why I wanted to talk to you."

"I thought her training was scheduled for June."

"It was."

"Then why now?"

"Two reasons. First, I don't want to delay any longer on getting her the skills she needs to protect herself and to be useful to us."

"And the second reason?" Rick asked.

"The second reason is that she'll be safer at the academy, surrounded by some of our best people than most anywhere I can think of."

Rick nodded. He saw the logic.

"But are you going to tell her about John?" he asked again. "She survived his attack. She's seen his face. She's definitely a person of interest to him. And if he is this Cincher..."

"I know." Wright straightened in his chair, balled his fists in his lap. "I just don't think she needs the added stress right now. She'll be somewhat insulated at the academy and she'll be concentrating on her training."

"Yes..." Rick said, letting the word hang.

"And," Wright continued, "as an added measure, I'm sending you in as an instructor. To be there on the premises for her. Watching over her."

"Okay, good."

Chief Wright stood and straightened his tie.

"Go pack a bag, Rick. You leave in three hours."

CHAPTER 3

Taz Salih stared through the glass, sweat breaking out beneath his gas mask.

Two canisters, nestled in a clear acrylic holder, waited beyond the unbreakable glass. Two canisters, more deadly than anything he'd ever encountered.

Over the years, his work had brought him face to face with some of the most lethal substances known to man. Here, operating in Nuremberg, he was part of an underground laboratory team tasked with engineering a new, particularly vicious variant of Sarin gas. Commissioned by an ultra-secret international research committee, the project was intended to provide data useful in the prevention and defense against chemical attack.

But Taz had recognized in it another potential.

In his eyes, the nerve agent had become a calling card. A way to send a message of terror and awe.

Beside him, Aludra tapped at her mobile phone, focusing and resizing the image sent from Raul's screen in the van outside. Their control center and getaway car.

A chill passed along the back of Taz's neck, partly due to the frigid temperature in the lab and partly due to the cocktail of dread and elation that coursed through his veins. He threw a nervous glance behind him. The low, constant hum of the ventilation system provided camouflage for the tiny noises he and Aludra might make, but they would also muffle the sound of someone approaching.

They were still alone.

Taz had used his credentials to get through the gate while Aludra and Marcos huddled in the trunk of his car, shielded from backscatter x-ray detection by a lead blanket stolen from the radiology lab. At 3:00 am, the facility was deserted, other than a periodic sweep of armed patrols.

But Taz knew a tactical team was kept on standby in a small barracks at the back of the property.

While Marcos kept watch at the lab's entrance, Aludra brought the high-resolution image of Dr. Klossner's eye into sharp focus. She looked at Taz and crossed her gloved fingers in a bid for luck.

Taz watched her place the screen of her phone in front of the retinal scanner which controlled the lock protecting the canisters. They'd tested this method with good results, but this was the only time that really mattered. He held his breath.

Nothing happened.

Taz trembled through four long empty seconds before the lock finally clicked, releasing with a faint whooshing sound. He snatched one of the canisters, gripping it hard to calm his shaking hands. Aludra seized the second canister.

Their eyes met through the gas masks they wore and Taz saw her excitement and triumph, echoing the emotions rocketing through his own breast. He snapped open the airtight titanium case designed to carry the canisters and pressed the one he held into the foam-lined space, feeling it settle into place.

An alarm blared, shrill and sudden, shattering the silence of the lab into a thousand dangerous pieces. Pulse throbbing in his eardrums, Taz nearly dropped the case. Fumbling it open, he held it out for Aludra's canister, but she was running to Marcos at the door, still holding the vessel of toxic gas cradled to her chest.

Raul's voice rasped in his earpiece. "Trouble's coming. Get out."

Marcos, armed with a rifle, nosed into the hallway, clearing it and motioning them forward. Taz ran, his heart pounding, Aludra at his heels. Before they'd gone five meters, four uniformed gunmen turned the corner and fired.

Marcos shot back. The clattering racket filled the corridor, multiplied by the canyon-like walls, a torrent of noise and confusion. Taz saw two of their attackers go down and then Marcos spun, hit in the chest.

He fell.

His rifle skittered on the tile and Taz made a grab for it, but was driven back by a rain of gunfire. He retreated into the lab and Aludra slammed the door, locking them inside.

"That will hold them for thirty seconds," she said. "No longer. What do we do now?"

"There's another door. On the other side of this divider. Help me!"

Taz shoved the carrying case under his arm and struggled with the locking mechanism holding the accordion divider in place. He knew it hadn't been used in years and it didn't want to budge. Aludra still clung to her canister, using her free hand to claw at the divider.

It did no good.

The door to the lab burst open with a crack like a rifle shot, spilling men into the room.

"Halt!" one of them shouted. *"Nicht bewegen!"*

Taz gave a final tug on the lock and it popped open, creating an instant gap three inches wide. As he punched his fist into the breach, straining to push the divider along its rusty track, one of the tac team men leaped forward and dragged Aludra back, pulling off her gas mask.

Taz turned, saw the grim, determined look on Aludra's face. He screamed, "No!"

Before anyone could stop her, Aludra sprang the cap on the canister, breaking the seal. A slight hiss, as if she'd popped the top on a can of soda, was the only perceptible indicator that something had happened.

The gas was invisible and odorless.

Taz watched in horror as Aludra doubled over, vomiting onto the immaculate tile floor of the lab. She collapsed, writhing with the effort to breathe but unable to do so. The two men dropped beside her.

A pool of urine spread from beneath one of them, reaching to Aludra's flailing legs, soaking her pants.

It was too late. Too late for him to do anything, even if he'd known of something to do.

He gripped the case and ran.

"Raul!" He shouted into his mouthpiece, reaching out to the last remaining member of his team. "Raul, can you hear me? Aludra and Marcos are down. I'm alone now, heading to the rendezvous. Meet me there."

He heard only a crackle, then silence.

Taz burst out of the building. Raul was blown. His bridges were burned. He'd have to think on the fly as he ran.

His car was no good. He wouldn't get three blocks in it. But he remembered a little-used gate at the far end of the research complex. A rugged galvanized steel turnstile. You could get out that way, but not in.

That worked for him.

Keeping to the shadows, Taz made his way to the turnstile and crouched low, scanning the area. He saw no one.

The longer he waited, the more time lab security would have to summon men and implement a planned response. Once outside the gate, he could get his hands on another car and proceed with the contingency plan put in place by the man in charge.

Someone they called The Cincher.

Taz grasped the handle of the titanium case and sprinted for the gate.

CHAPTER 4

Riley let her shoulders relax and pull back, opening her posture and feeling the tension release as her fingers moved across the keyboard of her piano. She finished running through the scales and Hanon exercises that had honed her technique over years of practice. They were no problem for her to execute with precision, even when her mind was a million miles away. Muscle memory prevailed and her fingers found the keys without conscious thought.

But she owed more than thoughtless automatic movement to her performance pieces.

Natural sunlight poured through the high clerestory windows above the mahogany grand piano, burnishing its varnish to a glowing, translucent red. Riley loved the piano and normally she cherished the time she spent with it, letting her fingers dance over the keys, delighting in their rich and mellow tone.

But very little about today felt normal.

She dug into a Mendelssohn *agitato,* felt the heaviness in her forearms bringing out the depth and volume of the tempestuous music. It suited her mood and she let it roar beneath her fingers, filling the room, feeding her irritated, restless temper.

Pressing her lips together, she tasted the peppermint of her favorite lip balm, savoring the subtle burning sensation as she rolled through the last crashing chords of the Mendelssohn. She sat for a moment on the bench, eyes closed, breathing deeply in and out, before turning her attention to the Bach Prelude she'd been studying. She started working through the complicated fingering, trying to find the patience and focus the task required.

And failing.

She pushed away from the piano in frustration. On her way into the kitchen for a glass of water, she indulged in a primal scream, letting it echo around the house where she lived. Alone.

How had her life become this fragile, this empty? Less than three years ago, she'd had a husband, a son. She had a promising concert career and a bulldog agent helping to make it happen. She was on track for the life she'd always dreamed of.

And somehow, it had all derailed.

She'd lost Jim and Tanner in a horrendous fire, set by a man she'd believed to be her friend.

Her ability to perform had shattered, robbing her of everything she had left and plunging her into a deep mire of depression. It had taken the better part of two years and every ounce of courage she had to thrash free from that sucking hole.

She'd struggled to rebuild her career through slow, painful effort, believing it could be her lifeline, a slender thread to happiness.

Only to have her comeback tour destroyed by a spurting volcano and a fiendish killer.

And now, out of these ashes, she'd been given a small burning ember of hope.

But could she do it? Did she have the grit, the stamina, to do what Devin Wright and his Olivero agency expected of her?

They wanted her to go undercover, to use her identity as a concert pianist to move in certain circles and gain access to key people and locations. They wanted her to uncover secret information, to pass along messages and critical communications.

They wanted her to be a spy.

She'd spent enough time with Rick, with Chief Wright, and inside the annals of the agency to be convinced their values coincided with her own, that they supported the cause of freedom and justice.

But could she accomplish what they asked of her?

Would it be enough?

Could she build a new life with substance and meaning sufficiently deep to bring her—if not happiness—a sense of fulfillment?

Riley looked down at the glass of water in her hands. She didn't remember pouring it. Tipping the tumbler, she gulped the water, nearly choking as her throat closed, thick with tears.

She slammed the glass down on the granite countertop, watching a crack spread up from the heavy base to the delicate rim. Dragging in a ragged breath, she straightened her spine and lifted her chin, standing with eyes closed, feeling the cool of the tile spread across the soles of her bare feet.

Just breathing.

She was made of rugged material. She had steel in her DNA.

She reached for it now.

Her great-great-grandfather had gone down on the Titanic, still playing with the orchestra as frantic passengers stormed the life boats.

As a young man, her granddad—Zach Riley, for whom she was named—had traveled with the USO, giving battle zone performances during WWII. More than once, he'd been wounded in the course of his duty but that hadn't stopped him from returning.

Her own parents had braved hazardous situations to bring music where it was most needed and Riley had once or twice gone with them. She'd played charity concerts in war-torn nations and to benefit the victims of the September 11th attack and other terrorist actions.

Not only could she do this, she *needed* to do this. She needed to rise above the forces crushing her down. To make something meaningful of her life.

To honor those who had gone before, and give hope to those yet to come.

Hell, yes!

She would ace her spy school training and become the best damn agent Olivero ever produced.

Riley shook herself and headed for the bedroom. She pulled a suitcase out of the closet and opened it on the bed, making sure it still contained the large laundry bag she used as a hamper for dirty clothes while traveling.

She pulled blouses from hangers, took down folded pairs of pants from the overhead shelf, arranging them on the bed for packing. Tossing toiletries into the zippered compartment, she wondered what kind of shoes she ought to bring.

She paused, absently running her fingers over the hard, pebbled surface of the suitcase while her mind wandered. Lifting her shoulders, she pulled in a deep, cleansing breath, letting the oxygen flow through her, willing herself into serenity. Into strength.

She'd faced her fear and anger, made peace with it and chosen to use it as an impetus rather than an obstacle. Yet her heart continued to beat with a trace of agitation. There was still something niggling at her and she knew she'd have to take it out and examine it before she'd truly be ready to go.

Nate.

Over the past months, the police detective she'd teamed up with to catch a killer, had become a significant part of her life. She and Nate had grown close and in some ways she'd come to depend on him—his cheery optimism, his talent for having fun, his expertise and encouragement. They were friends.

And maybe something more.

But he had a daughter, Sammy. And an ex-wife named Marilyn. Marilyn wanted them to be a family again, and Riley knew Nate wanted that too. She couldn't blame him.

Family was everything.

She and Nate had talked about it, but left things between them up in the air. One way or the other, Riley would have preferred to settle the situation before she left.

She couldn't help feeling that by the time she got back, Nate would be lost to her.

Just one more precious part of her life...gone.

CHAPTER 5

Anton Forst trudged up the wide, dusty mountain trail. The spring air was cool, not yet warmed by the rising sun, and it nipped at the lobes of his ears below the knit cap he wore. The scent of insect repellent traveled with him, overpowering the fragrant budding wildflowers growing thick along both sides of the trail. He'd rubbed the bug spray over every exposed inch of skin, hating the smell and feel of it.

Hating what mosquito bites did to him even more.

As he walked, his hiking boots crunched on loose pebbles and stones, sending them skittering across the dirt. A noise from behind made him turn his head and he watched a mountain biker pedal up the path. A native Berliner, Forst was used to the German enthusiasm for cycling through nature but found it more prevalent here, in Bavaria, than anywhere else he'd lived.

While he applauded the practice in theory, at times it posed a potential hazard for him.

Like now.

However, at the turnoff up to the Rauher Kulm, a long-dormant volcano, the rider continued on, leaving the path less traveled by free and clear. As Forst started up its rocky incline, he understood why. It was more suited to a mountain goat than a bicycle.

Fortunately, he didn't need to follow it to the top. Using an app on his phone, he clocked off half a kilometer and found a faintly delineated trail, following it into thick pine and oak coverage as he'd instructed his contact to do.

The man was there, waiting for him.

'Were you followed?" Forst asked. "Did anyone see you come?"

"No, I made certain of it."

Forst studied the man, judging his sincerity, his competency, measuring the look and stature of him. Weighing it against certain data points and details.

He would do.

"Have you brought all your documents as I instructed?" Forst asked, holding out his hand to receive them.

"They're all here," the man said. "My passport, driving license, birth records, social security and residency cards."

Forst opened the packet and checked that everything was in order. "And you've told no one about this?" he asked.

The man laughed bitterly. "Who would I tell?" he said. "I no longer have colleagues. My family is gone. My last friend left months ago. Everyone believes I am scum."

Yes, they would. After the rumors and allegations of extreme sexual deviancy and child pornography Forst had engineered and strategically planted, destroying the man's career as a schoolteacher. His wife deserted him soon after, leaving him desperate and ready to grasp at the chance for a new beginning when Forst offered it.

As he had. Confidentially. In the guise of a friend.

"Good. Are you ready, then?" Forst asked.

"More than you can possibly know."

Forst stepped closer, running a finger along the man's jawline, lifting a hank of hair off his forehead.

"We'll have to make some changes to your appearance," he said, edging behind the man.

With swift, practiced movements, Forst wrapped one arm around the narrow chest, using his other arm to grasp and wrench the head in one sharp, abrupt motion, breaking the man's neck.

The crack of it echoed in the silence of the forest.

The body flopped heavily at Forst's feet. He kicked it over so that it fell supine, the pale face staring blank-eyed at the lacework of branches overhead. He searched through the pockets, removing everything, even the lint. He took off the shoes and socks, checking them carefully. In his experience, people often hid important items in their footwear.

Concealing the body under a pile of brown, crackling leaves, Forst surveyed the area and made sure it was ready for his disposal team. They would move in after dark.

He scooped up the packet of documents, tucking it inside his jacket, and made his way through the trees and foliage. Back to the rugged path, this time leading him down the basalt mountain.

A nice payday awaited him, but he had work yet to do. Running a service such as his—securing new identities for hunted criminals—was indeed lucrative. But also demanding and dangerous.

Some days, his work never ended.

As he neared the place where his car was parked, well back and hidden from the road, his mobile phone rang. He picked up.

"Forst."

"You got one coming in hot. The lab gig in Nürnberg didn't go off as planned."

"Only one?"

"Marcos and the girl are down. Police nabbed Raul."

Forst swore. "Not good," he said. "What about the chemical? Did they get it?"

"That's unclear at this point."

Forst ground his teeth and stared off into the trees. "This guy coming in," he asked, "is he the one? The one with the key?"

"Yeah, he's the one. Cincher said to take care of him until the next op. And make sure his exfil docs are ready to go."

"I copy," Forst said, ending the call.

He had one more important appointment that took precedence even over these orders. He'd take care of it before returning to base and preparing to receive the fugitive.

Letting himself into the car, he started the engine and pulled out onto the narrow, winding road. He used one hand to rub at the knot forming along the base of his neck.

It was going to be one of those days.

CHAPTER 6

Liesl Saunders descended the staircase from the apartment where she lived with her son and parents and entered the mezzanine surrounding the lobby of the Swanhilde convention center. Like she did every morning, she stopped and pinched herself.

Literally.

Astounded, amazed, and so utterly grateful to be living and working in this spectacular place.

The sun coming in the eastern windows tinted the massive towering fireplace that served as the lobby centerpiece, turning its stones to pale gold. Liesl stood at the balcony rail, flanked by enormous picture windows, and gazed out over the rolling fields and forests of the Upper Palatinate, spread like a patchwork quilt over the surrounding hillsides. Deep greens and rich browns alternated with squares of bright yellow rapeseed just coming into bloom.

Breathtaking.

From here, she could see two more basalt mountains in the distance, little sisters to the one on which the Swanhilde center was built. All part of a long-extinct chain of volcanic fissures. An old but still functioning church sat atop one of the sisters. The other was crowned by the ruins of a castle dating back to the Middle Ages and destroyed during the Second Margrave War. She'd hiked to the top and been as enchanted by that vista as the one laid out before her now.

Here, on her basalt mountain, the Swanhilde Sammelplatz had pride of place, a small private convention center which hosted anything from family reunions and weddings to diplomatic talks and peace summits.

Like the one she was organizing now.

Leaders from seven Eastern European countries, lately torn by high-tension relations, would be meeting to discuss and negotiate arrangements between their governments, with an eye toward cooperation and greater transparency.

General expectations for the outcome were optimistic. But, like anything political, that optimism rested on a knife edge and could teeter one way or the other into disaster.

Her job depended on the smooth and successful completion of the summit.

Liesl heard the snap of a heavy door closing and the click of heels on the polished marble of the floor below her. Margaret Vonnegut, the facilities manager, moved into view, running her hand along the surfaces of the lobby counters and furniture, checking for dust and seeming satisfied with her inspection.

"*Guten Morgen*," Liesl called down to her.

Margaret turned, looking up, squinting against the streaming sunlight. "*Morgen*, Liesl. Were you able to finish those estimates for the banquet?"

"Oh, yes. I did them last night and they look good. I left the file in my apartment, but I'll bring it down to your office."

"Thanks. Just leave it with Gisa."

Liesl turned and climbed the stairs, re-entering her apartment, still scented with the morning coffee and breakfast rolls. Her parents, Peter and Ingrid, sat at the table with her son, Max, the remnants of the meal laid out before them.

"Mama," Max said, surprise and delight spreading across his face. "Are you home?"

Liesl felt the familiar wrench at her heart, the surge of fierce love she often knew when looking at her child. She drank in his simple, open and honest face, made a bit owl-like by the glasses he wore and the blinking hazel eyes behind them.

He was fourteen years old, but Down's Syndrome made him seem much younger. His father had left shortly after the boy's second birthday, unable to deal with the child's condition or his own disappointment. Max and Liesl had seen him only a handful of times since. She thanked God her parents, patient and kind, were there to help care for her son.

She smoothed the hair over Max's forehead, planting a kiss there. "No, I'm not home yet," she told him. "I only forgot something and had to come back."

Liesl noticed the empty place at the table, the coffee grown cold, rolls and butter untouched.

"Julia's not up yet?" she asked.

Her father looked exasperated but said nothing. Ingrid shook her head. "Not yet. I think I'll go rouse her. She needs to eat and sleep on a regular schedule."

About a month ago, Liesl's sister, Julia, had come to stay. Straight out of a drug rehab program. They were all determined to keep her with them until she'd solidly recovered, but their worry over her and the disruption to the regular flow of their routine imposed a strain.

Just another layer on top of the stress Liesl already bore in connection with the imminent peace talks.

The head of the corporation who owned the Swanhilde Sammelplatz had made it clear to Liesl that she'd been hired on a trial basis. She and her family could live in one of the apartments attached to the center and she'd draw a good salary and a generous benefit package.

But if her event planning skills didn't hold up to the challenges of an international peace summit, they'd all be sent packing.

Message received.

Liesl delivered the file to Margaret's office, leaving it with her secretary. In her own office, she greeted her assistant, Joseph, and got right to work checking details and confirming the arrangements she'd made for the success of the summit.

After a busy few hours, the phone on her desk buzzed. She stood and stretched, pressing a hand to the small of her back, easing the ball of tension that always seemed to settle there. She pressed a button on the phone, putting Joseph through on speaker.

"Frau Saunders," he said, his voice sounding nasal over the wire, "Anton Forst is here for your eleven o'clock appointment."

CHAPTER 7

Riley wrapped her hands around the mug of steaming tea, breathing in the vapors of lavender and mint, letting them and the warmth of the cup soothe the wrestle in her chest. Her cell phone alarm clock still showed seventeen minutes before it was set to go off, but Riley hadn't needed the reminder.

She was wired to go.

Canceling the alarm, she stared out the window at the pink, iridescent fingers of dawn stretching up from the eastern skyline. Her packed suitcase and carry-on waited beside the front door, ready for Chris to haul out to the car when he came to take her to the airport. The thought set her heart thumping again and she gulped the tea, burning her tongue and the roof of her mouth.

Her phone jangled and she snatched it up.

Rick. She hit the green button.

"Hope I didn't wake you, Riley, but I figured you'd be up by now."

"I'm up," she confirmed. "Been up most of the night, to be honest."

Rick laughed. "Perfectly understandable. I hope it's as much excitement as nerves. This will be good for you, Riley. And I'm not just saying that as your recruiter."

Riley sucked in a long breath, let it fill the cramped corners of her lungs. "I know," she said, exhaling. "I'm sure you're right. I am excited. And nervous."

"Well, I'm here ahead of you, paving the way. I just got off the plane and someone from the academy is picking me up. I'll be here waiting when you arrive."

"Thanks, Rick. I can't tell you how much better I feel, knowing you're going to be there with me."

"I'm pretty happy about it, too. See you soon."

Riley moved her finger over the end call button, but before she tapped, Rick spoke again.

"Oh, Riley, one more thing. Give me a call as soon as you get to Germany."

"Okay."

"I want to see you first thing when you arrive at the academy. I'd like to be the one to show you around and introduce you to Stanley Edwards, the director."

Riley smiled. His dedicated enthusiasm was one of the things she loved about Rick.

"I promise," she told him. "I'll ask for you first thing."

"Great. Enjoy your flight, Riley. And get some rest."

Riley ended the call and went to the kitchen where she swallowed the last of her tea and rinsed the cup, finding herself grateful for good friends. Rick had been that for her since the day they'd met. And Nate, too.

Regardless of how that turned out.

Riley used the bathroom and brushed her teeth, smoothing on some of the peppermint lip balm she relied upon. Almost to the point of addiction.

She returned to the living room just as a swinging flash of headlights danced across the dim walls, signaling Chris's arrival in the driveway. Riley pulled on a light jacket, trying to quell the shaking of her hands, and grabbed her house key from its shelf near the door.

Time to go.

Acknowledgements

For Terry, the steady rock in my stream.

Thank you to everyone who has encouraged me during the writing of the book. A big thanks to all the faithful and helpful readers on my blog at .

I owe a debt of gratitude to my two best sounding boards, Terry Giles and Daniel Higley for their enthusiastic support and the many motivating conversations we had while I was formulating the book.

A big thanks to U.S. Army helicopter pilot, Mike Welch for giving me help and direction with the helicopter scenes. I'd also like to thank Chief Ryan Spurling, Chief Deputy North Mason Sheriff Department, Elizabeth Westby of the United States Geological Survey, Priscilla Fleischer, Ph.D., Nan Barker, U.S. Army librarian, Corene McDaniel, reference librarian at Timberland Regional Library, and Kyle Imhoff, a Pennsylvania State Climatologist.

Any and all errors and inaccuracies are purely my own and should not be laid at the feet of any of the experts I consulted.

Thank you to Dean Wesley Smith for helping me with the back-cover blurb and description, and for generously imparting great wisdom on the craft and business of writing.

I owe a healthy portion of thanks to Joanna Penn for her generosity in always sharing what she has learned for the benefit of others, and for her book mid-wivery efforts and skills. I never could have delivered this baby without her.

I'm grateful to Lisl Fleckner for help with proofreading and the final edits.

I thank my friends with an eye for design, Nick Thomas and Tyler Angel, for giving me guidance during my angst over the front cover.

Credit for the band name, Downed Illusion, and for the lead singer, Coby Waters, goes to Jay and Sherrie Johnson.

Dulcie Larsen came up with two of the T-shirt ideas: "Just when you thought it was safe to go hiking," and "This is Rainier. This is Rainier on crack."

A special thank you to my advance readers: Terry Giles, Sherrie Johnson, Jay Johnson, Daniel Higley, Dulcie Larsen, and Barbara Jensen-Marlow.

Most of all, I thank my family for giving me the time to make this happen.

About the Author

Joslyn Chase is a prize-winning author of mysteries and thrillers. Any day where she can send readers to the edge of their seats, chewing their fingernails to the nub and prickling with suspense, is a good day in her book.

Joslyn's story, "Cold Hands, Warm Heart," was chosen by Amor Towles as one of the *Best Mystery Stories of the Year 2023.* Her short stories have appeared in *Alfred Hitchcock's Mystery Magazine, Malice Domestic's Mystery Most Devious, Thrill Ride Magazine, Fiction River, Mystery, Crime, and Mayhem, Mystery Magazine,* and *Pulphouse Fiction,* among others.

Known for her fast-paced suspense fiction, Joslyn's books are full of surprising twists and delectable turns. You will find her riveting novels most anywhere books are sold.

Her love for travel has led Joslyn to ride camels through the Nubian desert, fend off monkeys on the Rock of Gibraltar, and hike the Bavarian Alps. But she still believes that sometimes the best adventures come in getting the words on the page and in the thrill of reading a great story.

Join the growing group of readers who've discovered the thrill of Chase! Sign up for Joslyn's readers' group and get VIP access to great bonuses—like your free copy of *No Rest: 14 Tales of Chilling Suspense*—as well as updates and first crack at new releases.

Visit joslynchase.com to get started now!

bookbub.com/authors/joslyn-chase

goodreads.com/author/show/16850235.Joslyn_Chase

facebook.com/StoryChase

linkedin.com/in/joslynchase/

pinterest.com/joslynchase/

youtube.com/@joslynchase5955/videos